THE BATTLE FOR ENGLAND

BERNARD NEESON

Bigpa Publications

Published by Bigpa Publications

ISBN: 978-1-4849-9626-3

Typesetting services by BOOKOW.COM

For Dee

They ask, "Why doesn't he come?"
Be patient! I'm coming, I'm coming!
ADOLF HITLER - BerlinSportPalast, September 4th, 1940

PART 1: OFFING

offing (n): the more distant part of the sea visible from shore

in the offing: close at hand, imminent

1

Someone was tugging on his arm, a voice telling him to get up. His body was trembling, his mind racing with violent images... searches ... arrests... deportations.

The firing squads were already at work. He saw broken bodies heaped in an execution site. It looked like a school playground. There were figures falling through the air. Pilots or paratroopers, alive or dead, he couldn't tell. On all sides, noise... sirens and explosions... machine guns... dive-bombers screaming down to attack a column of refugees, and then a different screaming, more terrible, from the carnage on the road below. There were flecks of blood on his clothes. He twisted away to deflect the horror.

Black uniforms in familiar London streets, tramping jackboots, panzers clanking along the Mall. Adolf Hitler was on the balcony of Buckingham Palace, ranting away to a crowd of supporters outside ... Fascists... *British* Fascists. Somehow, they could understand what he was saying. Standing beside the brown-shirted figure was a man in morning dress, tall, smug. He felt the bile surge in his throat; the Englishman had once been a friend.

But his anger was futile; it was over.

The Nazis had won.

"Prime Minister... Sir..."

The hand was on his shoulder, shaking him. He shied away from its grasp, until it dawned on him he'd been addressed by his title, not his surname, not a number. And the voice was English, not German. It wasn't a pitiless *Aufwachen!* A wave of confused relief swept over him. For a few, chilling seconds he'd feared worse, much worse. He rolled onto his back, still disorientated, his heart still thumping. A man was standing beside the bed. In the near-darkness he couldn't make out the face, but, as his head began to clear, he thought he recognised the voice. It was Colville, trying to rouse him from his troubled sleep.

"Jock... that you? God, what time is it?"

Without waiting for an answer, he turned and rummaged under his pillow, still only half awake. He fished out his pocket watch and held it up close to his eyes. In the dim light he couldn't read the dial, even squinting hard.

Colville paused for a few seconds to allow Churchill to gather his senses.

"It's half past five, sir."

"Eh? What's happening?" He was still trembling. "Have they landed? Are they...?"

"No, Prime Minister, not as far as I know. It's your wake-up call; half five, as you asked."

Churchill lay back on the bed and groaned.

"Damn and blast, Jock. Did I not tell you to put it back an hour?"

"No sir, you didn't."

A tetchiness crept into Colville's tone. The Prime Minister had managed a few more hours of sleep after the disruption in the small hours, but he'd been up all night.

Churchill rubbed his head, aching with lack of sleep and the self-inflicted damage from the evening before. The late whiskies shared with Bracken wouldn't normally have had much effect, but then, in the middle of the night, he'd been awakened by Menzies, with the shock news about Russia. The rest just seemed part of a dream, or part of his nightmare. It had been nearly four o'clock when he'd gone to bed for the second time that night and tried, with difficulty, to sleep.

Churchill pushed back the blanket and went to sit up, only to lurch sideways as his elbow slipped off the narrow sofa bed. The jolt seemed to wake him. He swore under his breath and slumped back, his eyes closing for the briefest of moments. He was feeling vile, but there was no escape, he had a war to fight. More immediately, his young tormentor wasn't going to leave till he rose.

He raised himself again, more carefully this time, and turned round to sit hunched on the side of the bed.

"You can go, Jock. I'm awake."

Colville waited a few seconds, until Churchill reached a fully upright position, then switched on the ceiling light and left.

The Prime Minister of Great Britain and Northern Ireland yawned, leaned down and groped around for his spectacles. In the light from the unshaded bulb, he took in the dull surroundings; his desk, a filing cabinet and a few chairs, one with his clothes lying on it. Plain grey walls with no windows. It felt like a prison cell or a monastery. Neither would be good.

He remembered; he was in the Paddock. They'd moved across from Whitehall the previous evening, from the dingy cosiness of the Cabinet War Rooms to this concrete mausoleum, hidden deep underground in north-west London.

He had delayed the transfer for as long as he could, and, he muttered half-aloud, with good reason. The place was as soul-destroying as he'd feared; dank and depressing, a world removed from the comfort of the flat in Number 10, or even the shabby domesticity of his little space in the War Rooms. For a moment he let his mind drift further afield, to the leafy surrounds of his house in Kent and the peace he found there.

He snarled at the brutal contrast. From the garden at Chartwell, in less than a year, to this Paddock. Even the name seemed to mock. There were no horses, no grass, not even a sky to gaze at, just a soulless block of concrete hidden away in the drab suburb of Dollis Hill.

But, for all its oppressiveness, he knew he'd better get used to it. This was now the national seat of government. From this bleak bunker he would lead the battle for England.

One of the juniors came in with a basin of hot water and his shaving kit, and placed them on his desk. Churchill stretched his stocky frame and put on his dressing gown and slippers. He took a few deep breaths. That would do for exercise; he was ready to face the day.

"Joccck! Call the Chiefs over. We'll start in ten minutes."

He didn't wait for a response; he expected his private secretary to be at his post outside the door.

"Bring me the Situation Report before they get here."

Since he became Prime Minister in May, the 0900 review with the Chiefs of Staff had been the established routine. Today, with the invasion imminent, it would start three hours earlier than usual. Colville put his head in and handed him the single-page summary of military events. He scanned the sheet and saw no surprises. He turned it over in case, against his instructions, there was more on the back.

There wasn't.

He sighed, with a just a hint of relief. It was a sign of how far they'd come. Back in June they'd faced each day in dread, with problems on every front, usually disasters. If the Nazis had come then, it might have been over. There wasn't the military capability to resist, perhaps not even the will to try.

But they hadn't come crashing through the door when it was unguarded, and the period of grace had been put to good use, re-equipping the Armed Forces and restoring their shattered morale. And so, on this autumn morning, there was no bad news, no surprises. Not that he expected any; they were keeping the surprise for Hitler.

He went over to the enamel basin and checked the water was still warm. A splash would do for now; he'd find time for a bath later. Some things weren't going to change just because there was a war on. He washed, thinking about the day ahead. Until a few hours ago, it had all been going according to plan, but the message from Berlin changed everything. He called out again to Colville.

"Tell Brendan and C to come round as soon as I've finished with the Chiefs; say, at half six."

He heard a brief acknowledgement.

Brendan Bracken, the MP for Paddington North, had been at his side for twenty years, helping him through the ebbs and flows of his turbulent life. Brigadier Stewart Menzies, alias 'C', was the head of MI6, Britain's network of agents around the globe. The two made for an unlikely duo, the wayward son of an Irish Republican and the Old Etonian, but, in these new, uncharted waters, Churchill knew he could depend on them. Bracken, the arch-schemer, would offer pithy advice on what they should do. Menzies, the spymaster, would tell him what they could.

He massaged his face with the cloth, pressing it gently against his forehead and cheeks, breathing deeply through the warm, wet material for a moment of contemplation. He had to deal with the Halifax situation as well; it couldn't be left to fester. With an invasion pending, a split in the Cabinet was the last thing he needed.

He called out again.

"And will you ask the Foreign Secretary to come around for a few minutes after the tour of inspection, say at nine o'clock."

"Yes sir."

It sounded as if Colville had got everything.

Churchill dabbed his face dry and sighed. Soon, very soon, the pivotal battle would begin. Despite the months of lacklustre effort under Chamberlain, he felt the country was on a war footing at last. Since becoming Prime Minister in May, he'd thrown every ounce of his strength into the effort. He had shaken up the senior command in the Army after its woeful performance in France, firing generals not up to the job and putting in new men, his own men, men he could trust. He'd demanded root and branch reform right across the Armed Forces, insisting the commanders put the disaster at Dunkirk behind them and ready themselves for the battle ahead. He had driven production in the armaments factories to new peaks and used the country's financial reserves to buy much-needed arms from America.

Ever conscious of the need to sustain morale, he had stomped around the country, cigar in mouth, with Bracken making sure the newsreel cameras were watching. At the very blackest of hours he'd made rousing speeches on the BBC to raise people's spirits. To everyone, at home and abroad, he was the leader of the nation, the embodiment of Britain's resolve to fight.

Then he glimpsed his reflection in the steamed-up mirror. A shudder ran through him. He was looking at a lie. The bulldog image portrayed to the world was not the whole truth. It was, in fact, far from the whole truth. He and the group at the heart of the Ethelred plan could not assert they had done everything in their power to prevent the Nazi invasion. They couldn't claim that Hitler's armies were so powerful it had been impossible to stop his advance on Britain.

That simply wasn't true.

They had invited him.

2

Two hundred miles from London, grey-uniformed troops were beginning to muster. On gravelled parade grounds and dusty fields across the north-west corner of France, tens of thousands of Feldgrau stamped their feet to keep warm or checked their weapons and equipment. A few tried to make nervous, unwelcome conversation with their comrades, some of the younger men even claiming they were happy to be marching against England at last. But most, anxious about the crossing, kept their feelings to themselves. They were soldiers, not sailors. The thought of spending the next twenty-four hours huddled in cramped ships or barges, under fire, had sobered them. For all the press reports hailing the Luftwaffe's victory in the skies, or the mess talk about a collapse in the British forces, they were nervous about what awaited them, at sea and on the other side.

Then it was time. Whistles blew. The steel-helmeted figures clambered on board lorries and buses, sitting impassively in rows as the convoys pulled out through the gates and set out on their journeys. In the early morning mist they drove along straight, poplar-lined roads, past farms and through tightly-shuttered villages, their unwelcome intrusion marked only by the barking of dogs and the crowing of insolent cockerels. It wouldn't have been hard for an onlooker to know where they were headed; the soldiers were carrying just their weapons and their combat gear and were travelling towards the Channel ports. But there was no-one on the roads to watch. Only the twitching of an occasional curtain showed there were other people in the world who cared, who feared.

* * *

At Boulogne, Hauptman Fritz Weber and his company of grenadiers had a short journey ahead, from their billets on the outskirts of town down to the quays. For the last three months, the unit had been enjoying the pleasures of the French countryside. They felt they'd earned it. After fighting their way through the Ardennes forest, they'd crossed the Somme in the van of the 16th Army and had been one of the first units to reach the Channel coast. There they'd stopped and waited, relishing, for a while, the sweet fruits of victory.

But now, on this autumn morning, they were on the move again. Sitting quietly in the back of their half-tracks, the grenadiers drove through echoing streets, past long lines of military vehicles half-hidden from the RAF's bombers in city parks and streets. They were part of a great phalanx of troops and equipment heading towards the port and, from there, onwards to England.

All around them Weber could see the stuff of Germany's military power; hundreds of tanks and armoured cars, hundreds more of field guns, flak units and supply trucks. This was the hard mantle of the Heer, the army that had swept all before it in the dash through France and was about to be launched upon England, to finish the fight for good.

In the lead-up to the attacks on Poland and France, these vast displays of armoured might had boosted the men's morale. They promised a battle that would be fought with German steel, not German blood. In those earlier campaigns the soldiers had moved up to the front line in high spirits, singing and joking, enjoying a sense of Teutonic invincibility, confident in themselves and in their Fuehrer.

This time it was different; the men were quieter.

This time there was a Channel to cross.

3

Brendan Bracken had no idea why he'd been woken at such an ungodly hour; Colville had just told him the Prime Minister wanted to see him and left without explanation. He was feeling wretched, after a long, fractious day and too many whiskies at its close. But when the instruction came from the PM's private secretary, there was no point in arguing. He did, however, wonder what might have happened in the four short hours since he'd left Winston's office.

He stretched his long legs and turned over in his bunk, looking around, trying to collect his thoughts. The room didn't give much away. There was a bluish light coming through a panel above the door, though he couldn't remember if there was a passageway outside or another room. For a minute he thought he was alone, then he heard snoring from the bunk above. He had company, but he'd no idea who it was; they'd been fast asleep by the time he'd crept in a few hours earlier. Though it might explain why Jock had been so tight-lipped.

Bracken lay still for a few more moments, listening to the muted noises in the background; footsteps, the murmur of voices and the occasional ring of a telephone. Nothing that wouldn't be expected in a command centre and nothing to give any more information. He tried to think. There'd been no alerts in force when he went to bed and there was nothing scheduled until the tour of inspection at 0800b. He looked at his watch. *Not yet 6.* Still dark outside... there couldn't be much happening at such an hour. Then he stopped, in the sharp realisation that, in this subterranean world, time of day would make no difference in either routine operations or crises.

He pulled on his shirt and trousers and went out into a brightly lit corridor. It was alive with activity – though a strange, confused activity. People were hurrying about, but making some effort to be quiet. His first thought was that the *Cromwell* alarm had been issued, the call to the country that the invasion was under way. However, he realised at once that that didn't make sense. If the Nazi assault had started, people would have been going about their assigned tasks, long-planned and well-rehearsed, and making as much noise as they liked, rather than scurrying around like headless chickens. *Did headless chickens make noise?* he wondered idly, thinking back to the farm in Tipperary a long time ago.

One or two staff nodded as they passed, but didn't give any more clues. If any of them were in the know, they weren't saying. A few yards further along he overheard talk about a Cabinet meeting during the night. *That would explain it.* Something had happened in the small hours of the morning – clearly unforeseen and obviously serious. He guessed it must have been a military incident or Winston would have called him at the time. He hoped it wasn't more bad news.

At least, if it was the start of the invasion, it shouldn't have come as a surprise to anyone. They'd been preparing for months. The Chiefs of Staff were saying the Forces were ready, the battle plans tested, the men in good spirits. Whatever the convoluted path that had taken them to this point, they seemed confident, prepared for the worst Hitler could throw at them.

Certainly, as far as he could tell, the command centre was working as expected. On arrival the previous evening, his own top priority had been to check the communications links to the outside world. In the desperate days ahead, he had to make sure they didn't lose the propaganda war. He'd tested one channel with particular care; the link to the BBC. He knew Winston would need to make use of it soon ... today, perhaps, or tomorrow... not long anyway. When the Nazis landed, the country would need the comfort of hearing his voice.

He went looking for Colville, but the young civil servant wasn't at his desk outside the PM's office and the office itself was empty. On his way across to the Operations Room he spotted Stewart Menzies in the canteen, alone, pouring a mug of tea from a metal urn. He went in just as Menzies spat the first mouthful into the sink.

"Stone cold! You'd think the people trying to run this damn war could get a cuppa tea when they need one."

The head of MI6 filled a kettle from the tap and switched it on.

"Forget the bloody tea." Bracken pushed his way into the kitchenette. "Can somebody please tell me what in the name of God's going on?"

Menzies looked round.

"Oh, Brendan... Sorry! Jock not spoken to you yet?"

The kettle began to steam.

"Thought he was going to. I guess we're all busy at... Actually, to be honest, I'm not quite sure what we're all at this morning."

He poured the boiling water into a teapot.

"Look, grab a mug and sit down – this stuff should be better. We need to catch up; Winston wants to see us in half an hour."

"At half six?" Bracken knew it wasn't Churchill's style.

They sat down at a corner table in the empty room.

"Go on, tell me!"

"Aw, Brendan, give me a moment, for God's sake. It's been a long night."

He gulped down a mouthful of tea, then pinched his nose for a second, thinking.

"Well, it hasn't started yet. I suppose I'd better go back to the beginning." He glanced up at the wall clock. "Christ, that was only four hours ago! Feels like days."

He took another sip.

"Anyway, about 2 o'clock, I was woken by my duty officer, straight over from H.Q. with a message from Admiral Canaris."

Menzies took another drink from his mug, leaving Bracken frustrated for a few seconds more. Canaris was the head of the Abwehr, Germany's military intelligence organisation. But he was also an implacable enemy of the Nazis, and Britain's highest source in the Reich.

Any message from him was important. With the invasion only hours away, it might be crucial.

Menzies looked straight at Bracken.

"Seems Hitler has given the order for the invasion of Russia, in the spring."

Bracken's mug slapped back on the table.

"Mother of God! Russia? Before he's... I mean, whether he's finished us off or not?"

"I know, hard to believe," Menzies said. "According to Canaris, we just have to hold on. Doesn't say win or beat the buggers back or anything. Just *'hold on'* and, oh, *'don't let the Realists have their way.'* Here, look for yourself."

He pulled a folded sheet of paper from his jacket pocket and handed it across the table. Bracken read it, screwing up his face in disbelief.

"Russia...? He's invading Russia! Christ. All our hard work to get Stalin to tear up his pact with Hitler and we needn't have bothered our backsides. Dear old Adolf's going to do the job for us?"

"Apparently."

Bracken ran a hand though his wiry hair, his face twisting as the implications sank in. It was the great battle in the East they'd been hoping for, a battle that would take the pressure of Britain.

"Hard to believe," he said. "The evil bastard's really planning to invade Russia before he knows the outcome here – or even what their losses are like, assuming he thinks they're going to win?"

"That's what struck me, too," Menzies said. "It's as if we're just a sideshow for the man."

Bracken stared at the wall opposite, thinking of the months they'd spent trying to unhinge the Nazi-Soviet pact, and of their own efforts to build a plan to deceive Hitler. They had baited a trap for the Nazis, ready to spring it as they struggled ashore in England.

He looked at the note again.

"But he still mentions the *Realists*. I'm confused."

As part of the charade, they'd invented a group of traitors, supposedly planning a coup against Churchill. They'd christened them *Realists* and fostered the illusion with leaks and false messages, hoping to lull Hitler into the belief that Britain's resolve was collapsing.

But they had dropped the pretence a few weeks ago, trying to goad Hitler into launching the invasion against the advice of his generals.

Bracken was shaking his head, still looking at the note.

"I'm totally confused... The head of the Abwehr isn't aware we dropped the whole Realists thing ten days ago?"

Menzies shrugged. He had been struggling to understand.

"Maybe he wrote his note before we pulled the plug. It would have taken some time for his courier to get to Spain – at least if he had to go by train."

"Spain?"

"Yea, Madrid. His courier handed it one of my people there, two days ago. Couldn't risk sending it on by cable, so it was hand delivery from there – train to Lisbon and flying-boat up to Dorset. The messenger got in late last night and we'd a car waiting to bring her up to London."

"But more than a week on the road without hearing from his boss? C'mon!"

Menzies took the empty cups over to the sink. He'd been wrestling with the same question.

"Unlikely, I grant you. Maybe Canaris himself hasn't been fully briefed... He's not invited to all Fuehrer conferences – only brought in on specific intelligence items."

"You'd have thought the sudden disappearance of the Realists would fit into that category rather neatly," Bracken said.

"I know, Brendan. It's bizarre. I suppose it's possible Adolf hasn't let everybody know he was fooled. A gentleman has his pride after all."

Bracken turned the note over in his hand and rubbed it between his fingers, as if testing the paper.

"You sure it's genuine?"

"Pretty much. The courier's close to Canaris, one of his department heads. And he's got a track record. Same chap who brought the news about our naval codes being broken, a few months back. That leak has saved a lot of ships... and men."

"Or written under duress maybe? If they've rumbled him?" Bracken was still testing.

"Don't think so. There's a formula in each message to verify it – built into the text. I'll spare you the details. In any event I can't see how it would be to anybody's advantage to make up something like that, about Russia."

Bracken scratched his stubbled chin, still trying to think of any other explanation that might fit the odd circumstances.

"Except, perhaps, Canaris himself."

Now Menzies looked confused.

"Eh? Why on earth would he do that?"

"Keep our hopes up, maybe? So we stay in the fight?"

"Hadn't thought of that... but it's unlikely," Menzies said. "If he's caught making stuff up – even once – we'd never believe him again. The channel would lose all value, for the German Resistance as much as us."

Bracken examined the letter again to see if he'd missed anything. He saw it also stated the invasion was imminent. Menzies hadn't mentioned that rather important detail – but again, they knew it anyway. He shook his head.

"Anyway, what did you do with it?"

"Woke Winston. Had to elbow my way past the sergeant to get in. Fortunately, he mustn't have had too heavy a night – was on top of it straight away."

With the taste of the night's whisky still on his breath, Bracken knew the assumption wasn't actually true, but saw no point in correcting him.

Menzies sat down again at the table.

"We talked it over for a while and he decided to get the War Cabinet together there and then, and the Chiefs, too – about 3 a.m."

"Bet that was fun."

Menzies looked around, then back at Bracken. He lowered his voice, as if personal tittle-tattle required greater discretion than the state secrets they'd been discussing.

"Some of 'em half-asleep, some half-drunk and some half-dead by the look of them."

Bracken raised an eyebrow, though not really surprised. He knew them all.

"I guess the Admiral's note woke them up pretty sharpish!"

"Too right! Even the half-dead. I didn't mention Canaris by name. Some of them aren't aware we've a source that high in Berlin."

"Did they get the message?"

"They got it alright."

Bracken handed the note back.

"Our prayers answered. Though I don't imagine the Russians will feel the same when it hits them." He winced. "You know, C, if we'd heard this a month back, it would've changed everything – undermined the entire rationale for Ethelred. After all, if we're not going to be on our own any more, come spring, why would we take the risk of letting the bastards land now?"

"That's the line Halifax took. Turned into a huge row. He wanted to pull the plug on the whole caboodle – and Chamberlain, too. Mind you, they didn't actually suggest how we might, at this stage!"

Bracken groaned.

"As I said, it's a month too late. No surprise about those two though. You'd think the way Hitler screwed them at Munich, they'd be itching to get their own back. Yet they're at it again? Ready to chicken out?"

"I know. It's depressing," Menzies said. "Winston should have got shot of them weeks ago. He's already announced they'll be leaving the Cabinet – so why doesn't he just get on with it?"

Bracken had argued the same point with Churchill; now he just shrugged. "Says it's about continuity... he's never met Hitler and they might be able to give useful advice on dealing with him."

"Your own view?"

"I think Winston can be too soft on people at times."

Menzies pulled a face. "Unfortunately, they weren't the only problem. Attlee and Eden were a bit wobbly as well, looking for an easy way out."

Bracken rubbed his chin slowly.

"Now that," he said, "is a lot more worrying."

Clement Attlee, the leader of the Labour Party, was key to maintaining the National Coalition welded together in May. The other waverer, Anthony Eden, was the Minister of War. After the Prime Minister, he was the most influential politician in the Conservative Party. Usually the two were Churchill's most dependable supporters in Cabinet. *If even they were losing faith in Ethelred...*

He swallowed his concerns.

"So, how'd it pan out?"

"Touch and go for a while. Winston was backed into a corner by Halifax – rather aggressively, in fact. Fortunately, the Chiefs came down in favour of seeing it through."

"The Chiefs?" Bracken looked surprised. "Thought they'd have been delighted to drop the whole thing."

"No. They were simply logical about it. In fact Alan Brooke was quite clinical, taking the Army's perspective. *'The plan's under way. There's no sign it's been compromised... More dangerous to abort than to see it through.'* Hard to argue with him – and Admiral Pound took the same line when he eventually woke up."

"Seems fair enough. I guess it's too late to stop the first wave landing."

"That's the point the Chiefs were making. Dear old Poundie said he couldn't get the Home Fleet down from Scotland in time, even if the PM ordered it there and then. Winston was not amused."

"I can imagine. Not much point having those bloody battleships sitting up there in a fog if you can't use them when they're needed!"

"He didn't quite put it like that, but..."

"What did he decide?"

"No change on Ethelred for the moment. Sent everyone off about their business. Just told them to keep an eye open for any chance to close it off earlier than we'd planned."

Bracken grimaced. "Makes sense, I suppose... Maybe not let Jerry so far inland? And the second wave, could we stop it before it lands?"

"Chiefs are looking at that now," Menzies said. "Seems to depend on how many days they are behind the first lot."

"So nothing really settled?"

"No. Winston talks, a bit grandiosely, about the Russians becoming the meat grinder next spring, instead of us having to do it all ourselves."

"As long as they don't collapse when the blitzkrieg hits them."

"That's the worry. Adolf would be back within the year to sort out his unfinished business here. Anyway, the PM wants to see us as soon as he finishes with the Chiefs; wants to talk over our options on the diplomatic side."

"Tch... some hard thinking needed on that." Bracken yawned. "And I'm not usually at my best after four hours' sleep."

"Count yourself lucky, old boy." Menzies yawned in sympathy. "Some of us didn't get any."

4

GrossAdmiral Erich Raeder stood at the window of the grand salon, peering through a gap in the sandbags as the men assembled in the square outside. For almost two hundred years, the Chateau of Wimille had been home to a succession of minor French nobility. Now it served a different master. Commandeered by the Germans soon after the fall of France, the chateau was now the naval headquarters for the invasion of England.

From the day he first arrived, Raeder had been pleased with the choice. Driving through the Picardy countryside in early summer, he'd felt like a tourist visiting in a time of peace, admiring vast fields of grain ripening under a hot sun and lush cider orchards that promised rich pickings to come. When he reached Wimille, he found a building that would provide well for their needs as they went about their work of war. It had a grand salon for formal meetings and half a dozen smaller rooms for the many planning sessions needed. A brief tour showed an adequate number of bedrooms, bathrooms and kitchens for the domestic needs of his staff.

As the Admiral went about his inspection tour, his cook looked around outside. To his delight he found a small herb garden, stocked with rosemary, fennel and thyme. Nearby he discovered an old greenhouse, leaning against a crumbling brick wall. Inside, the raised beds were filled with rows of tomatoes and aubergines. Raeder smiled wryly when his adjutant told his about the culinary finds.

"Well, Joachim, if nothing else, at least we'll eat well."

Three months into its new life, the aura of the house was very different. It was now a fortified military installation. Tiers of sandbags protected the elegant windows on the ground-floor. Upstairs, the wooden shutters were closed over and the glass was criss-crossed with tape. Scattered around the formal gardens, an array of defensive positions had been dug in, equipped with flak cannon and machineguns. Naval infantry in dark blue uniforms patrolled the red-brick walls and manned a checkpoint at the entrance.

Somewhat incongruously, amid all the military activity, the estate's old French gardeners continued to tend the leafy grounds. Raeder occasionally wondered if they didn't care that the property was under new management – or were they minding it in trust for the original owners, in the fond hope they might, one day, return?

The planning work was all behind them. Raeder watched in the dawn light as the naval infantry assembled. Until a few days ago these battle-hardened marines had been underemployed, protecting the site against an unlikely attack by the British. Now they'd been replaced on guard duty by a group of old reservists; the elite troops were off to war.

Raeder flicked at a fingernail. He was troubled. His last meeting with Hitler had been traumatic. For weeks he'd been anticipating there would be a settlement with the British. Their resistance was weakening by the day; the RAF was barely visible; their army and navy were in disarray. Abwehr agents had sent reports about civilian unrest in many cities and of huge marches for peace in Liverpool and Glasgow. He'd heard about eyewitness accounts of sabotage in British ports and of bloody clashes between striking dockworkers and troops. There'd been rumours of mutinies in naval bases, even hints of a split in the top ranks of the Royal Navy. Reconnaissance flights over Scapa Flow had shown strange manoeuvrings by the British battleships in the anchorage that seemed to suggest the local commanders were no longer answering to the chain of command from London.

He'd watched these developments with intense interest. If a split had occurred in the Royal Navy, his own task would be that much easier. Without the shield of their navy, it even seemed possible the British would decide it was futile to fight on and come to the negotiation table.

For weeks the flow towards an armistice had seemed unstoppable. Hopes peaked when an unknown group made contact from England, saying they were going to put an end to Churchill's war-mongering. They said they were realists about the situation. There would soon be a new government in London, with a new prime minister in place and the old king, Edward VIII, restored to the throne. The *Realists* said they wanted an end to the futile bloodshed between cousin nations and called for a new relationship based on mutual respect for each other's interests. In Berlin, optimism had grown that a settlement could be agreed and the need for a costly military invasion avoided.

But, about ten days ago, something had happened. He still hadn't been told the full story; the Fuehrer refused to talk about it. He did know that Churchill was back on top in England, broadcasting to the country, restored to his old belligerent self. Certainly, the battleships at Scapa Flow had returned to their original moorings, poised to oppose the Sea Lion crossing.

Raeder didn't know if there'd been a failed attempt at a coup in London or if there was some darker reason, but of all the Reich's military leaders he had most reason to fear the consequences. While Reichsmarschall Goering could boast about the supremacy of his Luftwaffe and Field Marshal Keitel laud the superiority of the German army, he couldn't say the same about his Kriegsmarine. Even as the Sea Lion operation cranked into motion, he knew the hard reality; the Royal Navy hadn't been defeated. It hadn't even been significantly weakened. The British fleet was nearly ten times bigger than his own. Even worse, he was going to have to fight them in their own back yard.

He paced up and down the salon, alone with his thoughts. The debate was over. He had lost the most important battle of his career, not at sea, but in a plush conference room in Berlin. Since the early days, he'd met Hitler many times, trying to convince him of the need to build a great fleet to challenge the British. It had started well enough, with the Fuehrer authorising a large naval construction programme and telling Raeder there was plenty of time; there wouldn't be a war in the west for at least ten years.

But his faith in the Fuehrer had been shaken. The war had started five years earlier than promised, with the naval programme only half complete. Even worse from his standpoint, the success of the Wehrmacht in France had brought them to the Channel coast in six weeks, with England just 30 tantalising kilometres away. The focus in the high command, the Oberkommando der Wehrmacht, had switched seamlessly to their next logical goal, the conquest of England.

At first, even the Fuehrer had shown an uncharacteristic nervousness about an invasion.

"On land, I'm a hero," he announced. "At sea, I'm a coward."

Raeder had worked hard to build on that reluctance, trying to guide the military strategy in a different direction, towards a blockade. Rather than fight the British head-on, he wanted to let Admiral Doenitz and his U-boats starve them into submission. But he'd lost the debate. Goering, bombastic as ever, and the fawning Keitel convinced the Fuehrer they could defeat the British without difficulty. And it suited Hitler to believe a quick victory was possible. He had other business to attend to in the east.

Raeder punched a closed fist into his palm in frustration. Even at a tactical level he'd been out-manoeuvred; he had lost the battle over timing. He'd argued that the crossing should be by day, but Keitel insisted the landings had to be at dawn, to give the troops the full day to consolidate their toehold on the beaches. He remembered the discussion, the shouting match, almost word for word.

"Feldmarschall, a night crossing is courting disaster. Two thousand ships exposed to attack by the British navy all night long – with the Luftwaffe not able to do a thing about it! We have to cross by day, under air cover all the way to keep the British navy off."

"We're at war, Admiral," Keitel snapped. "You can't afford to be so protective of your ships."

"If I lose fewer ships, Feldmarschall, you lose fewer battalions!"

He remembered the hard glares. He'd tried appealing to Goering's vanity.

"Reichsmarschall, you've created the most powerful air force in the world. My sailors need the protection of your flyers above them, their guardian angels as they approach the English coast."

Before Goering could reply, Keitel had interjected again.

"So they can dump my men on some lonely beach and sail away into the dusk?"

In a number of increasingly tense meetings, they'd failed to resolve the impasse. The decision had gone to the Fuehrer. Not surprisingly the old corporal backed the army.

And now, on this grey morning, it was under way. He had committed every seaworthy vessel in his navy, had gathered every steamer he could find. He'd requisitioned thousands of barges from the Rhine and the other great rivers of Europe. He had assembled a vast armada in the ports facing England, ready to carry across the assault divisions. Even as he watched and pondered, a hundred thousand men were stirring into action, the first wave of the great attack. They would sail this evening. The landings would be at dawn, *dawn tomorrow*.

He stared morosely into the dying embers of the fire. He'd waited until the marines were ready to leave before going out to see them off. They had enough to worry about without feeling the added pressure of an inspection.

Shortly before 0630 Korvettenkapitan Hans Weiser came in and saluted.

"Admiral, the men are ready."

"Five minutes, Kapitan."

On the way out, Raeder paused in the entrance hall to check his appearance, looking at himself in the gilt-framed mirror. He flicked a few specks of dust from his dark blue uniform, straightened his naval cap and walked out the door to the terrace. He went over to the commander, saluted and wished him luck. Without any formality, he took up position on a raised bank where he would be visible to the men – just him and Korvettenkapitan Weiser, not a large saluting party. He didn't want it to look like a parade ground review, just a demonstration of his respect for men he'd come to know well over the months. They were excellent troops, first blooded in Danzig on the opening day of the war and later carrying out daring river crossings during the Battle of France. Now they were to be in the van of the attack on England, among the first to land, using their skill in handing assault boats to carry out a vital mission. He knew they were brave men, ready to give their all for the Fatherland. He feared many of them might have to.

An NCO shouted out a command. The men slung their rifles and backpacks over their shoulders and marched out through the gates. Raeder stood to attention and saluted as they passed. He used the naval salute, not the raised arm of the Nazis; it wasn't the time for a political statement. He waited till he heard engines start up in the vehicle park and the lorries moving out.

When they'd gone, he lingered for a while on the grassy bank, listening as the sound waned in the distance. He turned away, feeling the loneliness of command, wondering how many of the men would return. He looked at the sky, his thoughts on the weather for the week ahead. In the east a faint sun was trying to break through the grey overcast. At least the early morning cloud was a blessing; the fleet would have some cover from the RAF's probing reconnaissance aircraft as the embarkation got under way. Every hour gained improved the chances of success – and they would need all the help they could get.

As he climbed down from the bank he heard distant gunfire, coming from the direction of the harbour. *Flak!* He wasn't too concerned; it happened most days. But thirty seconds later he heard the high-pitched roar of a plane. The guns in the grounds opened up. Raeder scrambled down the bank, snagging his greatcoat on a thorn bush, sprinting across the courtyard towards the nearest shelter. *Too late* ... With the entrance still ten metres away, he sensed the plane or its shadow race across the grass. He hurled himself to the ground, rolling across the gravel towards the skimpy protection of a garden wall... covering his head... hugging the earth...

The roar of an engine... dust...

Then it was over. As suddenly as it started, it was over. The aircraft flashed overhead and was gone. It didn't strafe or drop bombs, just climbed away at full power and disappeared into the clouds with tracer shells flaying harmlessly behind it.

Raeder lay still for a moment, then stood up and watched as the gunners fired off a last, futile burst in frustration. He brushed the dirt from his sleeve, bent down and picked his cap off the ground. A few withered leaves were caught behind the badge. He smacked the cap hard against his thigh to dislodge them, harder than needed, swearing quietly to himself. He'd recognised the aircraft, the sweet sound of its engine and the damned curved wings.

It was a Spitfire.

5

A thousand feet above Wimille Flight Lieutenant Paddy Fowley wrestled his aircraft onto the new heading. He was badly shaken. The flak over Boulogne had been intense, the heaviest he'd faced in the war so far. He was still coming to terms with what he'd seen below – the Nazi invasion fleet, hundreds of ships and barges, preparing for sea... and troops, thousands of them, stretching for miles along the quayside. In the staging areas behind the wharfs, he'd spotted long columns of tanks and guns. The images were captured in his camera. They'd give the Intelligence people all the information they needed – assuming he made it back. He had four more ports to photograph before he could head home to Blighty.

He turned in a wide arc to get out over the Channel. He hoped the change in flight path would confuse any fighters that might be tailing him, before he headed down the coast to his next target. The routing would also keep him away from the shore-based guns and flak-ships in the bay. He told himself he'd earned the few minutes of respite.

Fowley climbed back into the cloud. Over Boulogne it had been a mixed blessing, forcing him to fly dangerously low to get his photographs, but offering sanctuary when he'd finished his photo run. The weather briefing before take-off hadn't been encouraging; thick overcast covering the Pas-de-Calais was expected to clear as he went south. He decided to make the most of it while he could, staying in the greyness with just the comforting roar of his Merlin for company.

He flew on. Every few minutes he slipped out of the shadows to check his position, changing his heading slightly each time he emerged, trying to make it harder for any pursuer. Away to his left he could make out glimpses of the French coast, occasionally visible between the ragged footings of the clouds and the sea mist that clung to the shore. He kept checking over his shoulders, methodically, one side and the other, on guard against an attack by a lurking Messerschmitt. Travelling at high speed in the skirtings of the cloud meant there was little risk of being bounced, but the habit was deeply ingrained from his days as a fighter pilot. It had saved his life more than once.

Next on his list was Dieppe. In a minute or so he would be the target for every gun in the area. He tightened his harness and said a silent prayer. For a moment he thought of his family back at home. If anything happened, he hoped they'd be proud of him. He remembered his old school motto, *Fides et Robur*. Today he was going to need all that faith and strength.

He snatched a glance at the map strapped to his knee then checked his stopwatch, doing some quick calculations. The instruments again; course, altitude, engine temperature... all good. Fuel remaining... enough. A final check to make sure power was on to the camera. He started the countdown.

Just north of Dieppe he began a shallow descent, letting his speed build to over 300 mph as he broke through the cloud base. The port was straight ahead. He rested his thumb on the shutter button.

A mile outside the harbour entrance, a patrolling minesweeper spotted him and opened up with its flak cannon. The fire was poorly aimed, but it acted as a clarion for the rest of the defences. Twenty seconds later a second ship joined in, then a third. Soon the shells from dozens of guns were merging into a curtain of deadly colours. Streams of red and white tracer climbed towards his plane, languidly at first, before seeming to speed up viciously as they came closer, clawing at his aircraft, rocking it, trying to bring it down. Heavier shells burst orange and grey. He was scared, but he had to press on; had to run the gauntlet. If he faltered now his photographs would be worthless, the mission a waste, and he or one of his mates would be sent back to do it right.

The guns from a destroyer joined in, pock-marking the sky with oily-brown shell bursts. He pushed the nose down to gain a fraction more speed, but held tight to his heading. He pressed his elbows hard against the sides of the narrow cockpit, buttresses to stop himself flinching, and raced on just beneath the clouds, across the inner harbour and towards the quayside. The flak got fiercer; they must have been waiting for him after his pass across Boulogne. Tracer and explosions bracketed his aircraft. Every sinew in his body was protesting, his instincts screaming at him to duck, to weave, to turn away from the danger. But he held on, slouching low behind the windscreen as if the flimsy aluminium skin of his craft could protect him from shrapnel or cannon fire.

He could see the intense activity in the harbour. Ships, hundreds of them, of all types – destroyers, tugs, barg... *Christ!*

His aircraft bucked violently as a shell exploded just ahead of him. He was too close to avoid it and fought to retain control as he passed through the detritus. The Spitfire's airframe quivered, splattered with fragments of hot metal, zinging angrily. For a few seconds it was touch and go. But it kept flying.

He fought his way back on course. There were cranes below, dockside cranes. He was across the shoreline; his aircraft hurtling low over the town. Spread out on either side he could see the brute infrastructure of war, rail tracks and tank parks, vast tented encampments, yet more gun sites. He checked again... *Camera still running.*

The flak got heavier as the 88mm guns of the shore batteries joined in. Black shell bursts darkened the sky ahead of him. Just as he was beginning to fear the unequal contest could have only one end, he saw green fields below, sweet green fields. He slipped his thumb off the shutter button and pulled back hard on the stick, soaring upwards, banking and twisting, climbing, climbing towards the sanctuary above.

Freed from the straitjacket of a fixed course, he unleashed his aircraft's power. Now it was just him and his Spitfire against the enemy. A sense of exhilaration took over as the gunfire fell away behind. He was almost there... a few seconds more...

6

The door opened and Churchill swept into the conference room, a rotund figure in his silk dressing gown. He took his place at the head of the table, surrounded by the uniformed commanders. Despite the broken night and the early hour there was an air of anticipation in the room. After the agony of defeat in France and the early anxiety about the battle in the skies over Kent, they felt in charge of events for the first time since war started. Hitler was on the point of launching his armies against England, into the trap waiting.

General Sir John Dill, Chief of the Imperial General Staff, opened the review in his usual taciturn manner, though his sharp Northern Irish accent conveyed a sense of determination. He reported that things had been quiet overnight, with little change in the military situation since the last formal meeting twelve hours earlier. He didn't mention the dramatic events of the night; they had no relevance to the immediate battle.

Each in turn the heads of the three Services made their reports. The donnish figure of General Alan Brooke reported on the Army in Britain. Another Ulsterman, his accent had been softened by years of public school education in England. He put on his horn-rimmed glasses and began to leaf through his notes... a brigade transferred from East Anglia to the strategic reserve near London; a ship carrying munitions arrived from the United States; the men ready and on full alert.

It was all much as expected. Churchill turned to Air Chief Marshal Portal. At the meeting on the previous afternoon, they'd agreed to bring up the first cohort of fighters from the secret reserves.

"Did the moves go ahead as planned?"

"Completed yesterday evening, Prime Minister. About fifty aircraft."

Portal, impassive as usual, was letting Churchill lead the discussion.

"No trouble from the Luftwaffe?"

"No sir. They've been remarkably quiet – no serious raids for the last twenty-four hours. A few nuisance attacks on London and a reconnaissance flight over Scapa Flow. We got that one."

Churchill looked relieved. He'd been nervous about releasing aircraft from the reserve in case the Germans spotted the activity and became suspicious. But they seemed to have got away with it.

"And the Lazarus squadrons?"

"Ready to spring back to life, sir, as soon as you give the word."

Churchill nodded and moved on. He asked Admiral Sir Dudley Pound, the First Sea Lord, about the naval situation.

"It's much the same story at sea, Prime Minister. Unusually quiet. A noticeable reduction in attacks on the convoys over the last week. Hardly any, in fact, over the last forty-eight hours."

"So where are their U-boats?"

His question may have been partly rhetorical. In any event, Pound made a noncommittal reply, showing, worryingly, that he didn't know.

A few months ago this reduced level of activity would have been greeted with relief. Now it simply added to the tension. The very lack of German operations was the clearest sign that the day was almost upon them.

As the short meeting broke up, Churchill asked General Dill to stay behind to discuss a report left in earlier. They waited till the others left, then sat facing each other across the table; the dour Northern Irishman in his khaki uniform, the epitome of a professional soldier, the Prime Minister in his blue silk raiment. Churchill opened the report and threw out a few half-questions, which Dill answered rather curtly, trying to hide a growing irritation. The document had been updated to address some minor concerns raised by the PM and he didn't believe it warranted further discussion. As head of the Armed Services, there were a hundred other things he should be doing as they awaited the onslaught.

For several minutes the men continued a terse conversation, until Churchill finally appeared satisfied. He closed over the document, seemingly indicating that the meeting was over. Dill stood up to leave, but the Prime Minister had one final question. He looked up at the general.

"How long now, Sir John?"

Dill stopped, pursing his lips in concentration, trying to balance many factors in his mind; the weather forecast for the next few days, the tides and moonlight, the latest Ultra intelligence and a host of other considerations.

"Tomorrow morning, Prime Minister, or the day after."

Churchill grunted. After the defeat in France, he'd chosen Dill personally as the new Chief of the Imperial General Staff, but he still hadn't managed to establish a warm relationship with him. With battle imminent, he'd hoped that a few minutes of informal conversation would help build the bond between them, the political and military leaders of the country. But he wasn't having much success. He tried again, using a different tack.

"I suppose it's too late to change our minds?"

It was the first time he'd allowed himself to show an inkling of doubt, even if it was just a feeble attempt at gallows humour. Until this point he'd been so intent on bringing the Cabinet and the Chiefs along with him that he'd steadfastly refused to let any of his own misgivings show. He was sure it was the right decision, the only decision, but that didn't make it any easier to live with. Many a weaker man would have allowed fear of failure to outweigh the insistent logic behind the plan; would have chosen to delay, if only for a few months, the fateful battle rather than invite it upon them.

General Dill chose not to respond to the opening; he had no time for idle chat.

"I'm afraid so, Prime Minister," he said and excused himself.

7

Fowley had hoped the overcast sky would continue to shelter him as he headed across the Cherbourg peninsula towards the great port at its apex. He was soon disappointed. A few minutes after he settled on the final leg, a shaft of sunlight lanced through a gap in the clouds, lighting up his cockpit for a split-second. He flinched at the sudden brightness; a burglar caught in the beam of a probing torch. He eased the stick forward, forcing his aircraft lower into the cloud layer, hoping for a few more minutes of sanctuary before the cover finally disappeared. Even as he levelled out, just a hundred feet down, he glimpsed dark, flickering shadows below – the Normandy countryside.

His hands went clammy under his thick gloves. His modified Spitfire was designed to fly six miles high in the troposphere, keeping him safe from the enemy while his long-focus camera probed the ground below. Yet here he was, trapped at a fraction of that height, playing hide and seek in a rapidly thinning layer of cloud. He was almost out of time.

He had to assume he was being stalked. Although he was flying at his best long-range speed, he knew that wouldn't be fast enough to outpace any German fighters tracking him. He wondered who might be up there, above the cloud, waiting to pounce. A single *Expert*, perhaps, with dozens of kill markings already stencilled on the side of his cockpit, confident of adding to his score? Or a pair of flyers in their sleek 109s, an experienced leader and his wingman? Maybe more? They knew exactly the purpose of his mission and would be anxious to stop his vital film getting back to England. They would want to keep the British in the dark for every minute possible on this day of days.

Flying half-blind, in and out of the greyness, Fowley kept searching for pursuers. They had to be up there, watching and waiting, guided by radar controllers sitting at display screens in some comfortable hut. He didn't know much about the German radar. Some of the RAF intelligence officers dismissed the idea it was any good. It was easy for them; they didn't have to fly these dangerous sorties. Weeks ago, he'd decided to make the prudent assumption that their radar was pretty much the same as the British; that they would be plotting his course and altitude as he flew south, carefully positioning their fighters a mile or so behind him, ready for the last veil to drop.

At times like this he hated his reconnaissance role. In a fighter he would at least have his eight guns to fight back with; a fair contest, even if it was two or three against one. He ran his thumb over the top of the stick where the gun button would be, but on this mission he had no guns, only his cameras. His aircraft was exposed, near naked under the watch of the German radar, with only the cloud as a flimsy garment. And even that was beginning to slip. He would have to call on all his skills of airmanship to survive. That was how he was still alive after thirty of these dangerous missions over France.

He had to find out more about the odds he faced while he still had some cover to retreat to. A quick look-see to help him time his next move; a flash of petticoat to tempt his pursuers. If they tried an immediate attack, so much the better; a sharp turn back into the cloud as they closed would muddy the picture for the radar controllers. It might allow him to escape in the confusion. They probably wouldn't fall for it, but, in any event, it was time.

He pulled back gently on the stick and eased up into the brightness above, turning his head hard around to check behind him. No bursts of cannon fire as he emerged, thank God! A glint – no two – close to each other, maybe half a mile away; the sun on polished canopies. Two of them at least... He watched. They were pointing towards him, but were well out of range, keeping their distance. He waited for a minute to see if they would be tempted into an attack, but they held back. They were *Experten* all right; not going to be rushed. They knew the weather picture as well as he did.

8

Churchill's office was empty when Bracken and Menzies went in. They'd both been there on the previous evening, but it was their first quiet moment to have a look around.

The room was a bit larger than Winston's previous pen in the warren under Whitehall, though, with low ceilings, felt smaller. It had obviously been finished just recently and the smell of the new paint still lingered, but the colour was one of the grey institutional shades favoured by the Civil Service and did nothing to brighten the place up.

"Really quite palatial!" Bracken said as he surveyed the dull surroundings. On balance, he decided he preferred the plain concrete render in his own spartan quarters.

He could see there'd been a few additions over the last hours. The black desk was now furnished with the mundane accessories of office life; a telephone, pen holder and document tray. The bare bulb hanging from the ceiling had been fitted with a shade.

"Somebody's been at work early," he said, lifting the phone to check the dial tone.

In a corner behind the desk was a metal filing cabinet. It looked like the unit from the old office in the Cabinet War Rooms, but seemed somewhat battered, perhaps knocked about in the move.

The only touch of homeliness was a dark blue sofa, pushed up against a wall. It too had a clear practical function. Lying on top, in an untidy heap, were blankets and a pillow, obviously tossed aside just recently.

There wasn't so much as a painting or photograph to brighten up the walls, just a few maps pinned to a corkboard. Bracken stepped over to have a closer look. One, showing the western countries of Europe, was heavily marked with lines of green ink that tracked the progress, day-by-day, of the Nazi armies as they stormed across France and Belgium. Next to it was a matching map of the British Isles, as yet unmarked, though the green pen lay nearby. Bracken held the pen up and caught Menzies' eye, before putting it back in its holder.

On the other side was a larger map, a Mercator projection of the world. It was an old edition, dating back to the turn of the century. Bracken had often teased about buying him a new one, but he knew it was Churchill's favourite: a quarter of the globe was still painted red.

He looked around the dreary room again.

"Somehow I can't see Mr. Hitler moving in, even if Winston does have to vacate the place."

Menzies smiled. "Not really his style, I suppose. In fact, just between the two of us, he was on to me yesterday. Wants to know when Windsor Castle will be available and whether the carpets are included."

Bracken chuckled at the thought. At least he assumed it was just a thought; with Menzies it was sometimes hard to be sure.

A porter came in with an upholstered chair from the old office. He placed it behind the desk and left. A few minutes later Jock Colville appeared, carrying the Prime Minister's cigar humidor and a bottle of his favourite brandy, also, presumably, just brought over from Whitehall. He put them on top of the filing cabinet.

"That must be the manservant," Bracken muttered to Menzies, just loud enough for Colville to hear. It was a slight revenge on the young civil servant for the early morning call. The young Cambridge graduate smiled and refused to rise to the bait.

"He's just finished with the Chiefs... off to use the loo. Shouldn't be long. You wouldn't believe the trouble I had to find him a tin bath. Oh, I suppose I should apologise for the rude awakening, Brendan... couldn't say anything more with Rab in the room."

Bracken spluttered.

"Rab? Butler? What in the name of God is he doing here?"

"Didn't you know? He came over to see Lord Halifax last evening and got stranded with the air raid warning."

"For Christ's sake, Jock, this place is supposed to be secret... even from the other ministers."

"Maybe you should discuss that with the Foreign Secretary."

Colville chose not to argue the point. Brendan was a good friend, but he didn't see why he should take the grief for Halifax's actions.

"Does Winston know?"

"No."

"Well, I strongly suggest you don't tell him. And get Butler out of here fast."

A few minutes later the Prime Minister returned from his ablutions, wrapped in his dressing gown and carrying a towel. Tagging along behind him were Pug Ismay, his military advisor, and Max Beaverbrook, the Minister for Aircraft Production. They seemed to be engaged in an animated debate about defence of the aircraft factories. Churchill ended the discussion and muttered a gruff greeting to the two waiting for him, then grunted in a more agreeable tone when he spotted the recent deliveries. He dressed unselfconsciously in front of the group, putting on a green boiler suit over long underwear. He took a cigar from the humidor and smelled along its length before, looking somewhat sadly at the clock, putting it back in the box. He sat down and tested his old chair with a few childlike bounces. Finally, the cameo over, he looked up at Bracken.

"You've heard?"

"I have indeed. C's briefed me. Incredible news... changes everything. Though I hear certain of our colleagues are less than ecstatic."

"Huh. I will ignore those two... what was it you called them yesterday?" He fumbled for a moment. "*Begrudgers*, wasn't it? An appropriate word for those two gentlemen... unwilling to accept this unexpected gift and still trying to peddle their own fanciful ideas. They fail to understand that war, like politics, is the art of the possible. The Chiefs have already made quite clear what is possible in present circumstances and what is not."

General Ismay signalled his agreement, almost imperceptibly, though Bracken noted the PM had made no reference to the concerns expressed by Attlee or Eden.

"What about Ethelred? Has the news changed the Chiefs' thinking at all?"

Churchill let Ismay answer.

"They're still looking at it, Brendan. As far as the current situation is concerned, it doesn't seem to make any difference, at least in the next few days – much too late. Medium term, we've a decision to take whether to stick with the original plans, or try to cut Jerry off earlier than intended – say, after the first wave lands."

"And sink the second lot as they cross?"

"Or chase them back to France... Well, that's the debate – at least in theory," Ismay said. "In practice, it can be hard to distinguish between one wave of an attack and the next. The 'fog of war' and all that. Let's say that, up to now, we've been planning to wait until all their mobile forces had crossed from France or were on the high seas before springing the trap. With this news about Russia, we might decide to be less ambitious. Move earlier... go for a limited victory instead of a triumph."

"Seems a clear enough choice," Bracken said. "Any particular issues on the military side to worry about?"

Ismay pondered for a moment.

"Nothing too surprising. Assuming we manage to stop the second wave, it still leaves the first wave to be mopped up here. That shouldn't be too much of a problem once we cut off their supply lines. Overall, I'd say that moving early means we'll inflict less damage on them than we'd hoped – but, by the same token, should suffer fewer casualties ourselves. And, I suppose, take less of a risk along the way."

His words hung in the air for a moment as they each thought about the question. After all the effort to prepare a devastating blow against the Nazis, there seemed a reluctance to accept any lesser prize.

Bracken was first to break the silence.

"You know, Winston, with the Russians about to be dragged in, I think I'd settle for that. It's all well and good playing David against Goliath. But this Goliath's got a sling too, a big one."

"And more stones than us," Beaverbrook said.

Churchill was listening closely. He turned to Ismay. "The Chiefs, Pug... how are they likely to react? They pushed back hard this morning when Halifax suggested stopping the first wave."

"They'll go along with it, sir. I spoke to Dill and Brooke afterwards. Their reluctance earlier on was simply about timing. They're well aware that even a limited victory would be the first real defeat for Hitler since the war started"

Menzies had stayed unusually quiet and Churchill asked for his opinion.

"I agree with Brendan, Prime Minister. We should settle for the smaller victory – but maybe for a different reason."

He waited until he had their attention.

"If we knock his army about too badly, he might drop his Russian plans."

Churchill flashed a sharp look at Menzies; some things were better left unsaid. But it might have helped him come to a decision.

"Gentlemen, we don't have time for a protracted debate. It seems clear we can reduce the ambition of Ethelred while still achieving an epic victory over Hitler. A failed invasion is what the world will see, whether we kill fifty thousand of his stormtroopers or twice that number. General Ismay, talk to the Chiefs. Tell them my decision. I trust there'll be no insurmountable difficulties."

He paused for a moment and looked at Bracken.

"Brendan, you weren't involved in the row this morning, so you're the best person to tell the others. Talk to them before the Cabinet meeting this evening – one at a time, I suggest. Maybe you can un-ruffle some ruffled feathers."

Bracken smiled.

"I know what, Winston. I'll tell them they've convinced you."

Churchill grinned at his friend's insouciance.

"As you wish, dear Brendan."
Then he focused on the most difficult conversation.
"But I'll speak to Halifax myself."

9

Paddy Fowley took a deep breath and rolled his Spitfire onto its back, pulling the stick into the pit of his stomach, urging the aircraft into an inverted dive. Down he went, not levelling out in the thinning cloud or just below, but continuing to plummet earthwards. Ignoring the red lines on his instruments he plunged towards the ground, rolling his wings level again, accelerating to almost 500 mph. He kept glancing at the compass, holding tight to his original course south. Below, he saw dark fields looming. Countryside, open countryside. *Thank God.* At least there was no flak to add to his problems. His eyes were glued to the altimeter, now just snatching an occasional glance at the world outside. *2000 ft... trees getting larger... ease the descent; 1000 ft ... hedges, walls... start levelling out; 500 ft... too low for radar to follow him; 250 ft... flat and level...*

Now TURN!

He banked the aircraft hard to port and pulled on the stick with all his strength, wrestling the aircraft round. The Spitfire shuddered, protesting at the ungentlemanly piloting. He knew its springy wings could take the strain. *Could he?* His face distorted under the g-force. He could sense himself beginning to grey-out... vision narrowing... the danger sign. *Ease off on the stick.* Hard to see the compass. *Hold on, hold on.* He heard himself panting into his oxygen mask with the strain. Nearly there... a full 180 degree turn. He released the stick, straightening out, low and fast, still doing well over 300 mph, but now pointing due north, tracking back along the path he'd just travelled. Still clear behind. *So far, so good.*

He didn't know how quickly the German radar operators would react to his disappearance. With luck, he'd have a minute or two before they alerted his pursuers... that they'd assume he was still on his original course south, just down at lower level. He hoped that was the message they'd send to the Messerschmitts. Meanwhile, he would be hurtling back north at tree-top height, stretching the distance between them by the second. *One, two, three,* he began to count. If he'd timed it right, the 109s would now be miles away, heading away from him, confused by his vanishing trick. He hoped... He hoped... *Twenty-eight, twenty-nine, CLIMB!!*

He pushed the throttle forward through the gate to full emergency boost. Three hundred horsepower extra poured from the Merlin engine. His Spitfire zoomed skywards, towards and through the last scatterings of friendly cloud.

CLIMB... CLIMB... CLIMB... harder and faster than he'd ever climbed before. Pushing his engine to its limit and beyond. *Five thousand, six thousand, seven thousand feet.* At low altitude, the boost from his engine meant he could climb faster than any fighter in the world. But the power would fade away as he got higher, leaving his Spit and the 109s evenly matched. If he hadn't managed to get above them, he'd be in big trouble. He sought a second line of defence, easing gently to the east, towards the rising sun. It would be shining into his pursuers' eyes. If they'd spotted his feint and were closing in, the still-low sun would make him hard to track.

THERE! He saw them clearly for the first time: a pair of 109s... bright yellow noses, turning to climb after him, closer than hoped, *but a thousand feet below!* There was a flash of gunfire, but it was a futile gesture, the tracer shells falling away harmlessly below him. He watched the 109s for a few more minutes... *Thank Christ, they're not closing.*

Climb... climb... keep climbing. *Fifteen thousand feet.* He was almost safe. He checked again on his hunters. They were slowly losing ground, probably cursing their luck for missing the sitting duck or swearing silently at their useless controller for misdirecting them. He began to breathe more deeply in his mask. Higher and higher he went, leaving the 109s far behind, gradually making a gentle turn back onto his track south. *Twenty thousand feet.* Just a few more minutes ... *twenty-five thousand.* The sky was getting a deeper, richer blue. In another five minutes or so he would reach his ceiling, thirty thousand feet, maybe a bit higher, thirty-one or thirty-two, depending on the temperature outside.

He relaxed, to the extent he ever did over enemy territory. He felt at home up here. He knew the beautiful curved wings of his beloved Spitfire would cling to the thin air like no other aircraft, cradling him from danger. Six miles above the earth he could soar like a playful angel. *A lonely impulse of delight.* He remembered another scrap of Yeats's poem. Even if the joyous emotion rested uneasily with his work of war, it captured perfectly the thrill of flight.

A few short minutes later the thrill was forgotten. Before he even reached Cherbourg he saw his quarry, far below. A large convoy was making its way north, towards the Channel; he reckoned about a hundred steamships in total. On their seaward side he could see the long wakes of some faster ships, obviously escorts, racing up and down like harrying sheepdogs. His camera rolled for a full five minutes as he flew high above them, finishing only as he passed over the great port and its now-empty quaysides.

His task complete, he turned towards England.

10

As the lines of camouflaged trucks and armoured vehicles neared Boulogne, their progress slowed. More convoys appeared from more distant encampment areas, hundreds of lorries and buses full of troops, intermixed with dozens of panzers and support vehicles. All were moving in the same direction; all had to be merged into the great grey caterpillar.

At each junction military police drew on their experience from the Polish and French campaigns to keep them moving, shouting and gesticulating at drivers, alternately stopping columns or urging them on, conscious of the strict schedule to be maintained.

Fritz Weber was awed by the scale of it all. The lines of transports trundling towards the docks seemed to stretch for tens of kilometres. Just outside the main gate the column stopped at a level crossing to let a train rumble by, its freight cars loaded high with tanks, guns and supply wagons.

Inside the port area he was greeted with a scene of barely-organised chaos. Thousands of soldiers were milling around, seeking or being given directions. Most of the men were from the regular divisions of the Heer, from a wide range of infantry and panzer regiments, but at one junction Weber saw another group of men; tough-looking naval infantry with camouflage smocks over dark blue uniforms. He recognised one or two of the officers. The unit had been billeted nor far from his own men and, over the weeks, there'd been a few scraps in the local taverns. His grenadiers looked at the marines climbing down from their lorries with a mixture of respect and disdain. Weber knew it was time to put their differences aside. Whatever the mission the marines had to undertake next day, he knew it would be both dangerous and vital to the success of Sea Lion. He saluted their commander as they passed. He responded. They were all on the same side now.

A short distance further along the quays, his men were startled to come across a group of soldiers in British uniforms. A corporal was speaking to them in English. Weber thought it sounded like a regional accent, maybe from Liverpool or Manchester, maybe Scottish. He'd heard about a special force trained for operations behind enemy lines, the Brandenburg regiment. He guessed it was them, already in character for their mission in the morning. There was no sign of an officer with them and one of the grenadiers took advantage of the opportunity, shouting out from the back of the half-track.

"You'd better be careful, you lot, poncing around here dressed like Tommies."

The corporal switched in mid-sentence from English to a rich Hamburg accent and hurled a mouthful of expletives at the grenadier, ending with a vile allegation about his mother. The tension was gone. The soldiers laughed, both grey- and khaki-clad. Fritz Weber gave them a friendly wave as the half-tracks jerked into motion again.

Just a few minutes later, however, their humour changed again. They slowed to a stop at their marshalling point for embarkation. Standing outside a dock warehouse were some solders wearing field-grey, but with a different insignia on their collars. *Waffen-SS.*

There was an uneasy silence as the two groups looked at each other, eventually broken when one of the bolder grenadiers asked politely if they were lost. The SS men weren't normally seen this close to the front line. The rumours about them murdering British prisoners of war during the Battle of France hadn't endeared them to the Feldgrau either. No-one knew who might be a PoW tomorrow.

* * *

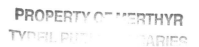

Half a kilometre from the entrance to the port, a young French-woman was also up early. Gabrielle Leman had been woken in the middle of the night by noise outside her parents' auberge; voices, German voices, and the sound of boots on cobblestones. She watched through a chink in the curtains as many hundreds of men walked in loose formation along the road. Driving alongside the ragged column were scores of vehicles, packed with soldiers or towing weapons, a seemingly endless line moving down towards the port. She heard another sound, in the distance but coming closer, the sound that had struck terror into soldiers across the continent, the clanking of tank tracks.

She knew it was the day. For weeks she'd been preparing, making friends with dozens of German officers in the town, ensuring they always received a cordial welcome in the inn. She'd even slept with one of them, a poignant half-pleasure, in her quest to build a picture of their forces in the area.

So far, the worst that had happened had been some vicious name-calling from neighbours and old school friends. It stung, but she could live with it.

If her real role had been suspected by the Nazis, if her meticulous notes on unit identities and equipment had been detected, if her couriers had been discovered in their hiding place, she knew the consequences. But for France and for freedom, she had taken the risk.

Now, on this calm, autumn morning it was finally happening. From behind almost-closed curtains she watched in the half-light for almost an hour, counting and noting, carefully recording the units as they made their way down to the quays. On they came, regiment by regiment, panzer by panzer. She saw Fritz's unit trundling past in their half-tracks. For a moment she thought she saw him, but it might have been any of the officers.

Down by the harbour she sensed a bustle of activity. With the help of a battered telescope left behind years earlier by a drunken sea-captain, she could just make out ships casting off from the wharfs and moving to the outer reaches. There, they seemed to halt, presumably at anchor, while others moved in to take their places at the quayside. She knew she couldn't spend much longer compiling her report. Her cell leader had told her it was vital to get some reliable information across at the earliest possible moment, rather than wait to record every detail. So, as the first glimmer of dawn tinted the sky, she folded the closely-scripted message page into a small container and entrusted it to her messenger.

An hour later, the first news that the invasion of England was under way was delivered to a loft near Dover Castle. It was conveyed by means of a centuries-old technology; a hand-written note, folded into a metal tube and tied to a pigeon's leg.

11

The party was waiting at the foot of the entrance stairwell when Churchill appeared, a few minutes behind schedule. He looked testy. He didn't expect the tour of inspection to be of any value to him personally; it was up to others to make sure the place worked as intended. Bracken had managed to convince him it was important that he and the top brass were visible. While the staff all knew they were in the countdown to the invasion, a walk-around was the simplest way of showing that the leaders were ready and confident.

Churchill acquiesced and then chose the rest of the tour party with some care. The Paddock was primarily a military facility, so he asked the Chiefs of Staff and General Ismay to accompany him, but not the civilian members of the War Cabinet. At the last minute, he told Bracken to come along as well, on the grounds he was responsible for press communications and radio broadcasts from the centre. In fact he wanted to continue a discussion from the previous night.

Their guide was the officer in charge of the facility, a ruddy-faced Royal Marines major, who introduced himself and led them along a white-tiled corridor. Even as they moved off, Churchill could sense the change from his previous visit a week earlier. People were hurrying along, brushing past them carrying folders or bits of apparatus. He sensed the unmistakeable buzz of a command centre commanding.

Their first stop was by a row of technical stations, crammed full of wireless equipment.

"Monitoring devices," the major said.

Most of the sets appeared to be in use, with uniformed personnel twiddling dials and listening to transmissions. A few of the units seemed to have been installed just recently and a handful of civilians, presumably well-vetted, were carrying out commissioning tests. They scrambled around on hands and knees, peering at wiring diagrams spread out on the floor and barely seemed to notice the VIPs.

At one station an operator pointed at his headphones and threw a switch on his set, diverting the output to a small loudspeaker. Bracken immediately recognised the hectoring voice of Lord Haw-Haw, broadcasting live on Radio Berlin. He began to listen, but after just a few seconds he spotted a Marconi recorder at the workstation, its tape reels slowly spinning. He could ignore the broadcast for now. When the tour was over, he would have the dubious pleasure of listening to the Nazi propaganda at his leisure.

A short distance further along they came across a locked room with grim signs forbidding unauthorised access, under pain of arrest. It looked like a cipher room or the like and no-one asked to see inside. They walked on past some storage rooms and came to a small open area at the end of the corridor. The major pointed out the first aid room, a mess, and some basic kitchen facilities. Inside, army cooks were busy preparing a meal. It looked like a stew of some sort, presumably for dinner that evening – though with people working around the clock, the names given to the different meals mattered little.

"If we get cut off, we have food and water for thirty days," the major added. He made no reference to the menu.

Churchill dropped to the rear of the party and signalled to Bracken to join him. Walking a few feet behind the others he whispered to him, "I don't mind being on show to the staff, but I really don't need to know the catering arrangements. Rather more important is the meeting with the ministers this afternoon. I still haven't decided what to do about Butler."

Bracken decided not to mention the overnight visit; what was done was done. But he understood Churchill's concern. Rab Butler was only a junior minister, one of twenty in the government, but he was a special case. In the years leading up to the war, he and Halifax had been leading lights in the negotiations with the Nazis. They'd been the main proponents of compromise, of appeasement.

"Is he that important anymore?" Bracken replied. "Or indeed Halifax for that matter? They're right out of favour with the party."

"That may well be true, Brendan, but it's not so long since the majority was with them. If things start to go badly for a while – and they might – is there a chance that sentiment might swing back?"

Weeks ago he'd decided to keep Halifax physically close-by, in the Paddock. It limited his opportunity for intrigue. But Butler was potentially a loose cannon.

"You could always just ignore him," Bracken said. "Rely on his patriotism to avoid any shenanigans. Knowing your feelings towards each other, that's probably no more than he expects."

He hesitated, thinking a bit more about his suggestion.

"Though I suppose there might be some element of risk with that approach."

Churchill gave him a sideways glance.

"There might indeed, Brendan. As if there aren't quite enough risks around at present."

The group moved on to the next station, with Bracken still mulling over the issue.

"I suppose he's in a different place from the others. If anybody else takes umbrage, they're not in a position to do much about it. But you're right, Rab's got contacts."

"And form," Churchill sniffed.

Back in June he'd discovered Butler had met the Swedish Ambassador and suggested that a deal with the Nazis might be possible. He'd even been reported as saying that no 'diehards' would be allowed to stand in the way of an agreement. Churchill had been incensed when he heard of the unauthorised briefing and came close to sacking the minister. On reflection, however, he was secretly pleased with Butler's blunt description of him. He hoped the sentiment had reached Hitler.

They moved along a corridor with sleeping quarters on either side, a couple of small dormitories and a few rooms with tiered bunk beds. The major told the group they were using nearby apartment blocks for staff, rather than sacrificing precious working space for bedrooms.

"If the fighting gets close, staff billeted outside will move in and sleep in the corridors," he added.

Bracken recognised the room where he'd spent the night and sneaked a look inside to check if his unexpected roommate had gone. For one anarchic moment he tried to imagine Winston's reaction if he found Butler there in his underclothes. Perhaps fortunately, he'd gone.

They came to the wash rooms. No-one needed to look inside; they were already familiar with the primitive facilities.

"Wash basins and toilets. No baths or showers, I'm afraid."

The major was beginning to sound like a prison governor, though Bracken knew there was one tin bath hidden away somewhere.

They walked along another spine, glancing into more side rooms filled with equipment: switchboards, clicking teleprinters and radio sets. One private gave a cheery thumbs-up to Churchill, who grinned and responded with a rude V-Victory sign.

Bracken picked up the discussion about Butler. "I suppose we better make sure he doesn't become a malign influence now we're all down the coalhole."

"That's what worries me," Churchill said. "Him up there in the daylight with his fellow-travellers – and there's still a few around – while we're closeted away in the catacombs, out of touch. Gives him far too much opportunity for mischief."

"I suppose we could always invite him down here with us."

Churchill snorted and gave his friend a baleful look. "It *has* been suggested," he drawled. "But I'm sure that, between us, Mr. Bracken, we can find a better solution."

Bracken laughed, mindful of the antipathy between the two men and of the close call a few minutes earlier.

They reached the plant room, crammed full of generators and air-conditioning units. The equipment was in full operation, noisy and throbbing, with tendrils of pipes and conduits snaking out to the rest of the building. From one of the ceiling pipes, water was dripping slowly, splashing into a puddle on the concrete floor. A plumber was perched on a step ladder, twiddling away at a connection.

"Temperature and humidity levels are controlled," the major said. "That's not a luxury. With two hundred people in such a confined space, it's a necessity." He sounded almost apologetic, then added, as if to justify the expense, "And the air is filtered for poison gas."

They passed the Prime Minister's office, but didn't stop. They'd all become acquainted with it over the last twelve hours. A few yards further on they were shown a little broadcasting cabin, sparsely equipped with table, chair and microphone.

"What about massaging his ego a bit?" Bracken said. "Get him to buy into the plan. Getting him on board might be the easiest way to avoid problems. Anything you could offer to keep him sweet?"

"Unfortunately, there aren't a lot of goodies to hand out in present circumstances."

They moved along in echelon, as the major droned on about some defensive features inside the complex, revolver slits and so on. The generals seemed interested, but Churchill knew it was all quite meaningless. *If the Germans got that close...*

"Maybe it doesn't have to be a goodie," Bracken said. "Why don't you give him something else to do on top of his day job – keep idle hands busy and all that. What about making him one of your new Regional... what are they? *Commissars?*"

"*Commissioners*, Brendan, please... This *is* still England."

Churchill mulled over the suggestion. Even if London fell he was determined that the fight would continue. He had mandated that political and military authority would be delegated to a number of regional bunkers, from where the remaining forces would be commanded. If, in extremis, the Regular Army was finally defeated, the struggle would be carried on by the secret British Resistance, operating from hides in farms and woodlands. He had already made that pledge in a speech to the House of Commons. *We will never surrender.*

They shuffled along.

"Actually, Brendan, that's not such a bad idea. In fact, it's smart thinking, very smart. Move Butler from hen to pig in this fine English breakfast we're serving up for Hitler. Not just involved, but committed."

"Mind your heads, please." The major warned as they came to some ventilation trunking. The tall Bracken ducked beneath it and helped Churchill through behind him.

"I was half-joking, Winston, but the more I think about it, the more I feel it could be the answer. Get him up to his neck organising one of the doomsday centres; his very own underground bunker, without actually giving him any real power."

"Somewhere out of the way, mark you!" Churchill interjected. Bracken ignored him, now warming to his theme.

"And while we're at it, Winston, we have, what, twelve or thirteen of the things? How many of our opponents could we account for? Let's see, one per hole in the ground. Couldn't put more than one in each, in case they start conspiring!"

Churchill laughed. At the front of the party, the major looked round in surprise.

"I'm quite taken with that idea, Brendan. Bury the naysayers underground... the Meerkat opposition party, just able to pop their heads up once in a while, before disappearing into their burrows again."

"Exactly! Hard to organise a rebellion when they're down below – short of burrowing from one hole to another!"

Bracken turned towards the tiled wall of the corridor and made a digging gesture, mole-like, with his hands. Churchill laughed even louder. The major was now quite unsettled.

"Unfortunately, Brendan, we don't have time to indulge our political fantasies for the moment – I'm told there's an invasion on the way. Besides which, my opponents might just notice a certain pattern."

He went quiet.

"But for Butler... yes, it might be the answer."

* * *

They came to the Operations Room, the hub of the citadel. At last Churchill began to show interest. On their last visit, a week earlier, the room had been empty and dark, now it was a brightly-lit hive of activity. People were edging round a large plotting table, some twenty feet square, which dominated the centre of the room. The top of the table was a contoured model showing the Channel and the south-east corner of England, the anticipated battleground. Sculpted in bold relief were the beaches and cliffs, roads and rivers, marshes, hills and woodlands. Prominently marked were the main airfields and naval bases, the coastal artillery sites and other key strong-points. Stretching out across the counties of southern England were several brightly coloured ribbons. They showed the series of stop-lines that guarded the approaches to London; natural barriers of rivers and escarpments, man-made obstacles of canals, trenches and fortifications.

Fifteen feet above the great stage was a gallery with a dozen glass-fronted booths, positioned in a semi-circle around the room. From these vantage points the commanders from the Army, Navy and RAF would monitor the battle, minute-by-minute, hour-by-hour.

In the pit below the gallery, a dozen young women were at work, bustling about checking equipment and accessories. There didn't seem to be a lot of movement on the table itself, but the plotters were busy, sorting out wooden blocks of various shapes and colours. These children's playthings were the symbols for the stuff of war; infantry and armoured divisions, artillery batteries, fighter and bomber squadrons, ships of various types. The plotters were wearing headsets and didn't appear to notice the illustrious visitors above.

The group watched the activity for ten minutes, impressed, but saying little. Although the room had been completed less than a week earlier, there was already an air of practised efficiency.

Churchill noticed an array of slotted boards on a partition wall behind the table, with cards showing unit identifications. Beside each slot was a set of indicator bulbs. He asked about them.

"*Green* shows a unit that's fully operational," the major said. "*Orange,* one that's not at readiness or is seriously degraded, and *Red,* one that is no longer a viable unit."

He spoke without emotion, as if uncaring of the fact that a division 'no longer viable' could mean ten thousand young men dead.

As they watched, a light beside an RAF squadron number changed from orange to green. Now they all showed green.

"We completed the final commissioning test two days ago," the major said, "and we've been fully operational since yesterday morning. As you can see, though, things are fairly quiet at present."

"That means we're just in time, Major," Churchill said.

As they watched one of the plotters paused and held her headphone close to her ear. She glanced up at the gallery and nodded. She reached out with a long croupier's pole and pushed a thimble-shaped block across the board, nearer to Cherbourg. It was marked with a red, white and blue roundel. The major identified it for them.

"One of our aircraft, Prime Minister, on a reconnaissance mission – though the position shown is just an estimate. It's been out of radar range for the last hour."

Churchill nodded, thinking for a moment of a lone, brave pilot over France.

The party moved to the adjacent Map Room. In the centre was a large conference table, and mounted on the walls around it were half a dozen large charts. They showed the other potential battle regions, the North Sea and Irish Sea, the land masses of the British Isles, and the Atlantic approaches.

Churchill's eyes scanned the scene. His mind drifted back to happier days, before the war, to Florence and its Palazzo Vecchio. He'd been captivated by the ornate map room in the palace, the *sanctum sanctorum,* the repository of world knowledge in the 16th century. In its bosom that small room held information about vast land masses and oceans, great rivers and mountain ranges, wild animals and strange peoples. As Florentine adventurers returned from their travels to the ends of the known world, the charts were updated with the information they brought, pushing back the frontiers of *terra incognita*. The secrets in the heavily-curtained room were guarded night and day.

In those distant days months would sometimes pass without any new information arriving. Time moved slowly then. In the coming battle for England the data would flood in, minute-by-minute, from radar sites and forward observation posts, from reconnaissance aircraft and patrol craft. But for all the difference in time pulse, the underlying principle hadn't changed in four hundred years. In London, in 1940, as in Renaissance Florence, knowledge was power.

12

Thirty metres deep, U-31 slipped along beneath the surface of the English Channel. Running silently on her electric motors she was hidden from the eyes and ears of the enemy above. In the submarine's control room, Korvettenkapitan Juergen Moeller looked relaxed; his crew was handling the boat well. Over to one side the navigator was crouched over his chart – a British Admiralty edition, Moeller had noted earlier, with a sense of irony. He watched as the navigator marked in an update on their track. They'd been forbidden to raise the periscope to confirm their position and had to rely on ready-reckoning for now. But from everything he'd seen so far, the staff officers at H.Q. had done a good job on the voyage planning, factoring in the fast-running currents in the Raz de Sein and routing them safely along the rocky coast of Brittany. He caught the eye of the watch officer and signalled his approval, then moved over to the hydrophone station and stood beside the operator. After a few more seconds of intense concentration while he completed a sweep, the seaman took off his headphones and looked up.

"Anything?" Moeller asked.

"No, Kapitan. Nothing."

Moeller nodded. The answer said it all. *Nothing*. Not the slow, thumping diesel of a steamship or the pitter-patter of a fishing boat's motor; not the high-pitched turbines of a warship. Nothing, in what a few months ago had been the busiest sea lane in the world.

He went back to his tiny cabin and sat thinking for a moment. He took a beige folder from a cubby hole and spread the contents on his desk, a dozen documents, his own hand-written notes and the letter from Admiral Doenitz with its blunt message. On top were two manila envelopes, one still unopened.

* * *

It had been a busy week for the twelve skippers of his flotilla. They'd gathered at a seafront villa in Brittany, in the small town of Kernevel. A year ago it had been a popular holiday resort and the villa a comfortable retreat for rich Parisians. Now it was the U-boat headquarters in France. To their annoyance the young officers had been given little time to enjoy the amenities. Instead, from early morning till late evening, they'd been schooled intensively in new battle tactics.

Doenitz's note told them they had to increase the rate of sinkings in their attacks on British convoys. They were going to switch from their current tactics, stalking their prey underwater and usually alone, to a radically different technique. In future, they would attack on the surface, in groups, relying on speed and surprise to overwhelm the enemy defences. *Wolf Packs*, Doenitz called them, conjuring up vivid images of their grey shapes roaming the Atlantic wastes.

For five days the skippers role-played the new tactics, using ship models on a billiards table to represent the players, the convoys, escorts and U-boats. They simulated approaches from the front and from the flank, by day and by night, learning what worked and what didn't. Their chief instructor, a veteran submariner from the Great War, played the role of the British convoy commander. He won the first four of the ten war games they ran. Over the course of the week, however, the U-boat skippers began to improve.

On the final evening they received a visitor, Admiral Doenitz in person. He made a short speech exhorting them to even greater efforts for the Fatherland and commending the new tactics to them. He also hinted at a more immediate reason for the change.

"In the coming months, we're going to rip the heart from the enemy convoy system – if there still are such things as enemy convoys. Because, before then, you have another mission to carry out, which may help bring the war to an early end."

With Sea Lion imminent it didn't take much imagination to know what he was alluding to.

When he finished his talk, he shook hands with the skippers and handed each of them a pair of sealed envelopes. Then, the strange little ceremony over, he stayed on to share an awkward supper with them. Some of the young officers thought there were too many uncomfortable parallels – the Admiral and his twelve skippers.

"Plenty of bread but no wine," Moeller said to Gert Schmidt, an old friend, who laughed rather too loudly.

When the meal was over, Doenitz's aide told Moeller to stay behind as the others departed. He was left alone with the Admiral in the dining room, nervous for a moment that his irreverent banter with Schmidt had been overheard.

The thin-faced admiral came over to him, not smiling, but showing no sign of censure.

"Korvettenkapitan, you'll have time enough to study your mission orders when you return to your boat. But there's something else you need to know; the written orders don't completely spell out the critical role your flotilla has to play in Sea Lion. In fact, you, Moeller, have the honour of firing the first shot. It's vital that you succeed in your mission; the outcome of the entire invasion may depend upon it. Make sure you carry out your orders meticulously and with courage, for the Fatherland and for the Fuehrer."

Doenitz straightened up and looked Moeller in the eye. He saluted.

"Heil Hitler!"

Fifty minutes after the unnerving encounter, Moeller rejoined his boat. He went straight to his cabin to open the first envelope. Their orders were straightforward, if unusually detailed. They had to leave base in Lorient in less than an hour and start passage northwards to the Channel Islands. Their destination was a secluded cove on the southern coast of Guernsey. It was a clear indication of where their mission was going to take them. Captured without a fight in June, after the fall of France, the Channel Islands were the first British soil to be occupied by an enemy for hundreds of years. More significantly, Guernsey was only 60 miles from the coast of England.

Moeller talked through the mission with his watch officers as the crew readied the boat for sea. One aspect of their orders was unusual. On previous patrols out to the Atlantic battleground, they'd left port on the surface, with lookouts on the conning tower scanning sea and sky. As long as they stayed alert, they could spot a threat in good time and submerge before a British destroyer or aircraft could reach them. In a crash dive, practised regularly, they could take the boat from klaxon sounding to twenty metres below in less than thirty seconds.

The orders for this mission were different. For the 250-mile journey from Lorient to Guernsey, they were forbidden to sail on the surface during the hours of daylight. Instead of being driven along at a brisk 15 knots by their powerful diesels, they would have to crawl along underwater at a third of that speed, using their electric motors and keeping a watchful eye on the batteries. There was a further, unwelcome adjunct to their orders. Even in the event of an emergency, they were forbidden to surface. Instead they had to drop to the bottom and await rescue. Clearly, it was vital to the success of the mission that they weren't detected.

* * *

Close to midnight on the day after leaving Lorient, U-31 had reached its destination off the sheltered south coast of Guernsey, Icart Bay. Three miles offshore they switched off their noisy diesels and slipped into the bay under the electric motors. As the boat slowed to a halt, the navigator climbed the con to check their exact location. He took transits from landmarks just visible in the moonlight, then slid back down the ladder and marked up the fixes on the chart. He stood back, satisfied, and allowed the skipper to inspect his work.

"That's good." Moeller nodded. The tight little triangle pencilled onto the chart showed the fix was precise.

He turned to the watch officer. "Depth?"

The officer checked the dial and matched the reading from against the tide tables. It was close. So far, so good. They were in the right place, at the right time.

Moeller leaned over to examine the chart more closely. "And the seabed is *sand*."

He nodded in approval. It was another sign the mission had been planned with care. *Weed* or *rock* would have made for a lot less comfortable cradle overnight.

The skipper climbed up to the con for one final scan around, watching as another U-boat glided past them towards its resting point. He dropped back down and locked the hatch above his head.

"Take her down."

With the crew hanging onto stanchions and pipes they descended and settled gently on the seabed. He waited while the boat was secured and then ordered the off-watch crew to stand down. The seamen made for their hammocks, to rest and conserve oxygen during the wait.

The first stage of their mission completed, Moeller retired to his cabin. He lay down on his bunk but couldn't sleep. His mind was on the second envelope.

13

"The Foreign Secretary, Prime Minister."

Colville announced Lord Halifax and stood back as the grey-suited figure ducked his six-and-a-half-foot frame under the lintel. Churchill looked up from the papers on his desk and greeted him.

"Morning again, Edward! Thanks for coming round."

He gestured for him to sit down and waited as Halifax settled.

"Look, I wanted to talk about our disagreement a few hours ago. It was all quite unfortunate. I think it would be best for everybody if we could clear the air."

After their fierce row earlier on, it was as pleasant an introduction as he could manage.

Halifax sat upright in his chair, not sure what way the conversation would develop. He eased his withered left arm onto the arm of the chair.

"That would be good, Prime Minister, though I believe our differences are quite profound."

"I'm not sure they need be. The decisions which led to our differences earlier this morning, were driven by military minds, not mine."

"As far as I'm aware, sir, we still live in a democracy. The Armed Forces remain answerable to the government."

"You know what I mean. This news about Russia has broken so late we're left with little or no choice how we might respond. Whether we like it or not, for the first phase of the battle at least, the lines are drawn."

"I'm afraid I don't totally accept that, Prime Minister. This news about Russia gave us one final opportunity to avoid the risks associated with Ethelred. But, to be frank, it's not just about this latest decision. This has come as the culmination of a series of issues I've been unhappy about."

Churchill hesitated for a moment. The conversation was heading in a direction he wanted to avoid. It was no time for a split in the Cabinet.

"I recognise that, Edward, absolutely. And I'm grateful you've continued to give your support even when you haven't fully agreed with me. Look, this battle's going to be decided in the next two weeks, maybe three. If I'm right, and I pray to God I am, you'll be associated with our victory – and deservedly so. You'll carry that legacy into your new posting in Washington. It will make for an excellent start there."

"And if you're wrong, Prime Minister?"

Churchill hesitated. Being wrong was something he hadn't given much thought to, except in the occasional nightmare.

"If I'm wrong, I won't be in my current position much longer. Whatever accommodation needs to be reached with that vile Austrian corporal, I won't be part of it. In fact, if it comes to it, I think you've shown sufficient independence of mind to take up the cudgel – whether you're here or in your new position in America."

"It's not a prospect I relish, Prime Minister."

"In that case let's both do our damnedest to make sure it doesn't happen."

Halifax responded with a nod.

Churchill wasn't sure whether it signalled agreement or just that he'd heard the request, but he made the positive assumption and moved on. "There's something else I'd like you to do for me," he said. "Our meeting with the junior ministers is confirmed for this afternoon, to brief them about Ethelred. I think Rab's earned the right to hear before the others. Will you speak to him beforehand?"

"Of course, sir."

Churchill smiled at Halifax. It was a bit forced, but he was happy enough with how the meeting had gone. It could have been a lot worse.

The Foreign Secretary stood up and left, also looking quite content. He wanted to see Butler anyway.

14

With the Halifax problem at least confronted, Churchill had another thorny question to consider. He sent Colville to find Bracken. When his friend came in, he sat still for a moment, pursing his lips and being careful to avoid his eye, clearly uneasy about something. Finally, after some long seconds, he spoke.

"We have to decide whether to tell Stalin."

Bracken looked at him, astonished. He felt that the impending, violent break-up of the pact between Hitler and Stalin was the best news they'd had in months.

"Tell Stalin? Why in God's name would we do that?"

"Why, Brendan, why? In the hope that Uncle Joe will stop killing off his own generals and leave them to face up to Hitler."

For years they'd watched as Stalin's purges scarred the face of Russia. Month after month the show-trials had rolled on in the House of the Trade Unions in Moscow. Dozens, perhaps hundreds, of generals had been put on trial and found guilty on a range of trumped-up charges. Their fates weren't hard to guess.

Bracken was still shaking his head.

"The Red Army generals would certainly thank you, but I don't know who else. Personally, I can't think of anything better than letting the thieves fall out and get stuck into each other. Will make our own prospects a lot brighter. In any event, even if you did try to warn him, there's no chance he'd believe you – you're not going to tell him the source, are you?"

"Tell him about Canaris? No, of course not."

"So he'd probably think you're just trying to wind him up... probably call his mate Hitler on the phone and tell him. We'd end up letting both the Russians and the Germans know we've a source in the top circles in Berlin, or we've broken the Enigma code – or both!"

Churchill was still framing a reply to Bracken's outburst when there was a knock on the door. General Ismay came in, sensing at once the atmosphere in the air. He paused for a moment, waiting for the tension to ease.

"Prime Minister, I wonder if you could join us in the Operations Room?"

Churchill left behind a still-fuming Bracken and went with Ismay. They went into an empty booth overlooking the great table. On the other side of the gallery, a naval commander was holding a telephone to his ear, at the same time gesticulating to his colleagues to be quiet. He tucked the phone under his chin and lifted another one in his other hand. Down below at the plotting table, a young woman glanced up towards the officer. She pressed her headset close to an ear and nodded an acknowledgment. Reaching over, she took a blue and black chequered block from the storage rack.

"That's the symbol for a group of steamers or barges," Ismay whispered. "Fifty or more."

The plotter laid the block on the edge of the table and pushed it across the surface until it settled just outside the port of Boulogne.

Churchill said nothing, just looked at Ismay and nodded slowly. The Stalin question would have to wait. They had more immediate things to worry about.

* * *

Within an hour information was flowing in to the Paddock. The initial report from Boulogne was followed by more messages, sent by carrier pigeon or transmitted, at great personal risk, by wireless operators. The reports from the resistance workers were soon being supplemented by information from military sources. In the last hours of darkness, a flotilla of motor torpedo boats had dashed across the

Channel to check the French ports. As they withdrew with the breaking dawn, a pair of submarines ventured close inshore to monitor the Dutch and Belgian ports. The reports back from all sources were consistent; the invasion convoys were forming up.

Just before 1100 the flurry of intelligence reports took on concrete form. An RAF intelligence officer told them the photographs were ready. Churchill and the senior commanders filed back into the Map Room and waited as Squadron Leader Miller mounted a large print on a tripod stand. He stood back.

"Just north of Cherbourg, gentlemen."

He let them look at it for a few moments before going on. Even then, he didn't have much to say.

"Prime Minister, they're on the way."

He paused. The rest, when he continued, would be detail.

"The convoy from Cherbourg left port about six hours ago – over a hundred steamers and a dozen escorts. They're heading north and should reach the Channel about dawn. Looking at the other ports south of the Dover Straits, the progress of the embarkations is consistent with that schedule. Based on what we can already see, we anticipate more than a thousand vessels crossing tonight, in the southern sector alone."

He hesitated, expecting questions. But no-one spoke; they knew there was more to come and let Miller continue. One at a time, he mounted the photographs from the other ports. He identified the groups of escort vessels swinging at anchor in the outer harbours and, inside the ports, the dozens of ferries being loaded with armoured vehicles. At the quaysides, hundreds of steamers and barges were rafted up, with long lines of troops ready for embarkation.

There was silence in the room as they absorbed the visual information. Eventually, General Dill asked the question on all their minds.

"Any prediction yet where they're going to land?"

"We can't be absolutely certain, sir, but we've done some estimates based on the speed of the first convoy. Assuming a landing at dawn, it looks like they're heading for the Channel beaches. The south coast doesn't appear to be a target."

General Brooke had been impressed with the quality of the intelligence data, but he knew it was only half the picture.

"What about the ports to the north of the Straits, Squadron Leader? No photographs of them?"

"I'm afraid the plane sent out to cover the northern sector didn't make it back," he answered. "We've sent out another Spitfire to complete the mission... same pilot who took the shots you've just seen. He's probably our top man, but won't be back for another hour."

Brooke nodded sympathetically. "Let's hope."

The group returned to the Operations Room and watched as the level of activity began to build. Around the table, staff were laying out new pieces, adding blocks of different shapes and colours, pushing them out across the surface. It painted a tableau of a great army on the move. Another wave of activity began as staff began tagging the blocks with identifications labels.

Churchill asked the major how they knew.

"Wireless traffic, sir. We've been monitoring their signals for months," he said. "Thousands of messages... clear language or code, it doesn't matter. Once a unit gets identified at its base in France, we can track it after that from its signals."

The Prime Minister nodded, but he noted that, for all the volume of reports now flowing in, one mushroom-shaped symbol still hadn't moved. The most-feared unit of all, the 7th Fallschirmjaeger Division, was still sitting on the airfield at Beauvais. Its 8000 paratroopers were likely to be in the van of the attack, but they might descend anywhere in southern England.

Churchill returned to his office, but couldn't sit still for more than a few minutes. He flitted in and out of the Operations Room, watching the plotters at work. He recognised the mood of quiet efficiency. It was similar to what he'd seen many times in Bentley Priory, as the RAF controllers directed the fighters in the battle over Kent. This morning, though, the action seemed to be in slow motion; ships didn't move as quickly as aircraft.

He spotted Dill and Brooke in one corner, deep in conversation, and went over to listen in. Dill told him the photographs from the northern sector had arrived. They confirmed there was no attack pending on the flat beaches of East Anglia. The generals said they were looking at transferring another brigade south from Suffolk to bolster the reserves near London. Then they stopped talking. Churchill walked away, leaving them at it.

In another booth, he saw Admiral Pound and Air Chief Marshall Portal closeted together, fingers hovering over a map, talking and pointing. They seemed to be sketching out the routes of the German convoys, perhaps with a view to making a co-ordinated attack. He walked over.

"Everything in order?" he asked quietly, with no particular question in mind.

"Yes sir." They answered in unison, but didn't elaborate. The two commanders excused themselves and left the booth, presumably to set in motion some carefully-orchestrated scores.

For almost the first time since becoming Prime Minister, Churchill didn't know what to do with himself. There was no point in loitering around as people went about their tasks; he would simply get in the way. There was no sense calling a meeting of the Chiefs of Staff; they were busy. Even though the fate of the nation might be decided in the next twenty-four hours, there seemed nothing more he could contribute. Finally, he responded to some gentle prompting from Pug Ismay and went back to his office.

15

Nine miles away, two besuited figures emerged from the Foreign Office. They stepped over the heaps of swept-up glass on the pavement and crossed into the cleared lane in the middle of King Charles' Street.

Lord Halifax had come over to see Butler ahead of the ministerial meeting scheduled for early afternoon. To his junior's surprise, he then insisted on going outside to talk.

Butler blinked as he moved from the sandbag-darkened interior into the brightness of the day, then wrinkled his nose at the stench of burning in the air. Just across the narrow street, the faux turrets of the Treasury building stood blackened with fire.

Halifax guided them right, towards St James' Park. Going down the Clive Steps at the end of the street they could see the gaping holes in the streetscape around them, where buildings had been razed. It was a city changed beyond recognition. Few of the landmark blocks had escaped unscathed. As they reached the foot of the steps, the horizon opened up and Butler could see a pillar of black smoke in the distance, still rising after the attack on the docks two days earlier.

"Oil or rubber by the looks of it," he said.

They crossed over to St. James's Park. Beneath their feet the autumn grass was flecked with grimy ash. Butler sniffed the air again. "Or maybe sugar?"

Halifax still hadn't said anything.

There were few other people in the park. Over the previous weeks, much of the civilian population had been evacuated to safer lodgings in the west of the country. The only passers-by were military personnel, striding along purposefully with briefcases or despatch boxes under their arms, and a few civil servant types, taking a brief exercise in the gap between air raids. With London suffering attacks by day and night, only those with easy access to a shelter if the sirens sounded would risk going out in the centre of Whitehall.

They walked past sandbagged defence posts, nodding at the surprised soldiers inside. When the first emplacements had been dug in the park, some suggested they were whimsical, a gesture to show the nation's switch onto a war footing. No longer. The German army had built up its paratrooper force to a full division in strength and they'd already demonstrated their capability for shock attacks in Belgium and Holland. While it seemed unlikely they would launch an assault into the heart of London, the defenders had to be ready.

Halifax steered them onto a path well away from other walkers and started to explain the reason for his sudden visit. He began to unveil the secrets of Ethelred.

Butler listened, dumbfounded, as he heard about a great deception under way to fool Hitler, pretending Britain was on its last legs, in the hope he would be tempted into launching an invasion before his forces were ready. He heard that the RAF hadn't been decimated, as he'd feared, but withdrawn to secret bases in the west, allowing the Luftwaffe free rein over Britain. Even as he walked along, he could see around the consequences of that reckless ploy, the bomb sites and the devastated buildings.

He listened in disbelief as Halifax told him how false rumours had been put out about mutinies in the armed forces, and how a phantom group of dissidents had been invented who were allegedly planning a coup in London. He wondered – though Halifax gave no such hint – whether the bogus messages had implied he himself was one of the conspirators.

Butler wasn't just shocked by the news, he was humiliated. With scheming and skulduggery all around them, he and his fellow ministers had been kept in the dark. When Halifax finally went silent, his reaction was acerbic.

"Has the man gone completely mad?"

Halifax looked around, as if nervous that someone might be hiding behind the ash trees, eavesdropping.

"A number of us would have some sympathy with that point of view."

"How on earth did he get you to agree?"

"We didn't actually volunteer," Halifax sniffed. "He pulled his usual trick, manoeuvred us into a corner before announcing his scheme. Played off one against another..."

"The Chiefs must be mortified. Dill, at least, is no fool."

"He'd managed to get them on board first – God only knows how. Though I sense Dill's none too happy."

"Playing at toy soldiers, the lot of them, with the fate of the country at stake. Outrageous," Butler said.

There was a tone of resignation in their voices. Two years earlier the two had been at the centre of the diplomatic efforts to avoid war. They'd worked together, exchanging reams of correspondence with the German Foreign Office. Swallowing their personal distaste for the Nazis, they'd arranged meetings with Hitler in Berlin and at the Berghof, trying hard to reach an agreement, some said *too* hard. Their efforts had paved the way for the summit meetings at Munich between Prime Minister Chamberlain and the Fuehrer, and they had acted as cheerleaders when an agreement of sorts was signed.

"Peace for our time!" The image of Chamberlain waving the scrap of paper with Hitler's scribbled signature had spread around the world.

Peace for twelve months had been the reality; six months for Hitler to complete his annexation of Czechoslovakia and another six months before he'd launched his invasion of Poland. If Hitler had been a man of his word, if even, perhaps, he'd shown some decorum as he pursued his territorial ambitions, the two would now be heroes, in line for the highest offices in the land. As it was, their positions were in jeopardy. They were marginalised, reviled from all sides as 'Appeasers'. Worst of all, they now had to serve in a government led by their arch-critic, Winston Churchill.

Halifax was in the better position; he'd soon be leaving to take a new position in Washington, as British Ambassador. Butler, however, faced an uncertain future when his mentor moved on. He listened, with growing alarm, as Halifax filled in more details. He heard how Churchill had dreamt up the plan and forced it through the War Cabinet. Even the codename, *Ethelred*, seemed a cheap jibe, a reference to an English king who'd failed to protect his kingdom from invasion a thousand years ago.

"Arrogant knave," he muttered, "comparing himself to a king."

He couldn't come to terms with the news. Instead of continuing to resist the Nazis with every ounce of their strength, Churchill was going to gamble everything on an attempt to fool the Germans.

His initial distress turned into a growing rage.

"The callousness of the man... Young pilots sent to their deaths in obsolete planes, while brand new Spitfires are hidden away in the woods... the Luftwaffe raiding the country at will. Bomb sites all over London... dismembered bodies lying on pavements, wrapped in tarpaulins... casualty wards overflowing. Is he blind? Or mad?"

Halifax had more to tell him, even more alarming. Butler heard, to his dismay, that Churchill intended to let the first waves of German troops land in England before unleashing the full strength of the Forces against them.

If the plan had simply been a ruse to tempt the German armada into mid-Channel, where it could be destroyed by the Royal Navy, he might have had some sympathy, or at least understanding. The plan didn't even have that merit.

"Disgraceful... English soil, to be casually conceded in pursuit of a gambler's fantasy! Absolutely disgraceful!"

Butler was in shock. Until now, he'd tried to be supportive of the government. Despite his efforts to reach a deal with the Nazis before the war, he'd come to accept it was necessary to fight Hitler, as the Reichsfuehrer broke agreement after agreement. But to hear that the thousands of deaths and the dreadful damage done to London were all the result of a crazy experiment!

"It's madness, Edward, megalomania! That contemptible man. Are there no depths he won't fathom?"

They walked for a while in silence, turning back towards the Foreign Office along another quiet pathway. Butler's questions dried up. There were a thousand more things he could have asked, but he was so overwhelmed by the enormity of what he'd heard it seemed futile to raise them.

Halifax had gone quiet as well, for a different reason. He was worried he might have gone too far... Butler would be meeting Churchill within the hour.

"Rab, I understand exactly how you feel – but let me urge caution. It won't do either of us any good to have a public row with him just yet. We've got to keep our ammunition dry until the right opportunity appears. Believe me, there'll be more twists on this road before it's over."

Butler just continued to shake his head.

16

Jock Colville checked his watch. It was one o'clock. *In the afternoon*, he had to remind himself. Even after just a day underground it was easy to lose touch with the world outside. He manoeuvred his way past the cardboard boxes still stacked in the corridor from the move and knocked on the Prime Minister's door. There was no reply. He opened the door a fraction, to be greeted by the aroma of a fine Havana. It was a pleasant change from the other odours permeating the bunker; the sweat, urine and over-boiled cabbage. Once he stepped inside, however, the atmosphere was thick with the fug. The cigar lay untended, smouldering away on a metal ashtray with a thin column of smoke rising towards the ceiling grille. The PM was at his desk, motionless, swathed in the bluish cloud and focused to the point of distraction on a folder in front of him. Colville recognised a report he'd left in earlier on RAF pilot casualties. He knew it was bad news. With most of the fighters withdrawn to the secret bases, the few left in the front line were suffering heavy losses even before the decisive battle had begun. He watched for a few seconds as the Prime Minister penned a comment on the edge of the top page, took an ink stamp and pressed it to the document. Colville saw it was the red one, commanding *'Action this Day'*.

Almost in slow motion, Churchill put the stamp back on its pad and closed the folder, then reached out again for the cigar. Colville coughed gently.

"Prime Minister... the cars are here."

Churchill looked up, taken aback. "Oh... is it time already?"

He took off his reading glasses and rubbed his face with his hands, slowly unwinding from the intense concentration. His eyes seemed quite red.

Colville knew the pilot casualty report wasn't the only bad news the Prime Minister had received that morning. Already stacked in the out-tray were two other folders. One held a despatch from the army commander in the Western Desert, saying unless more tanks could be spared for the Middle East, they risked being pushed back to the Suez Canal. The other report showed the shipping losses on the Atlantic convoys during the previous month. The numbers were alarming. With most of the Royal Navy's destroyers withdrawn to guard against invasion, protection for the convoys was threadbare. They were losing merchant ships twice as fast as the shipyards were building new ones.

With a final stare at the RAF report, Churchill put it in the out-tray with the others and gestured to Colville to take care of them.

"There's a lot riding on Ethelred, Jock."

He straightened up in his chair and composed himself.

"Let's get on with it. No air raid warnings, I presume?"

"Nothing at the moment, sir," the young civil servant answered. "I don't think they'd let you go if there were."

Churchill seemed to emerge from his melancholy cocoon.

"Don't be so sure, Jock. There's one or two around who'd see my demise as a career opportunity, even in present circumstances. But I'll take your word for it – you're coming with me."

"Of course, Prime Minister. I'll just check the air raid status again."

"Faithless servant," the statesman growled benignly. "Go and round up Ismay and the others – and tell Bracken to come as well."

He took a final long pull on his cigar, leaned across and stubbed it out in the ashtray. The trademark Havana wouldn't be on view this afternoon.

The large figure of Pug Ismay appeared at the door. In his dull service uniform, he looked ready for the front line.

"Brendan's on his way."

Churchill grunted. He didn't like being kept waiting, even though he'd given no warning he wanted Bracken to come with them. He lifted his walking cane from a stand behind the door. With a long climb ahead, he would need it.

Three minutes later a lanky figure came loping along the corridor.

"You're late, Bracken," Churchill grumbled.

"Sorry, Winston, I was caught up in a war."

Churchill showed no irritation, just sighed pensively.

"Aren't we all, dear Brendan, aren't we all?"

They climbed the flight of bare concrete steps, with the Prime Minister's detective staying two steps behind him, ready to break any fall with his body. Churchill was soon breathing heavily with the exertion, his shoulders slumped. At the top they waited for the steel blast door to be opened, then stepped outside. Churchill stopped for a moment to catch his breath, leaning against a wall with his cane propped in front of him. Although back in the open after less than a day underground, he seemed morose, almost depressed.

Ismay moved to cheer him up.

"Nice to breathe some fresh London air again – though it's perhaps not quite as bad as I feared down below."

Churchill responded with a loud rumbling noise.

"Nonsense, Pug. It's like one vast public urinal."

Ismay glanced across to Bracken. They both knew the early warning signs of a change in his disposition.

"Didn't know you ever had to use one." Bracken gently mocked the Prime Minister's privileged upbringing, with some effect. Churchill seemed to perk up.

"Perhaps not, Brendan, but I've read about them in books."

There were a few quiet chuckles.

He turned round to Ismay as they walked across to the cars. "How long do you think we're going to be stuck down there, Pug?"

"I'm afraid I've no idea, Prime Minister."

"No idea, Ismay? Aren't you supposed to know these things?"

"Well, sir, if you can just tell me how long the war's going to last…"

They went over to a corner of the yard where two army saloons were waiting, engines idling. Churchill grumbled when he saw the dark green Humbers, sinister-looking in their green camouflage paint and blacked-out windows. "Government transport? Huh. They look more like Mafia staff cars."

The others ignored his petulance. They knew he preferred to travel in grander vehicles, but today there was an absolute need for anonymity. This afternoon's business wasn't about motivating troops or boosting civilian morale. The last thing they needed was people on the streets cheering 'Winnie' on his way through the suburbs. It was vital that the Paddock's location wasn't revealed.

The drive into central London was tedious, with long detours around collapsed buildings and half-blocked streets. In a few places smoke was still rising from the previous day's raids. At one crossroads they stopped to let a military ambulance pass, though they could guess the sad reason it didn't appear to be in any hurry. Near Paddington station an entire block was cordoned-off by police barriers, with signs warning of an unexploded bomb. A dozen residents from a nearby apartment block were being shepherded away from their homes, clutching a few belongings. They'd have to wait their turn for the overstretched bomb disposal squads to come and defuse the munition. In the meanwhile they had a long, uncomfortable night ahead in some cheerless shelter.

The meeting was in the Reform Club, one of the few undamaged buildings in the vicinity. It was the first time in weeks that Churchill and the War Cabinet had met with the junior ministers. Most of the ministers expected it would be last such occasion for many weeks to come. *Perhaps forever*, a few of the more pessimistic ministers muttered, though they didn't voice their fears too openly.

A hush descended as the senior officers came in and sat at one side of the room. Behind them, the members of the War Cabinet filed in. Clement Attlee clutched a thick folder and seemed his usual careful self. Chamberlain shuffled in, a shadow of the man who had been Prime Minister just five months ago. Antony Eden, usually such a debonair figure, looked white and tense. Lord Halifax came in on his own. Normally the epitome of an upright English gentleman, he seemed on edge.

A few minutes later the Prime Minister appeared, with barely a sign of recognition to anyone and no greetings exchanged.

All eyes focused on him as he took his place at the head of the table. He sat quietly for a few moments, as if gathering his inner strength, then began to address them, without preliminaries, in a clear and determined voice.

"In a few short hours our trial will begin. The Nazis are about to launch their invasion upon our shores. It is the battle we have long been expecting, have long been preparing for. It is the battle that will determine the fate, not alone of our country, but of western civilisation. Of its vital importance, there can be no doubt. But neither can there be any doubt what the result of this battle will be. It will be victory!"

The ministers listened in silence. To some of them his opening tone sounded flat, the words, at best, bravado. They'd watched with increasing foreboding over the weeks as the crisis worsened. It had been obvious for some days that the invasion was imminent, and most were fearful of the outcome. They waited anxiously, glued to his words, wondering if he would give them some reason for hope. After a brief pause, he continued.

"To this battle, this historic battle, there are many dimensions. With some of them you are familiar. We think of our gallant fighter pilots, without whom the nation would be on the precipice of defeat. We see the British Army and the Royal Navy ready at their posts, defiant, full set to face the Hun. We watch with admiration the civilian population, defying the Nazis in so many ways; stoic in the face of the onslaught."

He took a slow sip of water from a glass, punctuating his speech and allowing the tension to build.

"We stand united, a small and plucky nation, admired by free men across the world; fighting ferociously at sea and in the air, preparing for the battle that will shortly begin on our own sacred soil. This much you know already. But in recent hard days, it may have appeared that the pendulum was swinging in favour of the enemy. It may even have looked, in darker moments, as if one more great heave by the Nazis would see us on the edge of the abyss."

For the first time, he looked around the table, scanning the drawn faces, the unspoken fear now spoken.

He leaned forwards, his arms resting square on the table. "I can tell you now that this is not the case. This is, indeed, far from the case. There is another dimension to this great battle, which, until this moment, has been kept a close-guarded secret. Even now it is only being shared with you, ministers in the King's government, in the strictest of confidence."

The silence was searing. Only Chamberlain's cough, echoing faintly around the room, disturbed the quiet.

Churchill's voice began to build.

"We have shied away from the Nazi assault, not through weakness, not through exhaustion, but in the manner of a great spring, coiled, ready to rebound and smash the enemy in the throat. Even as our warriors in the front line have fought the good fight, we have assembled behind that shield a great reserve of forces, hidden away in forests and inlets. When the Huns land upon our shores, we will not just resist them, not even just rebuff them, we will smite them! We will wreak upon them a crushing defeat. We will hurl them back from our island home, battered and bloodied."

There was a ripple of surprise in the room, then a surge of relief as they grasped the import of Churchill's words; *the situation was not nearly as bleak as they had feared.* When summoned, many had feared the worst; that they would be confronted with dire news of impending military collapse or of moves under way to negotiate a humiliating deal with Hitler. *Instead there was hope!*

Churchill waited for the clamour to subside.

"We have hidden, safe from the enemy's eyes, hundreds of aircraft, tanks and warships. We have lulled the monster into the false belief that our country is on the point of collapse; that the RAF is beaten, the Navy will not fight, and that the very institutions of state are on the verge of crumbling. We have pretended that, like the Saxon King Ethelred a thousand years ago, we are unready.

"I can tell you, most assuredly, we *are* ready."

Churchill sensed people sitting up straighter in their seats, their eyes brighter than before. He could see he was winning their support, but he knew the more difficult part of the briefing was yet to come.

"These secret reserves are powerful, more powerful than any we have yet put in the field. However, much as I would like it otherwise, we are not yet in a position to cross to France and engage the enemy there. We have had to wait for the enemy to come to us. We have, in fact, enticed him to do so. And from the moment Hitler launches his assault upon us, we will respond with a ferocity that will astound the world. We will smack that evil man back so hard his aura of invincibility will be shattered forever. We will restore across the free world, and to those currently enslaved, the unshakeable belief that tyranny shall not prevail."

Despite the crescendo in his voice, the word *'enticed'* punctured the swell of optimism. What had begun a few moments earlier as a murmur of support now became more staccato, as muttering and questions were heard in the background.

It was no more than Churchill expected. He had known he couldn't take their support for granted; he had to earn it. In powerful language, he began to outline the reasons for Ethelred. He described the challenges the country would soon have faced if they'd simply waited for Hitler to choose the moment. He spread his arms wide as if to encompass the magnitude of the threat.

"We are an island nation. Our freedom depends on our ability to trade the seas. But from north to south, in a great arc around us, the Nazis have established lairs for their submarines and long-range aircraft, the teeth of a vicious mantrap preparing to snap shut on our trade routes. Thus far, thanks to the bravery of our sailors, we have survived. We have succeeded in importing large quantities of arms and supplies, sufficient unto the day. But our shipping losses creep up by the month. A point might soon have come where bravery alone would no longer suffice to sustain the great bridge across the Atlantic."

There was silence. Few had been ready to look beyond the current battle; to think about what lay further ahead.

"And while, every moment of every day, we fight this insidious threat, while we throw our physical strength and our financial wealth into the battle, the Nazis are free to exploit their pirate's booty. From Calais to the Vistula, they plunder the riches of the conquered countries; the coal mines of Poland; the steel mills of France; the factories of the Low Countries; the oil fields of Rumania, now a vassal state. The riches of Europe, serviced by a vast pool of slave labour, are diverted to their evil purpose."

Churchill had forced them to face not just the military, but the economic reality of war. He clenched his jaw and waited. In a sombre, almost-threatening tone, he made his stand.

"We have determined to reverse this foul Nazi tide, this tide that seeks to undermine and erode that which it is unable to breach by frontal assault. We have decided to destroy that monster, Hitler, by playing to his vanity, by confusing him – yes, if you want, by deceiving him. We have seduced him into the belief that Britain's resolve is crumbling; that we no longer possess the resources or, indeed, the stomach for the fight. We have lured him into launching an invasion before his forces are properly prepared. And when they come, we will not simply repel them, we will smash them. We will emasculate his brutish army as it straddles the English Channel, one foot in France, the other in England, with its nether regions suspended above the deep waters."

The ministers listened, their faces pale. But no-one raised any objections; there was no point. It was clear that the opportunity for debate had long since passed. There was no turning back.

Churchill finished his discourse and waited silently for a time, allowing his words to sink in. He did not invite any questions.

He sat back in his chair and allowed General Dill to provide some information about the military implications. Within the constraints of security, Dill described how they had been able to build powerful reserves, while leaving just sufficient forces in the front line to frustrate the Luftwaffe's blitz.

There was a ripple of dissent in the room. Not everyone agreed he'd left enough. But there was no argument. It was clear the generals weren't the decision-makers.

When he finished, Churchill sat forward again and turned to another aspect of Ethelred, a most delicate one.

"There is another dimension to Ethelred I must now share with you. No military position exists in isolation from its political environs. To support the illusion of weakness it has been necessary to create another chimera; that civil and political disunity is growing in Britain. We have pretended there exists in our land a peace movement, a subversive movement undermining the country's will to resist. We chose to fabricate the notion that there is amongst us a disloyal group of politicians aligned with that peace movement, a group which terms itself *Realists*, willing to parlay with the Nazis. This fictitious group has been the honey in the centre of the trap."

People shuffled in their seats as he went on to describe the concoction of lies and innuendo fed to the Nazis. No-one interrupted to ask the names of the suggested Quislings; the answers might have been embarrassing.

With a final few words of patriotic encouragement, Churchill ended the meeting, stating that he had to return to battle headquarters. He pushed his chair from the table and walked from the room, leaving behind a stunned group of ministers.

* * *

Bracken had waited in the lobby of the club. He wasn't a minister and wasn't universally popular with those that were. As they got back into the Humber saloon, the air raid sirens started to wail. Churchill told the driver to keep going.

"How'd it go?" Bracken asked as the car moved off.

"Well enough, I think." Churchill looked out through the darkened windows. The streets were unusually quiet, with a sense of foreboding in the air. The only activity seemed to be military in nature, with just a few civilians scurrying towards the shelters. There wasn't a woman or a child in sight.

In the distance they heard the crump of anti-aircraft guns.

"They were expecting bad news; that much was clear... all conscious of the drop-off in the RAF's visibility and had drawn grave conclusions. Some of them had read the stories we planted in the Irish newspapers about riots in Liverpool and Glasgow."

"So you had some good news for them, anyway."

"One or two had an inkling something was going on; had heard stories about secret airfields in their constituencies and so on. The relief was quite tangible when they heard what we've been at. In fact, it all started out quite positively."

"And when you got to the bit about holding back the reserves for a while?"

"I handed over to Dill and let him deal with it. He did well; talked about it from a purely military perspective... *the only possible tactical decision*. He avoided any reference to the strategic purpose."

"How'd they react?"

"They became fairly subdued again."

"Guess they'd prefer us to bat Jerry for six as soon as he comes up the beaches."

"Indeed... especially the ones from constituencies in the front line. I suppose that's understandable. It got distinctly personal... wives... families... homes..."

"Just as well you brought the Chiefs along."

"Dill was good, and Brook even better; gave them assurances about the evacuation of civilians and so on; a soupçon of comfort, I suppose."

A stick of bombs exploded half a mile behind them. The driver saw the black plumes in his mirror and accelerated away, the Humber swaying and swerving, narrowly avoiding a fire engine racing past in the opposite direction. Churchill's detective looked out the window, scanning the sky, not sure what to do if he saw a German plane coming towards them.

Bracken picked up the conversation.

"And the *Realists*? How did they react?"

"They went even quieter. Though, to be fair, it ended up well enough – one or two saying they were glad we're finally getting off our posteriors and doing something."

"And Butler? Did he say anything?"

"Not a word. I got the impression he was just sitting there simmering... sulking, more like it."

"Didn't like being hinted at as a future Prime Minister, under His Majesty King Edward VIII?"

"I thought he might not respond favourably to that particular detail, so I didn't dwell on it."

"Chicken!" Bracken laughed. He knew Churchill had ducked it. "Still, I suppose there's no point in provoking him. Think there's any chance he'll get up to mischief?"

"Too late now. The Nazis will be in England tomorrow by the looks of things. I don't think he's time to stir up trouble, even if he wanted to. And to be fair, for all his misjudgement about Hitler before the war, he's been moderately supportive since it started."

"Except for a certain gaffe with the Swedish Ambassador in June?" Bracken said.

"Well, apart from that."

"Apart from that, he is the very model of a modern junior minister? Perhaps, Winston, but I'll keep my ears open."

The gates to the courtyard swung open, and the Humber pulled into the car park atop the Paddock.

17

Two ministers stayed behind in the Reform Club after the meeting, withdrawing to a small dining room as the others departed in their government cars. Halifax and Butler told their colleagues they had some Foreign Office business to clear up before the various departments dispersed to their emergency locations across the country.

After their tempestuous meeting earlier in the day, Halifax approached the subject gingerly.

"Well, Rab, did it sound any better coming from the anointed lips?"

Butler snorted.

"Worse, far worse. Just watching him sitting there, spelling out his grandiose plans – his '*vision*', he had the nerve to call it! All I could think about was Gallipoli in 1915 and the fiasco in Norway six months ago. Look where his vision got us there! Good grief, has the man no ability to learn from experience? And, by the way, I'm quite sure I wasn't the only one feeling that way."

"Wouldn't surprise me. I must say I'm torn about the whole situation. On one hand I have a sense of loyalty to the Government and, of course, honour. On the other hand..."

"We have to stop him, Edward, the risks are appalling. The Army's in dire straits. Our troops are no match for the Germans. Our tanks are feeble and most of our generals seem to be idiots. The Navy's not much better. Look what happened the last time they sent out a battle fleet – an aircraft carrier sunk in the middle of the North Sea, for God's sake! I know the RAF's doing its best, but the fact that they've hidden a couple of hundred fighters in the backwoods doesn't mean they can beat the Luftwaffe. And now that renegade invites them to a duel in England! Good grief, did he learn nothing about their abilities in France? It's madness. We have to find a way stop it."

"It's gone too far, Rab. He's won over the rest of the War Cabinet, apart from Chamberlain, perhaps, and he's on the way out. I'm afraid we're stuck with it now."

"But it's absolute lunacy! He acts like a tin-pot dictator, a madman, and nobody does anything about it! I expect Beaverbrook and that mongrel Bracken are up to their necks in it as well."

Halifax shrugged. "Churchill says it's all his idea, but, I will admit, it does seem to have Bracken's greasy fingerprints all over it, certainly some of the wilder elements… the Duke of Windsor and so on."

"And the Chiefs? They must be horrified!"

"They were nervous to begin with, but none of them had the *co-jones* to stand up to him – all conscious how their predecessors were dumped a few months back."

"The King?"

"Just between ourselves, I've spoken to him. He's sympathetic – but you know the constraints. No power to intervene unless the government looks like falling."

"Well, if the House were to find out that…"

"There's no time, Rab; the Germans will be here in a day or two. No time to get a backbench revolt under way."

"Good Lord, there must be someone we can talk to."

Butler looked at Halifax, but the Foreign Secretary said nothing, just pursed his lips and turned his face away, looking out the window.

The hint was enough. Butler realised there was no point in simply railing at the situation and expecting a solution to appear. Someone had to take the lead, had to act immediately with whatever resources they could muster. The fate of the country was at stake.

"Edward, we need to remind ourselves that Churchill wasn't elected Prime Minister by the country. It was a cosy political arrangement in Westminster – and that can be overturned just as easily. If he's leading the country to disaster, and there's only a few of us who might be able to stop him, how could it possibly be dishonourable to try?"

"Rab, be careful. Some might see that sort of thinking as bordering on treason."

"For God's sake, we're talking about using our influence to stop a German invasion of the country. How could that possibly be treasonous? In fact, 'treason' is a better word for what Churchill's been at."

"Rab, as I said, be careful. There's not much any of us can do at this stage."

"Maybe not, but I still see the Swedish Ambassador from time to time. I might be able to... to do something. Come to think of it, my last meeting with him was a bit funny. Prytz mentioned the Duke of Hamilton had been round to see him; something about RAF aircrew interned in Sweden. I was a bit peeved at the time. Serving officers shouldn't be interfering in the diplomatic arena. But I thought he was looking at me a bit... how can I put it? A bit slyly. Wonder was he fishing... testing me out to see if I was one of these Realists?"

"Could be. Hamilton was used as a go-between to pass messages to the Swedes. In fact, that was the main conduit to Berlin. Prytz must have been in a difficult enough position – obviously, we couldn't let on it was all a charade. I'm sure he wasn't too happy being stuck in the middle with the conflict about to get even wider. The Swedes know, if we go down, they're right in line when Hitler decides on his next move. God knows, with the man's record they won't have long to wait."

Butler was quiet for a few moments.

"You're right. But I know the Swedes," he said. "They'll box clever ... want to make sure they're on the right side of whatever new dispensation emerges. I suppose it's hard to blame them. Mind you, the ambassador didn't actually *say* anything to me and it wasn't hard for me to play dumb – as I knew sweet damn all about it!"

"Anyway, Rab, I'm afraid I won't be able to help much from now on – be buried in the Paddock with the rest of them. Not easy to stay in touch. By the way, have you found out where you're off to?"

"A country house somewhere in the Cotswolds, along with the consular department. Near enough to Oxford, I suppose... though

Bracken wants to see me about something or other, some 'emergency' regional responsibility, he says. I suppose I'll have to humour him. Anyway, Oxford should be fine. I'd prefer Cambridge of course, but it should still be fairly comfortable and I'll be able to get up to London without too much trouble."

"Well, at least until our visitors start arriving," Halifax said.

Butler turned away, a distant look in his eyes.

"Unless we can find a way to revoke the invitation."

Halifax raised an eyebrow; they were getting into dangerous territory. He made no comment and let Butler continue.

"Edward, you may recall that, in the aftermath of my discussions with Ambassador Prytz in June, I was given certain instructions by Mr. Churchill. I was asked, indeed directed, to meet the ambassador again. I was to inform him that, contrary to any impression he might have mistakenly obtained from me, the country was united; there was no question of negotiation; the Armed Forces were fully prepared to take on the Germans and our strength was growing by the day. You may also remember I had to make sure the message made its way to Berlin through diplomatic channels."

"I'm missing your point, Rab. That was months ago – long before Ethelred."

Butler gazed into the middle distance and spoke quietly, almost to himself.

"Those instructions came to me directly from the Prime Minister. They have not been rescinded."

Halifax said nothing, in either support or discouragement. Quite abruptly, as if embarrassed by the direction the conversation was taking, he stood up and left the room.

18

There was no point in delaying any further; the landings were imminent. On his return from the meeting Churchill gave the order for the *Cromwell* alarm to be sounded.

The counter-invasion plans, long under preparation, rolled into action. Along the south-east coast the last civilians were evacuated from the seaside towns, with just a few old men staying behind to feed the remaining farm animals. A small number of policemen and firemen remained at their posts to guard against incidents, hoping to be evacuated at the last moment. The authorities had asked for volunteers, knowing there was a risk they might end up working for the enemy, in occupied England or further afield.

The Armed Forces went to the highest state of alert. In damp dugouts and pillboxes along the coastline, troops made final checks on their weapons and laid out ammunition. Sentries scanned the sea and beaches through binoculars, alert to the threat of commando raids even before the main invasion force appeared. Further inland, artillerymen checked their guns' elevation and traverse, and moved shells up from the magazines to positions beside the guns.

On the front-line airfields, RAF aircraftmen worked feverishly on the Hurricanes and Spitfires, checking oil levels and hydraulics, radios and gun sights. The airfield defences were fully manned, with steel-helmeted soldiers patrolling the boundary fences in makeshift armoured cars, to guard against paratroopers or Fifth Columnists.

At the secret bases in the west, however, no activity was permitted. The orders to the commanders were clear: no flying unless specifically authorised; maintenance work prohibited, except at night. Even airfield security was to be monitored from fixed hides in the cover of the woodlands rather than by mobile patrols.

In naval bases from Plymouth to Harwich, the crews readied their ships for sea, topping up fuel bunkers and loading the ready-use ammunition lockers. A final hot meal was served up, after which the order was given to clear out the messes; they might be needed as casualty stations in the hours ahead.

At the final briefing ashore in Plymouth, the destroyer captains listened intently to the orders issued by the flotilla commander. The message they received was reassuring. A hundred RAF fighters had been assigned to protect them. Free from the threat of overwhelming attacks by the Luftwaffe, they could focus on their traditional mission – protecting the nation from assault by sea.

As Commander James Acton returned on the ship's cutter, he spotted a squadron of Hurricanes wheeling around, high above the mastheads. They were there to protect the ships against air attack until the cloak of night descended, and they would be there again in the morning to shield them on their return from battle.

Back on his ship, HMS *Kelvin*, Acton briefed his officers. He sent them about their tasks and went out to the open bridge as the final consignment of weapons was brought aboard. They were a vivid portent of the close-quarters fighting ahead – old Lewis machine guns and boxes of hand grenades. He watched as a party of sailors hauled the heavy boxes up the gangplank.

"Everything but fucking cutlasses," he heard one old tar mutter.

For the first time in several days, Acton smiled.

He was proud to lead these men.

19

Rab Butler was shown into Ambassador Prytz's office. The men had been friends for several years, though they'd met less frequently since the embarrassing episode in early summer. After his meeting with Halifax, the Foreign Office minister had telephoned the Swedish Embassy and spoken to the ambassador, insisting they meet straight away.

On his arrival at the embassy, he seemed flustered, brushing past the Third Secretary at the door and pacing up and down in the hallway as he waited to be received. He even refused the customary offer of a cup of tea.

As soon as he was alone with Prytz, he moved straight to the purpose of his visit without exchanging any of the usual pleasantries.

"Thank you for seeing me promptly. I believe you'll recognise the urgency of the situation as I expound."

Prytz stayed silent, waiting for Butler to explain his unusual approach.

"Your Excellency, you may recall that, at our meeting after the Dunkirk evacuation, I advised you that there was a slight possibility a compromise peace with Germany might be achievable. I also indicated that certain parties in Britain were open to the idea of negotiations with such an objective in mind."

The ambassador's face went red, surprised the British minister had brought up the delicate matter, one they'd both been trying to forget. Butler hesitated for a moment, seeming to search for the right words.

"A short time after that meeting... on reflection and after full consultation with, er, my colleagues, I clarified that statement to say that there was, in fact, *no* possibility of compromise; that Britain would fight on until the war was won. With the full support of those colleagues, some of whom are in most senior government offices, I encouraged you to pass that message on through appropriate channels, to ensure all parties to the conflict understood the position clearly."

"That request was complied with by the Swedish government," Prytz said, being careful not to show any sign of his personal feelings on the matter. He watched the British minister who was now breathing heavily, his face flushed.

"Ambassador, in the context of certain other discussions which may have taken place here in recent weeks, I would like to restate the position I conveyed to you in that second meeting in June, using the most powerful language at my disposal. There is no question of any weakening in Britain's military or political position. In particular, I can advise you that any messages to the contrary provided by any serving officer of the Crown, acting in an unauthorised manner, should be disregarded. The officer in question has been relieved of his position."

Butler knew the last remark was half true. Wing Commander Hamilton was no longer acting as an intermediary, but only because he was back with his fighter squadron.

Prytz squirmed. He'd known the approach by the Duke of Hamilton in August had been unusual. Nonetheless, he assumed it had been made in good faith by a growing peace faction in the British government, in an attempt to end the war.

At the time he'd surmised that the original approach had been made in an indirect manner so that it would be deniable if it leaked out. That was long-standing diplomatic tradition. *Perhaps today's meeting was the denial!* He liked Hamilton and hoped he hadn't suffered too badly. At least this wasn't Nazi Germany or Soviet Russia – and he did have the advantage of being a duke.

"I understand, Minister." He sat poker-faced, waiting for Butler to continue.

"Ambassador, I would like to re-emphasise the assertions I made in that second meeting in June. Britain is in its strongest-ever military position, determined and well able to resist any attempt at invasion. The British Army has been re-equipped; weapons have been pouring in from our factories and from America. And from the Empire, tens of thousands of soldiers have come to help the mother country. The Royal Navy has reached its greatest-ever strength, with morale at the highest level. From Lords of the Admiralty to Able Seamen it is united in the fight. Most important of all, despite any appearances to the contrary, the RAF has not been defeated. It has hundreds of fighters in reserve, ready to deploy as the invaders approach.

"And, whatever you may have been told to the contrary, there is no group of politicians looking for any settlement other than the defeat of Nazi Germany. As someone who, in the past, has done his utmost to prevent war, I can state categorically there is no split in the Government's resolve. Anyone who believes otherwise is living in a fool's paradise. Anyone who thinks they can invade Britain successfully is deranged. Any enemy that tries to do so will be annihilated in the attempt. And any faction which tries to understate our military strength or our determination to fight is spreading falsehoods, seeking the glory of a battlefield victory, uncaring of the cost in British lives. Any person, no matter how senior, who lends encouragement to such a course of events is a traitor."

He paused, gasping for breath, patting his flushed brow with a white handkerchief. The last, damning word hung in the air, shaking Prytz to the core. He was struggling to comprehend just how high in the British government Butler's harsh indictment might extend.

Prytz sat back, stunned and silent. There was nothing he could say in the face of such a torrent. He stared at Butler, unsure how to interpret his actions or his motivation. He went across to the drinks cabinet and poured him a glass of water. After a few moments of recuperation, Butler continued, now speaking with more composure.

"Your Excellency, at the conclusion of our second meeting in June – after I had clarified my previous misstatement – I asked that your government bring the position to the attention of all parties to the conflict. I now urge you to do so again, with this firm restatement of

Britain's military and political determination. Furthermore, in view of impending events, I ask that this be done with the utmost urgency."

Without waiting for a reply, Butler stood up to leave. Anything else said would simply dilute the message. Without pausing for even a word of social conversation, he left the Embassy and walked down the steps into the evening sunshine.

For several minutes Prytz sat at his desk in shock. He'd listened with growing alarm to Butler's words, his most uncharacteristic and undiplomatic words. In all the years he'd known Rab, he'd never heard him speak with such passion about anything. His message was in direct conflict with what he'd been told by the Duke of Hamilton over recent weeks. He didn't know what to make of it. He was even further disquieted that Butler had left without leaving a note on the position he'd just expressed so forcefully.

The issue was far above his career grade. He asked his secretary to bring him a message pad and to put the cipher clerk on stand-by for an urgent transmission to Stockholm.

He would gladly leave it up to Head Office to handle.

PART 2: MAELSTROM

maelstrom (n): a powerful whirlpool, a state of violent turmoil

THE ENGLISH CHANNEL

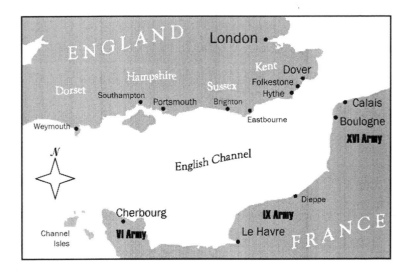

1

At Chartwell, deep in the garden county of Kent, the morning had been quiet. The little cluster of buildings round Churchill's home was peaceful, swathed only in the traditional sounds of the countryside; the cattle and sheep in the nearby pastures and a few tractors at work in the fields. There was little sign of a great conflict taking place around them; the skies were empty of the swirling air battles that had been a reminder of war for months past. Today, only the occasional sound of a shotgun punctuated the rural idyll, echoing round the outbuildings as someone tried to supplement their rations with a rabbit for the pot.

In her cottage in the grounds of the estate, Jessie Wilson had been up since dawn, determined to make the most of the fine autumn day. Although the main house had been closed and shuttered since the Churchills moved to London at the outbreak of war, the young housekeeper felt she was busier than ever. With most of the young men of the village called up and gone away, it was a struggle to keep the place in some sort of order.

After breakfast, she spent a few minutes tidying the cottage and then went out to the garden to start on the long list of chores. She let the hens out of the coop and scattered a half-bucket of meal for them in the run. The reward for her care was a handful of eggs lying in the nesting boxes. She put them in a basket and left them on a low wall by the woodshed.

The plants in the greenhouse needed attention. She'd been putting it off because the door was jamming hard against a paver outside, and it took all her strength to move it. She must have asked her brother a hundred times to fix it before he signed up. But it didn't do to feel annoyed, not now.

When she managed to shift the door and get inside, she found the tomato crop beginning to redden. She picked a dozen of the ripest, then thought for a moment, but decided to leave the rest. With luck, there'd be a few more days of sunshine before the night temperatures dropped. She might get another crop out of them. After that, they'd only be fit for chutney.

When she finished in the greenhouse, she decided to tackle the vegetable garden. It had been neglected for the last few weeks; there was just so much else to do. However, she found that even without much attention it was doing well; nature was still at work. The runner beans were ripening and she popped a few to try them. In the lower garden, the onions were doing well, too. She knelt down with a trowel and tidied them up, tying over the tops to help them on. After twenty minutes bent low, she straightened her back and turned her attention to the potato patch. As ever, it needed work. She spent the next half-hour hoeing the rills and then lifted a few King Edwards for dinner. There would be enough in the plot for herself and her mother for a month or two, maybe right up to Christmas. After that, she didn't know. No-one knew.

The work was tiring and at midday she stopped for a quick dinner, soup and some pie left over from the day before. Later in the afternoon she been planning to cycle over to her mother's with some freshly-baked bread, but as she was waiting for it to rise she got a telephone call from Mr. Colville. He was as polite as ever, but seemed under a lot of stress. Usually he would enquire about the house or her well-being, but today he just asked her to dig out a manuscript from his study. She knew the one, a thick volume in a blue binder that she'd often seen Mr. Churchill working on. Mr. Colville asked her to parcel it up and have it ready for a despatch rider to collect later in the afternoon.

Jessie loved being asked to do these little tasks. Once or twice she'd even had to find a passage in one of the books in the library and read it out, word-by-word, over the telephone. She imagined the quotations were needed by the Prime Minister as the finishing touches to one of his speeches. Sometimes she'd listened to him on the BBC next day, and had the thrill of hearing him speak the words she'd found. She told her friends it was her own little contribution to the war effort.

When the bread was baked, she took it out of the oven and put it on a rack to cool, before making her way over to the house to look for the manuscript. The lawn was overgrown after a year of neglect and she skirted round it, climbed the steps at the back and let herself in through the French windows.

Unoccupied now for so many months, the place felt strange and echoey, especially this long, low garden room. Sometimes she would talk to herself as she went around – her mother told her she was talking to the house, that it needed company, too.

Jessie hated the oppressive silence. For years this low-ceilinged dining room had been full of life, rich with the sound of family and friends. She could still hear Mrs. Churchill's instructions to the cooks and household staff in the mornings; brisk, but always polite. She remembered the many days when famous men or women would be down for lunch or dinner with Mr. Churchill. And the debates, always the debates. Most of the visitors were civil, some quite friendly – except for one or two. Still, it wasn't her place to criticise her betters. The most thrilling memories were of those evenings when the house was almost deserted, silent but for the sound of Mr. Churchill in his study upstairs, rehearsing a speech. Sometimes she would just stop and listen to his wonderful voice.

On the rare day when the place was quiet, Tom would sometimes come over, bringing a message from their mother or a pot of home-made jam, or maybe just offering to lend a hand with little jobs the old house constantly needed. There was always something to be fixed up, creaking doors and windows, leaking taps and broken handles. At this time of year, when the trees were losing their leaves, blocked drains and gutters were a real nuisance.

Tom had always been handy with things, ever since he was a boy; repairing toys and bikes; sometimes, she suspected, breaking them on purpose, just to have the excuse to fix them up again. And his motorbikes... As a teenager, he'd spent hours tinkering with his beloved, battered Triumphs. There was still one in the shed; she found it hard to let go. When he was called up, he'd hoped to become a despatch rider, but the training sergeant spotted his country boy shooting skills and selected him to train as a Bren gunner.

How such a little quirk of fate could change everything. It might have been Tom coming to collect the package this afternoon.

This war. This awful, awful war.

It was just a month since his best friend had come to see her. He told her how Tom had volunteered to stay behind at a crossroads a few miles outside Dunkirk, to hold off the Germans for as long as possible. It gave the rest of his platoon the chance to escape. She sobbed for a few moments, imagining his stocky frame outside the kitchen door, and his smile, the crooked smile she would never see again. She missed him desperately.

She dried her eyes and smoothed down her apron. There were things to do, a long list of things. In the hallway, some cobwebs needed to be brushed down, and she noticed a torn seam on a cushion in the drawing room. Funny how she'd missed it before. She put it by the door to bring over to the cottage when she finished. In one of the traps in the scullery she found a dead mouse, with a trickle of dried blood on its neck. As she disposed of its little body she felt a fleeting shudder. There was too much killing in this world.

She climbed the stairs to Mr. Churchill's study and found the blue binder in a few minutes. The courier wasn't due to arrive until 5 o'clock and, with an hour to spare, she had time to go around and open the windows. It might help rid the house of its mustiness. She decided to start where she was, in the study. It was always the hardest room to clear and she knew it would never be rid of the smell of cigar smoke until the furnishings and wallpaper were all replaced.

As she opened the shutters she heard aircraft, coming closer.

They didn't sound like Spitfires.

2

Earlier in the afternoon, Hauptmann Willi Rall was grumbling as the crews hung around the mess at Calais-Marck airfield, waiting for the signal. He'd been in foul humour since the previous evening when he heard the details of their mission for the day. He finished his cigarette and flicked away the butt.

"What d'you think, Uwe? Where shall we go while we're stooging around over England?" He was addressing Weser, his gunner. "Stonehenge? Windsor Castle? Or maybe we've enough fuel to get up to the Lake District?"

Their unit, Erpr. Gruppe 210, was the Luftwaffe's elite fighter-bomber squadron. On the previous evening, the crews had been given their orders for the strike that would launch Sea Lion. What annoyed Rall was the detail. Instead of the usual dash across the Channel and back before the RAF could react, he and his four aircraft would have to fly around over Kent for half an hour before making their attack. The base commander just told them the three sections had to cross the Channel at the same time to give no warning to the British, and that the attacks on the targets had to be made simultaneously. As Rall's was closest to the coast, that meant flying a dog-leg to get to it, burning up time as the other sections made their way to London.

Major Erich Schulte, the squadron commander, was getting annoyed at his peevishness.

"If it upsets you that much, Willi, do you want to swap?"

Schulte's own target was in the centre of London. He stubbed out his cigarillo and tucked the long butt into a silver case for later.

"Anyway, let's leave the sight-seeing till next month. When the army takes London, we can hire a car and do England in style."

He snapped shut the lid of the case and stood up from his canvas chair.

"Let's just get this one over with."

The crews lifted their parachutes and walked across the dispersal to their planes.

On the warm afternoon the Messerschmitt 110s lined up close to the boundary fence. Laden with 500kg bombs under their wings, the pilots wanted as long a run as possible for take-off. At 1630 the first section began to roll, led by Schulte, and cleared the high bocage at the end of the runway with a few metres to spare. Behind them, the second section got on its way. Then it was Rall's turn.

The twelve aircraft formed up into a loose gaggle and, staying low, headed west over the French countryside into the low sun. Leaving the coast behind, they dropped to wavetop height and made their way across the empty Channel. Eight minutes later they crossed the coast near Deal, attracting a few ill-aimed bursts of flak as they flew fast and low across the still-peaceful gardens of Kent. It was time to split up. With a final wave to Schulte, Willi Rall led his section off to port, leaving the others to head for London.

The expert crews of the unit were specially trained to make pinpoint attacks. While most regular bomber squadrons could just about find their way to a target the size of a city, the pilots of Erpr. 210 boasted they could hit any given street in a city. This afternoon, they would have to do even better. Their targets were not just streets, but individual houses.

Schulte's section avoided detection by radar as they crossed into England. Flying at high speed just fifty metres above the ground, they were safe from the British flak, but the pilots had to keep a sharp eye open for barrage balloons. As they approached the outskirts of

London, their luck ran out. Anton Bayer, his gunner, spotted a flight of Hurricanes turning into them. He shouted a warning and Schulte pushed the throttle forward. Normally the 110s could outrun a Hurricane, but the heavy bombs were slowing him down.

"They're gaining!" Bayer yelled.

Out of the corner of his eye, Schulte saw his wingman hit hard and going straight in. Another plane was streaming smoke from a burning engine. The pilot pulled up out of formation, trying to gain enough height to bale out.

Schulte pushed the throttle again, but it was already hard against the stop. He heard Bayer open up with his machine gun and fire a long burst, but a few seconds later the Messerschmitt shuddered four or five times. A Hurricane had got them in its sights. He heard Bayer scream. Twisting his head, he saw him slumped down in the rear cockpit. Now they were defenceless. The Hurricane was closing in for the kill. Another burst... more strikes... losing power... He saw his target just ahead. Still under pressure, he released his bombs as the building filled his sights; a large terraced house in Downing Street. Number 10.

The second section came in from the south, undisturbed by fighters or anti-aircraft guns. They slipped across the Thames Embankment in the wake of the confusion from the first attack and headed for a target not shown on any map.

Two weeks earlier, Goering had ordered Luftwaffe Intelligence to scour London, looking for possible sites for a British command bunker. After hours of painstaking research, an alert photo-interpreter spotted suspicious activity at an office block in Whitehall. At first glance there wasn't anything of interest, but a series of images taken over the months caught his attention. Taken individually, the changes weren't significant, but, after three days spent studying old guidebooks, he reached a tentative conclusion. A series of works on entrances, concrete sills and ventilation outlets suggested he might have found his quest. It was enough to have the site designated as a target.

The four Me110s approached in a shallow dive and released their bombs, devastating the block. Within minutes it was burning fiercely, with the staff who hadn't gone to the shelters when the sirens sounded now struggling to escape. The third bomb caused catastrophic damage. It passed through the building and exploded against a great concrete slab at basement level. For a few minutes the structure held, then another bomb struck, bringing the higher floors concertinaing down onto the weakened structure. The slab gave way. A thousand tons of masonry crashed down into the Cabinet War Rooms underneath. Melded together in the ruins were offices and conference rooms, plant and equipment. And people; the luckier ones killed outright by the blast, the rest half-crushed and trapped as darkness and dust enveloped them.

After their detour across the English countryside, the final section of Messerschmitts formed up over the Weald of Kent and headed for their target.

Chartwell was so close to the coast, and so easily recognisable, that even Churchill accepted it couldn't be protected. Besides, as an officious civil servant pointed out, it was private property with no military significance. As a gesture to the Prime Minister the lake in the garden had been filled in to make the property less visible from the air. Wooden shuttering had been installed over the windows. The security people didn't expect it to stop any bombs, but they hoped it might signal to the Luftwaffe that the house was unoccupied.

The hope was in vain. With no flak or fighters to oppose them, Rall's section were able to take their time. One after another they lined up on the large country house. Rall came in first, his bombs striking the east face of the building, bringing it down and laying open the interior. The bombs from the second aircraft exploded inside, rupturing the internal walls and half-collapsing the roof. The next released its weapons a few seconds late. They overshot the house and landed among the outhouses and cottages.

The fourth plane dropped a pair of 500kg bombs into the ruins of the devastated house, rupturing a gas pipe and starting a fire in the downstairs drawing room. Within minutes it was spreading out of control. It was fed by the rich contents of Churchill's home; fine tapestries and curtains, furniture, paint and oils from his studio. Soon the blaze reached the shattered library, licking at the hundreds of books scattered across the broken floor: histories of England and biographies of great men, drafts of his writings, years of correspondence with leaders and pretenders across the world. All were now just fuel to the fire. All were consumed in the flames.

The Luftwaffe pilots headed back to France in buoyant mood. They didn't know whether Churchill had been in the house – but, if he had, he was dead.

However, the risk had been foreseen. The Prime Minister's security advisers had stopped him visiting many months earlier. There was only one casualty, a young woman, crushed by a falling beam as she ran towards the air raid shelter in the courtyard. Clutched in her hand as she fell was the draft of a thick volume, *The History of the English-Speaking Peoples*. Page by typewritten page it flared and burned, and the ashes fluttered away in the fire winds.

3

Bracken was at work in a side office when he heard a crashing noise in the corridor outside. He had barely time to look up before the door burst open and Colville tumbled into the room. He looked frantic.

"Brendan! Thank God – I didn't know where you were! They're trying to kill Winston. They've attacked Downing..."

"Whoa... slow down, Jock! Who? Who's trying?"

"The Germans, damn it! The Luftwaffe! They've bombed Downing Street and the Cabinet War Rooms and Chartwell too."

"Christ! When?"

"In the last half-hour..."

"God Almighty. Are there casualties... or much damage?"

"Awful. Number 10's destroyed... staff missing... not sure how many. A dozen, maybe fifteen... in the kitchens. They're trying to dig them out... can't get near them. The War Rooms too. The roof slab's collapsed. They don't know who's inside... thirty people, maybe more, underneath."

"Dear God," Bracken said, badly shaken. He probably knew them all. And this time yesterday he'd been there himself, along with Winston and the others.

"What about Chartwell?"

Colville said nothing, choked with pain.

"Jock... Chartwell?" Bracken spoke more sharply.

"Oh Brendan, how do we tell him? It's gone. On fire... the roof's down... all gone. No chance of saving anything."

"Sweet Jesus..." Bracken was shocked at the meaningless assault. "Why? They must have known it's empty."

"It's supposed to be – but nobody can find Jessie." Colville looked distraught, tears welling in his eyes. "Oh Brendan, I called her this morning... Asked her to dig out a manuscript the PM wants." He began to sob. "God, if she was inside..."

Bracken reached out and grasped his arm, unsure how to console the young man in his distress.

"Jock... look, Jock, she may have been out somewhere. Let's wait before we... Oh God! Does Winston know yet?"

"No – still having his nap. I'm supposed to wake him in a few minutes. But I... I thought maybe you would... you might be the best person to break it to him."

Bracken turned away from the grief-stricken young man, trying to control his own anguish and focus on the consequences. He was fearful, desperately worried about the effect on Churchill. The casualties in Number 10 and the Cabinet War Rooms would be hard on him; he'd know most of them, at least their faces. But Chartwell! He knew what it meant to him. He'd been with him since the early days there, helping during the restoration, digging him out of the financial mess he'd got into over the cost. He knew how much a part of his life it was. For a moment, he thought of the days he'd spent there, listening to and learning from his hero. But his own feelings were irrelevant. The Nazis had failed to kill Winston; he had to make sure they didn't steal his spirit.

"How many people have been told?"

"In the Paddock? Oh, I'm not sure..."

"Think, Jock. It's important."

"Well, Downing Street and the War Rooms. I think word's gone around. I guess everyone's heard by now. Not many about Chartwell yet... in fact nobody else as far as I know. The call came in directly to me. I came straight to find you. You're the only one I've told. Outside, I'm not sure. I assume everybody in the village and..."

"Outside doesn't matter. We can't tell him about Chartwell, you know that. It would break his heart. Probably why they bombed it, the bastards."

Colville was still trembling.

"No, we have to, Brendan. It wouldn't be... No, I couldn't face him if we try to..."

"Jock, we've no choice. He's got enough bad news to bear, with the other attacks."

He blinked a tear away. "Look, go and wash your face. Leave him another ten minutes; we'll find some excuse. Just go in and wake him and leave. I'll come and see him about something or other... and I'll tell him about the other raids. We'll let Pug know about Chartwell, nobody else. He can tell the Chiefs if he must. You stay well away from Winston... Keep yourself busy. God knows there's enough to be doing at present."

Bracken could see Colville was close to breaking point, sobbing, shaking his head, unwilling to be party to any concealment.

"Jock, I hate this as much as you. But sometimes we have to, at times, do things we hate. We just have to. For the country... for people we love..."

He took a deep breath, fighting to conquer his own emotions.

"Our personal feelings are irrelevant. The Nazi landings are going to start at dawn. Winston will have to be speak on the BBC at 1 o'clock. The entire country will be listening. He mustn't sound like a broken man. We have to support him – by saying nothing."

He waited for a few seconds and saw Colville still wavering. The considerate approach wasn't working. He stood directly in front of him and hardened his voice.

"Jock, look at me. I'm afraid you've no option. Now do your duty. Go in there and waken him."

He stared at the distressed young man for a painful moment and took a long, sad breath.

"I'll speak to him tomorrow, as soon as the broadcast's over."

4

Fast and purposeful, the destroyers of the Plymouth squadron headed out past the breakwater, steering east. As they left their moorings, the ships went straight to action stations. The crews were trained and ready, in the engine rooms, at gun positions and on the bridges. Their orders were simple: rendezvous with the Portsmouth flotilla at 2100; close with the enemy before midnight; use maximum force to destroy whatever they found. They were to disengage no later than 0430 and withdraw to Portsmouth to rearm.

The crews were confident. They knew these waters well and their task was one for which the Royal Navy had prepared for centuries, defending the country against invasion by sea. The biggest fear for the skippers had been the Stukas, and they'd been relieved to hear they'd have fighter cover during the hours of daylight. Right on schedule, a squadron of RAF Hurricanes appeared and took up station above them, the first in a relay that would protect them until nightfall.

The Hurricanes weren't the only aircraft in the vicinity. Fifteen miles away, an ungainly aeroplane was circling high above the English Channel. A radar station on the south coast had picked it up two hours earlier, but the sector controller was unable to do anything about it. Flying at a height of over 40000 ft, it was far above the ceiling of any British fighter.

The old twin-engined Junkers 86 didn't carry any weapons or even cameras. Everything had been sacrificed to save weight. Other than the crew, its sole military load was a pair of high-powered Zeiss binoculars and a wireless transmitter. At 1708 the observer spotted a ship exiting Plymouth harbour, its wake clearly visible in the late afternoon sunshine. He watched the wake lengthen as the ship began to build speed. A short time later it was joined by another ship, then more. In the space of a few minutes he counted a dozen or more warships leaving the base, heading towards the Channel.

The wireless operator tapped out a brief sighting report: *Twelve ships exited Plymouth at 1710, estimated speed 25 knots, heading 120 degrees.*

They had orders to repeat the transmission at five-minute intervals for the next two hours.

* * *

After a long slog underwater, U-31 had reached its station in early afternoon. Now it was loitering four miles off the English coast, at periscope depth, but with just the wireless antenna above the surface.

At 1714, Moeller was called over to the radio cabin.

"It's the message, sir."

The operator passed him a pad with the decoded transmission jotted down on it.

Moeller studied the chart for a moment and spoke to the navigation officer. It looked good. They were in position, not far from the harbour entrance and within the predicted time bracket. An hour earlier the hydrophone operator had detected a few patrol craft in the vicinity and they'd been staying clear until it was time. Now the skipper took command. He ordered a change in direction towards the nearest one, carefully easing the U-boat into position, the crew at the ready.

Five minutes after the first transmission, he wedged himself into the tiny radio cabin, waiting for the message to be repeated. It was all the confirmation he needed. He gave the order to surface. The crew moved to their stations, tense. The next few minutes would be dangerous; they'd be on their own until the others heard their diesels start up and rose to join them.

Outside the harbour, just two small vessels were on patrol. The little anti-submarine trawlers were beating up and down the approaches, pinging the waters to prevent a U-boat sneaking in past the breakwater. The converted fishing boats didn't carry much by way of armament; just an old 3" gun and a handful of depth charges. But their AS-DIC sets were good enough to strip any intruding U-boat of its main asset, invisibility.

On the bridge, Lieutenant Commander Richardson was still enjoying the sight of the Plymouth squadron steaming out at speed a few miles away, when the ASDIC operator reported a contact.

"Very faint, sir, about a mile away. Green 120. Moving towards the harbour entrance. And maybe a second one, at Green 020, though it might be a reflection."

Richardson began to map out a search pattern with his first officer, expecting the usual game of cat and mouse if there was a U-boat in the vicinity. They'd just marked out the first leg when a lookout shouted out.

"Submarine! On the starboard quarter, about a mile off!"

He was holding his arm out straight, pointing towards a dark shape breaking surface.

"Actions Stations!"

Richardson called the alarm before even looking to confirm the sighting. The siren sounded. Seamen hurried to their posts. The gun crew grabbed their steel helmets and rushed along the foredeck. The skipper ordered the helm to starboard and only then took a moment to lift his binoculars and check the sighting. He saw it, now ahead of them, about half a mile away. The loaders slammed the first shell into the breech and rushed to bring up more ammunition.,

The gunner trained his gun towards the target, dialling in the range setting, anxious to get a few rounds off before the U-boat's crew reached their deck gun.

He fired. It was close, but not close enough to do any damage. The shell flew low over the target and burst in the water 50 yards beyond it. The crew cleared the spent case and were loading up again as the gunner adjusted the sights down.

Before they could fire again, there was a frantic call.

"U-boat! Another one! Port side!"

They all looked. Richardson lifted his binoculars. It was much closer and pointing towards them; an immediate threat.

"Take the one on port."

The gunner swung the barrel round to engage it. Suddenly there was another shout... a third submarine, off to starboard... then a fourth. All around, U-boats were appearing, a pod of killer whales rising from the deep. Diesel engines cranked into life. The sailors on the trawlers could see crews leap to the machine guns in the conning towers. A hail of bullets raked the deck, scything down the British gun crew. As the submarines' decks cleared water, German sailors tumbled out of the hatches and loaded up the deck guns.

They swept towards the British ship, raking the decks with machine gun fire and pouring shells into their hulls. There was nowhere for the sturdy little ships to run. Caught in the crossfire from a dozen 88mm guns, almost the firepower of a cruiser, the ships were hit, and hit again. They burned, listed and succumbed, slipping beneath the waves. All that was left in the water were some patches of debris and, clinging to half-submerged floats, a few burned sailors.

The route was clear for the U-boats. They swept past the sinking craft, accelerating to top speed, the skippers driving them like torpedo boats towards the line of destroyers.

They could see the British flotilla in disarray. Some ships were holding to their original course, others seemed to swing towards them for a minute or two, before veering back to their original course east. Two destroyers had peeled off and were coming towards them, presumably to check out the incident. Even as the British ships were still sorting out their response to the confused action, the Germans were closing fast, the wolf pack surging towards the mass of British warships. It was what the U-boat skippers had trained for at Kernevel. For this mission they had no need to make a stealthy approach, to stalk their targets and work out the trigonometry to aim their torpedoes. As soon as they were within range, the firing commands rang out.

"*Loos! Loos! Loos! Loos!*"

From each submarine a salvo sped out, a total of forty-four torpedoes coning the narrow waters of Plymouth Sound, heading towards the unsuspecting British ships.

On HMS *Duncan,* a young seaman in the crow's nest was first to spot a wake. He flipped open the voice-pipe and screamed a warning to the bridge.

"Torpedo! Torpedo! 3 o'clock!"

A surprised Commander Jenkins sounded the klaxon and ordered the helm to starboard. The lean warship leaned over as they executed the well-practised manoeuvre, turning in to comb the track. But thirty seconds later the lookout called again, this time with a panicked tone in his voice.

"Torpedo. Another one! 5 o'clock, close!" he yelled. Fixated on the first track, he hadn't spotted the second until it was almost upon them.

The first torpedo was passing clear ahead, but the second was coming in from an acute angle, the late warning gave them only seconds to react.

"Hard-a-port," Jenkins shouted. The bridge crew could see the approaching trail of bubbles. The ship levelled back and swung to port, turning away. It wasn't going to be enough.

"Full astern port!"

In the engine room, the signal bell rang out three times. The petty officer slammed the port engine into reverse.

The lithe ship protested at the treatment, vibrating and rattling as the turn tightened. It was close, but the first torpedo had passed fifty feet ahead of the bow and they were running on a parallel track to the second as it overtook them. They seemed to have escaped. Then a third was spotted, running clear astern, thank God... Then a fourth, fifty yards away, coming at them amidships...

Across Plymouth Sound, ships swung left and right, several nearly colliding in the panic as they tried to avoid the tracks. The destroyers would have been agile enough to avoid torpedoes from a single submarine, but with dozens approaching them from different points of the compass, they were being overwhelmed. The powerful weapons began to strike home.

Already, *Duncan* was sinking, a huge hole in her side, with the crew preparing to abandon ship. Half a mile away, *Jackal* was next to be hit, losing her rudder. *Kashmir* survived for a minute when a torpedo failed to explode, but seconds later the next weapon did detonate. *Dainty* was hit twice in quick succession. The second struck her forward magazine with catastrophic results. In the explosion, the ship disappeared, with nothing but some splintered debris left behind in the water.

Ships were burning and settling in the water as their crews tried desperately to save them. On *Kashmir*, when the captain saw they were losing the fight he turned towards shore, hoping to beach his ship before she sank.

For fifteen minutes, the chaos continued. Torpedo alerts and SOS calls jammed the radio bands. Six destroyers were already sunk or sinking. Those that had survived the initial salvo opened fire at the dark shapes in the distance. They swung around and headed towards the launch points, the crews running to fix the depth charges for a shallow water attack. The squadron was turning into a shambles.

As the pandemonium increased, Commander Acton was shocked to realise he was the senior officer remaining. An officer in the Volunteer Reserve, he'd last seen action as a midshipman in the Battle of Jutland twenty years earlier, but he saw he had to take control. He barked out urgent commands to the signaller, ordering his two fastest destroyers to start an aggressive search for the U-boats. He ordered the rest to resume their course east.

One by one the remaining destroyers responded. Acton had managed to restore a semblance of discipline. The toughest call was to the skipper on *Jupiter* as his crew tried to save their comrades on the blazing *Duncan*. The signal lamp flashed out a blunt message.

"Leave casualty. Immediate. Resume position."

Finally, the depleted squadron formed up and headed east again. Turning their back on the enemy was hard; leaving behind sinking ships and many pals in the water was even harder. But their orders were clear; they had an invasion to stop.

5

The news from Plymouth filtered into a shocked Paddock. Losses of ships had been anticipated, but the danger was thought to be from the Luftwaffe, not the German navy. It had hardly featured in their thinking. Admiral Pound sent out immediate instructions to the commanders at the other bases, ordering them to increase the anti-submarine patrols. At Portsmouth, the news had been heard with anguish in the base. Many relatives and old shipmates were on board those destroyers, their fate unknown. The base commander ordered a third anti-submarine trawler to join the two already on station, with orders to push the ASDIC cordon further out to sea. As more details came in about the scale of the German attack, he despatched three I-class destroyers, his fastest ships, to act as pickets ahead of the squadron. They were told to carry out aggressive anti-submarine patrols within a five-mile radius of the base. They would shield the rest of the squadron as it cleared port and then follow after them at high speed, to regain station before they reached the Channel.

The other ships of the squadron waited at anchor till night fell. There was no reason to leave the relative safety of Portsmouth and expose themselves to the Luftwaffe. They were still an hour away from their planned departure time when another call was received. A radar station had spotted a group of ships breaking away from the convoy coming from Cherbourg and heading, recklessly it seemed, towards Portsmouth.

It was an easy decision for the flotilla commander. The night sky was already too dark for the Stukas, and they wouldn't be caught napping again by the U-boats. He ordered the destroyers to sea.

After months of boring convoy duty in the Atlantic, they now faced the enemy in a head-to-head battle. On board the ships there was a heightened sense of purpose, a resolve to protect the country, and now a personal commitment as well; to avenge their comrades.

As they passed Spitbank Fort, the ships went to action stations. As soon as they had sea room they began zig-zagging. On the bridges, the officers stayed on high alert. In the crow's-nests, the look-outs scanned the black horizon. Below decks, the ASDIC and wireless operators were glued to their sets, listening for any sign of U-boats.

* * *

Leutnant Hausmann, the skipper of U-28, had been disappointed when he opened his second envelope as they left Guernsey. They were not going to join their comrades in the wolfpack attack. Instead they had to break away from the flotilla and head, not northwest towards Plymouth, but northeast. Now they lay on the bottom off the Isle of Wight, silent, listening.

For the last hour, they'd been monitoring the high-pitched turbines of destroyers thrashing around in the Solent, with intermittent bursts of speed followed by periods of quiet with only the pings of the enemy's ASDIC sets audible. Hausmann knew it was a good sign. The attack at Plymouth must have been a success to have stirred such a response. The aggressive British patrolling would have made another wolfpack attack impossible, but that wasn't the intention. Instead, they waited.

At 2125 the hydrophone operator picked up different sounds, seven or eight warships, perhaps more, on a steady heading south, coming down the eastern channel of the Solent.

It was what they'd been waiting for. Their role, in the darkness, was to act as the ears of the German destroyer squadron. Now Hausmann watched as the navigator tracked the British ships. It was as predicted; they were heading south-east, towards the approaching German flotilla. But there was a complication, one of the screening patrol ships was on a different course, coming straight at them.

"Course and speed steady," the hydrophone operator whispered. "It's a destroyer."

Hausmann didn't think the British ship had detected them yet, but he knew it would as soon as they moved. He felt the tension rise in the control room. His task was to report the position of the Portsmouth flotilla as soon as it appeared. They had to do that now; and to raise the wireless antenna, they had to get up to periscope depth.

"Less than a mile, skipper."

The oncoming British destroyer was getting close.

U-boat against destroyer, one on one. In a duel, it could go either way. If they stayed undetected, if would give them the edge. A salvo of torpedoes down the throat of the enemy, turn tail and run, counting out the seconds and hope they scored a hit. If they missed, they had just one more fish in the stern tube against dozens of depth charges. The crew watched and waited for Hausmann to make his decision. The pinging was getting louder.

He had no choice. He gave the order.

"Periscope depth. Antenna up."

He would get the message out, then face the British ship alone.

* * *

Twenty miles away, the German destroyer formation headed towards Portsmouth. On the open bridge of Z-20, Kommodore Ruge looked out into the darkness. Against the blacked-out shoreline in the distance, not a light or a shape was visible. He felt exposed. For the moment, the British held the advantage. Their coastal radars would be tracking his ships and reporting their positions to the Royal Navy commander. He was running out of time. If they waited much longer, they'd be getting dangerously close to the inshore minefields, and coming within range of the coastal guns. If they didn't hear soon, the flotilla would have to veer off and run away, blind, from their pursuers.

There was a sudden movement at the side of the bridge. A seaman rushed in, clutching a message sheet. It was the news they'd been waiting for.

Ruge skimmed the page and handed it to the navigator. He watched as the rough position of the British ships were pencilled onto the chart. What he needed was the bearing. It had to be now; his own flotilla was already within 15 miles of the coast. He gave the command.

At the side of the bridge, signal lamps flashed out the order.

Zulu 1955. The time was set; three minutes to go.

On Z-20 they watched the turrets traverse 10 degrees to port and the guns were elevated. In the background, an officer was calling out a slow countdown.

"80... 70... 60..."

Battle was less than a minute away, but Ruge would not be there to witness the start of the engagement. As the count wound down, he handed control to a junior lieutenant, turned and retreated below decks along with the rest of the bridge crew. They donned red-filtered goggles and waited as the countdown speeded up.

"5, 4, 3, 2, 1."

The ship shook with the opening salvo. Still, Ruge and his party didn't move. The count moved positive. "1, 2, 3..." They waited as the shells soared out across the black sea, in the direction of the English coast. At the extreme range, there was no chance of hitting anything; but that wasn't the intention. In a ragged cascade, forty star shells exploded in the sky in front of the onrushing Royal Navy destroyers, illuminating them in an incandescent light and destroying the night vision of the British deck officers.

As the count reached 20 seconds, Ruge sprang into action.

"Komm! Komm!"

They rushed back to the bridge. In the dying light from the star shells they could see the distant shapes. For the next ten minutes or so they would hold the advantage, with the British night-blind from the searing white flashes. The distance closed. As they came within range they launched the first salvoes of armour-piercing shells. They turned broadside-on to the line of advancing destroyers and launched their torpedoes.

The German skippers waited. Shell hits! In the distance... a few small fires, good aiming points for the next salvo. More star shells were fired. Now the German gunners could see clearly the silhouettes of the British ships. Bigger explosions... torpedo hits, at least two. Still no serious return fire. The plan was working. They rushed on, firing salvo after salvo from their 127mm guns.

More hits in the now-shortening distance. More fires. Another torpedo hit.... One of the British ships exploding – the magazine going up or maybe a depth charge rail. They could see fires, explosions, ships slowing in the water.

Finally they began to experience some return fire, but it was spasmodic and poorly aimed. One German ship was struck and damaged, but kept going. The ambush was evolving into a confused night engagement, with more hits recorded. It was becoming difficult to tell friend from foe. Then Ruge saw flashes of shellfire from a different direction, from the west. Well behind schedule, the survivors of the Plymouth disaster were joining the fray.

The odds were now turning against them. Kommodore Ruge's instinct as a naval officer was to pursue the engagement, to drive home their advantage. But his orders were clear. They had achieved their goal, and he ordered a turn away from the battle scene. His ships withdrew east in the darkness.

The skippers and gunnery officers had done their bit, now they would have to rely on their navigators. Thirty miles ahead lay the German minefields, laid the previous day to protect the invasion convoys. The next challenge was to thread a careful course through the mine barrier, and dare the British destroyers to follow.

6

Admiral Pound's face was ashen. He stared through the window of the gallery at the table below, motionless. Staff were pressing in and out of the booth to speak to him, but he just ignored them or brushed them off with monosyllabic replies.

First Plymouth, then Portsmouth – ten destroyers lost in the initial engagements. It was the pivotal action they'd planned for, had prepared for. It was the *raison d'être* of the Royal Navy, to fend off an attack on the nation by sea. And yet, in the opening encounter, disaster. It wasn't just the appalling losses that had shaken Pound. Underpinning the entire Ethelred strategy was the assumption that, whatever challenges Britain faced on land or in the air, at sea, the Navy reigned supreme. *If that assumption was erroneous...*

Thirty feet away, Churchill stood on the other side of the Operations Room, alarmed but silent, watching the white-haired figure in the gallery opposite. There was no place for a Prime Minister in the operational conduct of a battle and there was no point in adding to the pressure on Pound by confronting him. But if the admiral began to crumble under the strain, he would have to act, would have to relieve him of his command. Churchill decided to give him a little time. General Ismay stood by his side, ready to support the Prime Minister in any hard decision he had to make. For a quarter of an hour the two watched on, side-by-side, with the single, unspoken issue in their minds.

With his time almost run out, Admiral Pound turned away sharply from the viewing window and said something to his deputy. He began to re-engage with his staff, first responding to the officers waiting in the booth for instructions. Gradually he became more animated, stabbing a finger at a map on the rear wall and snapping out orders. After one brief discussion with a staff officer, he looked across the gallery to where the Prime Minister was watching. He turned and stormed out of the navy booth, heading round to him.

Churchill waited. Fifteen minutes earlier he might have been the one initiating the conversation, a different conversation. Now the First Sea Lord was coming to him.

"Prime Minister, you're aware of the situation on the south coast. I'd like your permission to release the three cruisers at Portsmouth."

Churchill wasn't surprised. He had insisted the light cruisers be held in reserve for as long as possible, to be deployed as part of the strike on the second wave. But the cold reality was they were needed immediately. He knew it was a gamble. They were more powerful warships than the destroyers, but slower. And, starting out so much later than the destroyer flotillas, they might not be able to clear the battle zone in the Channel before daybreak. It meant a risk of more losses and many more casualties. But there was no real choice; Pound was doing what he had to do. More importantly, he was back in control.

"You have my permission, Admiral."

With the immediate crisis averted, Churchill walked back to his room with General Ismay. He poured himself a large brandy and slumped down at his desk, looking shaken. He stared deep into the amber liquid for a second and gulped down a mouthful.

"My God, Pug, have we been deluding ourselves? We've set the trap and primed it. We have all the advantage in numbers, yet the Nazis are outfighting us again! Have they overtaken us with their naval technology as they did with their tanks? Lord help us if that's where we've come to."

Ismay looked at him, torn about how to reply. He'd been struggling with the same doubts, but he realised he had to sustain the Prime

Minister's confidence. There was no alternative. He tried to frame a measured response.

"It's been a bad day, sir, but I don't think the analogy with the tank situation is completely fair."

"I'm not interested in fairness, Ismay, only results."

"I didn't mean *fair* in that sense, Prime Minister. I meant your concern that our ships aren't good enough, or our men. The Germans had the advantage of surprise. They knew exactly when the engagements would take place and used that knowledge to telling effect. We were caught out by their tactics on the day, not their technology, not even their seamanship. We will recover."

Churchill looked up, with sad, hooded eyes.

"I pray to God you're right, Pug."

Ismay excused himself. He had done what he could to lift Churchill's spirit, but it was far from enough. He went looking for Bracken, the one person who had the knack of boosting the PM's mood, whatever the situation.

"Brendan, he's pretty low. Could you pop round and talk to him… see if you can work your magic?"

Ten minutes later Bracken went to the Prime Minister's room, finding him hunched in his chair, a glass in his hand. A folder marked 'Urgent' was lying unopened on the desk in front of him. He barely looked up to acknowledge his friend's arrival.

"How do I tell the country, Brendan? How do I explain this catastrophe? For hundreds of years the Royal Navy's been our trump card; a line of steel that moves from sea to sea to shield us from the enemy. And now, in the very first battle, catastrophe, a crushing defeat on our doorstep. How do I sustain the nation's belief on the very day the Nazi parachutists start dropping from the skies and their panzers roll up our beaches?"

Bracken stayed quiet for a moment. In their long friendship, he'd often seen Churchill's mood swing between elation and depression, but he'd assumed he would be invigorated now battle had been joined.

Perhaps his close association with the Navy for so many years made him feel the losses more acutely. There was no way to dismiss his concerns, he just had to lift him for the moment. *Thank God, he still didn't know about Chartwell.*

"It's been a dreadful day, Winston. I hope to God casualties haven't been too heavy. But you have to put it out of your mind. Leave Pound to deal with it. You need to focus on the things you can influence – the battle ahead, not the one already fought. Single-mindedly... ruthlessly."

Bracken took the brandy bottle from the desk and shaped to pour himself a drink, but, instead, put the bottle out of reach on the filing cabinet.

"The broadcast tomorrow is crucial. You've got to get it right... Let people know you're in command. They want to hear you speak ... they're waiting for you to rally them. Do that right and then stop worrying about morale for a few days. Leave others to get on with it. The press will help. Give them their heads and they'll do the job for you. Bad and all as they are at times, they know we're in this together. Beaverbrook and I will speak to a few people to make sure."

Churchill was still slouched down, his elbows on his desk, breathing slowly and noisily into cupped hands. The fight seemed to have gone from him. The black dog was in the room. For a long minute, it was touch and go. Then he started. He sat up and pushed away the half-full glass. He looked up at Bracken. "I know, Brendan. I know what I have to do."

He took a deep breath.

"And I will do it. But these disasters... Plymouth... Portsmouth. What do I say?"

Bracken sat down in front of Churchill and looked straight at him. The corner had been turned.

"You don't say anything, Winston... you don't need to. We're in the middle of a war, not a bloody debate in Westminster. I'll think of something to put out: *Naval battles off the south coast. Several Nazi ships sunk.* That'll do for now."

7

The convoy from Boulogne was the last to leave port. With the shortest distance to travel they'd waited patiently while the other convoys plodded their way towards the crossing zone from as far away as Rotterdam and Cherbourg.

The massive task of assembling the fleet had been under way since early morning. First to push back from the quayside were the freighters carrying the tanks of the 8th Panzer Division. Now they rode at anchor just outside the port. The long wait wasn't a problem for them. The men had plenty of space to lie down, and tanks didn't get seasick. Four hours later they'd been joined by the first of the steamers, full to the gunwales with assault troops. The troops on board would have a long wait, with almost eighteen hours to go before the landings, but the ships were moderately comfortable. The Feldgrau settled down where they could find space, sleeping or playing cards.

While the soldiers embarked on these large ships were able to get some rest, the skippers had plenty to worry about... British aircraft... mines laid inside the harbour... enemy submarines sneaking in. But as the convoys formed up, at least the threat of collision was less of a concern for them. Whatever the convoy commander might order, or the law of the sea might say, they were the biggest ships in the fleet. The smaller vessels could damn well stay out of their way. However, the skippers knew their size was a double-edged sword. While it worked in their favour today, it would count against them in the morning. As they closed the English coast, they would be the prime targets for the British defences; the RAF, the Royal Navy and the guns.

On the powered barges the skippers were already under intense stress, trying to avoid collisions as they manoeuvred their awkward craft in the confines of the French harbours. With hundreds of vessels milling around, the crews had festooned the sides of their craft with every fender or tyre they could get their hands on. Already the wall of rubber had saved several from damage. But for one barge, it wasn't protection enough. Struck amidships by a wayward steamer, it turned turtle, spilling a hundred soldiers and seamen into the water. The crews on the other barges watched on helplessly as tenders rushed around trying to pick up the casualties. It was a bad omen. If steering in the calm French harbours was such a challenge, they could only dread what it would be like on the other side, as they tried to steer their way to a safe landing using the aero engines lashed to their sterns, all the while under English fire. They could only take consolation in their numbers.

Last to leave the quayside were the towed barges; small, rolling coffin ships, grouped in clusters of two or three behind each tug. Keeping the formations together was already proving a nightmare for tugmen and bargees alike. The unwieldy combinations would take almost twelve hours to crawl across the Channel. With little ability to manoeuvre and no armament, their survival depended on German control of sea and sky.

The soldiers had been on board the dilapidated craft since early morning, corralled below deck in foul conditions. Already nauseous from the sea swell, they were thrown about in the dark as the tugboats shunted the awkward craft into formation. Many of the men were already retching with the smell of the chemicals or livestock that had been the previous cargoes. These Feldgrau would have to spend the next twelve hours in extreme discomfort, tossed around in the flat-bottomed craft, with frightened and violently ill men all around. Drained of energy and almost of the will to live, the only decorum they could manage was to vomit into the buckets provided, rather than over their comrades.

For most of them, the landing, even under heavy fire, would come as welcome relief.

At 2200 the sequence began, as the Boulogne ships headed out to sea. Within minutes, the challenges became evident. With the constant threat of British attack, rehearsals had been limited to small-scale operations using just a few vessels and staying close to the French harbours. Now the crews experienced at first hand the difficulties of manoeuvres on such a vast scale. Even as they formed up, collisions occurred, with several barges sunk and dozens of troops drowned before they'd faced the enemy. But slowly, after scenes of near chaos lasting almost an hour, a semblance of order emerged. Out of the chaos, recognisable columns of vessels emerged. Well behind schedule, the ramshackle fleet cleared harbour and headed west, the leading steamers making a steady eight knots through the calm seas, the barges, a snail-like four.

Following in the wake of the fleets of Julius Caesar and William the Conqueror, the armada of Adolf Hitler set course for England.

8

In Berlin it was two o'clock in the morning. Reichsmarschall Hermann Goering was sitting at a conference table in the Reich Air Ministry building, wearing a powder-blue dressing gown. He stared at a single-page document in front of him, drumming his fingers on the polished mahogany surface.

It wasn't how he'd planned to spend the night of the invasion. The fleet was half-way across the Channel and the early naval battles had resulted in great victories for the Kriegsmarine. In a few hours' time he would be flying to France to watch the action from the cliffs opposite Dover. But thirty minutes earlier he'd been woken by von Ribbentrop, asking that they meet straightaway. The Foreign Minister told him he'd received an urgent note from the German Ambassador in Stockholm. He said he was conscious of the instruction that the Fuehrer's sleep was not to be disturbed, but he felt the leadership ought to be informed immediately.

The drumming got louder as the Reichsmarschall read the note again.

"Rubbish! Rubbish! Rubbish!"

He looked around at the dishevelled group of Air Ministry and Nazi Party officials gathered in the room.

"According to this piece of fiction, we're walking into a trap! The British are far stronger that we thought! We should cancel the invasion!"

He grunted noisily.

"It's complete rubbish, Ribbentrop!"

Von Ribbentrop cringed under the verbal assault as Goering continued to mock.

"It's pathetic. Somebody in London says 'Boo!' and we're supposed to be scared off! You wake me up in the middle of the night to tell me! Churchill will have to come up with a lot better than this to stop Sea Lion!"

He looked accusingly across the table. "You brought the damn note here. Why are we even wasting time discussing it?"

"I apologise, Reichsmarschall. It wasn't my intention to cause any disruption. I thought the message was, potentially, a matter of urgent concern."

"And how did it magically appear in Berlin, just as the invasion gets under way?"

"It originated in London yesterday afternoon – an impromptu meeting between the Swedish Ambassador and a source in the British government. A minute was sent immediately to the Ministry of Foreign Affairs in Stockholm and they passed it on to our ambassador late last night. From there to Berlin by cable."

Goering took a handkerchief from the pocket of his dressing gown, patted his face down and coughed a few times into the silk square.

"Reichsminister, correct me if I'm wrong, but isn't that route through Sweden the one used by those so-called Realists over the last couple of months? That pantomime! All a ploy to delay us until the winter storms set in. Now they're at it again, trying to confuse us. And you, Ribbentrop, are the unwitting tool they're using again!"

Von Ribbentrop shuffled his papers awkwardly as Goering continued.

"Well, you're not going to tell me it's the Duke of Hamilton who sent the message this time, are you? I can inform you he's back in Scotland heading up a fighter squadron. Or maybe there are two of them?"

Von Ribbentrop flinched under the sarcasm, but held his line.

"Reichsmarschall, this new message doesn't make any reference to the Realists. It's completely different in context – a record of a diplomatic meeting in London, like the ones in early summer. Probably even the same people in the British Foreign Office who put out the feelers about a settlement in June. They're quite separate from the Realists – and were in contact with us long before the Realists appeared on the scene."

Goering flung his copy down. It skidded across the varnished table.

"The British had their chance. It's too late to ask for negotiations now. Unless they're ready to surrender without a fight. In that case we might discuss terms, let them keep their red post boxes or whatever. But no more!"

Despite the intimidating bulk of the Reichsmarschall, Von Ribbentrop continued to press his point.

"They're not asking for talks. It's the exact opposite; a direct warning that the British have been conserving their strength for the battle. It says they've built up large reserves to ambush our forces when they land."

"Huh. Read it to me again."

Von Ribbentrop unfolded his copy and cleared his throat.

'From the Ministry of Foreign Affairs, Stockholm:

A message has been received from the Swedish Ambassador in London, minuting a meeting with a senior contact in the British government. This contact claims that, contrary to other reports received, Britain is determined to fight on and is well equipped to do so. Rumours of a British collapse are falsehoods put out by a group – he refers to them as traitors – trying to enhance their reputations as war leaders by achieving a military victory in the Channel, regardless of the cost in lives. The contact says the British forces have been conserving their resources for the invasion battle. Their army has received vast quantities of arms from their factories and from the United States, more than replacing their losses in France. The Royal Navy is at full strength, with morale high and the chain of command intact. The apparent decline in the RAF's strength is an illusion. Large reserves of aircraft have been built up to deploy against the invading forces. The source concludes by stating emphatically that the British are fully prepared, and will repel any attack on their country.'

"Rubbish! Rubbish!" Goering banged his fists on the table. "My flyers can see the real picture... only a handful of aircraft left opposing us... London and the south-east wide open. You think the RAF has been off on holiday? Absolute nonsense! Where's Canaris? Is he here yet?"

Admiral Canaris had been worried when he was called to the emergency meeting at the Reich Air Ministry. He checked with his duty officer in Abwehr headquarters, but they had no indications of anything about to break. As head of military intelligence, he was responsible for Germany's agents overseas. The role of his department was to consolidate the information gleaned from the network of sources and feed it to the three services. But if his own people had heard nothing?

Half an hour after being summoned, he joined the group in the Reich Air Ministry. He listened with growing apprehension as the Foreign Minister read out the Swedish note. Goering sat glowering until von Ribbentrop finished, before turning to Canaris.

"Admiral, have you received any reports that the RAF has huge reserves of aircraft hidden away in some fairy glen, ready to pounce?"

"Could I see the note, please?"

Canaris was playing for time. He read the document several times, caught in a dilemma. He would have been delighted to be able to confirm the possibility of large British reserves. Even though the first wave was already on its way, it might still be possible to turn the ships round, and have the whole thing treated as some sort of large-scale exercise. That might just be enough to save Churchill's government – and tens of thousands of young German soldiers as well. But he hadn't a shred of evidence to call on, and had to walk a tightrope to avoid being seen as a defeatist. Two months earlier he'd angered Hitler and almost lost his job, when he suggested the British resolve was stronger than portrayed in the messages from the Realists. Fortunately for him, his suggestion that that mysterious group might be a British deception now seemed close to the mark. Not that it had helped his reputation much in Hitler's eyes; the Fuehrer didn't like to have his errors pointed out. *Though at least he was still in his position, not in a concentration camp.*

He decided to stick to the known facts.

"Reichsmarschall, we've received no specific reports from Luftwaffe intelligence about possible RAF reserves."

It was a subtle response. Whatever might turn out to be the reality, he'd shifted responsibility straight back to Goering's Luftwaffe. If they'd failed to spot any evidence, it was hardly the Abwehr's fault. At the same time, if there was any chance he could build on the report to abort the invasion, even at such a late stage, he wanted to seize it.

"Of course, from time to time we've received vague hints from our agents in Britain that there might be reserves hidden away. But without hard evidence or corroboration from the Luftwaffe, I decided there was no justification to escalate those reports to the leadership."

He was taking a risk. He hoped he would be able to find something among the intelligence chaff to back up his statement. If Himmler had been running the meeting, he wouldn't have dared. The head of the SS would certainly have demanded to see all such reports and would have realised immediately there was no corroboration. But Goering was not so methodical.

He looked down at the note again.

"This new information is very worrying... we need to check it out. I will instruct my agents in Britain to look for evidence to support the claim."

Goering was still bristling at the late upset to the invasion plans.

"And where exactly would you start looking for these phantoms?"

"If they have significant reserves hidden away, the most likely locations would be in the western parts of England, or in Wales or Scotland. And as well as mainland Britain, there could be hideaways in Northern Ireland. I can get one of my agents in Eire to travel up and check out the airfields there."

It was the professional approach. If the British had any such reserves, those were the places they would try to hide them.

"How long would it take to get field reports back?" Goering barked.

"It's difficult to say. With so little to go on, we don't really know what we're looking for. If there are these secret reserves, we can assume they'll be well camouflaged, not easy to find. My staff people in Abwehr H.Q. can put together a list of possible airfields. We'll prioritise the ones we want to check out, and instruct the field agents. They'll have to travel up to the locations, gather whatever information they can... talk to locals about unusual aircraft activity over recent weeks – vehicle and troop movements and so on. The agents will have to be very discreet, of course, to avoid suspicion."

"And just how long would that take, Admiral?"

"I expect a minimum of two or three days in each location, Reichsmarschall. On top of that, it'll take at least three, maybe four days to alert the agents, give them time to arrange their travel and return to base to radio in their reports."

"What a surprise!" Goering snapped. "A week or more – even to look at a handful of sites!"

He turned to von Ribbentrop.

"Isn't that interesting? If we did decide to turn the fleet around to check out these reports, it would delay us just long enough us to miss the tides at the end of September. Does that look like a co-incidence to you, Ribbentrop?"

"No, Reichsmarschall, but I'm not an expert on military matters."

"You speak the truth, Reichsminister, you most certainly are not."

Goering stood up and lifted his Marshall's baton from his desk. He placed it under his arm, forgetting for the moment he was still in his dressing gown and not one of his flamboyant uniforms. He gestured to the group that the meeting was over.

"We will not take this matter any further. We shall certainly not raise it with the Fuehrer; he has enough real problems to deal with. The decision has been made. Sea Lion proceeds!"

* * *

Canaris went back to his darkened office, his mind in turmoil. He needed space to think. At one level he didn't place much trust in the

Swedish report. Undoubtedly, the messages back in June were genuine, originating in the British Foreign Office with either Butler or Halifax. But those feelers had been withdrawn just a few days later, abruptly. At the time, he'd concluded there was a group in the British government interested in reaching a settlement with Hitler, but it was in a minority, with, thankfully, no power.

The later messages, in August and September, were different in tone. That group of 'Realists' seemed to be associated with a military cabal rather than a political faction. He'd always had his suspicions about them, and now they seemed to have vanished in a puff of Churchill's cigar smoke. Perhaps they'd started there as well! Either that or they'd gone very deep.

And now this even stranger message! Someone trying to talk up Britain's strength – a last-ditch attempt to prevent Sea Lion being launched. Even by the convoluted standards of the intelligence war it was confusing.

He tried to be rational in his analysis, professional, looking at the issue from different perspectives. In a matter of minutes, he realised it boiled down to just one question. *Did the British have these secret reserves, or not?*

Never mind what he'd told that gangster, Goering, he was sure there hadn't been even the slightest hint about reserves in any of the reports from his agents, or from reconnaissance flights. If there had been, he would have jumped on it immediately. He'd have used it to try to stop Sea Lion!

On balance, he felt the new report was false. There was nothing to suggest otherwise. In that case, who had sent the message? Someone in Britain. No, someone *in the British government*, the Swedes had said so. And someone at a high level, or they wouldn't have access to the Ambassador. So, someone in the British government was trying to stop Sea Lion. Understandable – *but such a pathetic attempt!* It wasn't MI6, anyway. He'd never met Menzies, but he'd studied him enough to feel he knew him; certainly, he knew the skill of his organisation. If they'd wanted to create a bogeyman to scare off Hitler, they'd have done it weeks ago, and produced some convincing evidence, whether real or made-up. This communication through Sweden was amateur-ish, garbled, and far too late to have any effect.

So, if it wasn't MI6, who else could it be? Not the Duke of Hamilton or any of the group around him. He hadn't made an appearance for weeks. Goering was probably right that he was back with his RAF squadron. Who did that leave? It came back to the obvious candidates – Halifax or Butler.

He buried his head in his hands, in deep confusion. It still didn't make sense. Why would they try to interfere at this late stage, with the invasion just hours away? What was it the British called their public servants? *Gifted amateurs?* Maybe not so gifted in this case, just amateurs?

He tried to think if there was any way he could use even such a du-bious report to stop the invasion. He had no back-up information – nothing at all – to make the Swedish note credible. Without collabo-ration, he'd just be seen as a defeatist, and he knew where that would lead.

He concluded, sadly, there was nothing could be done. If the British survived the next few weeks, despite not having these mythical re-serves, he'd get news of the note to Menzies and let him deal with it.

Then he stopped short, contemplating the other possibility, the startling possibility, that the British did in fact have powerful re-serves, hidden away and ready to fight off the invasion. If that was the case, the implications were frightening. Part of him would be hugely relieved; a defeat might be the beginning of the end for Hitler – though many young Germans would pay with their lives. He be-gan to think deeply, his mind drifting into some extremely disturb-ing waters... If the British did have such reserves, why hadn't they made them visible at an earlier stage? Why hadn't they used all their strength to stop the build-up of the Sea Lion forces?

His heart began to thump. *Could they have set a trap?*

He wouldn't put it past them. Much as he hated Hitler, he had no great love for the British. They were simply his last hope of saving Germany.

And if they did have these reserves, who had leaked that information to the Swedes? Who was trying to interfere? Should he tell Menzies in case the source did more damage next time?

He was frustrated that the head of MI6 had refused to meet him a month ago. He'd wanted to tell him at first-hand about Hitler's decision to invade Russia, and about the growing German Resistance. But if they had been able to meet, Menzies could have told him what was going on with the Realists. They'd have a better chance of getting rid of Hitler if they worked together. *If only they would talk to him!*

He froze, looking down at a spot on his desk, his gaze fixed, as another thought struck him. If there were these powerful reserves hidden away – and there hadn't been as much as a hint in any reports from his agents, what did that imply? If the only information getting through to him was what suited the British purpose – what they wanted Hitler to believe? What did that say about his agents? Incompetent... or worse? He felt a chill run down his spine. *Who were they working for?*

He found himself looking into a very dark space, full of mirrors and blind passages. He shivered. There was no point in even thinking about going there; he had to decide what to do immediately. He'd suggested to Goering he'd send agents out to try to verify the information – but the Reichsmarschall had refused. Not that he cared about his opinion; he would normally do it off his own bat anyway. But there was a risk. If he did send out those orders and they were intercepted, one way or another, the British would know there'd been a leak. They'd assume the Germans would take countermeasures. It was even possible they'd abandon whatever plans they'd put in place to foil Hitler.

He sat at his desk for another hour, trying to work through the possibilities in his mind. In front of him was a writing pad, but he didn't dare commit any of his thoughts to paper. There was no knowing who might find them. Then, through the haze, he glimpsed a path. As long as the British didn't find out there'd been a leak, there was no risk of them cancelling their plans. And this was exactly what he wanted – *because there hadn't been the slightest effect on the Sea Lion operation.*

9

As the long night wore on, the news in London got somewhat better. The southern naval battle had been a disaster but, to the north, the Harwich destroyers had broken through the German defences and were inflicting heavy casualties on the convoys heading for Kent. By 0300, however, the Royal Navy ships had exhausted their ammunition and reported they were withdrawing to re-arm. Plots from the radar sites showed the invasion armada regrouping and again making way towards England.

It was clear to the Chiefs that the southern fleet was the bigger threat. The attacks on the Plymouth and Portsmouth flotillas had fractured the first line of defence, and the remaining British warships had inflicted little damage on the approaching convoys. The radar stations showed the ships positioning for their approach to the Sussex coast. They seemed to be heading for the beaches between Brighton and Beachy Head.

At an early stage, the Chiefs had agreed not to send the RAF's light bombers against the invasion fleet in daylight. Bitter experience in France taught them that, against heavy German defences, it would be suicide. But at night there was an option. The Fleet Air Arm's torpedo squadrons were trained to operate in near darkness. The commanders came to a quick decision; they would leave the northern convoys to the guns at Dover; the Swordfish would all be sent against the southern fleet.

At the Naval Air Station at Lee-on-Solent, thirty-six ancient-looking biplanes waited in the gloom. The armourers finished their work, hoisting a sixteen-foot-long torpedo into position between the under-carriage legs of each Swordfish. In the briefing room the aircrew were hanging around, some having a last cigarette, some chewing their fingernails as they waited.

At 0230 the reconnaissance plane arrived back. The pilot and observer ran straight to the briefing room to report. There was no need for photographs.

"They're fifteen miles east of Beachy Head, sir. Heading north-west. Several hundred vessels, five or six lines, stretching back about three miles."

It was all they needed. Guided by naval ratings with hand torches, the Swordfish lined up and trundled down the flare-lit runway. Flying just a hundred feet above the sea in dim moonlight, they were safe from attack by German night fighters and exposed only to a few bursts of unaimed flak as they passed over the out-riding auxiliaries.

Five minutes later, the observer in the lead aircraft was the first to see something in the water. Hanging over the port side of the open cockpit, he spotted the luminescence of a wake. He leaned forward and thumped the pilot on the shoulder, pointing at it. They turned to follow the trail until they reached the ship, a large freighter. They climbed to 2000ft and dropped their flares.

For a moment the pilots of the other planes, still at sea level, were startled by the magnesium light. Then, silhouetted against the brightness, they saw a sight they'd been expecting, but stunned them nonetheless; hundreds of ships and barges.

The formation split up into small groups. They slowed to 80 knots and turned towards the convoy, coming in from different points of the compass, staying low to avoid the flak. Most of the flak went high above them, but four of the outdated biplanes were hit on the approach and fell, all crumpled wood and canvas, into the sea. The rest kept going, under and through the hail of fire. They dropped their torpedoes into the dark waters.

It was angry retribution for the losses at Plymouth and Portsmouth. Now the German ships were on the receiving end as torpedoes began to strike home. Six of the fast merchantmen carrying the first echelon of troops were hit, slowing under the blows and beginning to settle, with water pouring in through gaping holes in their hulls. In the black of night, hundreds of frightened troops discarded their weapons and fought their way on deck. Many leapt into the sea, hoping to find a raft or some wreckage to support them, as they saw the ship's crews unable to launch lifeboats before the decks flooded.

Three of the destroyer escorts had been hit. A few hours earlier they'd been celebrating their success against the British navy at Portsmouth, now their ships were sinking fast, with sailors struggling to escape in the darkness.

The aerial torpedoes had been set to run eight feet below the surface, to take them under the hulls of less valuable targets, but one miscued, porpoising along on the surface at 35 knots. Just visible in the moonlight, it sped towards one of the barges. Tethered by lines ahead and astern, the barge was unable to steer out of its way. The doomed crew watched in terror as the torpedo approached. Under the impact of 300 lbs of Torpex, enough to sink a cruiser, the barge and its occupants disappeared forever. Astern of the pulverised vessel, the next barge in line drifted helplessly across the path of ships behind. Within minutes it was run down in the confusion. In the line of craft, there was chaos, with more barges driven under in collisions. Unable to escape, hundreds of soldiers were dragged down in their vessels, others jumped or were thrown overboard.

Supported by their kapok lifebelts, they would survive for a while, but, in the cold English Channel, few would see out the night.

10

Across southern England, the final troop movements were under way. During the late evening and early hours of the night, the regiments reassigned by General Brooke from East Anglia travelled in lorries and hastily-camouflaged London buses to new positions near the southeast coast, or to the strategic reserve in front of the capital.

At Dover Castle, the garrison had been on full alert since midnight. Shortly after 0300 a company of reinforcements arrived on foot, infantrymen from the Royal Norfolk Regiment. There was some confusion about their papers at the first barrier, but the sentry allowed them through to get it sorted. With the extra layers of barbed wire and mine fields, installed at Brooke's insistence, they still had several checkpoints to pass before reaching the main gate.

From inside the castle they didn't see exactly what happened at the next barrier; the sergeant in charge didn't get the opportunity to phone through. Whatever occurred, a flare had gone up, followed by a burst of shooting.

"Can you see anything, Sergeant-Major?"

Captain Browne was confused. The gunfire sounded like Brens, but he knew the sentries at the outposts were equipped only with rifles.

"Call them again."

The sergeant-major was still trying to make contact by telephone when one of his men saw shadowy figures running towards them. They didn't stop when challenged.

Browne reacted at once. For weeks they'd been alert to the threat of paratroopers or fifth columnists. His training clicked into action.

"Get the searchlights on!"

Now he could see the figures, coming closer, in attack formation.

"Order them to halt!"

The figures didn't.

He waited, uncertain what was happening. They were getting close.

"Open fire!"

His men didn't stop to wonder why the soldiers' uniforms were khaki-coloured. They opened up with their Vickers machine guns, targeting the wave of men coming towards them. The rest of the gate detail joined in with rifles and Bren guns. Under the heavy fire, the attack faltered, then stalled. The assailants were cut down, dozens falling before they even got close to the gate. A handful of survivors turned and disappeared, like shades into the night.

The guns went quiet. Inside the castle, they waited nervously until there was no more movement outside. A reconnaissance squad was sent out. They found a scene reminiscent of the Great War; bodies lying on the ground or impaled on the barbed wire. A few seriously wounded troops lay moaning in the coils of wire. The squad dragged them into the castle for interrogation. Only when they got the prisoners into the light inside did they realise the implications. They were wearing British uniforms.

Twenty minutes later, Colonel Gibson, the C/O, came over to see for himself what had happened. With the numbers of Poles and other foreigners now serving with the British Army, he had to make sure there hadn't been a ghastly mistake. He was met by Captain Browne, who had already started to interrogate the prisoners.

"They're Jerries, sir, no question. Landed about a mile away in collapsible boats; were trying to infiltrate the castle."

Gibson commended the captain on his prompt action and went into the guardhouse to speak to the prisoners, a corporal and two soldiers. One of the soldiers was lying quiet, obviously badly hit; the other was crying. The corporal lay on the ground trying not to scream as a medic applied a tourniquet to his leg. Someone gave him a shot of morphine and a cigarette, and, over a few minutes, his pain seemed to ease. He began to talk quite lucidly, in English. He told Gibson his name was Juergen. Before the war, he'd worked for a year in Liverpool, a shipping clerk with the Hamburg Sud line. He talked about his life there … walking the Pierhead and Sefton Park… his girlfriend from Scottie Road and the football scene in the city. He even claimed he'd had a trial for Everton reserves. Gibson looked at his mangled lower leg. Whatever else, his football days were done.

Browne told the colonel it looked as if the impostors had been discovered at the second barrier, presumably by the sergeant in charge, who hadn't been heard from since. He guessed the assault troops' English hadn't been quite good enough or, perhaps, their identification papers weren't up-to-date. Or maybe the giveaway had been the corporal's passable Scouse accent jarring with his East Anglian uniform.

The injured corporal listened to the officers talk. He didn't argue about the facts, but insisted they were prisoners of war, saying they'd worn British uniforms only for the night trek across enemy ground, a legitimate *ruse de guerre*. He claimed they'd been fired on as they were about to discard their outer gear before the attack on the castle. He was obviously well-rehearsed, adding that the main invasion force would capture Dover in a few hours and it would be in the Englishmen's interests to treat him and his men in accordance with the Geneva Convention. Gibson listened politely to his argument and asked a sergeant to check if they were wearing German uniform beneath the khaki battledress. They were, but it didn't make any difference.

Gibson made sure the prisoners were receiving medical treatment and that their wounds had been dressed. He went back to his office, distressed, but with his mind made up. There was no time for a formal military trial, but it was clear the Geneva Convention didn't apply.

They had been fighting in British uniform.

They would be shot at dawn.

11

To begin with, the famous cliffs didn't look that white, more a dirty grey. But, as the sun came up they began to lighten, and then, to glow. For a moment, Hauptmann Fritz Weber thought they looked almost welcoming. Then the shelling started. The troops who'd been watching the English shoreline from the open deck dashed for shelter, first crouching low behind the bow ramp, before moving, as the fire grew fiercer, behind the armour of the tanks.

For more than three centuries, the castle at Dover had been Britain's frontal shield against invasion, a bastion strengthened over the years as the nature of warfare evolved. Whether facing Dutch or French cannon, or modern German naval guns and bombs, the threat to the citadel had changed only in terms of the calibre of the weapons and the depth of entrenchment needed for protection. At dawn, the fortress faced the latest military threat, the dive-bomber. Shortly after first light, the Stukas appeared, a great phalanx protected by more than a hundred fighters. They swept over the armada towards England. Even with four squadrons of Hurricanes thrown up in desperate defence, the RAF pilots were unable to break through the swarms of 109s to get at them.

One by one the dive-bombers targeted the guns sited in sandbagged emplacements. Blast after blast convulsed the surrounds of the fortress as German bombs and British ammunition stores exploded in a hellish inferno.

From the approaching ships, still a distance out to sea, it looked as if nothing could have survived the conflagration. For a moment they lived in hope of an unopposed landing, but no sooner had the Stukas withdrawn than the artillery fire started again. It came from the heaviest weapons, buried deep in the white cliffs, and unscathed in the attack.

The guns turned their fire on the already-weakened northern convoy as it approached the coast, sinking the handful of auxiliaries trying to lay a smoke screen and then targeting the biggest ships they could see. Heavy shells began to strike home on steamships and escorts. Soon a dozen ships were burning or slowed to a stop with water pouring in through holes gouged in their hulls. Coming on top of the losses inflicted during the night by the Harwich destroyers, the northern wing of the assault was almost stalled.

On Fritz Weber's vessel, two miles to the south, the troops waited apprehensively as they began their run in towards the beach at Hythe.

So far their crossing had been uneventful. Their converted ferry was more seaworthy than most of the fleet. A bulk transporter in her previous life, she had hauled sand and gravel around the Bodensee between Switzerland and Germany, before being requisitioned for Sea Lion. The crew had sailed the sturdy craft down the Rhine to Rotterdam, where she'd been fitted with crude loading ramps. In a series of nightly hops, they'd taken her the rest of the way to Boulogne. Though small in size, she was one of the more suitable transports in the makeshift fleet, open-decked and double-ended. The panzers and half-tracks had been able to roll on from the stern, ready to surge out from the bow ramp when they grounded.

"So far, so good," Weber said to his driver, as they came closer to shore. He knew they'd been spared the worst of the British reaction, but whatever excitement the men might have felt about Sea Lion was long gone. From the battle noises just to the north, they could tell that their colleagues were taking a pasting. There was little sympathy expressed, however. The more the defences focused on them, the better their own chances of staying alive.

But, a few minutes later, they came under fire.

After a few shots bracketing the leading ships, the British artillery began to get the range. First one, then two and more of the ferries were hit or swamped by near misses. Soon half a dozen ships were foundering. The ship beside them was on fire, belching a column of black smoke into the air. Weber could sense their own skipper hard at work, swinging the ferry from side to side on their run-in. An old hand, he was doing his best to make his ship a more difficult target for the guns.

A shell whistled overhead and exploded 30 metres behind them. They crouched in fear of the next shot. Weber could hear angry shouting from his men. *Where's the goddamn Luftwaffe?* They'd been told Germany had control of the skies. They expected it to have taken out the British coastal artillery before they came within range.

They didn't have much longer to wait. From the direction of the French coast, another group of Stukas appeared, in tight formation, heavily escorted by fighters. For a minute the cheers rang out. But then more aircraft appeared, from a different direction.

Christ... Spitfires!!

They'd been told the RAF had been destroyed, so why were the vicious dogfights taking place above their heads? They could see planes being shot down... smoke... parachutes. For a few minutes it seemed touch and go. Then, as suddenly as it started, the dogfight was over. The Spitfires had been driven off and the remaining Stukas began their dive attacks on the gun sites ahead.

Weber watched as gun site after gun site was destroyed. Gradually the artillery fire faded away. The way to the beach was clear.

In front of them, the little coasters straightened up for their run-in, closing to within 200 metres of shore before launching storm boats from the davits. Weber saw the assault troops clambering down nets into the fragile boats, to be taken the final dangerous metres.

The battle sounds changed from shells to close-range fire, as machine-guns opened up from the pillboxes overlooking the beach. A few veterans from the Great War recognised the heavy thumping of Vickers guns echoing along the shore. Soon they could hear lighter bursts of fire, from Lewis guns and Brens. The mortars started, their range honed into the water's edge where the men were most exposed. Within minutes the surf was being stirred up, not by wind or tide, but by British gunfire. The shoreline turned dark with German blood.

Behind the storm boats came the motorised barges, their skippers calling out almost foolhardy instructions to the helmsmen.

"Full speed ahead."

At a sedate 5 knots, they headed towards the beaches, trying to avoid the booby-trapped obstacles and sunken craft from the first line of the assault, then ramming their flat-bottomed vessels up onto the shingle. Assault troops jumped off the ramps into the surf. They struggled ashore and rushed across the sand, still under fire, ignoring fallen and falling comrades, pausing for a moment of shelter to catch their breath behind lop-sided beach defences, before staggering to their feet again, driven by the NCOs shouting and roaring at them to keep going.

For fifteen minutes the outcome was uncertain, but slowly the troops who'd made it to the beach gathered themselves into squads and attacked the strongpoints. With rifle, bayonet and grenade they overwhelmed the beach defences, pillbox by pillbox, yard by bloody yard. The British gunfire died away. With little left by way of opposition, the towed barges approached the beach, chivvied along and pushed towards shore by the tugs that had hauled them across the Channel. Troops tumbled down makeshift ramps and ladders into knee-depth water, seasick but alive. Behind them a few Siebel landing craft appeared, carrying the second line of infantry, some dragging light guns or pushing motorbikes through the surf.

Next it was Weber's turn. Two hundred metres from the shore, the panzer commander gave the signal. Engines started up on the tanks and half-tracks. The men tensed as they waited, each with his own private thoughts or prayers. After what seemed an eternity, the ferry grounded, the ramp dropped and the little armoured column began to grind their way through the surf onto English soil.

They pushed through the detritus of the first echelon, trying to avoid casualties lying bleeding on the sand, forcing their way towards the line of dunes. At last the grenadiers were in their element. Dismounting from the half-tracks, they fanned out behind the low hills, ready to take out the remaining beach defences from the rear. After a firefight lasting just over forty minutes, they managed to clear a strip of dunes a kilometre wide on either side of the landing zone.

For another hour, spasmodic counter-fire continued from a few stubborn Tommies on the flanks, but gradually the resistance died away, the defenders killed at their posts or fleeing for cover as the tanks approached.

The first of the heavy Panzer IVs crawled ashore from converted river ferries. More barges were towed or shoved to shore, laden with field guns and the teams of terrified carthorses that would pull them to battle. On now-calmer sands, beach marshals got to work, marking out safe routes through the British landmines.

After clearing their sector of beach, Weber and his men regathered. They were missing just two men, and one half-track, lost to a culvert mine as it climbed up the exit road. The part of Sea Lion they'd feared most, the crossing, was behind them. The battle for Hythe beach was over. Weber went over and spoke to the panzer commander. They cross-checked their location on a map and agreed the route forward. Now on terra firma, they were back to what they knew best. They remounted their tanks and half-tracks, and formed up into battle formation, ready for the next part of their mission, a fast, armoured thrust towards London; a *blitzkrieg*.

12

At midday Bracken went into a side room, not much bigger than a cupboard, and switched on the wireless set, tuning in to Radio Berlin. He knew Lord Haw-Haw would have prepared his speech with great care, and had it cleared by his Nazi minders well in advance of the landings. The facts didn't matter to William Joyce. Anything he said would have been included for its propaganda value, nothing else. However, Bracken wanted to see if there were any nuances he might pick up. He placed a sheet of paper and a pen on the bench beside the set and waited for the familiar call sign.

"Germany calling, Germany calling."

Bracken cringed as he heard the familiar nasal tones across the ether.

"People of Britain, the hour of your liberation has come! This morning, powerful forces of the German Army landed on English soil and are now sweeping forward towards London. The Royal Air Force has been destroyed. The few Royal Navy battleships that tried to interfere with the operation have been sunk by the Luftwaffe.

"Just twelve months after the British government foolishly declared war on Germany, the consequences of their stupidity are now clear, a crushing military defeat for England.

It did not need to be so. The Fuehrer did not want these issues to be settled by bloodshed. Our countries – like others – have had their disagreements, but, after the British and French armies were defeated in France, he hoped that wiser counsel would prevail in London, seeking peace instead of war. He offered generous terms. However, the warmonger Churchill still refused to negotiate; still refused to listen to reason. For three long months after the great German victory in France, the Fuehrer waited patiently to see if Britain would see sense; to see if new leaders would emerge, realists who would respond to his yearning for peace. He waited in vain. Now, regrettably, battle has been joined. The young men of England – your husbands, sons, brothers – are paying for Churchill's obstinacy with their lives.

"Already, entire British Army units are surrendering. The Fuehrer has ordered that all soldiers who put down their weapons will be treated honourably. He has decreed that any Royal Navy ships that withdraw from the battle and head north to Scottish ports will not be attacked. As a further sign of his desire for an end to this conflict, he has stated that any surviving RAF aircraft which leave the combat zone and withdraw to rear areas will be left undisturbed.

"People of Britain, Churchill and his blood-sucking government are doomed! Do not resist the inevitable. Do not prolong your nation's agony. Rise up! Rise up and throw off the Jewish-Capitalist clique that rules your country, and their puppet, Churchill. Why should your young men die for their greed? No longer, I say, no longer! Rise up, working people of Britain! Rise up and join your Aryan cousins in building a new future for all of Europe – a National Socialist future!"

He paused.

"*Heil Hitler!*"

Bracken sat waiting for a few moments to see if there was more, but the transmission ended with some martial music.

"Lying bastard." He spat out the words. "Clever, miserable, lying bastard."

* * *

Forty minutes later, Bracken collected Churchill from his room and chaperoned him across to the broadcasting cabin, trying to sound as relaxed as possible.

"Just been listening to our favourite traitor, Mr. Joyce. Usual rubbish... nothing new. Though he still mentions the Realists, surprisingly! Clutching at straws, I suppose. Anyway you don't have too much competition in the oratory department."

He ushered the Prime Minister into the little booth, closed the door and stood, sentry-like, outside.

Churchill sat down and placed his speaking notes on the table beside the microphone. He contemplated for a few moments. Across the country, people would be tuning into the BBC, anxious for news; military personnel at their posts, civilians gathered in their homes, factories and farms. They would have been wakened two hours before dawn by church bells ringing out, the signal the invasion had started. They'd have heard brief news bulletins on the BBC about German landings in Kent and Sussex, and about British successes at sea and on the beaches. He knew that people in the south-east corner of the country would be particularly frightened, already able to hear the sound of artillery. He was conscious that the entire nation, military and civilian alike, needed the reassurance of hearing his voice, and he had prepared his words with great care. Now he cleared his throat and waited. The red light came on. He counted to four, letting the silence build. Slowly and powerfully he spoke to them.

"Fellow Britons!"

He waited, allowing time for his opening words to spread across the country, letting people recognise his voice and nod to each other, reassuring themselves it was him.

"Out of the darkness this morning, as we have long been expecting, enemy forces landed on our shores. Having failed to subjugate us through poisoned enticements or vile threats, Hitler and his thugs now try to impose their brutish will on us through force. Well, let them try. The fish need feeding.

"Along the English Channel, in the Straits of Dover and on the beaches of Kent and Sussex, battle has been joined. Our soldiers are fighting ferociously, defending our island and our way of life. Already, in the opening hours of the battle, we have inflicted heavy losses on them. Hundreds of Nazi ships and barges lie twisted wrecks at the bottom of the sea. Their dead lie strewn on our beaches. Hitler and his Hunnish army will rue the day they decided to invade this isle, this sceptre'd isle."

He paused for a moment, visualising little groups of people round kitchen tables, at workbenches in factories, in barracks, all tense and white-faced.

"In the days ahead, the battle will be hard, but we are strong and ready. Let no-one doubt what the outcome of this battle will be. It will be victory; victory over Nazism; victory over an unspeakable evil. We will hurl the invaders from our shores, back into the sea from which they crawled."

He left the words hanging in the air.

"To all of you, I say this. Be diligent in your duties. Be calm and follow the orders given you by the authorities.

"Be confident in your leaders and in our brave fighting men.

"Be stout in your hearts. Be confident in victory."

He waited.

"God save the King!"

The broadcast over, Bracken walked with Churchill back to his office, silent. Without asking, he closed the door behind them. Churchill was at once on edge. He could see the pain in his friend's eyes and waited, still standing, for him to speak.

"Winston, I have some very bad news about Chartwell."

13

Even from their vantage points in the gallery above the pit, the commanders were finding it difficult to stay on top of events. Things were happening fast. Phones were ringing, messengers rushing in with news. At the great table, the plotters were doing their best to keep up, pushing symbols around, trying to make sense of sometimes-conflicting instructions. Staff officers from the different Services moved between booths, usually agreeing on a course of action, sometimes arguing over facts or priorities.

With all attention focused on the landing zones. General Dill came into the Army booth and stood behind Brooke for a few minutes, watching him and his team at work.

"Well?" he asked, at the first quiet moment.

Brooke stepped back from the wall chart and unstiffened his body. He had hardly moved in four hours.

"We're holding them in Kent, sir. The attack on the beaches to the south of Dover has stalled. The coastal defences are making it hell for them."

"Are the guns still operational?"

"Yes – at least the big ones in the citadel. Still pounding away at the ships... seem to have taken out most of the tank-carrying barges. The Jerries are doing a bit better a few miles to the south, round Hythe. Assault troops ashore in some numbers. They've got about half-a-mile inland and there are reports they've landed some panzers and half-tracks."

Dill wasn't too surprised. He had approved Brooke's plan to position the main British forces inland, well back from the beaches. The defences on the coast were just a thin shell.

"Sussex is more of a worry," Brooke said. "There's a major landing in progress on beaches from Eastbourne round to Brighton. German troops ashore in considerable numbers. The coastal guns have been knocked out, and there seems to be little counter-fire against the beaches from the field artillery inland. There were reports, earlier on, of paratroopers attacking the gun sites. I'm moving a mobile brigade up to seal them off."

"Any more news from Newhaven?"

"I'm still worried. It was attacked about an hour before the main force appeared... German naval infantry, apparently, landing from small boats. It seems the men managed to hold out long enough to set off the demolition charges. The dockside cranes are definitely down. We're not so sure about the blockship. The decks are awash, but there was fighting on board even as she settled. We don't know if the sailors just managed to open the seacocks or if they'd time to smash them up properly before the Germans could get to them."

There was a movement behind. A naval officer came in carrying some photographs. He looked relieved.

"Just arrived, sir. The blockship's done its job. Not fully sunk, but she's well down by the stern... only about a ten-foot gap to the quay wall. Maybe a fishing boat could squeeze in, but nothing bigger. The RAF will try and put a few more holes in her this afternoon, to make sure she stays down – before they get any flak guns set up."

"What about Dover and Folkestone?" Dill asked.

"They're secure. The blockships were sunk as soon as the news came in about the attack at Newhaven," Brooke answered. "The Navy's confirmed they're in position. Harbour entrances blocked."

Dill looked at Brooke. They both knew the significance of the reports. The invaders had been denied use of the only ports in the landing zones.

Five minutes later, the mood changed. An urgent call came in for General Brooke and was patched through to the booth. It was from Brigadier Galligan, an old friend of Brooke's. He was the commander of the troops defending the Brighton sector. He sounded desperate.

"Sir, the men can't hold out much longer. Swimming tanks came out of the water, straight up the beaches... used flamethrowers on the pillboxes. We've no artillery support. It's bad. I want to pull the men back a mile or so before they're overrun and then get the RAF to gas the bastards. Think it's the only way to stop them."

Brooke listened, and asked him to keep the line open, saying it would take a few minutes to get an answer. Galligan pleaded with him.

"Hurry, Alan. For God's sake, hurry."

Brooke went straight over to Dill and repeated the message, but added his own rider.

"I'll approve his request to allow a tactical withdrawal to the next defence line, sir. It's well within our plans. But I don't see any justification to use gas."

For a moment Dill didn't reply. Weeks earlier, the Prime Minister had insisted on reserving the decision on the use of gas to himself. Now, under pressure of battle, Dill had to decide what Churchill actually meant.

"I think we need to discuss his request with the PM," he said.

Brooke was taken aback. He looked at Dill.

"Why, sir? Surely he was just insisting on a right of veto if we want to use gas? We're a long way from that point."

Dill had a high regard for Brooke, but, on this occasion, he took a different view.

"There are political considerations as well," he said. "Even if we decide against it in this case, the issue's going to arise again. I expect he wants to be made aware of the circumstances each time it's being considered. Possibly wants a set of precedents to refer to as things develop."

There was no further argument. As the senior officer, Dill made the decision; he would consult the Prime Minister.

Before sending for him, he asked Ismay and Air Chief Marshall Portal to come to a meeting room behind the gallery. He suspected the discussion with Churchill could take some time, and they might have to execute any decision taken at short notice. He apprised Portal of the situation at Brighton and asked him to put a squadron of aircraft on standby for a gas attack on the beachhead, if it was so decided.

When he'd issued the instruction, he turned to Ismay and addressed him in a formal tone.

"General Ismay, you're aware of the situation. Please take a message to the Prime Minister, asking him to join us as soon as possible."

Five minutes later, Churchill appeared in the gallery. He looked grief-stricken. The generals knew why; Ismay had just told them about Chartwell.

"I've heard the news, Prime Minister. I'm sorry," Dill said.

He acknowledged Churchill's loss, but only briefly; there were too many other battles being fought, too many lives being lost, to worry about one house, no matter how special. In a conciliatory gesture to General Brooke after their difference of opinion, he asked him to explain the position to the Prime Minister.

Brooke understood. He turned to Churchill.

"Sir, I have Brigadier Galligan on the telephone, from Southeast Command. He says the beach defences at Brighton are being overwhelmed. He wants to withdraw his men to the next line, and has asked that the RAF make a gas attack on the beachhead."

For some seconds there was no response from the Prime Minister. His eyes narrowed. An uncomfortable silence seeped through the group. Brooke's alarm rose. He could see Churchill was in an emotional state, fraught, the look on his face a mixture of desolation and rage. He heard him mutter something under his breath. It sounded like 'Vermin,' although it might have been 'Verdun'. He seemed on the point of ordering a poison gas attack without even bothering to seek the opinions of his generals.

Dill caught Brook's eye, in silent acknowledgment that he'd made a mistake involving the Prime Minister. They both waited nervously.

Still, Churchill made no response. He turned away from the generals and stood slightly apart from them, sighing deeply as he contemplated the awful decision.

Brooke took the opportunity afforded by the pause. He lifted the handset again, speaking loudly enough for the others to hear.

"Brigadier, is there any indication that the Germans are using chemical weapons?"

There was a tense delay while the question was passed from Galligan's command post to the front line.

Brooke listened and repeated the reply aloud for Churchill and Dill.

"There are no such reports."

He decided not to mention the flamethrowers.

In the frightened weeks after the fall of France, with the country almost defenceless, they'd all been quite prepared to use gas if the Germans landed. But the strategic position had been transformed. To the outside world, it might still look like a battle for survival, but the group at the core of Ethelred knew different; they were now intent on a victory that would change the course of the war.

There was another lengthy pause. In his distraught state, Churchill seemed on the point of ordering a gas attack.

Brooke saw the hard look forming on the Prime Minister's face and decided to square up to any decision he saw as ill-judged. He had experienced the grotesque effects of gas in the trenches of the Great War and knew both its potency and its limitations. As a weapon, it was indiscriminate. Depending on the vagaries of the wind, it could be as dangerous for the users as for the intended targets. His worst nightmare was the Germans attacking English towns with similar weapons, inflicting appalling casualties on the civilian population. He was determined not to be the instigator in this new war. Most of all, he was concerned about Churchill's bitter state of mind. He decided to make a stand.

"Prime Minister, in my opinion there is no military necessity to take that step at present."

It was a calculated response. By limiting his advice to the military dimension, he hoped he wouldn't be accused of overstepping his brief. He looked straight at Churchill, who still seemed undecided. Brooke decided to throw caution to the wind.

"We're going to be on top of them in a few days' time, sir, with our conventional weaponry. There's no point giving Hitler the excuse to use gas on our cities and towns as soon as things start to go badly for them."

Churchill continued to stare at the general. He knew his authority being challenged, but he recognised the strength of the Brooke's convictions. He was also conscious that neither Dill nor Ismay had distanced themselves from the blunt opinion expressed. After a few more tense moments, he nodded slowly. He decided he would lead his generals in the direction they were determined to go.

"Tell the Brigadier we will not be first to use these weapons; not unless the fate of the nation depends upon it. The troops have permission to pull back to the inland defence lines as the situation warrants."

General Brooke passed the message on to Galligan and put down the telephone.

"I believe that's a wise decision, Prime Minister," he said, much relieved.

The tension from the exchange hung in the air and General Ismay moved in to defuse it before serious damage was done.

"Prime Minister, Admiral Pound would like to speak to you about the cruiser squadron in the Clyde."

With a final stare at Brooke, Churchill shuffled out of the gallery.

* * *

A hundred miles away, at Binbrook airfield in Lincolnshire, the Fairey Battle bombers remained in their revetments. The euphemistically named Smoke Canisters under their wings stayed empty. The road tankers, with their lethal loads of mustard gas and phosgene, were driven back, carefully, to their concrete shelters.

14

With the battle less than twenty-four hours old, GrossAdmiral Raeder was reluctant to leave his command centre in Wimille, but the order from OKW headquarters in Berlin left no room for argument. As dusk fell, he began the two hundred kilometre journey to Brûly-de-Pesche, just across the border in Belgium.

Shortly before 2300 they arrived at the village. A military policeman checked their papers and directed the driver down a narrow forest road. The Mercedes bumped along the rutted track for about a kilometre, past another checkpoint, till they came to a heavily guarded farmhouse. They had reached the Fuehrer headquarters for Sea Lion.

The Admiral stepped out of the car and was greeted by Kapitan Ernst Schmidt, a veteran from the Great War, now assigned as naval liaison to the field headquarters.

"Welcome to the *Wolfsshlucht*, GrossAdmiral."

Raeder was not impressed by the title – the *Wolf's Glen*. While his men in the front line were embroiled in deadly battle, someone with a Wagnerian sense of drama had been dreaming up fancy names. He couldn't see the Fuehrer wasting time on such frippery. He presumed it had been one of the hangers-on.

He took off his dark blue greatcoat and spruced himself up in the bathroom. Schmidt briefed him, telling him how the mood had been building since the first news came in about the naval victories, followed by the success of the parachute drops and the beach landings.

Raeder was shown to the conference room in the large kitchen space of the farmhouse. As he entered, he recognised the positive atmosphere; tense but optimistic, much like the early days in France when things were just beginning to go their way. Goering and Keitel interrupted their discussion and came across to greet him. After the fierce rows about the plans for the crossing, he found it a pleasant change to have the Kriegsmarine toasted as the heroes of the hour.

At midnight the Fuehrer arrived. Raeder heard someone say he'd travelled from Munich in his private train and been collected by armoured limousine from a railway siding nearby. He came into the room looking cheerful, exchanging cordial greetings with the commanders and singling out Raeder for special attention. He grasped his hand and shook it warmly.

"This is a day of honour for the Kriegsmarine, GrossAdmiral. Your sailors have shown what National Socialist spirit can achieve, even when our forces are heavily outnumbered. You may send a Fuehrer message of congratulations to the men. Be sure to include the staff officers who created the plan as well. They deserve recognition for their brilliant work."

Raeder bowed slightly in acknowledgement. He was indeed proud of his men's achievements. Despite his own reservations about Sea Lion, they'd achieved their objective; they had, in fact, exceeded his most optimistic hopes. He was conscious he had some difficult messages to give the Fuehrer later, but, for the moment, he accepted the words of praise.

Hitler moved over to the old kitchen table, covered with a large map of the Channel area. He clucked with satisfaction as he looked at the routes the invasion fleets had taken and the toeholds gained by the first wave of assault troops. He called Raeder over to stand beside him.

"The crossing, GrossAdmiral; it's the only thing I was worried about. Now our forces are ashore in England, I'm a lot more comfortable. And if I'm comfortable, think how Churchill and his gang are feeling... traumatised! They've discovered their vaunted Navy is impotent... can't even defend their own coastline. Without their navy to protect them, the British have nothing! They'll be in despair ... bleating for negotiations before the week's out. You've done well, Admiral. Now show me how the naval operation was carried out."

Raeder stood looking down at the map. It showed the complex picture of fleet movements and enemy counterattacks, of minefields and landing zones. Just twenty-four hours ago, he'd been in his headquarters, standing in front of a similar chart, riven with apprehension. Yesterday it was still a plan; today it was reality.

"Fuehrer, I can report that, in overall terms, the operation went as planned. We carried the body of troops and tanks committed across the Channel, and we inflicted heavy losses on the British navy in our engagements with them. Our own casualties are in line with expectations."

Hitler stood with feet apart and arms firmly folded, taking in the panorama on the chart, the English Channel and the German lines transcending it.

Raeder left him a minute to enjoy the picture, then lifted a pointer, trying to gauge the right moment to continue.

"There were, however, some differences between the sectors. In the south, protection of the convoys was the responsibility of the Kriegsmarine. I concentrated my naval resources there, and we made the crossing with relatively few losses. Anywhere the British navy tried to intervene, we got the better of them. We sank more than half of their destroyer fleet in the sector. At Plymouth, six sunk and no losses. They were in total disarray... couldn't make their minds up whether to chase our U-boats or head for the Channel crossing zone. Later that evening, in a separate action, my destroyers sank five of their ships off Portsmouth and suffered hardly a hit in return, though we did lose one U-boat. As a result, the Royal Navy didn't get close enough to the southern convoys to do much damage. However, we did suffer some casualties from other causes – minefields and a surprise night attack by torpedo planes."

"Those aircraft have now all been shot down, Fuehrer," Reichsmarschall Goering interjected, heading off an unwelcome question.

"What about the northern assault, Raeder? Why were the losses there so much higher?"

"Fuehrer, at the OKW meeting in August, it was agreed that protection of the northern fleet would be the joint responsibility of the Luftwaffe and the guns at Cap Gris-Nez. The subsequent decision to make the crossing at night meant the Luftwaffe was unable to provide effective air cover. Protection had to be left to our minefields and the coastal artillery. These did claim a number of British ships, but a small group of enemy destroyers broke through the defences and inflicted serious damage on the convoys."

Raeder hadn't quantified the scale of the losses, but Hitler didn't seem particularly bothered.

"GrossAdmiral, losses at any time are unfortunate, but are to be expected in war. History will simply record that the crossing was a success."

The final decision on timing had been taken by Hitler and he moved rapidly to pre-empt any discussion about it.

"In view of the changed circumstances, I assume the second wave will cross by day?"

"Yes Fuehrer." Goering and Feldmarschall Keitel answered in unison.

Raeder had won the anticipated argument without saying a word. The other issue he'd intended to raise was the hard reality that, so far, the British had committed just one fifth of their fleet to the battle. At the last moment, he decided not to spoil the party too early. That particular discussion could wait.

Still in buoyant mood, the Fuehrer looked across the table at Goering.

"Reichsmarschall, the Kriegsmarine has played its part. Is the Luftwaffe ready to wipe out the rest of the British fleet?"

"Yes Fuehrer. Air attacks continued until dark and we sank several more enemy ships. During the night, we're laying more minefields outside their naval bases. Bombing missions will start again at dawn."

Hitler turned back to Raeder.

"What about their Home Fleet? Has it left port?"

"No Fuehrer, still at anchor in the north of Scotland. No sign of any movement, even though they must have had at least twelve hours' notice of our crossing."

Hitler clenched his fist and made a comical little half-hop which embarrassed the more traditional officers present.

"It's exactly as I predicted." He looked around the assembly. "I told you all not to be so pessimistic. Every time the British Army tried to confront us in France, we defeated them. When the RAF tried to resist us in the aerial battles over the Channel, we swept them aside. Now we're doing the same to their much-vaunted navy. Even the so-called invincible Home Fleet is staying out of the action, hiding away in the Scottish islands. I tell you once the British lose their navy, or their navy loses its guts, they have nothing. We'll be in London even faster than I'd hoped. Even that dinosaur Churchill must realise the war is lost."

His generals went quiet; they weren't ready to celebrate just yet. Field Marshall Keitel had received reports that the troops were meeting fierce resistance as they tried to push inland. He was also getting concerned about the supply situation. A few small coasters had managed to get some fuel and ammunition across the short sea crossing to Kent, but on the longer trip to the Sussex beaches, none of the freighters had made it through the British patrols.

In the air battle, Reichsmarschall Goering was conscious that many more RAF fighters had appeared than his intelligence staff had predicted. The Stukas had suffered badly at the hands of the Hurricanes when they tried to finish off the destroyers heading back to Portsmouth. By this point, his dive-bomber squadrons were down to less than half-strength. They couldn't carry on much longer at such a rate of attrition. He just hoped his Messerschmitts could swat aside the remaining Spitfires in the morning. He had a lot to be worried about, but chose to say nothing.

The Fuehrer switched his attention to the battle ashore and immediately seemed more at home as Keitel discussed progress on the different beachheads. The only irritation he showed was at the failure to take Dover Castle, but, for the rest, he congratulated his commanders. The invasion of England was going according to plan.

At 0300 he brought the meeting to an end, without any discussion about the next phase or its challenges. He left in his armoured limousine to go back to train for the journey, presumably, back to Germany.

* * *

Tired as he was, Raeder didn't have time to dine or sleep at the Wolfsshlucht. As soon as Hitler left, he said his goodbyes to the others and called for his car. He had a long drive back to Wimille.

For all their success in the opening battle, he was filled with a mixture of relief and worry. The British still had many more warships than his Kriegsmarine, in the Channel sector alone. He knew the ambush tactics wouldn't work twice. He had also received reports that the cruiser squadrons in Scotland were preparing to move south. And, although the Home Fleet had not moved from its base at Scapa Flow, it hadn't gone away either. But for the time-being, he could relax; he'd been spared a tongue-lashing, or worse, from the Fuehrer.

He sprawled out on the back seat of his Mercedes and closed his eyes, hoping to catch a few hours' sleep before he would have to turn his attention to his next problem, getting the second wave across the Channel.

15

For more than 60 hours, the commanders in the Paddock had hardly slept. The staff were tiring too. Even with a sophisticated network of sources feeding information into the centre, they were finding it hard to stay on top of events. Over the first day or two, the battle had been relatively easy to follow, shaped as it was by the fleets of ships and aircraft committed by the sides. By the third day, however, the fighting had disintegrated into a patchwork of attacks and counterattacks. The picture was changing by the hour, getting more complicated and confusing.

The mood in the bunker was no longer one of excitement. Although the Ethelred plan had always envisaged a gradual withdrawal in front of the invading forces, the consequences of that decision were proving hard to stomach, hearing the names of the English towns fallen to the Nazis: Folkestone, Hythe, Eastbourne, Brighton.

Despite that pain, the battle seemed to be going roughly as expected. The RAF had been feeding just enough fighters into the fray to frustrate the Luftwaffe's attempt to gain air superiority. On the ground, the defenders were doing well in most areas. Despite the fury of the Nazi assault and the grinding pressure on all fronts, casualties were on the low end of expectations.

At midnight, Churchill called a joint meeting of the Cabinet and the Chiefs of Staff. He had been moving restlessly between the floor of the Operations Room and the gallery above, keeping abreast of the battle during the two days. However, he had to make sure the other

Cabinet members were fully briefed. It was no time for uninformed opinion to be at large in high places.

There was a tense atmosphere in the room as the meeting convened. Added to the natural apprehension about the progress of the battle, they now had another worry – Churchill's state of mind. The destruction of Chartwell had struck deep and his mood was difficult to read, swinging from fits of depression to a violent rage against the Germans.

After the scare about the use of gas, Pug Ismay and Bracken had been keeping a discreet eye on him, doing their best to steer him away from any decisions that involved fine judgement. Dill had discussed the situation with Ismay before the meeting and they had decided to limit his reporting to the bare facts of the battle, hoping to carry the Prime Minister along on any difficult decisions that needed to be taken.

Churchill took his place at his head of the table. Unusually for him, he said nothing, just gestured to General Dill to begin.

Dill confirmed what they knew already; the Germans were ashore in strength and were in the process of linking up the various beachheads. They now controlled most of the coastline from Dover to Brighton and had advanced a few miles inland in several places. Although no-one voiced the sentiment, they all knew their most optimistic hope had not materialised; the sea landings had not turned into a fiasco. They would have to beat the invaders back the hard way.

Though clearly still distressed by the losses in the early battles, Admiral Pound seemed reasonably composed. He reported that the Royal Navy had inflicted heavy casualties on the German transport fleet.

"We estimate they've lost about a third of their total capacity so far, to air attack, mines and the Navy during the crossing, and to natural obstacles and beach defences as they approached the shore."

With obvious signs of relief, he confirmed the most important fact.

"They've failed to capture any ports in working order, Prime Minister. The second wave, like the first, will have to come over the beaches."

Churchill made an approving noise and turned to Portal.

"Tell me how the RAF is doing, Air Marshal."

With the focus on the action at sea and on the landing beaches for the last three days, they'd been paying little attention to the battle in the skies. But it was critical to the Ethelred strategy. The struggle between the Luftwaffe and the RAF would determine who controlled, not just the sky over southern England, but the sea as well. They all knew it was a numbers game.

"Much as expected, Prime Minister," Portal answered. "So far, I've I released eight squadrons from the reserves, roughly a hundred fighters. They moved up to the forward bases without serious incident, and they've prevented the enemy gaining superiority over the battlefield. Unfortunately, sir, it's impossible to stop every air raid."

He waited for a few seconds, in silent sympathy for the losses suffered in the attacks on Whitehall and Chartwell.

"As we agreed last week, I've kept our day bombers away from the combat zone, but our heavy bombers been carrying out hundreds of sorties at night against the beachheads. To be honest, though, it's practically impossible to do any serious damage to such a dispersed target in the darkness. The raids are really just to keep the Germans awake."

Churchill moved back to the only issue that mattered.

"What's our remaining strength in fighters?"

"Two hundred and twenty now in action in the front-line squadrons, sir. Another two hundred still in reserve, half of those earmarked for the defence of the Home Fleet if it has to come south."

Churchill looked down at a notepad on his desk and grimaced. The total was a hundred less than on the eve of the attack, two days earlier.

"And pilots?"

"Enough to man those aircraft, sir."

Lord Beaverbrook had been called into the meeting to report on aircraft production. Churchill knew he had been working wonders at the factories. The squeals of protest reaching his office from people he'd steamrollered were proof enough.

He put the direct question to him.

"How many fighters are we producing, Minister?"

"About ten a day, Prime Minister."

"And we're losing fifty?"

The arithmetic was frightening, but it was only one side of the equation. He turned again to Portal.

"How are we doing against the Luftwaffe?"

"We're destroying at least two of the enemy for each aircraft lost," Portal replied.

Churchill had learned to be cautious about the RAF's claims, but there was no point in having a debate at this point.

"We'll find out if you're correct soon enough, Air Marshal. If they run out of planes before we do."

He turned to Brooke. His other big worry was the battle on the ground. The army had not done well in France.

"General Brooke, how are our soldiers fighting?"

"They're doing well, sir. Holding out as long as possible in each strongpoint and then withdrawing to the next line before they're overrun."

He chose not to mention the poisonous argument about gas.

"The garrison at Dover had a tough test. The Germans tried a false flag operation to take the Castle. Fortunately we'd heard about their ruses in Poland and Holland, and the men were ready. They did well... killed most of the attackers and saw the rest off. They captured a few prisoners and dealt with them appropriately."

Churchill didn't enquire any further.

"Are the guns still operational?"

"Yes sir, at least the big ones, in the emplacements. They're concentrating their fire on the tank-carrying vessels, and that has certainly reduced the firepower of the forces landed."

Clement Attlee had been listening attentively to the briefing. He hadn't involved himself in the military discussion, but had one tough question for Brooke.

"General Brooke, the defenders at Dover have put up a remarkable resistance, surpassing anything we could have expected of them. Will it be possible to relieve them before they're overrun?"

The silence from Brooke gave him the answer he feared.

Throughout the discussion, Lord Halifax had stayed quiet. The operation he had tried to prevent was in full swing, and there was little he could do to affect things. He'd sat fiddling with a pencil as the generals claimed things were going much as expected. To his ears, it was a meaningless assertion. Ethelred had always envisaged German forces landing and beginning an advance on London.

It hadn't taken a lot of clever planning on the British side for that much to happen.

The problem would come when they tried to stop them.

16

On the third night, the OKW assembled at the *Wolfsschlucht,* summoned again to brief the Fuehrer. Admiral Raeder made the long journey from Wimille by car, the others travelled by train or light aircraft. To begin with, Hitler seemed impassive, but the mood was chillier than on the day of the landings. The planned numbers of troops and armour had been landed on the shores of England and he'd expected the Heer to be finishing off the task they'd started in France, the obliteration of the British Army. Instead, things were slowing down.

He didn't waste time getting to the point.

"We're running behind schedule. What's the reason?"

Field Marshal Keitel moved over to a map spread on a table. He pointed to the beachheads established and the inroads being made through the dunes.

"Yes, Fuehrer, unfortunately. We're about a day behind our most optimistic scenario as a result of the delay in capturing Dover and difficulties in clearing beach defences elsewhere. It's also taking longer than planned to get supplies across, particularly fuel. The British have learnt lessons from the campaign in France. They've drained or set fire to the petrol in filling stations and abandoned motor vehicles. As a consequence, we're having to allocate more of our shipping capacity to the transport of fuel. It's all slowing us down."

Hitler showed no emotion. He turned to Goering.

"What's happening in the air battle, Reichsmarschall?"

"Fuehrer, the Luftwaffe has kept the RAF's bombers at bay and has prevented any attacks on the landing grounds."

The generals shuffled their feet in embarrassment. One or two glanced towards Keitel to see if he would contest Goering's statement. They knew it was disingenuous. The measure of the Luftwaffe's success was not their defence of the landing zones, but their ability to support the army's advance – and, in that, they had fallen far short. Keitel decided not to challenge the Reichsmarschall.

Perhaps with a sixth sense for hidden tensions, Hitler turned to Goering. He asked the direct question. "How many aircraft have we lost since S-day?"

Goering squirmed in discomfort, nervous where the conversation was heading.

"About 80 single-engined fighters since the landing and about the same number of Stukas. Perhaps 30 other types, bombers and twin-engined fighters."

The senior Luftwaffe officers in the room looked away, trying to avoid Hitler's gaze. They knew the number was a gross underestimate. Goering had ignored the many aircraft written off or seriously damaged on their return to France.

Even without the full facts, Hitler was startled. He glared at the Reichsmarschall.

"Nearly 200 aircraft in two days! Last week you told me the RAF had been destroyed!"

He continued to stare at Goering.

"Where did the British get these aircraft?"

"It appears they may have had a small number of aircraft held in reserve, Fuehrer, maybe 100 or so, all of which they have now committed."

"What sort of aircraft? A month ago you said they'd been reduced to a few obsolete biplanes."

"Most of the aircraft are old Gladiators, but there are some Hurricanes appearing too. It looks as if they've moved their final reserves from bases in the west to airfields near London. From there they can cover the landing zones, while the further our forces move inland, the further our aircraft have to fly from airfields in France to the battlefront."

"Our troops are only 5 kilometres inland; that shouldn't be too much of an extra burden on the Luftwaffe!"

"No, Fuehrer, that is correct. But our plans envisaged us having forward air bases in England by now. We're still waiting for the Heer to take an airfield. As soon as we have a base in Kent, our fighters will have twice the endurance over the battlefield area and a much greater range inland."

Hitler snapped at Keitel.

"When are you going to capture an airfield?"

Keitel stepped across to a wall map of the Channel sector and lifted a pointer.

"Tomorrow, Fuehrer, RAF Lympne. That's here." He tapped the chart.

"The plan was for three forward air bases by now. Why just one?"

"We've had to reject Manston, in the north of Kent. The delay capturing Dover means our front line is still compressed in that direction. Also, it's only five kilometres from the sea."

"Has it moved since you made your plans?"

"No Fuehrer, but British warships are still active in the Thames Estuary. The airfield would be within range of their guns at night. It's the same problem with airfields on the Sussex coast, around Brighton. Too close to their naval base at Portsmouth."

"So, that leaves two?"

"Yes, Fuehrer, Hawkinge and Lympne. And Lympne first, because it's nearer our front line – just a few kilometres away."

He looked down and ran his finger over the map till he found the other two airfields, near each other in the south of Kent.

"But they're close to the sea too!"

"That is correct, Fuehrer, but the British don't have the same freedom of operation there. That part of the coastline is under surveillance by the Luftwaffe day and night. Also, it's protected by our minefields and the guns at Cap Gris-Nez. A few of their destroyers might be able to make a nuisance of themselves in hit-and-run attacks, but they can't carry out a sustained bombardment."

Hitler didn't argue any further. "All right, Lympne. When?"

"Tomorrow morning, Fuehrer. A group from the 15th Panzer Regiment and a unit of grenadiers will move up during the night and storm the airfield at dawn. Should be operational by mid-afternoon. We'll fly in fighters and Stukas straightaway. They'll support the advance inland and cover the second wave as it crosses."

It was a day later than planned. Hitler folded his arms in front of him and seemed to accept the revised schedule. He turned to Admiral Raeder.

"Is the second wave ready to cross?"

"Fuehrer, the transport ships are waiting, but it will take longer than originally expected to get the men and equipment across. The Heer has failed to capture a port in working order, so we must land over the beaches again. That will slow us down. Also, we've lost about a third of our shipping capacity as a result of our losses on the first day. Some of the freighters will have to make a double run to compensate."

Hitler nodded. He didn't care how it was accomplished. It was up to Raeder to sort out the logistics details.

"What's the British navy doing?"

Raeder asked for a pointer and turned round to the map.

"Their destroyers haven't moved out of port, since we gave them a bloody nose three days ago. However, they're using torpedo boats to attack our supply ships at night, particularly off the Sussex coast. They're fast and hard to defend against, so we've had to switch the resupply missions to daylight hours. My big concern is their cruiser fleet. Two squadrons are moving south from Scotland, one along the east coast from a base near Edinburgh; the other down the west coast from the Clyde. About a dozen cruisers plus escorts in each squadron."

"Preparing to intercept the second wave?"

"That is the prudent assumption, Fuehrer," Raeder said.

Hitler turned to Goering.

"Can your Stuka squadrons reach them?"

"Not at present, Fuehrer. They're outside the range of our dive-bombers until we get air bases established in England. However, if they come much closer to the Channel, my flyers will see to them."

"What about the British Home Fleet, Raeder? Any sign of it moving towards the Channel?"

Raeder had heard the exhortations on Berlin radio, offering the Royal Navy ships safe conduct if they sailed for Scotland. But he didn't know the full extent of the contacts with the Realists, or whether there was still any possibility of a split in the Royal Navy. In the Fuehrer's presence, he didn't intend to raise any awkward questions. He kept his response brief.

"No, Fuehrer. They're still at anchor in Scapa Flow."

Hitler nodded, looking satisfied at the news.

"It's just as I predicted. They're not going to risk losing their battleships by sending them into the Channel."

Raeder realised he'd been outmanoeuvred. He shuddered, poised over the map, worrying about the next battle. The Home Fleet wasn't the problem. The threat was from their cruiser squadrons. From their bases in the Humber and Plymouth, they could reach the crossing zone before the second wave was halfway across – unless the Luftwaffe stopped them. This time the battle wouldn't be decided by feints or decoys in the middle of the night; it would be a bare-knuckle fight in mid-Channel between the Stukas and the British cruisers. If the Luftwaffe won that battle, the second crossing would be easy and the war as good as over. If the British won... it didn't bear thinking about.

He decided not to voice his concerns, waiting quietly with his colleagues until the Fuehrer announced his decision.

"The second wave will proceed as planned. The airfield at Lympne and Dover Castle are to be taken before they sail. Show no mercy to the defenders there. The British have to learn that war is not a game."

Amid a flurry of stiff-armed salutes, he left the *Wolfsschlucht*.

17

Fritz Weber and his company of grenadiers started their day early. They ate breakfast from the field kitchen and began loading up the half-tracks for the assault. It wasn't far to Lympne, but they would still ride in the sturdy vehicles and save their strength for battle. As they were getting ready, however, there was one disturbing note for Weber. A pack train of horses had brought up petrol in 20 litre cans to the front line, but there was only enough to top up the panzers; there was none for the half-tracks. He radioed back to ask if more was on the way, but the answer was negative; they would have to make do with what they had. He knew they had sufficient for the day's mission, but it was a bad omen.

As the sky lightened, they prepared for the off. Weber and two others were to pull the company's anti-tank guns. They hitched up the Pak36s to the tow bars. The final step was to drape large swastika flags across the rear of their vehicles, recognition signals to stop the Luftwaffe targeting them by mistake. They waited for the signal, arrayed in battle formation, sixteen powerful Panzer IVs in the van, followed by the twelve half-tracks.

Right on schedule, the Stukas arrived. They'd been asked to hit a target about half a kilometre away, a church tower that dominated the exit from the seaside hamlet. It seemed a likely vantage point for snipers or artillery spotters. Within five minutes it was destroyed, with the tower collapsed and the roof in flames. The battle group mounted up and moved past the burning church and onwards towards Lympne.

They didn't get far. Just two kilometres along the road, the column ran into the first defence line. Six Matilda tanks were concealed in a wood, supported by anti-tank guns and a company of the Royal Warwickshire regiment. As the German armour came within range, the British opened fire. The leading panzer came to a halt and brewed up as its ammunition exploded, leaving the twisted body of the commander hanging half out of the turret. Three more panzers were immobilised, their hulls punctured by armour-piercing shells.

In the face of the fierce resistance, the others withdrew out of range and waited.

"Dismount! Get the Paks!" Weber shouted. The grenadiers couldn't hear him over the battle sounds, but it didn't matter; they could see him gesticulating. They'd practised the manoeuvre over and over. The men jumped down from the half-tracks and unhitched the guns. A squad of soldiers broke into an empty farmhouse and dragged a machine-gun to a window to give covering fire. The gunners pushed the Paks forward, looking for a firing position.

"Fire!"

The first ragged salvo went out. In France, the tactic had worked well; but it didn't now. The problem was the heavy armour of the Matildas. The shells from the German anti-tank guns bounced off their thick hides. The gunners paused for a moment, uncertain what to try next. A minute later a shell hit the armoured shield of the most exposed Pak, smashing gun and crew into the undergrowth.

Weber rushed across, shouting at his men.

"Keep firing... try again. Go for the visors."

After a dozen rounds, they finally knocked out one of the Matildas, but the rest kept up their fire on any German unit that moved. For thirty minutes there was stalemate. The panzer commander, Major Beck, was getting agitated. He'd lost four tanks and the attack was now well behind schedule. He put out a call for Luftwaffe support, but the Stukas had returned to France to refuel after destroying the church.

It was an hour before they appeared again, loaded up with 250kg and 50kg bombs. Without any interference from the RAF or British anti-aircraft fire, they swept in from the coast, taking their time to identify the targets. Carefully picking out the British tanks, they destroyed them one at a time. The skirmish was over.

Frustrated by the delay, Beck and Weber got their column on the move again. The panzers and the half-tracks crawled past the burning Matildas and tried to rebuild their momentum. But ten minutes later, they were stopped again. The British anti-tank gunners had learnt from bitter experience in France. They had known better than to wait around for the Stukas. They had pulled back half a mile and taken up new positions. As the panzers approached, they opened fire again. Two more Germans tanks were knocked out.

Beck jumped from his immobilised tank and ran across to Weber, now shouting and swearing.

"Get your soldiers to shift them. We can't wait for the Luftwaffe!"

The Warwicks fought hard. One group of grenadiers were cut down by a Bren gun hidden in a thicket. Their colleagues reacted furiously. A squad attacked the machine-gun post and killed all the British soldiers inside. The half-tracks moved up behind the grenadiers and added their fire. For another fifteen minutes the firefight continued. Eventually the German pressure won over. Under the combined fire of the panzers, half-tracks and the grenadiers, the British troops were dislodged, post by post. The survivors retreated, abandoning their anti-tank guns and fleeing into the woods.

The final defence line had been breached. The armoured column formed up and moved forward. Bloodied, and much later than planned, they reached the perimeter fence of Lympne. The final assault was the easy part. The panzers smashed through the barbed wire and the half-tracks followed close behind. Inside, the grenadiers spread out and scattered the garrison of half-trained soldiers and untrained airmen. Within half an hour the firing ceased.

They rounded up the defenders and forced them into one of the hangers.

Finally, Weber could allow his men some rest. They sat around in the sunshine and ate some field rations. They watched on while a company of pioneers went round surveying the damage to the buildings and runways. The British prisoners were brought out from the hangar and put to work at gunpoint, filling in the trenches they'd dug just a few days earlier.

The grenadiers were exhausted, but they'd achieved their objective. The Luftwaffe now had the airbase it needed in England.

18

The loss of Lympne hadn't come as a surprise, but it still made the Chiefs of Staff nervous. The Army had suffered too many defeats at the hands of the Germans in France, and the bitter taste still rankled. Dill decided to speak to Churchill on his own.

"Prime Minister, you've probably heard they've taken Lympne and are moving towards Ashford. I'm concerned they're building up too much momentum. I wonder if it's time to slow them down a bit – perhaps commit the in-sector reserves to seal off the salient. Maybe not try to push them back, but at least stabilise the front in Kent."

Churchill squared himself against the pressure.

"General Dill, we expected to lose RAF Lympne. That's why we didn't fortify it heavily or position a large body of troops there; we knew it would be suicide. We've also received confirmation that the fuel stocks at the airfield were all destroyed before the assault began. Indeed, as I understand it, all we've left behind for the Nazis are a few little surprises scattered around the place for this afternoon, and a big surprise for later on this evening!"

Dill looked restless. Despite the clarity of intent in Ethelred and the deliberate strategy of sucking in the enemy before springing the trap, he was uneasy. It was against his instinct as a soldier to concede ground to the enemy so readily. Churchill could see his concern and spoke again, reiterating his decision.

"I understand your discomfort, General, but nothing has changed. This is the hard plan to which we committed ourselves. We shall see it through. We shall wait until the second wave is on the high seas before we commit our reserves."

He hesitated for a few moments, then decided to soften his uncompromising line.

"If it's any consolation, Sir John, we won't have long to wait."

19

Paddy Fowley sat in the cockpit of his Spitfire, the Merlin ticking over, waiting to set off. The reconnaissance sorties were less demanding now, but there were more of them. It looked as if the intelligence people couldn't wait the extra half-hour for an aircraft to cover several targets before getting back with the evidence. So it was straight across to one or other of the French ports, take the pictures and head for home.

It was his fourth mission of the day, but he'd been at it long enough not to be annoyed at the delay. He knew the ops people wanted the latest possible picture before night drew its cloak over the port. They'd be in the tower, watching the light and running the numbers on his flight time.

At 1635, the signal came. Fowley gave his mechanic a thumbs-up and slid the canopy closed. He revved his engine and began to roll.

Twenty-five minutes later, he arrived over Boulogne at 32000 ft. Even from that height, above the flak and fighters, he could see the level of activity in the harbour below. Ships were manoeuvring around, their long shadows etched on the water by the evening sun. It mirrored what he'd seen on the first morning. The time of day was different but the conclusion was the same; the second wave was embarking.

* * *

With the news from the French ports, Churchill pulled forward the War Cabinet meeting by an hour. They'd expected to be discussing the progress of the land operations, but the agenda had changed. The photographs showed the second wave would cross next day, during the hours of daylight.

From the moment the timing of the second crossing became known, the shape of the battle was determined. It would be the Royal Navy's cruisers against the German troopships; the Luftwaffe's Stukas trying to sink the cruisers; the RAF's Hurricanes and Spitfires doing their best to hold off the Stukas.

Churchill began the Chiefs of Staff meeting by asking a tired-looking Admiral Pound for an update on the naval situation.

"I released the ships at Plymouth about an hour ago, Prime Minister, as soon as the news came in. It's a ten-hour sail to the Channel, so they had to leave at once. The east coast squadron doesn't have as far to go. They'll be leaving the Humber shortly. The two groups will reach the Straits of Dover at the same time in the morning, at about 0700. I've assigned every destroyer that's capable of going to sea to shield them against submarines and every minesweeper I can lay my hands on to clear the sea lanes."

Churchill nodded. They'd spent many hours discussing this moment. Now it was all about execution. Pound had said nothing about his critical dependency on the RAF. He didn't need to; they all realised it would be the deciding factor in the battle.

Churchill took charge of that discussion, turning to Portal.

"Air Chief Marshall, please provide us with the details of the air cover for the fleet."

Portal looked first at Churchill, then at Pound, before replying.

"We're ready, Prime Minister. I released the fighter reserves an hour ago. There was just enough light remaining and I ordered them up straight away. They'll be reaching the forward bases about now. The ground crews are moving up in buses overnight."

"How many fighters do we have in the battle zone?"

"Including the new arrivals, about two hundred and eighty, sir. Two-thirds Hurricanes, the rest Spitfires. Maybe four or five times what the Luftwaffe is expecting."

Churchill nodded. There was no posturing, no arguing. Instead, there was a quiet sense of purpose. Tomorrow's battle would be the denouement. The Royal Navy would throw its entire force of cruisers to engage the invasion fleet. Then, out of nowhere, hundreds of fighters would rise to confront the Luftwaffe. It was the culmination of the great plan they had been working on for months. It was the blade on the Ethelred guillotine.

The Prime Minister sat silent for some time, allowing the group to deliberate on the day ahead. But the feeling of solidarity was interrupted by one discordant voice, as Lord Halifax leaned forward and directed a question at Pound.

"Admiral, what if these German embarkations are just a feint?"

Pound was taken aback for a moment, but he answered without any sign of rancour. "In that unlikely event, Foreign Secretary, I will turn my cruisers back as well."

"Unlikely, you say? Isn't it wise to prepare for 'unlikely' events in wartime? Wouldn't you be caught high and dry if the Germans just sit fast in port tomorrow and disembark their troops instead of making the crossing? Your cruisers will be approaching the Channel, with daylight breaking and the Luftwaffe ready to pounce. Meanwhile, the German invasion fleet will be all tucked up in harbour. What then, Admiral?"

Pound remained calm.

"Foreign Secretary, as I said, in that hypothetical scenario our cruisers will withdraw as well, under the RAF cover already committed. The Germans might succeed in misleading us for a while but, if they do as you suggest, they'll have failed to reinforce their bridgehead in England, which is, after all, the objective of the second wave."

Halifax's long-standing scepticism about Ethelred was now reinforced by what looked to him like casual incompetence in the planning. His voice began to rise.

"We will have exposed our cruiser squadrons to air and submarine attack, Admiral Pound, all for nothing. We'll have unveiled our secret fighter reserves! After that, do you think the Germans so naïve they'll walk blindly into a trap? All they have to do is wait, take their time to grind down our last few fighters. At that point they'll control the air over the Channel – and will be able to cross at their leisure."

Churchill glared at Halifax, tapping his pencil loudly on the table as the Foreign Secretary pursued his argument. Although the questions were directed at Admiral Pound, it was clear that he was the intended target. The issues raised by Halifax were awkward, but he suspected the answer would lie in a combination of intelligence reports and careful timing of the fleet's movements. In any event, it was for the military to sort out. In the worst case, of Halifax's prediction coming true, there might indeed be a period of shadow boxing between the fleets of ships and aircraft, perhaps for days, before one or other landed a killer blow. But the strategy had been agreed months ago. It was no time to be diverted by hypothetical questions – especially as Halifax, for all his complaining, never suggested any alternatives. *The sooner he got him across to Washington, the better...*

He moved to seal off the damaging line of attack.

"Foreign Secretary, in the event that Hitler decides to abort the second wave and leave a hundred thousand of his men stranded in England, without ammunition, without fuel, without food, you ask what shall we do? I will tell you what we'll do. We shall round them up in our own good time and celebrate that as our victory."

He had answered a slightly different question to the one raised, but the argument had gone on long enough. He locked Halifax in a piercing stare.

"We shall now return to the actual battle at hand."

20

Paddy Fowley was awake early. After his reconnaissance flight the previous evening, he hadn't expected to be rostered for a dawn sortie, but the C/O had summoned him and Flying Officer Andy Smith to the briefing room at 0700.

"Wonder what's up?" Smith said as they waited. "Would have been nice to have a lie-in for once."

Despite the banter, neither of them was surprised to be called. Their sorties the previous evening had shown embarkation getting under way. The only question was what their role would be in tracking it.

They stood up and saluted as Squadron Leader Wilson came into the room. He explained the tasks the PR Spitfires had for the day.

"There'll be close to a thousand ships trying to cross this morning – nearly as many as the first wave. This time, the Royal Navy intends to stop them. Our job is to give them all the help we can. We'll be putting up aircraft every half-hour or so, to get a fix on what's happening."

The two pilots listened in silence. It didn't take much imagination to foresee the scene in a few hours' time, with vast fleets of ships and planes thrown into a fierce battle, a battle that might decide the outcome of the invasion, and of the war.

"The first sorties have already gone out," Wilson continued. "I sent Carling and Allen out to photograph the convoys leaving harbour."

Fowley and Smith understood. The two new pilots had been given the first mission of the day. By now it was a well-practised routine, and much less risky than the later flights. They would have headed across to France while it was still dark, staying high, ready to turn and make a fast run over the ports as soon as the light was good enough for their cameras. If they timed it right, they'd be on their way back to England before the 109s could interfere.

Wilson moved on.

"You two gentlemen will fly the second mission; to get some shots of their convoys before the Royal Navy gets to them. Take off at first light, get your snaps and high-tail it back to base as fast as you can. The photographs will give us some idea of their tactical formation, and will help our radar operators identify the blips on their screens. That's not as good as the Fleet Air Arm having its own spotters up to provide a running commentary, but their Swordfish wouldn't last five minutes over the Channel."

The two pilots looked at each other. Smith asked the question on both their minds.

"What's the weather like, sir?"

They didn't usually care much, but the amount of cloud would determine the height at which they'd have to make their overflights.

"Overcast, I understand. Seven-eighths cover at about 15000 ft. Sorry."

Fowley grimaced. With the cloud, they wouldn't be able to take their photographs from the safety of high altitude – and they couldn't go low either, with the amount of flak from the German ships. They would have to go in right through the middle of the dogfights, where every Luftwaffe fighter in France would be pitted against the RAF. Fowley and Smith looked resigned at the news.

"Fighter escort, sir?" Fowley asked, more in hope than expectation.

"No, 'fraid not. They'll be busy with the Stukas. In any case, they'd only slow you down. Get in fast and get out, no hanging around for an escort to appear."

Wilson gave them their routings. Fowley's would take him across the Isle of Wight, to pick up the trail of the Plymouth cruisers and then fly along their planned course to intercept the German convoys. Smith was to cover the route of the cruisers from the Humber to the invasion fleet.

The higher-ups were obviously hedging their bets; assigning two aircraft doubled the chances of at least one of them making it back.

* * *

Twenty minutes after taking off, Fowley headed out across the south coast of England, following the route of the ships from Plymouth. Just past Selsey Bill, he came upon a scene of devastation below. Two large warships were sinking – they looked like cruisers. One was dead in the water, burning fiercely. The other had lost its complete bow section and was sinking fast, its foredeck awash. It was a bad start. He ran his cameras for a minute as he passed overhead, then refocused on his mission. The German convoys were still 60 miles away.

21

James Acton glanced up at the lone plane as it passed over. In the half-light he couldn't tell if it was friend or foe, but at that height it didn't matter. It was when you could see their shapes clearly you had to worry, especially the bent wings of the Stukas, coming straight down at you, sirens screaming.

Since they'd left Plymouth, *Kelvin* had been hard at work, scurrying around behind the cruiser squadron to guard against an attack by torpedo-boats. Other destroyers from his flotilla were off to the south, shielding the flank against U-boats.

The explosions came within a minute of each other, about three miles ahead. He raised his binoculars. *Damn!* Two of the cruisers... Now there were seven.

He scanned the skies. *Nothing.* He trained his glasses on the screening destroyers... no sign of an ASDIC search under way.

"Could be a minefield, sir," his first officer said. Lieutenant Campbell sounded agitated. They were getting close.

Acton had been assured that the channel would be swept for magnetic mines before they sailed. Maybe the Heinkel seaplanes had seeded more during the night. In any event, it looked as if the cruisers had run straight into it. As he closed the scene, he could see the casualties, *Arethusa* and *Galatea*. They were sinking, the crews abandoning ship. He could make out Carley floats being launched. His instinct told him to stop, but his orders were clear; he couldn't.

"Course, sir?" the first officer asked, this time with an urgent tone in his voice.

Acton snapped back to his command. They were still heading for the minefield. He had an immediate call to make. Staying close to the stricken ships meant a chance they could get through the gap in the field left by the detonations. But there were survivors in the water. Staying further away reduced the risk of running them down.

Acton made the hardest decision of his life.

Still 50 miles short of the Channel, the cruiser squadron was hit by the first air attack. A group of Ju88s from France reached them before the RAF fighter cover had taken up station. They came diving down through the anti-aircraft fire from the ships, not in the near-vertical plummet of the Stukas, but accurate enough to score hits.

Without fighters to protect them, the cruisers were left to their own devices. Twisting and turning, they threw up a hail of fire from their pom-poms. One of the Junkers was hit and veered away, but the rest kept coming. The first bombs missed, but it was only a matter of time. HMS *Aurora* was the unlucky one, hit by an armour-piercing bomb that penetrated through to the engine room. The pillar of smoke and steam rising from the aft funnel showed its predicament. Acton watched as she slowed to a stop, not listing yet. He thought she might float for a while, if she was lucky. She might even survive a tow back to Plymouth if she wasn't attacked again. But she was out of the battle. *Kelvin* raced on past the stricken ship.

Another group of bombers appeared, targeting the wildly manoeuvring warships. HMS *Phoebe* was hit and slowed down. A light cruiser, HMS *Dido,* was hit near her stern. As they came close, Acton saw that a fire was raging near the rear turrets. This time his decision was easy.

"Starboard 30."

They steered well away; near the turrets meant near the magazines. And now they were down to five.

The Hurricanes finally arrived. They chased away the last of the bombers, heading after them as they fled towards France. Too slow to catch the fast Ju88s, they turned back and took up station over the ships.

The hiatus was brief. Ten minutes later, the Stukas appeared: twenty of the ungainly aircraft protected by a swarm of 109s, coming from the north, obviously from Lympne. The British waited, gunners at the pom-poms, ready to throw up a curtain of fire as the dive-bombers came down at them.

"Sir!" Campbell was pointing. He'd spotted another large group of aircraft coming towards them, from the direction of England. But that didn't mean they were British...

Campbell tried to identify the formation. Being tossed around on the bridge of the fast-moving destroyer made it difficult.

"Fighters, sir, I think."

It wasn't a lot of help for Acton. From a distance, the Stukas looked much the same as fighters.

Campbell propped himself against the compass housing, trying to steady his hold on the binoculars.

"Fighters, yes... Spitfires! Jeez, dozens of them."

The two officers watched as they came closer. A full wing, by the looks of it – thirty or forty planes, more than they'd seen for months. They could see glimpses of a raging dogfight, the contrails interlaced in the gaps between the clouds. There was a parachute, then another one... of different colours. The Spitfires seemed to have a height advantage; they came slashing down, trying to avoid the 109s as they went after the dive-bombers. A few Stukas fell away, but the main part of the formation kept coming, separating from the dogfight and heading towards the British ships. Even as they lined up for their dives, another group of aircraft appeared, unnoticed by the German fighters entwined in the dogfight.

"They're Hurricanes, sir." The bridge crew watched as they tore into the unwieldy dive-bombers. They began to hack them down. Within a few minutes the Stuka attack faltered and petered out. The survivors dropped their bombs into the sea and tried to escape.

The depleted cruiser squadron sailed on.

Leaving the damaged and sinking ships behind, they closed on the German armada. Acton was pushing *Kelvin* to the limit. Once in among the troop convoys, he knew they'd be safe from the Stukas. The war ships spread out into attack formation. As they closed the German convoy, they could see indications of a fierce action already under way, about ten miles away. It was a good sign; the northern cruisers had got to the German fleet ahead of them.

Now the invaders were on the receiving end of the fury. Within minutes the handful of Kriegsmarine destroyers trying to protect the steamers were sent to the bottom by the cruisers' six-inch guns. A few weakly armed auxiliaries turned towards the powerful warships and began firing with their puny weapons. The German sailors expected to die within minutes, but, for the moment, were spared; the cruisers had more important targets to see to. The British flotilla swept past the little trawlers and opened fire on the mass of transport craft.

The bloodbath began. The largest freighter, SS *Ceuta,* was first to be hit, struck amidships by a broadside. Within a few minutes she was foundering. Her crew rushing to abandon ship, leaving behind a thousand soldiers struggling to escape the floods inundating the lower decks. The steamships and ferries were next to be targeted. Tank landing barges, burdened with their heavy cargoes, disappeared without trace under the water.

As the cruisers continued to shell the bigger ships, the destroyers turned to the barges. Speeding to almost 40 knots, they sliced through tow lines and swamped the craft with their bow waves.

In the feeding frenzy, the crews were having difficulty aiming their main guns, managing just a few rushed shots against the steamships. But they had more success against the smaller vessels. With the barges' low freeboards, even a near miss was enough to swamp them. The destroyers' machine guns and pom-poms raked the unseaworthy vessels as they went by. As *Kelvin* passed another tow group, they dropped a pattern of depth charges, primed for a shallow setting, blowing the bottoms out of tug and barges.

Soon, a tsunami-like scene of broken ships and bodies littered the sea. Dozens of the motley craft were sinking. Thousands of troops were floating amidst the debris, most face down, some still struggling. The destroyers did not spare them, their captains driving at high speed through the human flotsam as the sailors tried not to look. The nicety of whether enemy soldiers in the water were combatants or survivors would be left for history to decide.

Only in late afternoon did the Germans finally get some respite. The British ships were almost out of ammunition and the squadron commander ordered a return to base. The gun encounter was over, but they now faced the most dangerous part of the mission. Untangled from the German armada, they were exposed again to attack from the Luftwaffe. Horrified by the destruction wrought below, the bombers swept in again, determined to exact revenge.

Despite the efforts of the RAF fighters, two more cruisers and three destroyers were lost as they withdrew. The last to go was the gallant HMS *Phoebe*. Another bomb struck her on the port quarter as she limped homewards behind the rest of the fleet. A weakened bulkhead gave way, and the seas finally dragged her down.

The battered survivors of the squadron headed for Plymouth, the ships blackened, the sailors exhausted. The crews had seen the destruction inflicted on the enemy, but they knew they'd lost many comrades as well. The empty spaces in the anchorage told their own story.

Behind them, they'd left a scene of devastation. Spread across a hundred square miles of sea, the detritus from the battle burned or floated away, half-submerged. Barges idled without power in the failing light, the men hoping for rescue before the British returned to finish the job. Rafts and lifeboats drifted about in the dark seas, with half-drowned soldiers and sailors clinging to them. Thousands of bodies were lapped by the oil-slicked waters, with just a few lucky survivors picked up by launches from the French side of the Channel.

22

The day's actions were still not over. Deep in the Port of London, another warship was being readied for action. In the evening darkness, crew began to remove camouflage nets and carefully positioned debris from the decks of HMS *Erebus*.

Erebus was an aberration of a ship. At 7000 tons deadweight, she was the size of a light cruiser, though with a speed of just 12 knots, much too slow to travel with the fleet. But perched on top of her hull was an outsized turret from an old battleship, mounting two 15" guns. *Erebus* was a monitor, a floating fortress.

At 2100 hours she left her berth and made her sedate way down the Thames estuary. Just past the Isle of Sheppey, she slowed and moved at a crawl into Whitstable Bay. The navigation officer watched the depth carefully, taking her as far inshore as he dared.

She hove to. He checked his bearings.

Fifteen minutes later, she fired her first salvo. Two high explosive shells weighing almost a ton each flew into the air, twenty miles across the Weald of Kent. Eighty seconds later they exploded just outside Lympne, obliterating a train of horse-drawn supply wagons trudging towards the airfield. Two miles away, circling in the darkness, a Royal Navy spotter in a Swordfish watched the fall of shot and radioed back an adjustment.

"Left 100. Down 200."

Three minutes later, she fired a second salvo. This time the shells landed on the edge of the airfield near a group of recently arrived Stukas, damaging several of the dive-bombers. With another slight adjustment called by the spotter, the next rounds were on target, wrecking a hanger and the six fighters being serviced inside. After that it was carnage. For two hours, salvo after salvo crashed down on the field, destroying aircraft, fuel tanks and munitions and killing, without discrimination, airmen, ground crew and British PoWs.

By 0100, Lympne no longer existed as an air base. There wasn't an airworthy aircraft left. Even if any had escaped damage, the shocked survivors of the bombardment were in no fit state to fly them.

Her task completed, *Erebus* turned away. She headed back up the Thames, hoping to hide again among the cranes, chimneys and warehouses of London's dockland.

23

Churchill had delayed the meeting till he heard the news from Lympne. With the picture complete, he summoned the War Cabinet and the Chiefs of Staff to the conference room. The Chiefs were in their places early. They huddled in solitary concentration, using the final minutes to read the latest despatches from the battlefronts, still trying to calculate the final reckoning on the day.

The Cabinet members appeared and sat down at the table, making no attempt at conversation with the commanders. They could see there was work in progress. A few minutes later, the Prime Minister came in. He looked ebullient, greeting the assembled group warmly. Without asking the Chiefs for their reports, he made his pronouncement on the day.

"Gentlemen, the Battle of the Channel has been won. The trap has been sprung; the rat spiked. It is an historic victory for the Royal Navy; it is all the sweeter as revenge taken cold for our losses on the first day. With this brave action, the Navy has defeated Hitler's plan to conquer England."

Despite his bullish words, there was no sign of celebration in the room. Admiral Pound sat leafing through some papers on the table. The reports suggested that more than 500 enemy vessels had been destroyed; barges, steamers and escorts, and many more damaged or scattered to the four winds. But the Royal Navy, also, had suffered grievous injury. He looked up, obviously under intense stress from the loss of the ships, and, he feared, many friends and colleagues.

"Prime Minister, we have been victorious on the day, but I must counsel restraint. Nine of our cruisers have been sunk and twelve destroyers, almost half the ships committed. Others have been seriously damaged and won't be fit again for sea for months. If the Germans mount another assault like yesterday's, we may not have the wherewithal to stop them."

The Prime Minister appeared flustered by the response, but was still determined to savour the moment. Without engaging further with Pound, he turned to Air Chief Marshall Portal and asked about the RAF's success during the day.

"It's a similar story in the air battle, sir. We shot down close to two hundred enemy aircraft, and *Erebus* has probably destroyed several dozen more at Lympne. But we've lost nearly seventy fighters in return."

Churchill still resisted the plea for caution.

"Air Marshal, that is also an outstanding victory, you should be proud of your pilots' achievements."

"I am, Prime Minister, intensely proud. But I have less than two hundred fighters left."

There were sharp intakes of breath. The arithmetic was easy, and frightening. At the current rate of attrition, that was three days' worth.

Before Churchill could restate his satisfaction with the outcome, Clement Attlee interrupted the debate.

"Prime Minister, I share your opinions about the bravery of our fighting men. However, we must be careful not to use the language of victory. The measure of victory is not in the number of enemy destroyed, but in the consequences of the battle."

There were some murmurs of agreement. In his understated way, Attlee had captured the sentiment of his colleagues. With the first gentle breach made in Churchill's euphoria, Halifax saw his opportunity.

"Prime Minister, you claim a historic victory. But Admiral Pound and Air Marshal Portal have given us an alarming insight into the consequences. If the Nazis try again, we may well be overwhelmed. Today's battle will come to be seen as a Pyrrhic victory."

Step by step, Churchill's elation was being dampened. Antony Eden was scribbling down the details given by the Chiefs of Staff. He hadn't involved himself in the controversy about the air and naval actions, but realised that one crucial issue had been ignored.

"Admiral Pound, do you have any indication about the number of German troops who managed to escape the Navy and land in England?"

Pound didn't need to look at the reports in front of him.

"Our best estimate is that about a third of their craft made it ashore, Minister. With perhaps another 20000 men."

It was not the answer they'd been expecting. Halifax's mutterings got louder.

"To add to the 100000 already here?"

Churchill tried to ignore the interruption.

"It is an historic victory, gentlemen, notwithstanding the fact that some of the Nazis escaped."

Halifax's tone moved from scepticism to bitterness.

"If this is victory, Prime Minister, I find it difficult to imagine your definition of defeat. Now we can see the harsh reality of Ethelred. For all your plans to set a trap for the Germans, we now find ourselves with over 120000 enemy troops in England, equipped with hundreds of tanks and guns, heading towards London. More than half of the Royal Navy's cruisers and destroyers lie at the bottom of the Channel, and the Royal Air Force is down to a few hundred fighters. And you call this a victory? How many more 'victories' like this will we have to endure before we are finally overwhelmed? The whole Ethelred strategy's been a disaster, Prime Minister, from start to finish, and it's quite clear who is responsible."

There was an ominous silence in the room. No one added their voice in support of Halifax, but neither did anyone take issue with his harsh conclusion.

Churchill leant forward, glaring at him.

"If Ethelred should fail, Foreign Secretary, I will indeed shoulder the responsibility. But Ethelred has not failed. It is succeeding. It has achieved its goal of luring Hitler's armies to invade England before they were ready. It has denied them control of our skies. It has now achieved its aim of destroying their navy and their armada of transport craft. Have we suffered? Sadly, we have. Many brave warriors have lost their lives in defence of our homeland. But, from the moment Nazism took hold in Germany, the need for such sacrifice became a sad inevitability. There was no other way of confronting the evil."

"An inevitability, Prime Minister?" Halifax answered, his voice rising. "Was it inevitable we chose to ignore Hitler's peace offer in July? Inevitable that we refrained from opposing the first wave with all our might and were willing, instead, to concede English soil? Was it inevitable we chose not to inform the Russians and engage them as an ally when we heard about the German plans in the east?"

"Foreign Secretary, the decisions you refer to were taken democratically by this War Cabinet, of which, until now you have been a valued member." Churchill was breathing loudly, his face red. He seemed barely able to maintain his calm. "Should you no longer feel able to support those decisions, there is an appropriate course of action open to you."

Someone gasped. The strain in their relationship had been obvious for weeks, but it was the first time the bitter argument had been aired in public. The two men glared at each other. After a long, tense silence, Halifax edged back from the brink. He chose neither to pursue his attack nor to respond to the implicit threat. He broke his stare with Churchill and looked down at a folder on his desk, but made no effort to apologise or withdraw his remarks. He stayed firmly in his seat. He refused to make it easy for Churchill by resigning. If the Prime Minister wanted to fire him, he would have to do it the hard way.

24

The conference in the Berghof was fraught, more heated than any since the beginning of the war. Hitler had forced the generals to make the 300km journey to his retreat in the Bavarian Alps rather than meet at the *Wolfsshlucht*. He was demanding answers. He screamed that the losses suffered in the second crossing were completely unacceptable. The destruction of the base at Lympne was a disaster. On land, the lack of progress was an insult to the honour of the Fatherland. Six days after Sea Lion had been launched, they had only reached the line that should have been achieved by the third day.

He listened angrily to the reasons, the excuses...

Keitel was first to face his rage, coming under a tirade of criticism ... the slow advance... the failure to take Dover... the disaster of the second wave...

"Fuehrer, it's taking time to break down the British defences. They are defending with great tenacity... totally different from their gutless performance in France. Now they're fighting the way they did in 1918."

It was a shrewd way to make the point. Corporal Hitler had been part of the losing German army in the Great War, and it was the Field Marshal's subtle method of pointing out the doggedness of the Tommies.

Keitel then tried to share the blame around.

"I must also point out that our forces are short of fuel and ammunition. The Kriegsmarine has failed to establish the required chain of supplies. And now it has also failed to get the second wave across in fighting shape."

Admiral Raeder interrupted his superior. It was better than waiting for Hitler to turn his venom on the Kriegsmarine.

"Fuehrer, the Heer has failed to capture a port for the Kriegsmarine to use. Our logistics plan assumed one would be available by the third day. We still don't have one. The only ports captured are so badly damaged that only small motorboats can use them. All supplies still have to be brought across in small craft and unloaded over the beaches. These vessels are much smaller than the steamers planned for the resupply missions. They're also slower, which reduces the number of supply runs each day. As far as the second wave is concerned, I must point out its protection was entrusted to the Luftwaffe. They failed to protect my ships from the British cruisers."

Goering had decided he didn't want to be in the Fuehrer's line of fire about the Luftwaffe's performance. He had brought his chief of staff, Hans Jeschonnek, to face his anger.

The Reichsmarschall asked him to explain how the RAF was still offering resistance despite intelligence reports showing they'd been practically eliminated before the invasion was launched. Goering had rehearsed the answer with Jeschonnek, but still pretended to listen attentively as his Chief-of-Staff offered his explanation.

"I can only conclude that the economic intelligence service must have provided incorrect data about the British aircraft production rates. It seems the British have been able to draw on a hidden reserve of fighters. I understand that the Abwehr received information about this possibility before Sea Lion started, but failed to act on the intelligence."

Hitler turned angrily to Canaris.

"Admiral, is this true? Did you fail to follow up on reports about British reserves?"

Canaris took a thin folder from his briefcase. Inside were the minutes of the meeting with Goering a week earlier. He didn't open the file, just put it beside him on the table.

"Fuehrer, the report from Reichsminister von Ribbentrop on the eve of the invasion was the first suggestion the British might possess secret reserves. There was no corroboration from Luftwaffe reconnaissance. I recommended we send field agents to verify the reports, but Reichsmarschall Goering decided it was unacceptable to divert them from their role of watching British military activity in southeast England."

He put his hand on the folder, a gesture more telling than reading out the minutes.

Hitler fixed Goering with a glare, but said nothing.

He broadened his attack to the entire OKW.

"These excuses are unacceptable. I don't have the time for another war bogged down in fields and ditches. If the plans of my generals have failed, I will have new plans. Or new generals."

He stormed out of the room.

25

General von Leeb was not surprised when the call came in from Field Marshal Keitel's headquarters. He'd heard rumours about a fierce row with Hitler at the Berghof and knew that his 6th Army, still in its encampments on the Cherbourg peninsula, was the only major resource in the west not yet committed to the battle.

He decided to take the call in his study and waited for it in front of a wall map showing the invasion plans. Long arrows on the chart showed the planned route of the advance from the landing zones in Kent and Sussex. They reached out towards Objective Line 1, stretching across southern England, from Dover to Southampton. When the advancing troops reached the line, it would be time for his 6th Army to land on the south coast. From there, they would strike north-west to Bristol, cutting off the south-west corner of England and shielding the western flank of the 9th Army as it made its enveloping movement round London. The thrust would force the British defenders to face both ways. It would make their position untenable.

That was the plan; the updated markings on the map showed the reality. The advance in the south-east was less than half way to their objective. Von Leeb's four divisions had been waiting for the past ten days, frustrated as they watched the snail-like progress of the Sea Lion forces. Already, the date for the landing in Dorset had been pushed back by a week.

* * *

The call went much as anticipated. Keitel asked him to come to a meeting in Versailles next morning, to discuss the deployment of the 6th Army. Von Leeb decided to gamble; he asked if he could bring Erwin Rommel with him. The young general had been pushing a radical plan to break the deadlock.

Rommel had made a name for himself in the blitzkrieg through France, but had been forced to sit on the sidelines as the Sea Lion battle was fought across the Channel, with his 7th Panzer division transferred to the 6th Army and consigned to the third phase of the assault. The rumour mill was suggesting there were pockets of resentment in the OKW in Berlin, with some of the generals jealous over Rommel's success in France. Von Leeb guessed it wasn't his success they minded, so much as the attendant publicity he'd received. However, he knew Keitel was desperate for a breakthrough and thought there was a chance of sentiments changing. Von Leeb hoped that petty agendas would be put aside to allow the plan to be considered.

He was right. After a brief hesitation, the Field Marshal agreed.

* * *

They arrived at Versailles two hour ahead of the start time. Von Leeb said they'd done enough preparation on the drive up and brought Rommel on a tour of the palace. They walked around admiring the building and the grounds, then toured some of the opulent state rooms and bedrooms, that had been graced by heads of the French state from the days of Louis XIV.

When they reached the great Hall of Mirrors, von Leeb stopped and began to talk about the scenes of history that had taken place there. It had seen both the signing of the armistice after Bismarck's victory in the Franco-Prussian War and its antithesis, the humiliating treaty forced on Germany at the end of the Great War. There was method in von Leeb's approach, letting Rommel absorb the grandeur of the scene. As they reached the Queen's Guard room to join the conference, he had a final word of advice for the young general.

"Just remember, Erwin, he's a Field Marshal – old style."

* * *

They gathered in the plush room, the grey of their uniforms in stark contrast with the 18th Century splendour. Around them, the walls were covered with portraits of French statesmen and rich tapestries with fleur-de-lis motifs.

Field Marshal Keitel looked tired after the stressful meeting at the Berghof and the early morning flight back to France. He didn't waste any time on preliminaries, just brought the meeting to order. He told them of the Fuehrer's dissatisfaction about the slow rate of progress in England, and his demand that, in future, the Wehrmacht live up to his expectations. General von Leeb scanned the paintings on the wall and made no reply. It was hardly the 6th Army's fault if others had failed to achieve their objectives, but he knew when to bite his tongue.

After the brief preamble, Keitel asked about the readiness of the 6th Army. Von Leeb stood up. It was as much of an invitation as he could expect.

"Feldmarschall, my soldiers are ready to play their part, as soon as they're called upon."

The remark was slightly barbed, but Keitel didn't react, allowing von Leeb to proceed.

"I can report that the infantry and panzer divisions are at full strength, awaiting only the order and the assignment of shipping capacity to carry men and equipment across the Channel."

He paused. He'd told Keitel why he wanted to invite Rommel, but had to prepare the other senior officers for the discussion.

"My staff and I are conscious that the first stage of the operation has met with unforeseen difficulties, and we understand the reasons why. We have examined some ways we might adapt to the changed situation. With your permission, Feldmarschall, I would like to ask General Rommel to describe one possible line of approach."

Keitel nodded and sat rigidly in his place, showing no sign of either encouragement or hostility.

Rommel stood and looked around the hard-set faces at the table. Only von Leeb, back in his place, showed any sign of empathy. On the battlefield, his preferred approach was speed and manoeuvre, always with an element of surprise. All of those attributes would be needed today, with a layer of deference on top.

"Feldmarschall, as General von Leeb has stated, the 6th Army stands ready to carry out its assigned tasks, as soon as the order is issued. We recognise this has not yet been possible due to the setbacks on the existing battlefront. With General von Leeb's approval, a group of staff officers have been evaluating whether we might be able to support the operation in a way that reflects the new realities. We have asked ourselves whether, instead of waiting until the difficulties in Sussex are overcome, we could support the assault in a more direct manner."

In the field, Rommel was a dynamic, sometimes brash, young general, but he had listened to von Leeb. He recognised that suggesting changes in strategy to a field marshal was a topic to be approached with considerable caution. Keitel, however, gave no sign of any misgivings. He removed the monocle from his left eye and began to polish it with a small cloth, allowing Rommel to continue.

"Feldmarschall, we recognise that the difficulties with supplies and the lack of air support have slowed the advance in England. So far, we've received no indication when 9th Army will reach Objective Line 1. As per the current plan, the 6th Army is not scheduled to land and strike for Bristol until that line is reached. Clearly, if we were to move earlier, our flanks would be exposed to British counterattack. The suggestion I would like to put forward is that, instead of waiting for the 9th Army, we should deploy our forces straightaway to assist them, and leave the advance on Bristol until later."

Keitel put his monocle back in his eye and looked at Rommel.

"General, are you suggesting we land your divisions in Sussex in support of the forces there?"

The OKW staff in Berlin had discussed the possibility and rejected it, but Keitel wanted to hear Rommel's view. It would be a test of his thoroughness.

"If those are your orders, Herr Feldmarschall, of course. But our feeling was that such a landing would just put more pressure on the bottleneck. We'd still have the same issues about air support and the lack of supplies – in fact, it's likely to make those problems worse."

Keitel nodded; they were the same problems his own staff had raised. He waited to hear what else Rommel might come up with.

"My suggestion is that we land in Dorset, as planned, but strike north-east rather than north-west."

"Towards London?"

"No, sir... too ambitious for the four divisions I've got. I suggest an objective that may seem more limited, but is more effective in terms of the overall strategy. I propose we land as planned in Dorset, but with the objectives of capturing and holding a port and an airfield – the things we haven't been able to do in the south-east. That would re-energise the entire Sea Lion operation."

Without waiting for a response, he unfolded a large-scale map of southern England on the table.

"We would use the landing zones already identified for our assault, here and here," he said, pointing to a cluster of beaches on the Dorset cost. "From there, we push two columns of panzers forward. One swings left, to the west, to take the port of Weymouth, here."

He pointed to the map. Weymouth was 40 kilometres west of Southampton.

"My main thrust goes north-east, to capture an airfield, here, in Hampshire. Eastleigh is a Fleet Air Arm station, well away from the front line. It's unlikely to be as well defended as the RAF airfields."

He pointed to the base, a few kilometres north of Southampton.

Keitel listened, now with a mixture of interest and scepticism. He walked over to the wall map and stood beside the young general.

"Your right flank would be completely exposed, Rommel."

"It would, sir. But as I strike north-east from Dorset, I suggest the 9th Army in Sussex turns its point of attack left and comes towards me. We would plan to meet somewhere near..."

He circled his finger on the map. "About here, near Bishop's Waltham. That would take the British by surprise."

"I'm sure it would, General. The 9th Army would have turned away from its strategic objective!"

"Yes, Feldmarschall, but once we have a port and an air base in England, our whole offensive will be revitalised. We'll control most of the south coast, air and sea. We cut off a vital port, Southampton, and their largest naval base, Portsmouth. The British defences around London will be unhinged; they'd have to face two ways."

Rommel had spoken persuasively. Keitel raised an eyebrow and looked around the conference room to gauge the reaction of his staff officers. No-one had raised any objections as Rommel set out the ambitious, but carefully thought-out plan. After a few minutes thinking about the proposal, Keitel lifted a pair of protractors and began to measure out distances on the wall map.

"It's a long drive from Dorset to Eastleigh – as far as the armies in Kent have managed in eight days. What makes you think you can do it so much faster?"

"We did it in France, sir."

The answer sounded smug, but it was unarguable.

"And, though it's further in kilometres, there's less in the way to stop us. The British defences in the southern sector are much weaker – just two divisions, compared with the eight in Kent and Sussex. And, by this stage, most of their reserves of artillery and tanks have been sucked into the south-east."

"It's still a good distance, General."

"Agreed, as the crow flies. But half of it is through the New Forest. I want to strike right through the forest, same as we did in the Ardennes. The British don't seem to have learnt any lessons from there; maybe they didn't get a chance to speak to the French generals."

Keitel was impressed. Their experience in the Ardennes had taught them how to move armour rapidly through wooded terrain. While Rommel had commanded just a single division in the Battle of France, he had shown great flair in planning and execution. He had always achieved his objectives.

"Suppose we did try what you're suggest, General Rommel, would we not have the same problem as Lympne – the British destroying everything before we got there? And even if we managed to take the airfield intact, would we not face devastating attacks by the British Navy before we can build up the air wing?"

"I agree those are risks, sir, so we mustn't give them time to carry out a scorched-earth action. We need to use the Fallschirmjaeger division, a *coup de main* by the paratroopers to take the airfield and hold it for the three days it will take me to get there."

"Three days?"

"Yes, Herr Feldmarschall."

For the first time, Keitel showed signs of scepticism; there was a fine line between ambition and foolhardiness.

Rommel saw the doubt in his eyes.

"Light armoured vehicles and motorcycles, coming right off the beaches to clear the way, followed by fifty tanks straight through the New Forest."

He pointed to the map. The plan now showed two beaches, one just west of Weymouth, the other thirty kilometres east of the port.

"From the western landing zone, here, at Chesil Beach, a column goes right. It captures Weymouth and shields my left flank from any British forces in Devon and Cornwall. The larger force lands here, at Swanage and heads straight up through the New Forest to relieve the paratroopers at Eastleigh. We end up with a port and an airfield, the things we failed to get in Kent."

The field marshal listened. There were risks, and he could see why Rommel had made enemies in the OKW, but he was becoming absorbed in the plan. It was audacious, but looked achievable, and it might just get Hitler off his back.

"It's a possibility, Rommel. Let me talk to Reichsmarschall Goering to check if the Fallschirmjaeger division is up to strength again. They suffered badly on the first day, and are back in France to regroup. However, they might be able to carry out this one specific mission. Now, what about my other question? Are you not ignoring the lesson we learned at Lympne – naval bombardment?"

Keitel took the protractors again and began measuring out distances.

"The airfield is only 3 kilometres from Southampton Water! Even Admiral Nelson's old sailing ships could have hit it from that distance!"

"It might look similar, Feldmarschall, but the geography is quite different."

It had been Rommel's biggest concern as the plan came together, but his staff officers had done their homework. He turned to the map.

"The problem at Lympne wasn't the distance from the sea, it was the distance from the Thames Estuary. That was our Achilles' Heel; we didn't control the estuary, and nobody had thought about the big guns on that old monitor. Although it's true Eastleigh airfield is only a few kilometres from Southampton Water, there aren't any warships based there, apart from a few minesweepers. The airfield is actually 30 kilometres from the open sea, outside the range of any British naval guns."

"What's to stop them sailing their battleships right into the Solent," Keitel said.

"Mines, sir. We seal off the Solent with hundreds of mines – more than the British can clear. The Luftwaffe should be able to do that before the British battleships can get down from Scotland."

"And Portsmouth?" Keitel took the protractors again. "Less than 20 kilometres from Eastleigh. They've plenty of ships there!"

"But all destroyers, Feldmarschall. Their little four-inch guns can't carry the distance. Even if they tempt fate and send in a few cruisers, it would be on the limit of the range of their six-inchers. And, remember, the damage at Lympne was caused by fifteen-inch guns firing 1000kg shells, not six-inch guns firing 50kg shells. In any event, once we get our Stukas based in England, it would be suicide for enemy warships to try to get into either Southampton Water or Portsmouth."

Keitel was increasingly impressed with the young general's approach. His questioning moved from sceptical to practical.

"Coastal artillery? There's a lot around those ports. Would they not turn the guns against the bridgeheads?"

"There's a fair amount, sir. However, from what we can see, the big guns in emplacements all point to seaward. The only ones trainable to fire inland are in open sites. The Stukas can deal with them."

Keitel nodded.

"What are the landing beaches like?"

"They're fine, sir. We'd already surveyed the ones we intend to use as part of our original plan, Swanage Bay and Chesil Beach. They're both quite well defended, but not in sufficient depth. I intend to out-flank their defences by putting five hundred of my best troops ashore in Lulworth Cove, here." He used a pencil to point to a spot half-way between the two main landing areas. "They'll have orders to drive hard and take the defences on the other beaches from behind."

Keitel took a magnifying glass and looked at the tiny lagoon.

"We'd never get assault ships in there!"

"It's been used by tourist boats for years, sir, paddle steamers. We'll use ships of the same size and draught."

"Defences?"

"Two pillboxes, one at each end. A dozen or so glider troops on top of them at first light."

Field Marshal Keitel nodded slowly. After ten days of painful graft-ing in Kent, Rommel was again using the bold language of blitzkrieg.

"And from there?"

"The cove is sheltered and we can get some equipment ashore – but there's only one narrow track up from the beach. In any event, there won't be time to unload tanks. So I'll go for speed; motorcycles and sidecars. We've also got some British Bren Gun carriers, twenty or thirty, captured at Dunkirk. They're small and don't have much ar-mour, but they're fast and can carry a machine gun and a few troops. The familiar shape should also confuse the British defenders. From Lulworth Cove, a column in each direction; one in behind the de-fences at Chesil Beach and one behind Swanage as the assault ships approach."

Keitel thought for a few minutes. He was deeply impressed by Rom-mel's approach. With some junior generals, he'd have taken such a bold plan with a pinch of salt, but Rommel had demonstrated his ability to execute such fast-moving attacks in France. What was more, he had trained his troops to the high standards required for such an action. And they would follow him through hell.

If anyone could do it, it was Rommel.

26

With low, scudding cloud covering the Channel, the convoy from Le Havre had avoided detection until it was almost halfway to the Straits of Dover. The radar operators at Worth Matravers picked up a return at 0450 and provisionally identified it as a supply convoy, plodding its way towards the crossing zone. The controllers then switched their attention to a more immediate threat, a large formation of aircraft coming from the Cherbourg peninsula towards southern England.

The radar coverage along the Dorset coast was patchy. Further to the east, the next three stations had been put out of action by Luftwaffe fighter-bomber attacks on the previous evening. Worth Matravers had been damaged and was running at reduced power. It left a sixty-mile gap in the chain. As the aircraft formation moved further away, the operators were only able to get occasional paints on it. With limited data to go on, the sector controller had to make a call. He identified the likely target as the naval base at Portsmouth, and raised an air raid alarm.

Forty-five minutes later, Observer Corps spotters heard a group of aircraft approaching the city. Searchlights criss-crossed the sky above, but the formation seemed to have missed its target. No bombs fell on the city or the base. As news came in to the Paddock, the raid was marked up on the plotting table as minor. It was one less thing to worry about.

A few yards away, in the navy booth, it had been a relatively quiet night for the duty officers. There'd been little by way of action at sea overnight, just a few skirmishes between motor torpedo boats and German launches trying to get supplies across. They were looking forward to the end of their watch when an urgent call came in. It was passed to the officer-in-command, Commander Holmes. He listened for a moment before slamming the phone down at his side.

"Quiet! Quiet!"

It silenced the rest of the group in the booth. Holmes lifted the phone again and clicked his fingers for a pen. He had to make sure he got everything.

The staff watched. They could see Holmes was unsettled, not certain how to respond to the call.

He looked at them. "It's Eastleigh," he said. "The Naval Air Station. Being attacked by parachutists."

The reason for his hesitancy was clear. All their preparation work, all the procedures for the invasion battle related to incidents at sea. There was nothing in place to handle an emergency in the middle of Hampshire. Holmes snapped into action.

Call Admiral Pound now... and get General Brooke... quick! And tell Colville we'll need the Prime Minister in ten minutes."

He dashed along the corridor to the army booth.

"Colonel, there's a paratrooper attack on Eastleigh airfield. Hundreds of them. Just received a call from the control tower. It's a major attack; they say the defenders can't hold out."

Five minutes later Brooke and Pound rushed up to the gallery, still buttoning up their tunics. Communications from the Fleet Air Arm station had stopped. Another eyewitness had made contact, a police constable from a nearby village. He'd called the local army base and been patched through to the command centre in London.

Brooke took the phone from the commander and listened to the frightened policeman.

"Lots of aircraft overhead, sir. Hundreds, I'd say. And parachutes, hundreds, maybe thousands."

"Is the shooting still going on?" Brooke asked.

"Seems to have died down in the last ten or fifteen minutes."

Brooke looked at Pound and repeated the message. It was bad news. The lack of gunfire suggested that the defenders, naval reservists and Royal Marines, had been overwhelmed.

He had another question.

"Constable, can you see any black smoke rising from the airfield?"

"I haven't noticed any, sir."

It was their worst fear. It looked as if there hadn't been time to torch the fuel tanks.

Brooke handed the phone to the duty officer, telling him to keep the line open. He turned to a wall map, trying to identify the resources he could muster for a counterattack. He stood, hand on chin, thinking aloud.

"It doesn't add up. We've enough troops near Eastleigh to quarantine the airfield. They're not very mobile, but I'll be able to move them up in a day or so. We can handle paratroopers, no bother. But I'm worried... it only makes sense as part of a larger operation. So where else might they try?"

"It's five miles from Southampton," Pound said. "They can hardly be thinking of a direct assault there? Right into the teeth of our defences?"

"Unlikely – but we'd better put the troops are on full alert, just in case."

A courier came in with a message for General Brooke. He read it aloud.

"There's been a breakout across the River Arun, in Sussex. They've got some tanks across the river somehow."

Brooke has passed on the message, but was shaking his head. He looked at the map again.

"The Arun? Still doesn't make sense. It's 50 miles from Eastleigh, and we've two more defence lines in the way. It'll take them several days, minimum, maybe a week. And how are they going to supply the advance? They're already badly constrained by what they can get across the beaches in Sussex."

They had to act on what they had in front of them. Brooke put the garrisons along the south coast on alert and ordered one of his staff officers to start rounding up transport to move on Eastleigh. Admiral Pound sent orders to the naval bases for all seaworthy ships to prepare for sea.

Twenty minutes later, Pound was still discussing the situation with the naval staff, when an officer came across with a telephone.

"Sir, I think you better take this."

The call was patched through. It was a naval sub-lieutenant billeted in a guesthouse in Weymouth.

"There's an attack under way at the docks, sir. Some gliders crash-landed in the port area. Troops rushing the defensive positions."

The officer said he was hidden and had a partial view of the quay-side, a hundred yards away.

"The guard posts have been knocked out, sir. I can see German troops shooting up the port offices... looks like there are parties of men going round the cranes – could be sappers."

"Are the cranes still standing?"

"Yes sir."

"Any demolition charges going off?"

"None that I've heard, sir... Shit, they're coming this way. Gotta go."

The final pieces of the jigsaw fell into place just ten minutes later. Dozens of ships had been spotted, emerging from the mist off the Dorset coast. There was a report of a panicked call from a coastal battery, calling for help. They were under attack from the rear. An odd message received an hour earlier from a coastguard station near Lulworth Cove suddenly made sense. General Brooke ordered a warning to be sent to the other coastal artillery sites in the sector, but only a few acknowledged.

27

The Chiefs of Staff had always known that Ethelred came with dangers. Even as they had worked to prepare the trap, they had recognised the risks; a risk of British military failure; a risk that the elite German assault troops would, through skill and determination, achieve breakthroughs. The War Cabinet had only authorised the plan after Churchill forced them to confront the appalling vista of what otherwise lay ahead in 1941 or 1942.

The gamble, and the deception core to its success, had worked as planned in almost all respects. Even the early naval losses at Plymouth and Portsmouth had not detracted from what looked like an unfolding success. The Germans had succeeded in landing more than 100000 men in England, but, until today, it seemed the best they could look forward to was surrender, followed by a long spell in a PoW camp.

The critical strategy had been to cut off their logistics channel; to deny them access to airfields and harbours in England. The fact that the strategy had worked in Kent and Sussex was now of little consolation. Eastleigh airfield had fallen and the port of Weymouth taken. The defenders had been overwhelmed, the Auxiliaries, presumably, discovered in their hides and murdered. Most worrying for the commanders, despite the explicit standing orders, it looked as if the petrol storage tanks at Eastleigh had not been fired. Within an hour, reports were coming in of enemy fighters and dive-bombers flying into the airfield.

By late-morning, reconnaissance photographs from Weymouth showed the port had been captured intact. The cranes had not been toppled. Several ships had made it into the harbour and were unloading over the quays. Waves of troops and armoured vehicles were already moving inland.

* * *

The strategic threat was clear; the German forces intended to sweep through the weak British positions in the New Forest and link up with the airborne troops at Eastleigh. The attack exposed the entire defensive position in the south of the country; land, sea and air. For the RAF, however, the crisis had already arrived. Air Chief Marshal Portal described the situation to General Dill in blunt language.

"They're making things very difficult for us right across southern England. Our radars all point out to sea, not inland. Without radar, the controllers have only visual reports from the Observer Corps to rely on. It's chaotic. That system didn't work in France and it's not working now."

Brooke stood beside Portal and unfolded a map showing the troop dispositions in the sector. He had two infantry divisions, only one combat-ready. Their role had been to defend Portsmouth and Southampton. Now they also had to stop Rommel's advance through the New Forest and prevent the westward advance of the German 9th Army from Sussex.

"That's all I've got, Charles. Obviously, it's the PM's decision, but I think you've got to handle Eastleigh yourself."

During the afternoon, Portal sent every available light bomber to attack Eastleigh. The result was disastrous. The fighters and the flak guns were waiting. The RAF lost most than forty Battles and Blenheims, while doing little damage to the airfield. Even worse, twenty-five Hurricanes were lost as they tried to protect the bombers from the 109s. The loss rate was unsustainable.

At sea the situation was as bad. With their new base in England, the Luftwaffe now had air superiority over the south coast, and the Royal

Navy's destroyers had to fight their way through continuous air attacks. They were unable to stem the flow of ships bringing supplies to the Dorset beachheads. By late afternoon, four destroyers had been sunk by dive-bombers from Eastleigh. Reluctantly, Admiral Pound ordered the remaining ships to withdraw to Plymouth, where the remaining fighters and anti-aircraft guns could still offer protection.

* * *

The crisis hour had come. Three months earlier, Ethelred had begun in a spirit of optimism, with the Prime Minister's enthusiasm carrying along the doubters in the Cabinet. Despite the latest reverses, Churchill felt confident the military commanders would knuckle down and address the new challenge. He was less certain about his political colleagues. He decided to square away any issues with the Chiefs of Staff before speaking to the Cabinet.

At 1700 he summoned them from the Operations Room to the adjacent Map Room, away from the minute-by-minute pressures of battle.

Churchill and General Ismay were first into the room, and waited patiently for a few minutes while the Chiefs dragged themselves away from their command posts. Even when they came in to the meeting room, they seemed reluctant to sit down. No-one said anything. No-one was smoking. They didn't want to be away from the action, but they all knew there were some hard decisions to take.

Churchill addressed them in a subdued voice.

"In recent hours we have suffered grievous losses, and, sadly, will suffer more in the days to come. But we must put this setback into perspective. We have not been defeated. This is our Verdun; the ultimate test of our nation under fire. In Kent and Sussex, our brave defenders have stopped the Nazi advance. They have shown that our troops are more than a match for Hitler's stormtroopers. Now we must ensure that their brave efforts are not unhinged by this attack on our soft underbelly."

Churchill asked for their reports, and listened as the Chiefs summarised the battles that had been taking place during the day; the landings, the consolidation of the German beachheads, and their initial advance inland. He waited until they had finished their brief reports, then turned to Brooke.

"General Brooke, you have identified the extent of the Nazi penetration in Dorset and their apparent intentions there. We must take immediate action to forestall Rommel's panzers linking up with the parachutists at Eastleigh. As long as we succeed in keeping their forces divided, we will be able to sweep up the two separate components in our own good time. The hour has come to commit our remaining tank reserves to the battle in the New Forest."

He had spoken with quiet confidence, but was not prepared for Brooke's response.

"Prime Minister, we have no tank reserves."

Churchill went white. He remembered the words from the French High Command as the Battle of France reached its conclusion. "*Il n'y a auchun,*" had been the chilling response when they were asked about their reserves. "*There are none.*"

For a few moments he said nothing, sensing the nervousness in the air. He fixed Brooke with an iron look.

"If you have no tanks, General, your soldiers will find other ways to stop them."

His voice began to build.

"The Nazis have but a few score panzers ashore. The British Army shall hold its ground, shall use whatever tools it has to hand to stop the invaders; anti-tank guns and artillery, land mines and booby traps, sticky bombs and Molotov cocktails. They shall fell trees; they shall blow up bridges. They shall not withdraw!"

He shifted his gaze from Brooke and looked around the table at the other anxious faces. In France, the success of the German blitzkrieg had hollowed out the will of the French army and the government. He was determined that Britain would not go the same way.

"At no stage, as we envisaged this great undertaking, did anyone suggest the task would be easy, or that we would experience no setbacks. But let us remind ourselves of our goal in this epic battle. It is victory; victory whatever the difficulty; victory whatever the cost. For only through victory can we stop that man and his forces of evil."

He seemed to dig deep into his soul, gathering his strength and looking at his commanders.

"The time has come to take decisive action, to do whatever it takes to stop the invader in his tracks, to dislodge him from his toehold in Dorset and Hampshire. If we have no tanks, we will throw in the other reserves we have been holding back – General Brooke, the infantry divisions from the north and Scotland; Admiral Pound, the Home Fleet; Air Marshal Portal, our heavy bomber force. And if that great onslaught fails, we shall gas them."

His eyes went round the table, fixing the commanders, one by one. In a few short sentences he had given them each an order that took them into territory previously sacrosanct. He had underlined his determination with a threat to use a weapon that repelled them all.

"There will be no caveats, there will be no reservations," he continued, in a sombre tone. "We will complete our task. We will ensure the survival of our nation."

After a few moments of deep silence, Admiral Pound was first to respond.

"Prime Minister, three months ago, when we first envisaged this battle, you agreed that the Home Fleet was to be held in reserve, a counter against an attack on northern Britain, a guarantor of our ability to control the Atlantic sea lanes. You acknowledged that, while a foray into the Channel sector would wreak devastation on their supply lines, the threat to our battleships in the confined waters made the risk unacceptable. With German air bases established on both sides of the Channel, that threat has doubled. I must advise you that if we commit the Home Fleet, as you have directed, there is every possibility it will be destroyed."

He paused, knowing the impact of his words. Since the days of King Henry VIII, the navy had been the ultimate protector of the island's freedom. For 400 years it had made Britain the most powerful maritime nation in the world. Without its fleet, Britain would be an isolated, vulnerable island.

Churchill waited. He didn't argue, just looked hard at Pound.

"What is a Home Fleet, Admiral... without a home?"

Each word was powerfully weighted. For a few, tense seconds, he was silent, then spoke again.

"How long will it take them to get to Dorset?"

Pound took a slow, deep breath, knowing the sacrifice Churchill was demanding. He had feared this moment might come. Although dismayed about the grave threat to the Fleet, he had prepared unreservedly in case the order was issued. It was the reason that, despite their frequent disagreements, he retained Churchill's confidence.

"About fifty hours, Prime Minister."

"Which route? East coast or west?"

"West, sir. Down the Irish Sea and around Land's End. It's further, but the ships will be exposed to air attack for less time, and they won't have to run the gauntlet of the coastal guns at Cap Gris-Nez."

"When can they sail?"

"They can leave Scapa Flow tonight. They will reach Dorset before dawn on Thursday."

"And to support them?"

"The destroyers withdrawn from the Atlantic convoys are refuelling in Londonderry as we speak. They'll provide a screen against U-boats, from the Scottish Isles down through the Irish Sea. I've arranged a relay of minesweepers out of the Clyde and the Mersey to clear the sea lanes of mines."

"Do you need to use Irish waters?"

"That could help, sir. As far as we know, the Germans haven't laid any minefields there, and the risk from U-boats will also be reduced if we sail close inshore."

Churchill nodded. "You have my authority to take advantage of that shelter if you need to. I shall seek forgiveness rather than permission from the Irish. And even if I fail to get that, I will live comfortably with the stain on my character."

He scanned around the table at the other military commanders.

"What can the other Forces do to assist you? In fact, what must they do?"

"Keep the dive-bombers off my ships, Prime Minister. It's by far the biggest danger they face; a hundred or so Stukas in Brittany, and now several dozen more at Eastleigh."

Churchill turned to Portal.

"I trust it is evident, Air Marshal, this is the most important mission the Royal Navy has undertaken in its long history. The RAF shall assign whatever it takes to protect the Fleet, over and above any other priorities you have."

Portal returned Churchill's look and nodded his understanding of the order. It would mean throwing in the last few Hurricane squadrons from the reserve. He might even have to withdraw some Spitfires from the battle in Kent, with all that that implied.

Churchill let the instruction hang in the air for a moment before turning his attention back to Admiral Pound.

"Admiral, you will have the full co-operation of the RAF to protect your ships. They will provide air cover during the voyage south. Now tell me how you will carry out the attack."

Pound looked across at Portal and signalled his recognition of the commitment received. He turned back to Churchill.

"We will make the attack at night, sir. The ships will be most exposed on the final leg, along the south coast from Land's End to the target area. So they'll make that transit in darkness; a six-hour sail on Wednesday night, reaching Weymouth about two hours before dawn on Thursday. They will launch a bombardment on the port facilities, and will sink any German supply ships they find there. After they've destroyed the port, they will turn their attention to other targets – the lodgement areas at Chesil Beach and Swanage Bay, and any other targets of opportunity the Army identifies for us, as far inland as the edge of the New Forest. Our guns will inflict immense damage on the enemy for an hour or two, after which..."

"Good." Churchill interrupted him, quietly but decisively. "You've heard the Air Marshal give his commitment of air cover."

Pound continued. "I appreciate that assurance, Prime Minister. However, I must again draw your attention to the fact that, after the attack, the fleet will not have sufficient time to recover out of the combat zone back to the Irish Sea, or to a secure port – Plymouth being the only option – before dawn. They'll have to make their withdrawal under constant attack from the Stukas from Eastleigh."

"Can your battleships not eliminate that threat before they leave the area?"

"I'm afraid that's not possible, Prime Minister. The Germans have chosen well. The airfield is 22 miles from the open sea and the range of our biggest guns is less than 20. We can't take our ships into the Solent to get closer because it's thick with mines – both east and west channels, either side of the Isle of Wight. They wouldn't get a mile in before they were sunk."

"So be it. The RAF will also assign fighters to shield your ships as they withdraw after the raid."

Pound nodded.

"I understand, sir."

He knew it was as much as he could expect.

Churchill turned to Portal.

"Air Marshal, you have heard from Admiral Pound that our battleships cannot eliminate the enemy lodgement at Eastleigh. You will, therefore, assign your entire heavy bomber force to do so."

The order was crystal clear; Churchill left no room for ambiguity. Although Portal had many concerns about the execution, he chose not to argue.

The Prime Minister looked at his commanders. He had given them hard orders, now it was time to encourage them.

"This is not the first time our nation has faced such a threat to its existence. Three hundred and fifty years ago, we faced conquest by the ships of the Spanish Armada. We confronted that threat. We saw off Philip II and scattered his galleons around our rocky shores. Two centuries after that, Napoleon's army waited in their tents at Boulogne, preparing to invade our island. The Royal Navy spoiled their picnic when they destroyed the French fleet at Trafalgar. We eliminated the threat and saw off Napoleon Bonaparte. Those great victories ensured our survival as a free people. Today we are engaged with another enemy, many times more powerful, driven by a tyrant a hundred times more evil than Philip or Napoleon. The threat to our nation is not just defeat, but enslavement; in time, perhaps, annihilation. We shall do whatever it takes, we shall employ every asset we possess, we shall use every ounce of our strength to see off this tyrant as we did the others."

He waited a moment for his words to be absorbed, then turned to Pound.

"Give the order, Admiral. Let slip the men-of-war."

28

Brigadier Menzies asked to see Churchill before the late evening Cabinet meeting, which, he suspected, was going to be a long one. He was shown in by Jock Colville, to find the Prime Minister poring over a nautical chart of the south-west approaches. Beside the map was a typed document which looked like a voyage schedule. Churchill barely looked up as he came in.

"You wanted to see me, C? You'll have to be quick, I don't have much time."

"Prime Minister, I've received another message from Admiral Canaris. He wants to meet me – says it's extremely urgent."

Churchill put his pencil back down on his desk, thought for a moment, before shaking his head resignedly. "We discussed this a month ago, after his last approach. You know my decision; the risks are much too great."

Menzies left the words to hang in the air for a few seconds.

"Sir, a month ago we were confident that Ethelred would result in a crushing defeat for the Nazis. With the current situation in the south, might the balance have changed? The Germans in Kent are now forty miles from London and the Dorset front is wide open. Are those not, perhaps, the bigger risks?"

"The Nazis are bogged down in Kent, Brigadier, and the Dorset front is a narrow opening, not a wide one," Churchill growled, though he didn't seem totally convinced. Despite his immediate counter, he hadn't dismissed the request as abruptly as he had in August. There was some truth in Menzies' remarks, and he considered the request again for several long seconds.

"Is there a possibility he might be able to influence the current battle?"

"We won't know unless we ask, sir."

Churchill looked down at his desk, breathing heavily, deep in thought.

"In any event, by the time you could set up a meeting it'll all be over – one way or the other."

"Prime Minister, arrangements can be made within an hour. He's established a wireless link from the Dover area."

"What! Canaris...? In England?"

"Not him, sir, one of his people – presumably with the landing forces. He made contact over short-wave radio this morning. Camouflaged the initial message as being about an exchange of wounded prisoners. As you can imagine, it took a while for their radioman to convince our signals people it was genuine. Eventually, after an hour or two's delay, it was patched through to London and my own people were informed. We've taken over the link."

"A trap, C? An elaborate trap...? If not the Abwehr, then the Gestapo or the SS."

"I don't think so, sir. They used the agreed codes. We issued the standard challenge and they came back with the correct response within the hour. I assume their operator in Dover, or wherever, can make direct contact with Canaris over the Abwehr's own field network."

"Hmm. Anyway, what did he say?"

"Says he's going to be in Spain for several days, from tomorrow on. Suggests we meet up there. I get to choose the location."

"No matter where... the danger..." Churchill looked away from Menzies, unconvinced. "If you were to be taken... the things you know... Ethelred, Ultra, our entire agent network, not to mention the devil's work going on in the Uranium Committee."

He turned and looked straight into Menzies' eyes. "They'd get it all out of you, you know that?"

"I do, sir. But if we don't manage to stop them on the south coast, we might as well not have any secrets anyway."

Churchill was still shaking his head.

"In any case, how would you get to Spain? Weren't the flying-boats all destroyed in the attack on Poole Harbour?"

"One of the BOAC boats escaped. Was on its way in from Lisbon and managed to divert to Foynes, on the Shannon. They're far enough west of the combat zone to keep a makeshift service running to Portugal two or three times a week. There's a connecting flight across to Foynes from Pembroke Dock – an RAF aircraft painted with civilian markings to avoid upsetting the Irish. So, a drive to Wales tonight, two flights and a longish car journey from Lisbon – maybe 36 hours to get to Spain. Something similar on the way back, depending on, well, a number of things, let's say the situation at the time."

"Nonetheless, the risks... for you personally... for the country ..."

"Prime Minister, it strikes me we're running low on options. I'd rather take my chances in the field than risk a firing squad in London in a few weeks' time."

"You can't be taken alive, C. You know that."

"I do, sir. I'm prepared to take the chance. I'll bring a squad of men with me, well-armed. We can smuggle them into Spain on a fishing boat from Gibraltar. They'll have clear instructions about their priorities if anything goes wrong."

Churchill looked at Menzies for a few moments more and came to a decision.

"Brigadier Menzies, your request to meet with an enemy representative is denied."

He waited, then held out his hand.

"Good luck."

29

As General Brooke returned to the Operations Room, he was handed the field report about the River Arun crossing. He read it with deep concern. It wasn't just the breach of the defence line in Sussex that disturbed him. That had always been a possibility, and there were several more stop lines behind it. What alarmed him was the speed and the seeming facility with which it had been done. The essence of Ethelred was to withdraw slowly in front of the Germans, to weaken them yard-by-yard in a fighting retreat, before finally unleashing the reserves to destroy them. But the Nazis seemed to have walked across the defence line on the river without stopping for breath.

The Germans had made a leap forward, just as he was gaining confidence that the situation in the south-east had been stabilised and he could focus his attention on the south coast.

The details were alarming. Shortly after dawn, three huge gliders had dropped out of the sky, crash-landing in fields behind the defence line. The anti-glider posts had been smashed like matchsticks. Another of the brutes had been discovered on the British side of the front line, twisted and broken in a wood, still tethered in death to the three fighters that had towed it across the Channel.

The report made chilling reading. From the nose of each glider, a heavy tank had emerged, crawling into an English meadow. The panzers hadn't moved west to lead the next wave of the advance. Instead they'd turned back towards the Arun, moving methodically along the river bank, clearing pillboxes and strongpoints. It had been brutal and effective. Within thirty minutes the defence positions on the river had been shattered. In the wake of the tank attack, assault troops had swarmed across in light boats. Behind them, engineers had erected a pontoon bridge for the tanks and half-tracks of the 1st Panzer Division. Then had come the second shock. They didn't head for London; they turned west, towards Hampshire.

Brooke put the report down. He took off his reading glasses and looked down at his desk, chewing nervously on one end of the frame. He felt alarming flashbacks to the blitzkrieg days in France. He hadn't thought it could happen again; not when his men knew what to expect; not on English soil.

* * *

At 1930 the Chiefs assembled again in the Operations Room, this time with an anxious War Cabinet in attendance. Churchill had his bulldog face on. The other ministers fidgeted nervously as the Prime Minister began to ask the tough questions.

"General Brooke, can you please explain the reason for our sudden dislodgment from the River Arun, and tell us what you're going to do to stop the Nazi advance."

Brooke showed no emotion. For as long as he retained the Prime Minister's confidence he would continue to lead the battle in the most professional way he could. And if Churchill chose to replace him, he would accept that as well, without question.

"Prime Minister, we expected that the defences on the river would be able to hold out for twenty-four hours; instead they were dislodged after just six. The appearance of a number of tanks in their rear put them in an impossible position. Our casualties have been heavy. I'm afraid that the 70th Brigade has been destroyed as an effective force."

There was a shocked silence as the other Cabinet members learned what the Prime Minister had been told an hour earlier.

"That much I knew already," Churchill said. "I asked you why the defence line collapsed so quickly and what you intend to do about it."

Brooke held his ground.

"Sir, the men fought bravely, but were in an impossible situation. Their mortars and machine guns would have been adequate to defend against an attack by assault troops or parachutists, even from the rear. But they weren't any use against tanks. We were caught unawares by those giant gliders. The ones they landed in are now useless, stranded and broken in the fields where they came down. We don't believe they can have many more, or they'd have used them in the assault. But, in case they do, the RAF dawn patrols will now be on the look-out for any such large craft. In regard to the current breakthrough, my focus is to limit its extent. I've pushed a few tanks out on the flanks of the current breach, to stop any lateral development. I've also targeted all our sector artillery on the salient."

Brooke paused, expecting questions on the immediate counterattack, but none came. He continued with his response.

"And to guard against it happening again, I've deployed a small number of anti-tank guns directly behind each threatened defence line, just enough to prevent any similar attack in our rear."

"Closing the stable door after the horse has bolted?" Churchill complained, a bitter tone in his voice.

"That may be fair criticism, sir, but it isn't really feasible to prepare for every contingency in war – particularly when the enemy uses a weapon we haven't seen before."

Halifax had been listening with increasing agitation, his doubts about the entire plan no longer suppressed.

"General Brooke, you will recall that the fundamental military strategy in Ethelred was to confront the Germans at each point of their advance; to inflict casualties on them until they finally ran out of momentum. That strategy, clearly, has failed. How do you propose to stop them now, if our men are going to run away at the sight of a few tanks?"

Brooke face flushed. He had always been willing to accepted criticism, however blunt, when it was justified – particularly when it came from the Prime Minister. But he was angered by the insinuation of cowardice from a man who'd seen little or no military service. He glared at Halifax across the table.

"You are misinformed, Foreign Secretary. The men didn't run away; they were killed."

He continued to stare at Halifax.

"I must also point out that, almost two weeks into the invasion, the Germans are still short of where we expected them to be after the first week. The Ethelred strategy is working, however regrettable the setback this morning."

In the heat of the moment, Brooke had made a fatal mistake. The full extent of the likely withdrawal in front of the Germans had not been discussed with the War Cabinet. Halifax was startled by the remark, then recoiled in shock as the implications sank in.

"Where we 'expected' them to be, General? Where we 'expected' them to be, as presented to this Cabinet, was a distance of 10 miles inland! That was the assertion made to get approval for the Ethelred military plan. At this moment, the Germans in Kent are 30 miles inland, halfway to London! And you say it was *expected*?"

There was no response from an embarrassed Brooke, ill at ease at having strayed into a political minefield. The Foreign Secretary turned towards Churchill, looking at him with barely-concealed contempt.

"Prime Minister, if the War Cabinet has been deliberately misled in this regard, it is a most grievous matter. It is, in fact, a resigning matter."

Churchill sat silent. He was pinioned, caught between protecting his own position and defending Brooke. For a few seconds, untypically, he was lost for words. The delay told Halifax everything he needed to know. He stood up, lifted his papers and walked out of the room.

The others watched in stunned silence. They'd been aware of the tension building between the Prime Minister and Halifax over many weeks, and knew that the two had just about managed to tolerate each other. Now the equilibrium had been shattered, and Churchill's truthfulness, or lack thereof, was the cause.

After a short period of awkward silence, a gaunt-looking Neville Chamberlain stood up.

"Prime Minister, I regret I must inform you that I share the opinion expressed by the Foreign Secretary. The situation is such that I must also withdraw from Cabinet. I believe you have no choice but to consider your position."

He got up from his chair, obviously in great pain, and made his way out of the room.

Churchill sat immobile at the table, shaken by the departures. It wasn't simply the fact that the two had resigned – that had been on the cards for months – it was the realisation of how his enemies would portray their reasons. It wouldn't be about the ministers' effectiveness, or even a principled difference of opinion on war strategy. They would claim it was about his duplicity.

He asked the Chiefs of Staff to leave the room. When they'd gone, he addressed Attlee and Eden in a subdued voice.

"In the fullness of time there will be opportunity aplenty to discuss the military advice shared with the War Cabinet at different times, and to apportion responsibility or blame. For now, a critical battle is looming, and that debate must wait. I regret that the Foreign Secretary and Mr. Chamberlain have seen fit to resign in this manner. As you know, I have already indicated that they would be leaving the Cabinet in the near future, though, perhaps, in happier circumstances. It had been my intention to nominate Lord Beaverbrook and Mr. Bracken as their successors, and to bring that decision to the House for ratification as soon as practicable. I now intend to expedite those appointments, so that we may refocus our attention on the current crisis."

There was no response for almost half a minute, then Attlee responded in a subdued voice.

"Prime Minister, I fear these resignations require more than a simple reshuffle of government positions."

His eyes were glued to a spot on the wall opposite.

"Several issues of great concern have emerged, which demand serious consideration. It will be necessary for me to consult with senior party colleagues before deciding whether it's possible to continue in government with you."

He stood up.

"Now, if you will excuse me..."

30

Bracken came round ten minutes later, summoned to the scene by Colville. He spoke to the young assistant outside the Prime Minister's office to confirm the shock news, and then went straight in. He didn't knock. It might have given Churchill the opportunity to refuse him entrance. Inside, he found the Prime Minister slumped at his desk, deflated, his face white. Bracken stared at the ghost of a figure. In all the years he'd known him, he had never seen him so dejected; not after political defeats, not after the naval losses on the first day, not even after the destruction of Chartwell. He seemed unable to come to terms with the twin blows, a savage political attack inflicted in the middle of a military crisis.

Churchill didn't dismiss him, as Bracken had feared possible. Instead, he acknowledged his friend's arrival and drew him in with a half-hearted gesture. He was no longer alone in the blackness.

"Where to now, Brendan?" His voice quivered under the strain. "Hitler's armies rampaging across southern England and our political structures crumbling around us. What began as a charade two months ago now comes to pass."

Before Bracken could think of a response to pierce the veil of despondency, there was a sharp knock on the door. Colville came into the room, in a state of some alarm.

"Prime Minister, Mr. Eden has just left the Paddock. He asked me to tell you he's feeling extremely unwell and needs some time away to recover."

Churchill sat still, looking disconsolately at his private secretary.

"So now they're all gone?"

He let Colville leave and turned to Bracken, a tremor in his voice.

"Is this the end, Brendan... or at least the beginning of the end? Our Armed Forces yielding under the axe we ourselves helped fashion; our colleagues in government running for cover. And what comes next... defeat on the battlefield or political collapse? The country subjugated by that evil monster, either way. And my place in history? The fool who sent an invitation to Hitler."

Bracken looked at his hero, searching for a glimpse of his old pugnacity, trying to think of a way to lift him before the black dog descended.

"We'll think of something, Winston. Now that Halifax has some time on his hands, maybe you could ask him to pay Adolf another visit. Bring him a bunch of flowers. Yep, flowers; that should definitely work."

Churchill blinked a few times and cleared his throat, fighting to recover his poise.

"I don't think so, Brendan." He coughed again. "Unless it's a wreath."

Bracken's anxiety eased a fraction; it was the first glimmer. He sat down opposite Churchill and looked him in the eye, his voice now serious.

"Winston, we're not going to give up now. We still have plenty of time to get things sorted. Well, several hours, anyway."

From anyone else the words would have sounded manic, but Churchill knew what Bracken meant. They'd been in tight corners before. They would keep fighting, with every means at their disposal, until the end. He even managed a sad smile.

"KBO?"

"Exactly," Bracken said. "Keep buggering on. As far as Halifax and Chamberlain are concerned, you've already announced they're leaving the Cabinet. There's even one or two asking why they're still hanging around –a couple of undertaker's assistants, somebody called them."

"Unfortunately, the departures of Mr. Attlee and Mr. Eden aren't quite so easy to explain."

"You don't have to. They haven't resigned; just absented themselves for different reasons. In any event, the War Cabinet has no formal standing. You chose it yourself out of the twenty-odd ministers in the government. You can choose a new one any time you want from that group, or from outside – without going to the King or Parliament for approval."

"That's not the way our democracy works, Brendan, and well you know it. It will have to be explained to the House and to the country."

"No it doesn't, Winston – not yet anyway. I'll make sure it doesn't get into the press. We'll all have much bigger things to worry about over the next few days. In any case, don't give up on them – they might be back. We can always hope Attlee will have his mandate renewed and..."

"And Eden, his manhood?" Churchill completed the sentence.

He looked at his old friend with affection. They had been through many tough battles together, though this was beginning to look like the end of the road.

There was a sudden knock on the door. General Ismay came in, unannounced and grim-faced.

"Prime Minister, the Chiefs of Staff would like to see you at your earliest convenience."

Churchill looked at him, ashen. He didn't really have much choice. "Five minutes, General."

* * *

The uniformed figures were standing beside the table, almost at attention, when Churchill came in. In the centre stood General Dill, upright, clearly the leader in personal authority as well as rank. On his right-hand side was General Brooke, looking solemn. Behind the two generals, Admiral Pound and Air Marshal Portal waited, one on either side.

Churchill decided that he, too, would remain standing, for whatever was about to transpire. The only sound came from the wall clock, each loud second seeming like ten. He thought it might be ticking away the last minutes of his government. He wondered how many scenes like this had been enacted in corridors of power over the centuries as democrats and tyrants alike came face to face with their mortality.

For a few tense seconds he stared into Dill's eyes, trying, without success, to gauge his temper. He scanned round the gazes of the other commanders. He steeled himself and addressed them.

"Will ye also go away?"

General Dill stood tall in front of him, grey-haired and unsmiling. For a few tense moments there was a deep silence in the room. Then Dill answered, in a clear voice.

"Prime Minister, to whom would we go?"

Churchill eyes went around the commanders' faces, looking at each of them in turn. He addressed Dill again.

"Am I to understand it is not your intention to involve yourselves in the current trials of government?"

"That, sir, would be a most un-British thing to do, even if we did have such a leaning, and we do not."

Dill waited a few more seconds.

"We are conscious that you face a situation which is unprecedented. As you imply, however, our responsibilities are solely military. It is not for us to involve ourselves in political arguments, or to try to influence how they might resolve. We do, however, have strong views on one matter. Howsoever we reached this point, the country is locked in a battle for survival. There is no imaginable change of government that could take place before this battle is decided. We are equally certain there is no other military policy that could be implemented, except surrender – which, like you, we have no intention of doing."

Though Dill was doing the talking, the others seemed to draw physically closer to him as he spoke. Their body language conveyed a deep sense of unity and commitment. After another brief hesitation, Dill continued, still speaking in a formal tone.

"Prime Minister, at this critical moment in our history, your commanders speak with one voice. We urge you to hold firm to your position and allow us to hold firm to ours."

Churchill felt a welling of tears in his eyes. He might have been abandoned by his Cabinet colleagues; it was probably the end of his political career, but for the moment he remained the leader of the nation. Things might not, after all, fall apart. He nodded slowly at them.

"Gentlemen, so be it. You will appreciate that it is not appropriate for me to thank you for your loyalty; it is what you have recognised to be your duty. I will, however, thank you for your clarity."

He hesitated for a moment, then indicated they should sit down.

"Now let us proceed with the pressing business at hand, your plans to address the current military crisis."

31

Ships dead, ships living. The dark waters of Scapa Flow held both.

Beneath the surface of the vast anchorage lay the remains of the German Grand Fleet, the vessels scuttled by their crews at the end of the Great War. Not far away was the carcass of another battleship, HMS *Royal Oak*, torpedoed at its mooring by an intrepid U-boat skipper soon after the start of the new war. Nearly a year after that sinking, the bodies of drowned seamen were still being washed ashore.

Surrounded by rusting steel and the evocative memory of 800 dead sailors, the Home Fleet lay at anchor. The Royal Navy's battleships were alive, and waiting.

At 1955, Admiral-of-the-Fleet Sir Charles Forbes received an encrypted communication from the Admiralty in London. It was the despatch he'd been waiting for. An hour later, he faced the captains of the other ships in the wardroom of his flagship, HMS *Nelson*.

His message was simple.

"It's this evening, gentlemen. We sail at midnight."

There was little need for discussion. Ever since the Nazis landed on British soil, they'd been preparing, knowing that, sooner or later, they would be called. The ships were ready, the voyage plans prepared. Each day of the long wait they'd updated the detail, factoring in the latest intelligence about U-boats, minefields and German bombers.

With the preparation work already complete, Forbes had only one further brief instruction to issue. "We'll be using the western route."

He could hear the sighs of relief in the wardroom. It was a hundred miles further, but they would be spared the dangerous passage through the English Channel.

"And the Emerald option, sir?" asked Rear-Admiral Whitworth, the captain of HMS *Hood*.

"That remains to be decided, closer to the time."

Forbes had shown no leaning either way. He'd been authorised to use Irish territorial waters if necessary. But if they didn't need to, there was no point in stirring a diplomatic squabble with the Eire government.

An hour after nightfall, cloaked from any unwelcome observers, the ships raised steam and prepared for sea. At midnight they weighed anchor and left Scapa Flow, heading west in the darkness. With a strong current behind them, they made good time through the Pentland Firth, the narrow waters between the Orkney Islands and the northern coast of Scotland. High up on the bridges, the navigators monitored progress on their charts, ticking off the unseen headlands and lochs away to their left. Most of the geographical features carried old Gaelic names, bestowed thousands of years ago by ancient travellers: Thurso, Strathy, Faraid. In contrast to that rich Celtic legacy, the waypoint they were approaching carried a name bestowed by a later set of seafarers. *Wrath*, in Old Norse, was Turning Point, the headland where the Vikings turned from a westerly route to a southerly one, on their expeditions to pillage the scattered communities along the shores of the Irish Sea.

Nearly a thousand years after the last Viking longboats rounded Cape Wrath on their epic journeys, another great fleet turned the corner of Scotland, but on a mission to protect, not plunder.

Morning brought the breathtaking vista of the Outer Hebrides. The crews on deck were able to enjoy for a few moments the majestic sight of the islands, one by one, as they rose into view: Lewis and Harris, North and South Uist, each more stunning than the one before. Off to port, a watery sun was trying to break through the mist covering Skye and Mull.

The battle fleet steamed on, between the islands and the sky. On a grey, still morning, the war seemed a long way away.

Shortly after 0930 their luck ran out. For almost an hour they'd been tracking a contact on radar, an unidentified contact. It was still 40 miles to the north of them, but was following a fixed patrol pattern, to and fro, presumably dipping in and out of the cloud cover as it continued its search, gradually coming closer.

Captain Miles invited Admiral Forbes up to his bridge.

"Earlier than I'd hoped," he said as Forbes came in, pointing to the blip on the radar display.

The admiral looked at the plot for a moment. "Can we not get it before it sees us?"

Miles shrugged. "We've been trying. The air controller has vectored fighters onto it a couple of times already... got a glimpse at one stage, but she's a wily old bird... ducked back into the cloud before they could get close. It's a flying boat, a Dornier 18. They're usually found well out to sea. Must have been in the air already. Maybe somebody noticed we'd left Scapa and diverted her from an Atlantic patrol."

"They must think we've no fighters left," Forbes said, "sending her so close inshore."

"Either that or they're quite happy to sacrifice the old girl," Miles said. "All the more annoying our fighters haven't been able to get her yet."

Forbes and Miles stayed on the bridge together, watching apprehensively as the radar operator reported the aircraft coming closer.

"Twenty miles, sir."

They waited. There was still a chance it would miss them in the poor visibility, or that the Hurricanes would get it before it came within visual range.

Then came the let-down.

"Aircraft, sir! At six o'clock. A flying boat. About two miles."

"Damn." Forbes' swearword said it all. If they had spotted it, it had spotted them.

The officers watched through binoculars as three fighters closed in on the flying boat. Slow and ungainly, she was almost defenceless against the Hurricanes. Within five minutes she was shot down into the sea. But there was no celebration. Five minutes was long enough for the sighting report to have been sent out.

Now they could only wait.

32

Since the fall of France in June, the leading members of the government had rarely been seen in Westminster. With the main political parties working together in a national coalition to run the country, Parliament had lost much of its importance, becoming little more than a talking shop. There hadn't been a significant division or a confrontation across the floor for months.

On a regular basis, the junior ministers had continued to attend the House, fielding a myriad of questions about the incidentals of war; about food rations and the housing of evacuees; about blackout regulations and traffic disruptions. Usually, however, they were able only to give the blandest of replies. In total war, almost any information disclosed might be of value to the enemy.

From time to time, the Prime Minister had appeared in the Commons, sometimes to update members on the progress of the war, sometimes to make a ringing speech he wanted the world to hear. On a few occasions, he'd spoken to MPs in secret sessions, giving them more information about specific events, usually disasters, in one theatre of war or another. But within the Houses of Parliament, the political landscape had been transformed. The tradition of a loyal opposition as an alternative government-in-waiting was gone. There was no opposition; there was no alternative.

As the battlefront in Kent edged closer to London, another pressing issue emerged in Westminster. A more secure location was needed for Parliament, further away from the advancing Germans and less exposed to air attack. A committee of security experts and MPs identified a new site, a hundred miles from London, in Stratford-upon-Avon.

Standing proudly by the River Avon, the Shakespeare Memorial Theatre had been built between the wars to provide a home for the Bard's plays in his native town. Now, twelve months into the new war, it had assumed a different role. It had become the emergency location for Parliament. For the last week, the House of Commons had been holding its sessions in the main auditorium; the House of Lords in the neighbouring conference hall. Outside the Paddock, hidden away and known only to a select few, the historic town in Warwickshire was now the nexus of political activity in Free Britain.

* * *

On the morning after his walk-out from Cabinet, Halifax travelled up to Stratford. He was convinced that Churchill was leading the country to a terrible calamity, and was determined to do his utmost to prevent it. The whole Ethelred strategy was on the point of collapse under the weight of wildly unrealistic ambition on Churchill's part and the military skills of the German forces. Parliament was the only place where the doomed course might be overturned.

He was in a difficult position. With the generals refusing to take the lead, any action would have to be political – yet he couldn't lead the challenge himself. There hadn't been a member of the House of Lords as Prime Minister for half a century. The years since had seen the rise of the Labour Party, which would never countenance a reoccurrence. As a member of the Lords, he couldn't even address the House of Commons to try to influence the debate.

It wasn't going to be easy.

In the past, his link to the Tory backbenchers had been through Rab Butler, and, in Eden's absence, there was an even greater dependence on his good offices. But Butler, too, was proving hard to contact, now forced to share his time between his departmental duties in the relocated Foreign Office and his role as a Regional Commissioner in Shropshire. Halifax suspected the inconvenient locations weren't an accident; it smelled like one of Bracken's tricks.

Eventually, several hours later than planned, Butler reached Stratford and made his way to the Juliet Hotel.

Halifax was waiting in a drawing room overlooking the river. He didn't waste any time in getting to the issue.

"Things have got worse since we last talked, Rab, a lot worse – both the military situation and Churchill's megalomania. I'm afraid we've only a few days left to act, a week at most. After that, the Army will be broken, and London taken or surrounded. That'll end any possibility of a settlement."

"Can he not see that yet?"

"He's still full of bluster, ignoring the messages from the Chiefs of Staff... still talking about a British Resistance to carry on the fight if the regular forces are defeated. All so much twaddle. You've seen the reports from Poland; the Germans executing twenty hostages for every soldier killed. The Resistance wouldn't last a week once that started."

"Yet the Chiefs are still with him, despite everything?"

"So far... just about. I sense Dill's far from happy the way things are going – but they're all under the thumb. None of them will countenance any action outside the democratic process until the bitter end."

"It's appalling, Edward, the whole damned thing. Is there anything more we can do?"

"We've only one option left; overturn Churchill in the House of Commons and try to reach the best deal we can with Hitler."

Butler pulled a face. "Easier said than done."

"But maybe not impossible. In the circles I move in there's a growing consensus that something has to be done, something radical. What's your feeling about the Commons? Any sign of Churchill becoming isolated? If we move fast, there might still be time."

"Time for what?"

"Time to make a transition to a new government without handing the country on a plate to Hitler."

"Not that simple," Butler said. "Any idea where Attlee stands?"

"Still sitting on the fence. Or, should I say, in the process of consulting with his colleagues. We'll find out soon enough. Chamberlain won't be able to take any part; he's declining fast. And Eden's nowhere to be found; still unwell or whatever. Think we have to leave him out of the equation, too. That really just leaves the three of us."

Shortly after 4 p.m. Attlee joined them in the hotel.

After some uneasy preliminaries, Halifax began the delicate discussion. He was conscious that, in a time of war, he had to make a fine distinction between loyalty to the country and loyalty to the Prime Minister. He had to win Attlee's support.

"You heard him yesterday, Clement. The prime of the Army wasted in France and most of Fighter Command destroyed in the battle over Kent. Now he talks about throwing the Home Fleet and Bomber Command into the cauldron as well – our last military assets of any value. We have to stop him. I'm convinced that the decisions we take in the next hour will determine whether we survive as an independent nation."

Attlee settled into a settee and took a few long draws on his pipe. He nodded slowly, but didn't make any reply, waiting for Halifax to continue.

"We need to stand back from things for a moment. Two months ago he forced us to agree to his madcap Ethelred scheme – despite our deep reservations. It's turned into a disaster, just as you and I predicted. Now we're running out of time. We have to take action immediately if we want to salvage anything before the German army sweeps into London."

There was silence in the room, save for an irregular tapping as Attlee emptied the contents of his pipe bowl into a glass ashtray.

"What might we still be able to do, at this stage?" he said, looking at the two Foreign Office ministers.

Halifax answered immediately, a decisive tone in his voice.

"Gain the backing of Parliament for a new coalition government, with new leadership. Get the Armed Forces answerable to them, and then negotiate. It's our only chance."

"I don't disagree with any of that, in principle," Attlee said, "though I'm not sure how we'd go about it – or whether we'd have the numbers."

"That's why we're here, Clement. If you and Rab can win a majority in the Commons, I'll bring the House of Lords along. We'll have a united front, legitimate in the eyes of our military people, and of foreign states – friend or enemy. A new government with cross-party support would be in a strong position to approach the Germans about a settlement."

Attlee took a tin of tobacco from his pocket and began to refill the bowl, taking a few seconds to tap a loose flake down below the rim.

"Edward, I share your concerns, obviously, but I'm nervous about going to Parliament just yet. I'm still in discussion with the party. It's fair to say I'm getting a mixed response. Some of them still feel Winston's our only hope – others have come to realise he's the major part of the problem, not the solution."

"Will they support a vote of no confidence?" Halifax said. "We really don't have much time."

"I just don't know, Edward. Back in May we swallowed our pride as a party and supported him as Prime Minister. Certainly, a lot of us feel let down by what's happened – but the numbers are tight. Clearly, we can't tell them everything that's gone on – though maybe we need to be a bit more open with some of the more influential backbenchers. But, at the moment, even if we did table a motion of no confidence, there's no guarantee they'd vote for it. Could swing either way."

Butler had been nodding in sympathy.

"It's the same with the Tory backbenchers, Edward. The mood has changed completely from all that blood, sweat and tears nonsense of six months ago. They just want it to be over, and for us to salvage as much as we can from the debacle. But I don't think they'd vote against

Winston just yet. Our best hope, if we handle it right, is that a fair number might abstain."

Attlee lit the pipe and took a few draws.

"Part of the problem is that there isn't an obvious successor to Churchill. Another problem is there's no way of finding out what Hitler might settle for – if that's what's at the back of our minds."

Halifax shrugged.

"There's no point looking for a new leader until we know where we want to be led. Let's start with that... decide what we want for the country and figure out what bargaining chips we still have. If we can do that, we might find the bones of a deal with Hitler, and work a political structure around that – a joint leadership or something."

For the first time since the discussion began, Attlee seemed to nod slightly in agreement.

"Whatever else we come up with, Edward, one thing's absolutely clear; it has to be a genuinely collegiate government, not a one-man dictatorship like Churchill. So why don't we start with that as an assumption, and ask ourselves what it is we're looking for from the Germans?"

Halifax began to frame a reply, but Attlee took the lead in answering his own question, more comfortable with diplomatic manoeuvring than backroom conspiracy.

"First thing is an immediate ceasefire, before any more of the country's taken over. After that, a commitment for an early withdrawal of all German troops from England, and a long-term peace treaty between our countries."

"I've no problem agreeing with all of that." Halifax said. "It's what we should have done years ago. We agree to leave Germany alone on the continent and in Russia; they leave us alone in the British Isles and the Empire."

Butler leaned forward.

"That's fine from our point of view, but what have we got to offer in return, that they're not going to take anyway in a week or two?"

Halifax stood up and walked over to the window, looking out across the quiet-flowing river. Butler's question was a tough one. It would have been a lot easier to negotiate a year ago, possibly even as recently as Dunkirk.

"We do have one advantage when it comes to the negotiations, if we play it right." He turned around from the window and looked at them.

"We've found out about his Russian plans – and he doesn't know that we know."

There was a moment's silence. The information about Russia was supposed to be top secret, known only to the War Cabinet and a few senior staff. If Attlee had any reservations about it being shared with Butler, he chose not to make an issue of it.

"So, we have that one little nugget of information," he said. "How can we use it to our advantage?"

"That's the key," Halifax said. "The Russia news shows Hitler is already looking beyond Sea Lion. And we have to do the same... ask ourselves what we've got that would be of value to him in his eastern campaign. Obviously, it makes no sense for him to destroy it if he can get his hands on it instead."

Butler had been stunned an hour earlier, when Halifax had told him the news, but had already adjusted to the new geopolitical situation.

"Tricky. The Navy's always been our trump card in this sort of negotiation... in the Atlantic, the Med, even the Far East – somehow I don't think it's of much use in the Steppes of Russia. In any case, we'll need it in the Empire when all this is over. Keep Japanese hands off it – not to mention the Americans."

"Anything else we could offer?" Halifax said, content that others were making the running.

"I suppose we might scrape together a British Legion to help him," Butler continued, "if we can find a few thousand troops who don't mind the cold. Unfortunately, as far as tanks are concerned, we don't have many left to trade with – and the ones we do seem fairly useless anyway."

"That only seems to leave the RAF," Attlee said.

Suddenly Halifax became animated, rapping the table with his hand.

"That's it! Our heavy bomber fleet… the one asset we have that is still reasonably intact – assuming we can stop Churchill flinging it away over the next few days. And it might, actually, be worth quite a bit to Hitler. The Germans don't have any long-range bombers of their own. We could offer to transfer all Bomber Command's heavies to the Luftwaffe and tell them about the four-engined jobbies coming along – the Short Stirlings and the new Handley Page machine. Come to think of it, that's a double bonus for him. Removes the one threat we might pose to him on his western front, while giving him equipment he could really use in the East."

"Hmm…" Attlee showed signs of interest. "Could make sense. Just the planes, mind you; not the crews. Except, perhaps, a few for training. I don't think we'd have the country behind us if we wanted to join in a war against the Soviet Union. Certainly, there are quite a few in the Labour Party who'd object."

"So, the machines, but not the men. That's fair enough." Halifax accepted the point, then spotted an opportunity to bind Attlee in. "And maybe we could offer to build Spitfires for the Luftwaffe, to replace the Messerschmitts they've lost over England."

"Even better," Attlee said. "Would keep the aircraft factories busy."

"This has real possibilities." Halifax stood up, and walked up and down the room, beginning to enthuse about his own idea. "We get Churchill out of the way, to Canada or somewhere – maybe Australia, it's further away. After that, a peace treaty with Germany – a binding agreement for diplomatic and military cooperation."

Attlee had one final of pang of conscience. He looked away from them. "It does mean welching on the promises we made to France and the others."

"The promises Churchill made, you mean," Halifax said. "Look, Clem, we have to face reality. It was those stupid promises that got us into this mess in the first place. They can't become an excuse why we can't dig ourselves out."

Attlee got up from his armchair and walked over to the window. Outside, the wind was getting up. It took a scattering of leaves from a chestnut tree in the garden, and carried them in a flurry across the riverside path. A young couple were walking past, holding hands. The man was in uniform; the girl obviously pregnant. He watched as they batted playfully at the leaves in the air. It was the end of his reservations. He would do it, for them.

He turned around to face Halifax and Butler.

"So, how do we set about opening communications with the Germans?" he asked. "We don't have much time."

"I think the Swedish link may still be usable," Butler said. He didn't indicate how he knew.

Attlee looked sceptical. "Sweden? After the fiasco with the Realists? I can't see them engaging through that channel again. Once bitten, twice shy, I'd imagine."

Halifax shrugged. "Everything changes when they see Churchill overthrown in Parliament. They'll know it's for real."

"I thought the main problem with the Swedish route was that there's no direct channel back."

"It's a problem alright, but if Hitler wants to show us he's interested in talking, all he has to do is halt his panzers for a few days," Halifax said. "Same as Dunkirk."

Attlee jumped. *He'd no idea that...*

Halifax saw the shock on his colleague's face. "I'll tell you about it sometime."

He hadn't meant it to slip out, and tried to bring the conversation back to the current crisis.

"We'll need a face-to-face meeting with a German emissary as soon as possible."

"Well, yes, that's the traditional way, I suppose," Attlee said. "But I'm not sure how we'd set about it. It's hardly possible to get to Spain or Sweden in present circumstances – and, presumably, none of their military people will come near us in the middle of a battle."

"What about von Ribbentrop?" Butler said. "Or Hess? From what I hear, they're not allowed anywhere close to military operations. Could we get one of them to fly over and meet us in some remote corner of the country. Scotland perhaps? Maybe the Duke of Hamilton's place up in Lanarkshire – he's been in contact with them already. Or what about trying to arrange something in Eire? Suppose we went over to Dublin to talk to their ambassador – what's his name, Hempel, isn't it?"

Butler ignored the deep irony in his suggestion. Since the start of the war, they'd been putting intense pressure on the Irish government to close the German embassy. Now their very lack of success offered a possible lifeline.

"Dublin... tricky," Halifax said. "Too many people nosing around. Though maybe one of us could find a reason to get over to Belfast and slip down to the border to meet him somewhere quiet."

The group fell silent for a minute, but no new ideas emerged.

After the shock about Dunkirk, Attlee was cautious about the direction the conversation was taking. Talking to a Swedish Ambassador was one thing; talking to a German one was quite another. He had sense enough not to put his head into that particular noose.

"Rab, you've more freedom of movement than the rest of us, with your commuting between Oxford and Shropshire," he said. "Would you be able to pop over to Northern Ireland on some departmental business? Maybe visit the regional bunker there?"

Halifax stepped in to keep the momentum going.

"I've a good man in our High Commission in Dublin, Rab, very dependable. I'll see if he can make contact with Hempel to get things moving."

There was a pause for a few moments.

"Well, perhaps," Butler said. "But that's all going to take a few days to arrange. What do we do in the meantime?"

"Find a way to put the skids under Winston," Halifax answered straightaway. "Clement, why don't you revert to your role as Leader of the Opposition, and go to the Speaker straight away to ask for an emergency debate on the war situation. You've every right to do that. It becomes, effectively, a vote of no confidence in Churchill, even if it's not phrased in so many words – same as did for poor old Neville in May. Though a right disaster that's turned out to be."

Attlee began to suck on his pipe. "It's vital we don't imply we're any less committed to the fight – at this stage."

"Agreed," Halifax said. "Just that Churchill's making a total Horlicks of it and somebody else needs to take over."

"So who's that going to be?" Butler asked, back in a full circle.

"We don't need to decide that for now," Halifax said. "But I think we're all agreed on one thing. Anybody's better than Winston."

33

Shortly before 1900, as the twilight thickened to a dark grey, the Home Fleet came under air attack. The battleships were entering the North Channel between Northern Ireland and Scotland, with the crews beginning to hope the fading light would see them safely into the sheltered waters of the Irish Sea. Then the ships' radars picked up a formation of aircraft approaching from the south.

Ten minutes later they saw them; a group of Heinkel 111s which had sneaked up the east coast of Ireland at low level.

The RAF Hurricanes had gone for the night, and the fighter protection for the Fleet was in the hands of a squadron of old twin-engined Blenheim fighters. They threw themselves at the German bombers, but, lightly armed and not much faster than the Heinkels, inflicted little damage.

The battleships and escorts swung into sharp manoeuvres, slaloming wildly from side to side. The guns opened fire.

The response was enough to disrupt the bombers and prevent accurate attacks. The Heinkels had to content themselves with dropping their loads from medium altitude in a hurried pass, before beating a retreat down along the Irish coast again, slowly pursued by the Blenheims.

One heavy bomb exploded 50 yards from HMS *Rodney*, causing some superficial damage but no casualties. *Hood* was lucky. A 500kg bomb penetrated her thin deck armour, but failed to explode.

The British crews sailed on, with a sense of relief, but in the knowledge that they mightn't be so fortunate next time. The Germans knew where they were – and tomorrow the fleet would have a long stretch of daylight to sail through.

Admiral Forbes had delayed taking a decision on the Emerald option for as long as possible, but, once they'd been spotted, he really had no option. The fleet had to keep as far away from the German threat as possible. As they passed Carlingford Lough, the border between Northern Ireland and Eire, he gave the order. The battleships made a sharp turn to starboard. For the next eight hours of darkness, they would hug the Irish coast.

34

For the commanders in the Paddock, no news during the night was good news. With the scars still raw from the naval disasters on the first day, every hour that passed was a relief, and brought the Home Fleet 16 miles closer to Weymouth. Shortly before daybreak, they heard that the battleships had left the shelter of the Irish coast and turned south-east. Its new course would take it in a great dogleg across the Bristol Channel, to reach Land's End at nightfall.

It was the most dangerous part of the voyage. To add to the threat from the air, they were now exposed to attack by U-boats and torpedo boats from the northern coast of France. The escort destroyers that had stayed close to the capital ships on the journey down from Scotland now pushed ahead at 30 knots, to form a protective screen ahead of the Fleet. They were joined by the battered survivors from the Plymouth squadron, who had sailed west to join their colleagues.

The biggest threat remained the Luftwaffe. All day long, the ships would be within range of the long-range bombers from Brittany and the Cherbourg peninsula.

At the 0600 meeting with the Chiefs of Staff, Churchill asked about the air cover for the Fleet. He heard that every RAF fighter in the western part of England had been thrown into the action, including the last Hurricanes from the reserves, deployed to airstrips near the coast. With the battleships cocooned by dozens of destroyers and hundreds of fighters, he knew that the German attackers were going to be handled roughly in today's battle.

He expected the Fleet would be fairly safe during the night passage along the south coast.

But then, at dawn, they would have to make their withdrawal. The Stukas that had been helping Rommel force his way through the New Forest would change their bomb-loads from high explosive to armour-piercing, and switch their attention to the British fleet. Protected by the Me109s from Eastleigh, they would be hard to stop.

He put the blunt question to Portal.

"Air Marshal, you have been given the task of destroying Eastleigh airfield. How you are going to achieve that, by day or by night?"

He had gone to the nub of the problem. By day, the RAF's heavy bombers would face massive resistance from the hundred-plus Me109s and the scores of flak guns now based on the airfield. There was no reason to think they'd do any better than the light bombers had over the previous two days.

Portal knew that, by night, there would be less opposition from the Germans. The 109s couldn't fight in the dark and the flak gunners couldn't see. The Luftwaffe didn't have any nightfighters at Eastleigh, and even if they sent patrols across from France, their planes weren't equipped with radar. However, at night, the accuracy of the RAF bombing was lamentable. Rarely did they get a bomb within ten miles of a target. Over enemy territory they could live with such indiscriminate bombing – but against a small target like an airfield, and over England?

The hard choice had to be made.

"By night, Prime Minister. We will attack tomorrow night."

"And how will you ensure destruction of the target?"

"I've assigned my entire fleet of heavy bombers – three hundred aircraft, Wellingtons, Whitleys and Hampdens, each carrying a three-ton bomb load on this short mission. The challenge is to get them over the target accurately, at lowish level, to ensure a concentrated bombardment. If it was a daylight attack, I would commit all my remaining fighters to escort them and..."

"As you've just told us, Air Marshal, your decision is to attack by night."

"I'm sorry, Prime Minister, I was just going to make a brief comparison. By day, the problem would be the German defences; at night, it's navigation. The crews – pilots, navigators and bomb aimers – have great difficulty knowing precisely where they are. The countryside is dark, most landmarks are invisible and the target, of course, will be in darkness."

"I think we're all aware of the problem, Air Marshal. What are you going to do about it?"

"Use pathfinder aircraft to drop flares, sir, to give the bombers an aiming point. We think that's the best approach, although it's not a panacea – the pathfinders themselves have to find the target first, to make sure they drop their markers accurately. I've asked if the Royal Artillery can put illumination rounds over the target – though even that will probably only work for a few minutes before the Germans start firing decoys to confuse us."

There was silence around the table. They had all experienced night battles during the Great War and knew the confused nature of such fighting.

"It's even more difficult for the follow-on waves," Portal continued. "Once the first bombs explode, it's almost impossible to distinguish between things… marker flares, decoys, bombs. There's a progressive loss of accuracy, a reduced density of bombs falling on target, not to mention the risk of civilian casualties up to several miles from the airfield. But it's our best chance of success. If we fail on the first raid, we'll go back, and back again, until we succeed."

"Or we have no bombers left," Churchill said, a grim look on his face.

It was General Ismay who, accidentally or otherwise, found the key.

"Pity we couldn't get the Germans to leave the lights on."

The remark wasn't thought through, but no-one at the table regarded it as facetious. Since the Ethelred planning group was first established, they'd become used to thinking in novel ways.

"We thought about that as well," Portal replied. "Clearly they won't volunteer to, so we looked to see if there was any way we could control the airfield lighting from outside the perimeter. There isn't, unfortunately."

"Perhaps not," Ismay said, "but might we be able to control the lights outside the airfield?"

"Explain," Churchill grunted.

Ismay continued, hesitatingly, still fleshing out the idea in his head.

"Let's put ourselves in their shoes. Obviously, they're enforcing a total blackout on the field – the last thing they want is to attract an air raid. And our own people are doing the same in the towns and villages around the base – like the rest of the country. Let's have a look."

He walked over to the large map on the wall and peered at the little towns around the airfield.

"Look," he said, tapping the map. "Five or six villages within a mile or two of the airfield. Let's see… Eastleigh town itself – we've evacuated the civilians, but the Germans haven't pushed out their perimeter to take it… Redhill, Colden Common, the northern suburbs of Southampton. And there'll be lighting on some of the main roads nearby. Now, if we could switch on all those streetlights, suddenly, in a co-ordinated manner, wouldn't the dark airfield stand out in contrast?"

"It might work," Portal said, thinking through the suggestion. "It's an airfield we're talking about, not a point target like a building or a bridge. Though we'd still have the problem of getting the bomber stream to within, say, five miles of the target."

"Five miles? Is that really such a problem?" Churchill was pushing for answers not obstacles.

"Regrettably it is, sir. It's a night operation. Landmarks on the ground are hard to spot, and navigation by the stars isn't easy when the planes are being thrown around at low level. Not even possible if there are any clouds around. It's why we're having such mediocre results over Germany."

"What about these magic radio beams you've been talking about? Couldn't you use them?"

"I'm afraid not, Prime Minister. We have one or two experimental stations, but none that could be moved to the Hampshire area. Even if we had, we've only a handful of obsolete test planes with the necessary receivers."

"Your planes will be flying over England," Churchill said. "There must be plenty of other options, searchlights or beacon fires for example."

"Yes sir. It will take a lot of organisation – Home Guard, police and so on. But if the Army could organise that…"

"Assume it can and will, Air Marshal."

"We'll work with that, sir… find a way to get the bombers close enough to Eastleigh to see the pattern of villages and roads all lit-up. Head for the black space in the middle and unload their bombs. Complete surprise, no artillery, no flares. Yes, perhaps…"

"And don't bomb anywhere there are lights showing. That should keep civilian casualties low," Brooke said.

"Could we not evacuate the villages, say, an hour beforehand?" Ismay asked.

"I'm afraid that won't be possible," Portal answered immediately. "The Germans might spot what we're at. They only have to switch on the airfield lights and the plan's scuppered. The airfield would merge into the background again."

Portal's words sounded harsh, but General Brooke added his support.

"Prime Minister, I have to agree with the Air Marshal. Civilians in the open would have no protection from stray bombs. Better for them to take shelter in their homes as soon as the raid starts."

Portal had been scribbling some calculations in a notebook.

"The key to the whole thing is timing. The lights will have to be switched on shortly before the first bombs drop, say five minutes, maybe less, say three, to be on the safe side. At that point, our lead bombers will be about ten miles away. If the Germans figure out what's happening and manage to get their own lights on, the black space we're aiming for just disappears."

"We need to find someone who knows the switching arrangements on the airfield," Brooke said. "If it's a single master switch, we might only have a minute or two before they react. No, hang on, that's not possible! The generators will all be switched off to save petrol. They'll have to get them started up before they can do anything. Christ, I've just thought of something. Have we cut off the mains electricity to the airfield?"

"General Ismay, have that checked immediately," Churchill snapped.

Ismay left. Ideas were flowing fast. A mood of determination filled the room.

As the initial surge of thoughts began to slow down, Churchill brought the meeting to a close.

"This operation will need the coordination of thousands of people – RAF, Army and civilian. It must be kept top secret; no discussion by wireless or telephone. We will draw on those paradigms of English country society, the local bobbies and parish councils, to get word around – they'll know everybody in the villages. So get on with it. Turn it into a plan for execution tomorrow night. We can't delay even a day longer in case their armoured thrust makes it through the Forest. If Rommel's panzers reach the towns around the airfield, the whole plan's ruined."

The group prepared to leave, but Churchill had one final question for General Brooke.

"We must follow up the destruction of Eastleigh with a fierce ground action to occupy the airfield and destroy Rommel's forces in the New Forest. Who's our commander in the south-west?"

"Lieutenant-General Montgomery, sir."

"Oh yes, Montgomery. I've met him. Another Ulsterman, I believe?"

Brooke nodded. "On his father's side, I believe, and none the worse for that; he doesn't play polo."

"Well, that's a start." Churchill knew what Brooke meant: a professional soldier, not one of the wastrels who often seemed to end up in positions of command in the Army.

"Is he any good?"

"Yes sir, very good. Not quite as good as he thinks, but very good nonetheless."

"Hmm. Can he handle Rommel?"

"If anyone can, sir."

It wasn't quite the answer Churchill wanted, but he let it go.

"You'll give him all the support he needs?"

"He's been on to me already, Prime Minister, demanding just that."

"Good. Get him on a field telephone. I want to speak to him."

He stood up.

"This meeting is ended. We will reconvene in six hours' time, at midday. I want your full plans in place by then."

35

Just after 2100, Jock Colville came into Churchill's room, looking flustered.

"Prime Minister, I've just received an urgent telephone call from the Speaker's Office. An emergency debate's been called for tomorrow night, on the conduct of the war."

Churchill scowled at him over his glasses.

"A debate? At this time? Preposterous! Do they not realise we're locked in a battle for survival? They can debate all they like; I won't be there. I've more important things to be doing. Get Bracken in here. He can sort it out."

Brendan Bracken didn't appear for thirty minutes. He'd taken the time to make some telephone calls.

Churchill looked annoyed at the delay, grunting at the explanation.

"What sort of outlandish behaviour is this – a parliamentary debate called when we're trying to fight off an invasion? Whose name is it in, anyway?"

"Some Labour backbencher from the Midlands, had just about heard of him – though presumably he's only a stalking horse. I guess Attlee and Butler will wait until they see which way the wind's blowing before showing their hands."

"Democracy at its worst, Brendan. Do the fools think Hitler's going to wait around while they traipse through the division lobbies? I shall ignore them; make them look petty. Let them do their damnedest, the House has more sense than to turf out the government in the middle of a battle."

"That was my own gut reaction, Winston, but there's more to it than I'd like. Seems to be a feeling gaining ground in some quarters – in both parties – that it's their last chance to take action before London falls."

"London is not going to fall!"

"You know that, and so do I. So, presumably, do Attlee and Halifax. But maybe it suits their purpose not to proclaim it. And there are plenty of snakes in the long grass, waiting their chance. Looks like they're beginning to stir. I think you've got to take it seriously, and face them down in the House."

"Leave London at the height of battle to go to Stratford? Don't be ridiculous!"

"We could do it. The debate's not scheduled to start till after midnight. Everybody's got the same problem – can't travel by day with the Luftwaffe all over the place. The Chiefs and Pug can look after things here overnight. We could get a car up about 8 o'clock and be back by 6 or so in the morning."

Suddenly Churchill seemed to tire. He slumped back in his chair and closed his eyes, as if finally overwhelmed by the exertions of the last fortnight.

"If, indeed, I am coming back..."

36

At the best of times, the town of Aliseda was a sleepy place. Deep in the Spanish province of Cáceres, near the Portuguese border, it was only a few kilometres from the Madrid-Lisbon road. But there wasn't much to attract passing travellers, just a gloomy church and a cluttered market square set in a warren of plain streets. The elders on the council claimed the remote location had been a blessing during the Civil War, helping them avoid the savagery that had convulsed the country. Like every other community in Spain, however, they'd lost a lot of their young men. Grief still darkened many doors. To add to the sense of uncertainty about the future, few of the soldiers who'd survived the fighting had returned home to Aliseda when the war ended.

Once a week, the square came to life when the farmers came in from the surrounding hill farms. They would trade their produce and livestock, and enjoy some company for a few hours before heading back to their smallholdings. For the rest of the time, except for the occasional funeral, the hotel and the bodegas stayed empty.

On this warm autumn day, the market stalls were deserted. A handful of people were still on the streets, some on their way home from rosary in the Church of the Assumption, others catching up on the local gossip. From a street near the church, the chords from a guitar drifted soulfully into the heavy air. In one tree-shaded corner of the square, a group of old men were playing petanca. The lazy sound of metal glancing on metal split the evening stillness. At the side of the pitch, two youths were sitting on a bench, watching, but not saying much.

Just before eight o'clock, a battered Fiat furniture van drove into the square. It reversed into a space in the shade of some lemon trees, close to the petanca pitch. The driver, Pedro Serrano, seemed to know his way around. He rolled down the side window and waved to the players, watching the game for a few minutes. He wondered why the young men weren't playing, till he saw they were both missing limbs.

He waved to them as well.

It was Serrano's second visit in two days. On the previous afternoon, he had stopped to get a puncture repaired while he had lunch. He'd taken the wheel from the back of the van and rolled it across to a little garage just off the square, asking for it to be fixed while he ate.

The fitter grumbled that he had to eat too, but was mollified with the promise of a few extra pesetas for his trouble. As Serrano walked past the church on his way back to the square, he got a surprise. A gravedigger leaning on his spade on the edge of the churchyard nodded at him and then looked more closely.

"You're old José's son, aren't you?"

Pedro smiled. *Remembered* – even though he'd last lived there as a teenager. He'd forgotten the strength of the folk memory in these parts. He shook the gravedigger's clay-stained hand and told him he was indeed the young Serrano. It was a lucky break, he knew it would lend weight to his cover.

Even as he ate, the news spread around the town. Some of the townsfolk remembered him as a boy. Somebody said they thought he'd been on one side or the other during the Civil War. "Or maybe both, and smart enough to end up with the winners."

Someone else had heard a rumour he'd been spotted in London a few years earlier. It was all just gossip, but, they all agreed, he was a strange one alright.

Serrano told the bodega owner he was bringing a load of furniture from Madrid to Herreruela, a few kilometres down the road, for a retired doctor who was moving back to his home village. While he was still eating his meal, one enterprising urchin managed to sneak a look in the back of the van. *Just some tables and chairs and lots of old books,* he told his mates. *Nothing worth pinching.*

Serrano sat in the shade outside the bodega for an hour, taking an easy interest in the goings-on and chatting to the locals, though one or two noticed he did more listening than talking. When he finished his coffee, he walked over to pick up the wheel and loaded it onto the van. He waved to the men in the square, saying he might drop in again on his way back to Madrid.

* * *

Early next afternoon, another unfamiliar vehicle appeared in the town, a black Mercedes with five grim-looking men squeezed inside. They disappeared into the hotel on the other side of the square. Half-an-hour later, four of the strangers came over to the bodega. They had some lunch, without wine, without talk. When they finished their meal, they left in pairs, walking slowly down the streets as if searching for someone or something.

On Calle Calvario, a black-shawled widow was standing outside her front door with a neighbour, talking quietly and watching as two of the strangers walked down the street.

"Bloody Nazis."

She spat.

"Look at the swine, walking the streets in their long coats as if they owned the place. You know, Maria, in my entire life I've never said a kind word about Franco – but at least he sent those bastards home in '38, when they'd finished their dirty work here."

She didn't much care if they heard her. Anger had made her brave. She'd lost her husband to the German bombers in the battle for Madrid.

Two hours later Serrano arrived, on his way back from Herreruela. He reversed the van into a shady spot at the edge of the square, chatting to the men playing petanca as he got out. He went across to the bodega, ordered a meal and enquired about the cost of a room for the night.

"Tired of sleeping in that bloody van," he moaned.

As the light faded, the players finished their game and strolled off. Ten minutes later, the rear door of the van opened. Five men slipped out; four in combat gear moving swiftly; one in civilian clothes, more slowly. The group of four disappeared over the low wall into the churchyard. The man in civvies straightened his coat and walked towards the hotel.

He had some cover if stopped by an inquisitive Guardia Civil; diplomatic papers and a letter of introduction identifying him as the new military attaché in the British Embassy. His story was that his car had broken down outside the town while he was on his way to his post in Madrid. He knew it wouldn't stand up to scrutiny, but it might buy time for his friends to come to his rescue.

Admiral Canaris was waiting in a small room upstairs when the concierge knocked. She showed Menzies in and left. There was a moment of awkward silence as the two old rivals came face-to-face for the first time. The German stretched out a bony hand and, after a second's hesitation, Menzies took it.

"I see you didn't come alone," Canaris said, in fluent English. "Furniture removals – very innovative!"

One of his men had watched as the group of dark figures had slipped out of the van.

"I know you didn't either, Admiral. Is your heavy brigade here to impress me or the locals?"

Serrano had told him about the Mercedes and its sinister occupants.

Canaris shrugged. "Unfortunately, Brigadier, that's the world we live in. In fact, they're all fine young men, chosen by me personally. Two Catholics, one a would-be priest, and two Lutherans – all German patriots. They all have one thing in common; they detest Hitler. Though I agree, the long coats do make them look rather menacing."

"Let's hope it doesn't come to a shooting match, Admiral. My own friends are trained street fighters, Cockneys most of them, one a Jew. I can assure you they hate Hitler as much as your companions."

"Well, perhaps we can start by agreeing on something. It would be most regrettable if they get into a fight over who hates him most," Canaris said, with a hint of a smile.

Menzies didn't reciprocate.

"On the subject of our men, what about my officers from Venlo? Your operation was very professional – but why did you go after them? It's made it very difficult for me to maintain contact."

Menzies had lost most of his network in northern Europe after an abduction. Two of his agents had been lured to a meeting near the Dutch-German border, kidnapped and dragged into Germany.

Canaris shrugged. "It was none of my doing. Things acquired a certain momentum with the Gestapo and some local operators."

"You took some of the credit, though."

"That's true. Some people who didn't know any better assumed the Abwehr was involved. I didn't see any point in refusing a share of the credit. Like you, Brigadier, I've a job to hold on to. It might just be in your country's interest, as well as my own in the longer term, that I'm seen to be doing it well. Your agents are in Sachsenhausen concentration camp, near Berlin. Not very comfortable, but I have a certain amount of say in how they're treated. My office arranges interrogations with them from time to time, and I drip feed reports to impress certain others."

"I can't imagine you've much more to learn after the Gestapo got their paws on them."

"That may be true, but your insinuation is wrong. The Abwehr's techniques are very different from the Gestapo's – not too different from your own, I suspect. We both understand that the psychological approach is more effective than the physical. In any case, the real reason for the interrogations is to make sure the camp management keep them in reasonable health. At least they're still alive, which is more than I can say for any of my people who've ended up in the Tower of London."

"Enemy agents, Admiral. Civilian clothes, wireless sets... I can hardly be expected to send them off for a nice vacation in Canada."

"This war's a filthy business, Brigadier. Let me just say that some of my men have their hearts in the right place. It could be in both our interests for you to at least check that possibility before you despatch them."

Menzies said nothing. With so many German agents already turned, he didn't want to go there.

There was a knock on the door and the elderly Spanish lady appeared again, carrying a tray with a jug of coffee and two cups. She put it down and left. Canaris ushered his visitor towards the table and poured out the drinks. Menzies hesitated for a moment. He had a suicide pill hidden in his lapel in case of treachery. Churchill had insisted. *But if the coffee was drugged?*

The German smiled, understanding his caution.

"You have my word we either both walk out of here, or neither of us does. I assume that fits with our respective security arrangements. Please choose."

Menzies took the cup on his left and sipped.

"I was disappointed you refused to meet me in July," Canaris said. "It's a pity. Things have got a lot more difficult for us since then."

"More difficult? You seem to be doing quite well in Dorset."

"I meant for *us*, you and me, and people like us trying to put an end to this evil – not the Nazi thugs who have taken over my country."

"You were with them for a while, though?"

Canaris sighed.

"To my regret, yes; in the early days. At the beginning, I thought they were our best chance of stopping the Bolsheviks. Then I discovered what they were really like. It was bad enough in Germany, but Poland..."

"I've heard reports."

"You haven't heard the half of it. I saw it myself. Priests shot by the dozen... army officers... teachers... Hundreds of Jews rounded up into synagogues and burned alive. Sickening. I went to Keitel to try to get it stopped, but he told me to mind my own business, to forget it. Apparently, his moral position is that if the Fuehrer wants something to happen..."

"That's when you decided to act?"

"That's when all doubt disappeared. It's not easy turning against your country's leaders, no matter how evil you know they are. Talking of leaders, does Churchill know you're here?"

Menzies hesitated for a moment and Canaris didn't push him.

"Admiral, let's say I recognise that you run a greater risk from your countrymen than I do from mine. But I'm intrigued... how did you explain your visit here? You don't seem to have been trying too hard to hide it."

"A meeting with one of the up-and-coming Falangist leaders. Took place two hours ago, in this very room."

Menzies nodded. It was clever camouflage. It was not unreasonable for the Abwehr to be staying in contact with the hard-line faction in Franco's government.

"You have the distinct advantage, unlike me, of not having to travel incognito."

"That is true, Brigadier. In fact, I've another reason to be in Spain. Our dear Fuehrer is desperate to meet the Generalissimo. You can probably imagine why. However, the old fox is proving remarkably difficult to pin down. I think we might both be having a certain amount of influence on that."

For the first time, a ghost of a smile passed across Menzies' lips. He knew both secret services were playing a sophisticated game of chess, trying to keep Spain out of the war. So far, they'd succeeded.

"We have just a few hours, Admiral. Can I ask why you wanted this meeting so urgently? You know the battle in England is at a critical stage. Is there anything you can do to influence things?"

"I'm afraid not, Brigadier, unfortunately. Those wheels are in motion. There's nothing can be done until it reaches a conclusion, or perhaps a stalemate."

Menzies persisted, his eyes narrowing. "A few months ago you hinted that the Army was getting ready to remove Hitler. So why not now?"

"In the middle of a battle? If they did, he'd just become a martyr to the German *volk*. The 'stab in the back' lie – just like 1918. There's no point disposing of him and have Himmler or any one of a dozen others take over... Reinhard Heydrich, for one. You won't have heard of him yet, but he's the most dangerous of all. Makes Hitler look like a gentleman."

Menzies made a mental note and let Canaris continue.

"There'd be no boundaries then... mass expulsions... exterminations. Not just thousands, millions of people. If, on the other hand, you do succeed in holding out, Sea Lion will be perceived as a failure, and Hitler too. That will make it a lot easier for those of us trying to change things."

"And if we don't succeed?" Menzies knew it was a chilling possibility.

"It will be harder, much harder. With France and Britain defeated, Hitler will be acclaimed as the greatest German who's ever lived. But even if that were to happen, don't give up hope – though it will take a lot more time and some difficult preparation work before we can act."

"Well, I can assure you we're doing our best to hold on – just to make it easier for you."

For the first time, they both smiled.

"To move to a different subject, Admiral, is your warning about Russia still valid?"

"It is."

"Despite the mess that Sea Lion's turning into?"

"That has put things back by a month or two, maybe from spring to early summer. But I've already heard him dismiss the outcome in England as irrelevant – even if you manage to inflict such a defeat that not one of our soldiers returns. *Only a hundred thousand men; ten divisions. We'll soon have a hundred and fifty!* That's what we're dealing with, Menzies."

"You're opposed to the attack on Russia?"

"Not particularly; I'm no lover of the Communists. I'm not sure there's much of a difference between Hitler and Stalin. But if either of them wins outright, the future's black for humanity."

"So where does Britain fit into this battle of tyrants?"

"You just have to stay free. That's why I contacted you in July. It's why I tried so hard to stop Sea Lion."

Menzies didn't respond. Canaris had come closer than anyone to foiling Ethelred. Several Ultra decrypts had showed him exaggerating the size of Britain's forces in his reports to Hitler – at the same time as the Ethelred planners were doing their best to hide the growing British strength. He'd talked to Churchill about alerting the Admiral to their strategy, but the Prime Minister had forbidden it.

Canaris hesitated for a moment, before continuing, sounding subdued.

"I was desperately worried when the Realists appeared – the thought they might take over in London and align England with Hitler. The stupidity of them thinking a few token gestures would satisfy the monster. They've learned nothing, obviously, from Czechoslovakia and Poland... and now France and the others. Once they made a few concessions, they'd be on the slippery slope. In a matter of months, he'd be ordering them to hand over the Jews and the socialists. After that, any politicians he didn't like, the intelligentsia, the press..."

"You can rest assured that the particular group you mention won't be coming back."

Canaris raised an eyebrow, but didn't pursue his suspicions.

"Even if those defeatists have vanished, somewhat mysteriously, your military position still seems precarious."

"You don't think we'll be able to hang on?"

"The situation on the south coast must be worrying for you. I expect that's why Churchill let you come."

"Why didn't you warn us about the attack?"

"Didn't have time. Rommel conjured up the plan in a matter of days. He's one of our best young generals – and I have high hopes for him in other ways. However, for all the early success there, I know Field Marshal Keitel is still nervous. Our losses have been higher than anticipated. But the point is that it's not simply about fending off Sea Lion, either with a victory, or, more likely, a stalemate on a line somewhere across southern England. It's afterwards, even if you manage to hold out... in a year or two from now... maybe after he's conquered

Russia. You don't know Hitler and his gang, or what they're planning – jet-propelled aircraft, guns that can blast London from France, long-range rockets. Some physicists even talking about unimaginable new weapons, small enough to fit on one of those rockets, that can destroy a city."

Menzies studied the drawn face in front of him. *How could he call this man his enemy?*

"So get rid of him!"

"I've told you the problem. You can assume that his removal will be part of any upheaval – but the Nazis are a nest of vipers – worse, in fact, a malignancy spread throughout my country. We have to cut the cancer out completely – and that means action in every town, every barracks. And it means action on the British side as well."

Menzies was taken aback.

"Military intervention?"

"No, that would only make things worse. The nation would draw together round the current set of criminals and continue the fight. On a wider stage, the longer our countries keep fighting, the happier it makes Stalin. When we're both exhausted, we'll see the Red hordes coming from the east and agent provocateurs stirring revolution in our streets. And I mean British streets as well as German. So, no, not military; it must be political. Churchill will have done his life's work stopping the Wehrmacht outside London. When we dispose of Hitler, somebody else has to take over in England, somebody who can take the next step forward, to a ceasefire and a genuine settlement."

"Somehow I don't think Winston deserves quite the same fate as Adolf," Menzies said, without giving any indication of his reaction.

Canaris smiled, spreading open the palms of his hands in a gesture of understanding.

"You British are masters at handling things in your own subtle ways. Let him spend his remaining years rebuilding Chartwell, or painting the ruins or whatever. The German people have no quarrel with him."

He leaned forward across the table. "But there has to be seen to be compromise. There are others with whom it would be easier to reach an accommodation... Lloyd George? Eden? Maybe even yourself?"

Canaris hesitated for a moment, leaving time for the flattery to take effect, but there was no response.

"There's another subject I need to discuss with you, Brigadier. Somehow, I don't think you're involved, but it looks as if there might be something already stirring in London."

He took a copy of the Swedish note from his briefcase and passed it over.

Menzies went white as he read it. *Somebody had told the Germans about Ethelred!*

He swallowed once or twice, before handing the document back, trying to look as calm as possible.

"Even if this was genuine, isn't it exactly what you want to see – Britain showing the strength and determination to fight on?"

"No, Menzies. This isn't under control. Not on your side, obviously, and not on ours either. The source implies that Churchill is the problem, a traitor to his country. The existence of a group of dissenters in England trying to undermine him doesn't help get rid of Hitler. In fact, it strengthens his position."

"Do you know who sent it?"

"Again no, but the last correspondence like this came from Minister Butler."

"How did Hitler react?"

"He didn't get to see it. Goering stopped it. After the fiasco with the Realists, he said it was obviously a fake and ordered us to drop it."

"Goering?" Menzies said. It was the second shock he'd received within a minute. "Is he with you in all this?"

"Brigadier, the Reichsmarschall is a fat, useless drug addict. He just didn't want his boss to be upset unnecessarily. We were lucky."

Menzies nodded. He looked at his watch. He had a long drive back to Lisbon to get the flight next evening. He stood up to leave.

"This has been a most useful meeting, Admiral. I wish you luck in your endeavours. I hear your message we must be ready to act when we see the sign. Maybe, when all this is over, you and I will have the opportunity to work together on other matters of common interest. Perhaps in the east?"

He reached out his hand, willingly this time. The men looked at each other solemnly and shook hands.

Menzies left the room and went down the narrow stairs. Outside the back door he was startled by a sudden movement. A tall figure in a leather overcoat was waiting in the shadows. He edged forward and looked at the Englishman, as if unsure of his actions. For a moment, the two men faced each other. Then, rather awkwardly, the German nodded an acknowledgement and stepped out of his way.

Fifty yards away, hidden in a clump of bushes, a crouching Londoner in combat gear put down his carbine. For a few tense seconds, he'd been holding it trained on the centre button of a long grey coat – Menzies' coat.

37

At Mildenhall airfield in Suffolk, the chattering stopped as Group Captain Mitchell came into the Operations Room. The men stood up and waited till he set them at ease.

The Bomber Command crews had been busy since the threat of invasion first emerged, carrying out raids on most nights. In the early days, their targets had been the ships and barges in the French ports. After the landings, they'd switched their attention to the beaches and lodgement areas in England. But for all their efforts, they knew it was something of a shadow war. They couldn't see the Germans, and the Germans couldn't see them. So they'd gone out in the dark of night, did their best to put their bombs in roughly the right place and headed back to base, largely untroubled by flak or nightfighters.

There was a sense that tonight's mission would be different. They knew about the landings on the south coast, and the briefing had been called for 1100, three hours earlier than usual. Now they sat forward in their chairs, stone silent, as Mitchell addressed them.

"Until a few days ago, it looked as if things in the invasion battle were beginning to go our way. The Army has halted the German advance in the south-east, and the RAF and the Navy have just about stopped the flow of supplies across the Channel. However, you're all aware of the dangerous new situation that has emerged. The capture of Eastleigh and Weymouth has changed the balance in the battle, exposing our entire defensive position in the south. Our task tonight is to change the balance back."

There was no reaction. So far, Mitchell hadn't told them anything they didn't know already.

He handed over to Squadron Leader Jameson, the intelligence officer, to give the detail.

Jameson walked up to the front of the room where a trestle stood to one side, its board covered with a dark green sheet. The Nissen hut filled with the sound of metal scraping on wooden floorboards as the crews edged their chairs forward. His briefings always started with a detailed description of the target. Today the men already knew what to expect.

With something of a flourish, Jameson pulled away the sheet. The crews were right; it was a map of southern England.

"Gentlemen, since the Germans captured Eastleigh airfield, two days ago, they've flown in almost 100 Me109s and more than 50 Stukas, maybe a quarter of their total remaining strength."

There was a low whistling in the room.

"Clearly, this has changed the strategic air picture for the worse."

He turned to the map and pointed to a large circle marked on it, centred on Eastleigh.

"The Stukas have a radius of action of just over a hundred miles, the 109s a bit more."

He lifted a pointer and began to tap on the map, going round the compass quadrant by quadrant.

"To the east, they can now attack our forces in Kent from the rear. To the south, they can protect the supply ships coming into Weymouth, preventing our destroyers getting at them. Looking out to the west, they can threaten railways, ports, even ships in the nearer parts of the Irish Sea. Perhaps most worrying of all, to the north, they can range as far as the factories in the Midlands."

He pointed out the critical industrial targets. Birmingham was the power house of the country, hosting the factories making tanks and small arms. On its outskirts were the aircraft factories where most of the RAF's Spitfires came from. Not far away, in Derby, was the Rolls-Royce plant where they made the Merlin engines. Coventry was where the Army's field guns came from.

"On their own, the Stukas would be easy meat for our fighters, but the hundred or so 109s are providing air cover for them. They're also maintaining an air corridor for transport aircraft bringing in supplies from France."

The aircrew knew most of it already. The rumour mills in the mess had been at work. It hadn't taken much imagination to piece together the snippets of information and to appreciate the seriousness of the risk.

However, they were not prepared for the officer's next disclosure.

"Over the last two days we've sent in our day bombers to attack the airfield, but with the amount of flak and the 109s on the base, our losses have been heavy. We've lost over 60 aircraft in the last thirty-six hours."

The battle-hardened crews were shocked at the scale of the losses. Many of them had friends, some brothers or cousins, in the day bomber squadrons. Amidst the muttering, one of the senior pilots put his hand up and asked a pointed question.

"Squadron Leader, why can't the Army just storm the airfield, or let the artillery boys shell it to bits – instead of throwing away dozens of aircraft?"

The intelligence officer had asked the same question an hour earlier. Now he had to repeat the unwelcome answer.

"It's not as simple as that. The Nazi parachutists are crack troops, skilled in defending positions against infantry attacks. It would be easy enough with tanks; unfortunately, all our tanks and field guns are tied up in the south-east, holding the line there. Any trying to move towards Hampshire are being taken out by the Stukas. And the Army has another demand on its resources – Rommel's panzer divisions are fighting their way through the New Forest from Dorset, heading north towards Eastleigh. If they manage to link-up with the air bridgehead, it'll make things extremely sticky. They'll have out-flanked our defence lines in the south-east, with all that implies. So, the deal is that the Army looks after Rommel and holds the front in Kent. The Royal Navy takes care of Weymouth. Our job is Eastleigh."

Jameson had made it sound brutally simple. He sat down, leaving a shocked silence in the room.

Group Captain Mitchell took over again.

"You've heard the background. Our orders for tonight come directly from the Prime Minister. They are straight-forward. We are to eliminate Eastleigh airfield."

He waited while his words sank in.

"Once we've done that, the Luftwaffe will be removed from the scene. The Army will turn its attention to the New Forest and roll up Rommel's forces there."

Even as Mitchell was still outlining the objectives, the murmuring started. Squadron Leader Barry, the commander of 149 squadron, sensed the question in their minds. It had been a constant discussion in the mess. The RAF's accuracy in night bombing was woeful; they could just about get their bombs into a county, not onto a small target like an airfield. Over Germany, that didn't matter so much – it was the only weapon Britain had to strike back with. While civilian casualties were not intentional, few of the fliers were over-concerned. It happened in war, and they shouldn't have started it.

At the first break in the presentation, he asked the hard question.

"Group Captain, how are we supposed to hit a target the size of an airfield at night? And how are we supposed to avoid casualties in the civilian population for miles around?"

Mitchell bristled at the challenge so early in the meeting. He fixed Barry with a cool stare.

"I will address those questions shortly, Squadron Leader. For the moment, just accept it."

Barry didn't push it any further and sat quietly as Mitchell continued his briefing.

"We are going to put 300 bombers over the target tonight, at low altitude, 3000 ft. You'll be given detailed routings to get you close to Eastleigh and the target itself will be illuminated. You'll be informed of the precise way this will be done one hour before take-off."

The mutterings started again, louder this time. There'd been some attempts to guide bombers using radio beams, but none, so far, had been successful. The crew also knew that no new equipment had been installed in their aircraft or any special training given that might have offered a clue.

Mitchell ignored the rumblings and continued with his presentation.

"At this point, I'll let Squadron Leader Jameson give you a detailed briefing on the target. After that, we'll look at fuel requirements, bomb load and schedules. The sequencing of aircraft formations from the various Bomber Command bases will be critical. Squadron commanders will work through the take-off schedule, the forming-up, the routing and the approach to target. You can assume there'll be sufficient navigation aids to get you to the target area. You can also assume there will be no nightfighters or heavy flak to worry about. There is a large concentration of light flak around the airfield, but the German gunners won't be able to see anything in the dark. In fact, with so many planes in the sky, the main risk will be collisions. Your air gunners will have a special responsibility as lookouts. Assume all other aircraft in the vicinity are friendly, so no shooting unless you're absolutely certain you're under attack from a nightfighter; and I mean absolutely – that means cannon fire coming directly at you."

He paused for a few moments to let the message sink in.

"What if we can't find the target on the run-in?" one of the flight commanders asked. It sounded a simple question, but there were many implications, especially if only a few of the aircraft managed to navigate precisely enough to find Eastleigh.

"There will be no, I repeat, no go-rounds. If you miss your run, you will exit to the south, climb out over the Solent and Isle of Wight to 6000ft. Dump your bombs over the sea and return to base over Land's End, south Wales and the Midlands. Standard night navigation procedures. The same applies for bombers that have completed their run. There'll be no special guidance to assist you on the return flight; you've all been trained for it."

He pinned a chart to the wall. It showed the order of battle for the biggest air raid the RAF had staged.

"Our Wellingtons will lead the attack. 149 squadron will be first off, followed by 115 and 218 squadrons. We'll be joined at designated assembly points by five more squadrons of Wellingtons from the other 3 Group airfields, 4 Group's Whitleys and, finally, the Hampdens from 5 Group."

Barry was fidgeting with his notebook. He'd scribbled down most of what Mitchell was saying, but was marking many of the key points with exclamations and question marks. He'd been given the responsibility of leading the attack. It was a pleasing recognition of the reputation his squadron and crew had earned, but it still didn't answer the question. *How were they supposed to find the target in the dark?*

The discussion moved on to bomb loadouts. Again, Barry became confused. As lead aircraft, his task would normally be to drop marker flares to guide the bomber stream flowing behind. Not tonight; they would be carrying a full load of 500 pounders. He looked askance at his navigator, who shrugged his shoulders. They'd been given their orders, but had no idea how they were supposed to carry them out.

Mitchell noticed the negative reaction building in the room. He spoke again.

"Gentlemen, I can assure you the target will be well marked for you. When I explain how, an hour before take-off, you'll understand the need for the tight security. Remember, your job is to get your load of high explosives right into the middle of the target. We want maximum shock effect on the airfield defences. Once their aircraft and the fuel dumps start going up, the succeeding waves will have no difficulty in finding the target."

* * *

At midnight the pilots and navigators trooped back into the briefing room. Mitchell brought them over to a large table with a map of the target laid out on top. Stacked beside it was a pile of books, illustrated tourist guides to England.

"Take-off is at 0130. The weather forecast is for broken cloud at 8000 ft. You'll be underneath that and we've chosen waypoints you'll be able to find quite easily. We'll discuss them in a few moments. First, I want to talk about the target. It's a night attack, so listen carefully. We won't be using flares. They would only warn the Germans and make our aircraft visible. Instead, the airfield will be thrown into contrast shortly before you arrive. At precisely 0252, exactly three minutes before your planned time of arrival, the street lights in the towns, villages and on the roads surrounding the airfield will be switched on. The airfield itself will be in darkness. The short interval is to avoid giving Jerry any warning. Even if they do put two and two together, it will take them at least five minutes to start their generators and get their own lights on. Within that window, you've got to hit the target hard, starting with the control tower, before moving to the hard-standings and hangars. By the time we've finished, fifty minutes later, Eastleigh airfield will be flattened and nearly 200 German planes destroyed. The Army will move in to complete the cleaning-up."

Suddenly the plan made sense. Barry didn't have to worry about how the target would be illuminated. His task was to plan the flying manoeuvres for his squadron. But, to do that, he had to find out how they would get close enough to Eastleigh to see the lights.

The group captain waited as the airmen gathered round the map, chattering amongst themselves. He called them to order and began listing the waypoints on the route to the target. All of them were familiar English cities. One navigator happened to have his protractors with him and began calling out the distances between waypoints.

Mitchell relaxed. They were buying into the plan. Now he could move on to the detail.

"They're all easily identifiable, 40 to 50 miles apart. The forecast is for good visibility underneath the cloud base, so you'll be able to pick up each successive waypoint within ten or fifteen minutes of leaving the previous one. You'll be required to track around each of them with care. Do that and they'll lead you straight to the target. But remember, a precise approach for the bomb run is vital, to make sure we avoid civilian casualties on the ground. So, accurate navigation all the way. Do your homework; there'll be no excuse for drifting off course.

Your rear gunners can help by tracking the reciprocal course as you leave each waypoint behind."

"I wouldn't be too sure about that," a voice muttered from the back. "They're gunners, sir, not navigators. Most of them wouldn't know one end of a compass from the other, if you know what I mean."

Mitchell looked at him. The point was valid.

"If you've any doubts about their ability to use a compass, either teach them fast or put somebody else in the turret that can. You won't be needing your tail guns tonight."

"What about the formation, Group Captain? Line astern?"

"No. Wouldn't get the aircraft over target in the time needed. A vee formation. Three columns, wingmen stepped back on each side. You'll have to be stay close together to get a tight bombing pattern – but you can keep your nav. lights on till you reach the final waypoint. There won't be any German nightfighters around; the only planes in the sky will be British bombers. Just don't forget to switch them off for the final run-in."

The muttering had stopped; it was beginning to look doable. There was silence again as Mitchell continued with the briefing.

"Staying in tight formation will be crucial. You will have to maintain a precise cruising speed to get over the target at the exact time scheduled. As you're flying over England, there'll be no need for strict radio silence, so, within reason, you can use your wireless to help. No reference to the target or waypoints, obviously, just 'left a bit, right a bit'. Within each individual squadron, it will be up to the pilots to sort themselves out before they pass Salisbury. There'll be a ten-minute separation between the last plane of each group and the first of group behind. Within each group the squadrons will be stepped up at 500 ft steps to give a bit more clearance from earlier bomb blasts. That's about as tight as we can manage from the different airfields."

The aircrew set quietly on their chairs, waiting for Mitchell. He still hadn't answered the key unanswered question. *How would they find their way to Eastleigh in the dark?*

"Now let's look at the waypoints."

He handed out the prettiest route planners they'd ever seen.

38

The drive up to Stratford-upon-Avon was slow. Since the *Cromwell* alarm had been issued, the entire country had been on alert, with roadblocks on all main roads. At this hour of the night, however, there was little traffic, and the convoy of the four Bedford lorries and the Lanchester armoured car didn't attract much attention at any of the checkpoints. The major just showed their papers and they were allowed to pass through without inspection. In the back of the converted armoured car, Churchill and Bracken slumped down, cut off from the world. Bracken was talking over his difficult negotiations with the Speaker earlier in the day. Occasionally, Churchill sidetracked their discussion to practise some key parts of his speech. At one point he managed to irritate Bracken by wondering aloud what he should do if a motion of no confidence was passed.

"It's not going to happen, Winston. They've more sense. Even if a majority are still unhappy after hearing you, there'll be a fudge of some sort for the time-being – same as in May. You remain Prime Minister unless and until you submit your resignation to the King. And there'll be a result in the battle long before that happens – one way or the other. Put it out of your mind and focus on your speech."

It was well past 0100 when they reached Ettington, five miles outside Stratford-upon-Avon. Churchill looked at his watch and spoke to the commander in the Lanchester's turret, telling him to stop the convoy outside the village.

The soldiers jumped down from the trucks, glad of the chance to have a break and stretch their legs. Several of the men lined up at a roadside hedge to relieve themselves. They hadn't been told the identity of the passengers in the armoured car and were startled to be joined in line by the Prime Minister. Some found it hard to go, but were soon put at ease by a few earthy comments from Churchill. He chatted away light-heartedly and, to their amusement, named the hedge *Adolf.* That seemed to help them perform.

To the surprise of the major, the Prime Minister didn't appear to be in any hurry to move on to their destination. He kept glancing at his watch in the heavily masked light from one of the lorries. Finally, at 0145, he gave the nod. They mounted the vehicles again for the final few miles.

Ten minutes later the convoy pulled up outside the Shakespeare Memorial Theatre. Churchill dismounted. Still wearing his army battledress, he strode purposefully up the steps with Bracken tagging along behind.

A storm of noise greeted him as he entered the chamber. There was some ragged cheering, from about half of the MPs present, on both the Tory and Labour sides of the House. But there was some jeering as well on the Labour side. On the Tory benches no heckling was audible, just a nervous, perhaps embarrassed, silence in some quarters. Over the last few hours, the patriotic surge experienced in response to the German invasion had been dealt a blow as rumours began to spread about a deception at the heart of the war strategy. For many of the MPs, the hint of a deeper, unpalatable truth had undermined their faith in the Prime Minister.

Ignoring the noise, Churchill took his place on the Front Bench and Bracken squeezed into a space on the bench behind.

Across the floor of the House, a grim-faced Clement Attlee faced them, arms folded.

39

"Power on, engine 1. Start."

The port Pegasus spluttered for a few moments and burst into life. A minute later it was followed by its twin on the other side. Squadron Leader Barry scanned his instruments, watching the temperature and oil pressure rise. He tested the intercom and heard each of the five crew confirm they were ready. They were a few minutes ahead of schedule and he sat waiting for the signal to taxi.

The delay was unwelcome. It left space for the crew's fears to surface, time for them to think about the mission ahead. In the Wellington's belly hung nine 500 lb bombs, bound not for Germany, but for a corner of Hampshire. Barry was anxious, conscious of the power of his weapons. Over Germany he'd seen the destruction wreaked on enemy ports and factories and on the cities and houses surrounding them. While he was proud that his crew had been chosen to lead this raid, he was painfully aware of the difficulties of accurate bombing at night, and of the mortal risk to his countrymen below.

He'd drilled the message into the pilots and navigators of the squadrons. For this mission, like none before, pinpoint navigation was critical. He hoped the commanders on the other bases had been as fastidious. And he had a very personal interest. His sister lived less than two miles from the target.

Ten minutes later a green Very light was fired from the tower. Barry throttled up the engines and began to taxi towards the dim threshold, bumping and lurching over the rutted surface. Behind him, the other eight aircraft of his squadron lined up and waited their turn. Another Very light. Barry pushed the throttles fully forward. The bomber lumbered down the grass runway, slowly gathering speed until he pulled back on the control column and lifted the aircraft off into the night. At fifteen-second intervals the rest of the squadron followed.

One after another the portly Wellingtons climbed away and began closing up into formation; first into flights of three; then flights into squadrons. Finally, the three squadrons from the base came together into a full wing of twenty-seven aircraft and settled down at the assigned altitude. Flying much closer together than usual, the planes kept their dim navigation lights on as a precaution against collision. But, even with the side and tail gunners keeping a sharp lookout, there were one or two close calls.

They set course for the first waypoint.

At carefully planned intervals, the scene was repeated on ten other airfields across Suffolk, Norfolk and Lincolnshire. Within a space of twenty-five minutes, a great fleet of bombers had taken to the air and was climbing to altitude for their cross-country flight.

Ten minutes after take-off, Barry spotted the first waypoint. Standing proud on the flat earth of Norfolk, the cathedral at Ely was known to the local citizenry as the *Ship of the Fens*. For the first time since war began, they saw it illuminated, the two towers and vaulted naves shining silver-grey under the lights of the local searchlight company.

The navigator checked the bearing and called out to Barry. "On the nose, skipper. Take it to starboard, then the next four to port, and Wells to starboard. Just like going round the cans at Cowes." They were both keen yachtsmen.

It was the first of a series of beacons marking the route to the target, unmistakeable beacons; six of the great cathedrals of England. After Ely came Peterborough, then Coventry, Gloucester, Wells and, last in line, Salisbury. The navigators had studied the photographs in the tourist guides and committed their shapes to memory. All so different, there was no risk of misidentification. Peterborough Cathedral lay flat in the centre of the town with its long gothic nave and three great arches. Coventry's elegant spire reached 300 feet into the night sky. Gloucester's square tower was topped by four graceful pinnacles, and Wells sat squat with a gothic tower. Finally, there was Salisbury, twenty miles from Eastleigh. Its thin spire, over 400 feet high, was the highest in the land.

The guidebooks illustrated each of them in all its medieval or modern glory. The searchlights would do the rest.

Soon Ely was behind them. With a precise fix now made on the time and position, Barry turned the Wellington smoothly onto the second leg, steering 285 degrees magnetic towards the next mark, Peterborough Cathedral.

* * *

For most of the afternoon, Bracken had been on the phone to the Speaker's office, arguing and cajoling, alternately calling in favours and making discreet threats. The first concession had been relatively minor. He'd arranged that at the precise time the Prime Minister entered the Chamber, a backbencher would be on his feet, one of his firm supporters on the Labour side. The veteran MP was extolling the strengths of the National Coalition, in a somewhat long-winded speech, when Churchill walked in. Bracken looked across and made brief eye contact with the MP, who continued speaking until he saw the prearranged signal. His part completed, he finished his speech and sat down.

There was a murmur of anticipation. With tension building, the Speaker announced he was going to call next on the Prime Minister.

"But first, I have a procedural matter to address."

There was a sudden movement at the main entrance door. The MPs were startled to see the Serjeant-at-Arms move a few feet inside the chamber. Behind him were several uniformed figures. Those close to the entrance could see a squad of military police taking up position outside. They appeared to be carrying batons. Behind the redcaps, some MPs saw other troops appearing, in field dress and carrying rifles. Word flashed around the chamber; the murmurs grew into uproar. Parliament was being violated. Not since Oliver Cromwell had dispersed the Rump Parliament, three hundred years earlier, had armed soldiers entered the House of Commons.

"Order! Order!" The Speaker tried to raise his voice above the clamour.

He struggled to gain the attention of the House.

"I must remind Honourable Members that the House is in secret session."

His words were almost drowned out. He shouted again.

"Silence, please! This is, I repeat, a secret session. It is the practice of this House that debates involving national security are held in such sessions, to avoid the risk of information reaching the enemy. It will hardly stay secret if the racket you're making can be heard a mile away!"

The noise died down.

"I have an important announcement to make in relation to this morning's session. I have been advised that the information about to be shared with you relates to military operations currently in progress. In recognition of the consequent risk to our servicemen, no-one will be allowed to leave the chamber until..."

On all sides members rose in a fury of protest. A few left-wing Labour members tried to rush the exit, but were manhandled back, roughly, by the military police. Eventually the Speaker managed to restore enough order to make himself heard above the din.

"Order, order! Will you please restrain yourselves and let me finish? As I was about to inform you, because of the risk to our servicemen, no-one will be allowed to leave the Chamber from the time the Prime Minister begins to speak until the military operations are over. I understand this will be in approximately three or four hours' time. However..."

He waited till another burst of shouting died down.

"However, anyone who wishes to leave the Chamber before the Prime Minister begins his statement may do so now, in a dignified manner, please. If you do choose to leave, you will not be permitted to re-enter until the debate is over. Nor will you be allowed to leave the building."

He waited, but no one moved. What they were witnessing was an unprecedented breach of parliamentary procedure, but the MPs could see that history was in process of being made. Gradually the shouting became sporadic. The Speaker waited until the rumpus had died down. With calm restored, he spoke to the uniformed figures standing inside the door.

"I now instruct those strangers present to leave the Chamber."

He waited till they backed out and the door was closed behind them. He spoke again to the House.

"Honourable Members should know that the guards will remain on duty outside the door to enforce the instructions I have given. I also wish to remind members that, outside this Chamber, the military police have full powers of arrest under the Emergency Powers Act."

He waited again for the objections to die down.

"I call upon the Prime Minister."

"Dictator!"

"Traitor!"

"Resign! Resign!"

For several minutes the shouting continued, from backbenchers on both sides of the House. Churchill stood silent, until even his opponents tired and went quiet. He took his glasses from his battledress pocket and put them on. He looked down once at his papers and then over the half-frames, across the floor of the House. He ignored the final few catcalls.

"Mr. Speaker, two weeks ago, enemy forces landed on our shores. Ill-prepared and over-confident, they thought victory would come easily, that Britain would crumble without a fight. How wrong they were! How wrong to expect the nation of Wellington and Nelson to bow before the evil that has swept Europe.

"Hitler thought we were unprepared. He was wrong. For the sacred task of defending our island, we have prepared for centuries. Hitler thought our air force was defeated. He was wrong; the Royal Air Force has been harbouring its strength, ready for the day. Hitler thought our navy was riven with doubt and dissent. He was wrong; the Royal Navy stands united, resolute in defence of our coastline. He thought our army would not fight. He was wrong; the British Army has stopped his panzers in their tracks."

He looked over his glasses, as if challenging the members on the Opposition benches.

"And how did it come to pass that Herr Hitler reached these erroneous and dangerous conclusions? You may well ask. I can tell the House that his sorry misjudgement was not totally the result of stupidity. We may, at times, have lent a certain encouragement."

There were shouts from the Labour backbenches; the news about Ethelred had been leaking out.

"And why we would have done such a thing? Again, you may well ask. I will simply invite you to contemplate how much more difficult our position would be if we'd allowed the Boche to prepare for another year before they launched themselves upon us. But exactly how we may have encouraged their miscalculation must remain a story for another day."

He paused for a moment. This time there was no heckling.

"Our bold plan has proven successful. In Kent and Sussex our brave soldiers have stopped the enemy in their tracks. Day by day we have frustrated the Nazi advance; we have ground down their armoured formations; we have chiselled away at their supply lines. In the southeast of our country the enemy force now withers on the vine, starved of petrol, out of ammunition, short of food. They stare defeat in the face."

He glanced at his watch.

"But at no stage, as we prepared for this great battle, did we believe the task would be easy or that we would experience no setbacks. The Nazis have sprung one unpleasant surprise with their aerial assault in Hampshire and the sea landings in Dorset. I tell you it is but the last sting of a dying wasp. Having stopped them in Kent, we will now do whatever is necessary, at whatever cost, to dislodge the invader from his toehold on the south coast."

He looked at his watch again, waiting. The silence was intense. He stood at the Front Bench, saying nothing for a moment, as if in prayer. He had another ten minutes of speech prepared, just in case, but he hoped he wouldn't have to use it. Then he heard something outside, at first just a distant throb. He could use the abridged version.

"We are not content just to halt the invaders."

The sound outside was growing. He raised his voice.

"We are not content just to see them off, to send them back to France with their tails between their legs."

It got louder. He raised a clenched fist in the air, shouting to make himself heard.

"This night, we shall vanquish them!"

The building began to shake. Nothing else could be heard inside the chamber. Three thousand feet above, the RAF bombers streamed past in tight formation, squadron after squadron, wing after wing. Thirty miles after leaving Coventry cathedral, and half way to Wells, three hundred aircraft flew low over the Shakespeare Memorial Theatre.

Churchill's supporters leapt to their feet, shouting with excitement, throwing their order papers in the air, drowning out the objections of what was now a small rump of left-wing MPs.

Bracken leaned across to Churchill and shouted in his ear.

"Some parliament, Winston! Some theatre!"

40

Thirty minutes after passing Stratford, Barry's Wellington approached Wells. It had been his biggest worry about the route; a 90 degree turn onto their next heading. He'd raised it with Mitchell at the briefing, but had been told it was the only distinguishable landmark within twenty miles. The group captain said they just had to handle it. As lead aircraft, Barry wasn't too worried about the risk of collision, but those behind him would need their wits about them. He checked his watch. 0247... *Damn!* They were three minutes ahead of schedule after the cross-country flight. Maybe he'd kept his speed a bit on the high side, over-anxious to make the target in time. Or maybe the headwind on the last leg hadn't been as strong as forecast. He throttled back as much as he dared.

He banked the portly aircraft round the mark and straightened up on course for the final waypoint. The navigator began calling out adjustments over the intercom, but it was hardly necessary; the tall spire of Salisbury Cathedral was soon visible in the distance.

The bomb aimer confirmed he had the cathedral in sight and began a countdown. As the count reached zero, Barry eased the Wellington round the mark, leaving it to starboard. He straightened up on course 120. Twenty miles to go.

"Lights, Skipper."

"What? Too early... Oh shit." He'd left the navigation lights on. Lucky somebody had noticed. He switched them off. Now they just had to look for an island of light in the dark countryside ahead.

Another minute.

"How's it looking, Bomb Aimer?"

"Nothing yet, Skip."

Seven minutes to go. It was getting tight. They were still a few minutes early, but, with the rest of the bomber stream close behind, he couldn't reduce his airspeed. If they didn't get a fix soon, he'd have to overshoot and hope the leader of the next squadron would take over.

He heard a shout.

"Lights! Lights coming on ahead, 1 o'clock! More... more... that's it... there's the pattern... Clear as day! More lights! Six miles to go. Time to target: two minutes. Bomb doors open."

They droned on over the village of Romsey, past a Y-shaped junction on main road lit up by the headlights of a dozen army trucks. The lights stretched on for another couple of miles. Beyond that was darkness.

"Dark space ahead, twelve o'clock. Clear as night!"

The bomb aimer took over. His orders were to target the western side of the void, round the invisible control tower.

"Right, right, steady... left a bit, steady."

The darkness moved towards the centre of his bombsight. He began the countdown.

"5... 4... 3... 2... 1..."

* * *

On the airfield, the air and ground crews were asleep, the luckier ones in the original airfield buildings, the rest in tents and in the corners of hangars. For the most part they were sleeping soundly, exhausted by the exertions of the previous four days. A small number of paratroopers were on duty to guard against a sneak attack by British commandos, but, so far, the nights had been quiet and the sentries did not feel under threat. They had time for some easy banter with the NCOs going round to check the blackout.

In the flak posts, the gunners were resting, most of them were asleep, though staying close to their weapons. They had been busy since the assault on the airfield, on continuous duty during the hours of daylight. Their officers were telling them the British would soon run out of aircraft, but most expected to be heavily tasked again in the day ahead.

Shortly after nightfall the Luftwaffe supply flights had come in to the airfield. Forty ungainly Ju52s had made the trip from France, finding the airfield with the help of a radio beacon and a few gooseneck flares placed along the edge of the grass runway. As soon as the planes touched down, the beacon was switched off and the dim flares extinguished.

Now the transport aircraft had gone again, departing at low level to dodge any RAF night fighters probing around in the darkness. In three hours' time, the 109s would be rolled out from their revetments, to be readied for the dawn patrols. When they'd gone, the ground crew would ready the Stukas for the day's operations. For this morning's mission, they would be loading them up with armour-piercing bombs. The British Home Fleet was almost within range.

A sentry in an outlying post was first to hear the deep-throated sound of engines. In the darkness he could see nothing, either in the air or on the ground. But the noise seemed to be getting closer. He called in on a field telephone and was told not to worry. The officer said he wouldn't raise the alarm unless illumination flares started falling on the field.

Over in the control tower, Major Kurt Braun had been on duty since midnight. He was staring into the nothingness outside when a light appeared on the edge of the airfield, just beyond the defensive perimeter. He was reaching for his binoculars to check it out when he saw another one. A few seconds later, it was followed by a strip of street lamps, about half a kilometre to the north.

"Shoot those lights out before they give away our position," he snapped. A sergeant passed the order on to one of the guard posts. Within seconds, bursts of machine gun fire began to knock out the nearer lights.

But now Braun could see dozens of lights, then hundreds, appearing at all points of the compass. As he was still trying to make sense of it, he heard a distant throb. Something was happening... he made a snap decision.

"It's a commando attack!!!"

He ordered a corporal to sound the siren. Across the base, troops stumbled out of sleeping bags and headed for their posts. Aircrew raced for the protection of slit trenches. They were all wondering about the lights, now a faint Aurora Borealis illuminating the night sky.

The throb was getting louder. They could hear it over the klaxon.

One of the flak officers was first to realise the danger. Leutnant Schiller jumped out of his position and sprinted fifty metres across the tarmac to the electrical control room. He burst through the door.

"We're being set up! Get the field's lights on."

Private Eichel had no idea what was happening outside. His job was to protect the switch panel, to ensure the blackout was maintained. He couldn't make any sense of the officer's yelling.

"Soldat! Get the generators going!" Schiller screamed.

Eichel tried to stop the officer as he grabbed at the control panel. He thought he'd gone mad.

"Leutnant, stop! Please, sir. Please... get away from the switches."

Schiller ignored him. He palmed over the panel, looking for the master control.

The planes were getting closer.

"Leave them alone, sir." Eichel unholstered his Mauser pistol. There was no reply.

Leutnant Schiller began to throw switches.

The private fired one shot and the officer fell to the ground.

"The lights, Soldat! Switch on the..."

Eichel held on to his pistol, pointing it at the wounded officer, unnerved, not sure whether to fire again. He was spared the decision; there was no movement from the crumpled figure.

The frightened young soldier lifted the telephone and called the commander's office.

* * *

"Bombs away!"

The Wellington leapt as the bombs dropped from its belly. Barry pushed the throttles forward to climb away. Six seconds later he heard the explosions. He called the rear gunner. "Toby, can you see anything?"

"On target, Skip, whoa... Secondary explosions. Looks like fuel. Yes! Silhouettes... planes on the ground, dozens of 'em. Number 2's bombing and Number 3... going for the biggest group of planes, got the bastards. More bombs... more... Jeez, looks like Bonfire Night."

Barry sighed with relief. They'd done it.

"OK chaps, would love to hang around and watch the fireworks, but there's too much traffic. We're heading home. Give me a course to steer."

By the time the aircraft of 5 Group arrived, the airfield was marked, not by dark contrast, but by a cauldron of fire; buildings ablaze, fuel tanks burning, bomb stores and ammunition exploding. The approaching Hampdens bucked and reared as they flew though the turbulence. One was thrown into a steep bank by a fiery updraught. Too low to recover, it spun into the centre of the airfield and exploded. All around the airfield there was chaos. With individual targets no longer distinguishable, the rest of the bombers dumped their loads into the centre of the conflagration and climbed away.

Last over the target was an aircraft from 44 squadron, its task to photograph the airfield for the damage assessment report. The bomb aimer lay on his stomach, ready to switch on the cameras as they reached the target. He went through the routine, but there really was no need. For a mile in each direction all that could be seen was an inferno of fire and explosions.

The airfield had ceased to exist.

* * *

Three miles away, two thousand khaki-clad soldiers climbed onto lorries and Bren gun carriers. The engines started up. As the sound of the bombing died away, a wiry figure emerged from a farmhouse and walked across to an armoured car. Watched by his battalion commanders, Lieutenant-General Montgomery clambered up into the turret. He stood up and raised his right arm. He held it high for five seconds, then threw it forward, towards Eastleigh.

41

Around the chamber, MPs huddled together in the aisles. Most were loud in their support of the Prime Minister's actions, their confidence buoyed by the show of air power overhead. A few were still shouting furious objections to his war strategy and to their continued confinement. All semblance of debate had gone. Only one MP had been given permission to cross the security picket, Brendan Bracken. When Churchill finished his speech, he'd left the House, to a storm of abuse from opponents.

Two hours later, Bracken returned to the chamber and took his seat, close to the Prime Minister. Watched by clustered groups of MPs, he handed him an envelope.

For several long seconds, Churchill stared at his friend. He saw in his eyes an expression of total loyalty, but that didn't tell him anything. It would have been the same in victory or defeat. He had prepared a series of brief speeches, conscious there could be a range of possible outcomes, from total success to total failure. In the case of defeat, he accepted full responsibility. In the happy event of success, he shared the credit around. With six hundred MPs watching in stark silence, he opened the envelope. He read the note twice, folded it over and put it into the pocket of his battledress. He nodded to the Speaker.

Around the chamber, members rushed back to their places, scrambling over furniture to get as close as they could to the front bench. Even the small group still haranguing the Serjeant-at-Arms seemed subdued. The scuttling of feet and scraping of wooden benches peaked for a few minutes and then died away, leaving a fearful hush as Churchill rose to his feet. He looked over his reading glasses, scanning around the tense faces in the assembled House.

"Mr. Speaker, I would like to make a statement regarding the military operations under way this night."

He paused again in the intense silence.

"It is with heartfelt joy I am able to report that the Battle of Eastleigh has been won. The Nazi bridgehead in Hampshire has been eliminated. To the proud lexicon of our nation's military achievements has been added another outstanding victory, a victory that will rank in our history beside Agincourt and Trafalgar. Our bombers have devastated the airbase. They have destroyed the aircraft, fired the fuel tanks, exploded the armaments. In the wake of that fearsome air attack, our soldiers have entered the airfield through its smashed perimeter and are encountering no resistance from the enemy. Eastleigh airfield, ravaged and blackened though it may be, is back under British control."

Gasps of relief surged round the chamber, surpassed a few moments later by loud cheering, as the import of Churchill's words became clear. His supporters were jubilant, shouting and hugging colleagues, jumping on chairs, yelling. The neutrals joined in, their doubts forgotten. Even his opponents seemed relieved.

Almost five minutes passed before he could continue.

"The RAF has won a great victory; news of which we have been awaiting anxiously in this House. And there is yet more good news. I can now tell you that, in parallel with that operation, another great battle has been taking place, of which the House had no intimation. The port of Weymouth has been the gateway through which the Nazis have funnelled supplies to their forces in Dorset. It has been the lifeline that allowed them to keep fighting. I must advise you that, sadly but necessarily, the port has been reduced to rubble by the battleships of the Royal Navy. The German ships there have been sunk. The port infrastructure has been destroyed; the supply line to Rommel's forces in the New Forest has been severed."

There were more gasps of surprise, followed by another storm of cheers, even louder. Members were clapping, shouting, embracing.

Churchill waited until he could make himself heard over the clamour.

"Mr. Speaker, today we celebrate two great victories. What is more, I am pleased to inform the House that our military casualties in the two operations have been light."

Only a few noticed his statement had made no mention of civilian casualties in the English towns, but no-one asked. Churchill continued, now in complete control of the House.

"With these bold actions, we have eliminated the threat to our country on the southern flank. We have ended the Nazis' attempt to establish a supply port and an airfield on British soil. We have frustrated their efforts to open a second front in their assault upon our country. All that is left for us to do is to mop up, at our leisure, the remaining enemy forces still hiding away in the New Forest. You will forgive me for saying we are in no great hurry to do so. We will not begrudge them a week or two living on British nuts and berries. It will reduce the demand put on our winter food supplies by the many thousands of prisoners. The deer, however, should be safe; the Germans will soon be out of bullets."

On both sides of the House, his supporters laughed and cheered, some throwing their order papers in the air, others crying with emotion. Even the doubters were submerged in the tide of relief flowing through the House. Across the floor, Clement Attlee was grinning. He looked delighted that the battle had been won. He was also, perhaps, thankful that the news had broken before he'd joined the clamour for Churchill's head. Antony Eden, returned from his convalescent bed for the debate, looked pale but relieved. Rab Butler, however, was keeping a low profile.

As the cheering died down, Churchill took to the floor again.

"Mr. Speaker, we have won a famous victory. The German lodgement on the south coast has been destroyed. What was intended as the left pincer of the Nazi assault on our country is no more. It is clause for jubilation. However, much as I would like to stay and savour

42

Erwin Rommel had been woken by the noise of heavy aircraft over-head and distant explosions. He stood outside for a while, looking at a sky lit up in orange, powerless. He could see a heavy air-raid un-der way to the north-east, in the direction of Eastleigh. Unable to do anything but endure, he went back in to wait for news, pacing up and down the six-metre length of the caravan, the plywood floor shaking with his pent-up energy. His staff officers stood to one side, silent. As snippets of information filtered in from outposts, his aide-de-camp read out the depressing messages. The group didn't really need the details. Even from thirty kilometres away they'd heard the sounds, at first individual claps of thunder, then a rumble, eventually building into the never-ending shockwave of a great earthquake.

Without much hope, Rommel went over to the radio van and or-dered the operator to keep calling Eastleigh. There was no response. After fifteen minutes, he returned to his command caravan and stood staring at a map on the wall.

Even as he tried to come to terms with the attack on Eastleigh, an-other urgent message was brought in by the radioman. It was from the commander at Weymouth: the port was under naval bombard-ment. The dockside cranes had been destroyed; the warehouses were ablaze. The soldier told them the radio contact had been cut off in mid-sentence, and he hadn't been able to reconnect.

Rommel's staff officers stood around in a group, making occasional eye contact with each other, but saying little. It was the funeral wake for their mission. With the destruction of Eastleigh, they no longer had the means to carry on the battle. Gone were the fighters that had given them protection and the Stukas that had been their heavy artillery. Gone, with the destruction of Weymouth, was their supply line. Gone, too, was the strategic purpose of mission.

They knew it was over.

43

In the Paddock there was a hum of excitement. For the first time since war began, Britain had inflicted a heavy defeat on the German army. Shortly after midday Churchill came into the Operations Room. He looked tired but happy, wearing crumpled battledress and with a large cigar clamped in his jaw. He responded to some not-so-gentle prompting from General Ismay that smoking was forbidden in the area and didn't light the Havana, but he still played the part of a Roman conqueror.

For more than two weeks the staff had been buried in the Paddock, working in shifts, four hours on and four hours off, with barely a break in their routine. They were close to exhaustion. Even as the Prime Minister entered, they were still responding to a steady, though now less hectic, flow of incoming messages, updating the plotting table with zombie-like movements. But for a minute or two they stopped pushing the symbols around and turned towards Churchill, giving him a rousing cheer. He stood on the balcony overlooking the pit, returning the applause and whistling with a V for Victory salute. For the first time since he'd become Prime Minister it expressed an achievement rather than an aspiration.

He stayed just five minutes. The battle of Eastleigh had been won; the battle for England, not yet. There were still 70000 Nazi troops hunkered down in Kent and Sussex. They were low on fuel and ammunition; low on food; low, presumably, on morale. Their supply lines had been cut off, as had their escape route to France. They would have heard about the disaster in Hampshire. Churchill knew there might be more hard fighting; there would be more casualties before the invaders surrendered or were killed. But from now on, it was only a matter of time.

44

The pain for Rommel's troops started at dawn. Despite his urgent pleas to the air commander in France, it was soon clear there was no hope of getting effective air cover. With the destruction of Eastleigh, the Luftwaffe was now forced to fly from the Cherbourg peninsula, nearly 200 kilometres away and could only offer token support. In their absence, the supposedly vanquished RAF had taken back control of the skies. New twin-engined fighters were appearing over the battlefield, Beaufighters and Whirlwinds, armed with 20mm cannon. They wreaked mayhem on anything moving in the forest below. Only the mobile flak guns offered any defence against the British attacks, and they were running low on ammunition.

As Rommel watched the pummelling his troops were suffering, he knew this was more than a tactical defeat. Somehow, despite Goering's boasts, the British had managed to build a great reserve of aircraft and they were turning the battle in their favour.

In late afternoon Rommel himself became a casualty. A Beaufighter of 604 squadron caught a glimpse of his Kuebelwagen as he was driving over to the reserve command post. The heavy fighter came down in a shallow dive before his driver could get the vehicle into the cover of the trees. The driver paid for the delay with his life, as a hail of shells smashed into the car. Rommel just managed to jump clear into a roadside ditch and escaped with a deep wound to his thigh. He was rushed to a first aid station in a village primary school, given a shot of morphine and had the wound patched up by the medics.

During the night, the Ju52s did their best to sustain a supply line, making dangerous sorties over the New Forest at low level. Their crews scanned the dark tree canopy, looking for signal lights. As soon as they saw anything, they pushed the crates of food and ammunition out of the side doors into the darkness. But even if it had all been gathered up, it was only a fraction of what was needed to support four divisions in action.

As they made their return to France, the Junkers ran into unforeseen opposition. A squadron of Blenheim night fighters had been assigned to patrol the route. Even with their primitive and unreliable radar equipment, they took a toll of the lumbering transports. The RAF now controlled the sky over Dorset by night as well as day.

Late in the night, one last supply ship made it through the Royal Navy patrol lines to Weymouth and tied up alongside the cratered quays. With the dockside cranes destroyed, soldiers began the slow process of unloading by hand. They didn't get far. In the absence of the Luftwaffe, even the Fleet Air Arm's obsolete Skua dive-bombers were able to operate freely. At first light, they sank the German ship at the pier, before she'd unloaded more than a quarter of her cargo.

Rommel knew his mission had failed. Despite his wounds, he insisted on being carried back to the command post and continued to push his staff officers to find a way out. There were few options open. It was pointless trying to continue north towards Eastleigh. They'd all seen the scale of the destruction wrought on the airfield. Even if they'd wanted to try, a handful of British tanks had moved up to the front line and presented a solid barrier to any advance in that direction.

To their east was Southampton Water, easily sealed off by British patrol boats, and offering no possibilities for escape. To the west was open countryside, where, during daylight hours at least, they would have no protection from the RAF.

At night, they might have a chance. Rommel sought permission to attempt a breakout in that direction the next night. He wanted to lead the men down to the Dorset beaches, from where they could be picked up by small craft during the hours of darkness.

The request was refused. Admiral Raeder won the argument in the OKW about attempting a rescue. Freed from the threat of Stuka attack, the Royal Navy's destroyers now dominated the waters around Weymouth and the landing zones at Chesil Beach and Swanage. Raeder described to the dejected commanders the slaughter that would ensue if he tried to send in boats to pick up the men.

"If there was any way, the Kriegsmarine would go in to evacuate the men. But a Dunkirk in reverse is impossible without control of the air and sea. It would be a massacre."

The final indignity for Rommel was a direct order from the Fuehrer to report back to headquarters in France for recuperation. Late next evening, a tiny Fieseler Storch liaison plane crept across the Channel at sea level and landed on a cricket pitch near Lyndhurst. Without formality, just a rushed goodbye from his aide, the wounded general was bundled into the cabin. The plane bumped across the unmown grass and took off into the gathering night.

45

The British were now in no hurry. After the clearing-up operation at Eastleigh was completed, Montgomery turned his forces towards the New Forest, but General Brooke ordered him to halt. In a heated argument, Brooke told him there was no need for a costly advance through the woods. Instead, the RAF and the Royal Artillery could be left to do the job.

At Bracken's suggestion, loudspeakers were brought up to sheltered sites close to the front line and began broadcasting a constant message to the German soldiers: *There was no escape. They had fought fairly, and those surrendering would be protected under the Geneva Convention. The British were not Nazis.*

Gradually, in twos and threes, with ammunition and food exhausted, the troops of the 6th Army put down their weapons and moved out of their camouflaged positions with hands held high.

Two days later, Colonel Eggers, the senior officer remaining, ordered the white flag to be raised. At 1100 he surrendered the German forces in Dorset and Hampshire to Lieutenant-General Bernard Montgomery.

* * *

Ninety miles away in Kent, Fritz Weber and his men were exhausted. They had reached the outskirts of Tunbridge Wells, but two weeks of hard fighting, without relief, had worn them down. The early success of the landing and the battle for Lympne now seemed a long time ago. Since then, they'd been grinding away at the British defences, in pitched battles and skirmishes, inflicting casualties and suffering too; about half his unit now dead or injured. They'd made progress, but the supply situation was getting critical. The half-tracks were out of fuel. For the last attack, the grenadiers had had to operate as infantry, even the drivers, moving forward without supporting fire from their machine-guns or the towed Pak36s. They'd managed less than a hundred metres before being pinned down by British mortar fire. He'd lost another two men, one just 18 years old, killed by a booby-trap as he sought shelter from the mortars in a barn.

The strain was telling on them all. Every day the routine was the same, just harder. Fight to make a few hundred metres during the daylight hours, then dig in to defend against counter-attack. And they had to be mindful of their consumption of ammunition. They were getting low; almost out of anti-tank shells for the Pak36s. The men were hungry, too. A little food had got through, a few loaves of bread and some sausage, but not nearly enough to sustain men in action. So, in the evenings, after the soldiers had been fighting all day, he had to send out forage parties to scour the countryside for potatoes and turnips. If they were lucky, they might also find a few apples from a ruined orchard. At night, every night, the RAF bombers would come over. They didn't do much damage, but it was hard to get any sleep with 500lb bombs exploding at random, sometimes just a few fields away.

Each morning, the cycle would start again.

He tried to find little things to drive him on. His field map showed they weren't far from Winston Churchill's house at Chartwell. He'd like to reach it, even if they probably couldn't hold on for long. Maybe bring back a souvenir for Gabrielle when the war was over, a book, or something with Churchill's initials on it. Then he realised she mightn't appreciate it; he sometimes forgot she was French. Perhaps he'd bring it to his mother in Wiesbaden instead. She might value it more.

It was 2100; time for a final check on the defensive positions. The British hadn't been making any infantry or tank attacks in the dark, so they would probably have a peaceful night – except for the bloody bombers.

As for the morning, he didn't know what to expect. Five days earlier they'd been euphoric when they heard the news from southern England. The powerful landings on the south coast had brought hope that the British defences would soon be turned and their own advance made easier. But that hope, too, had now been crushed. The BBC was claiming a great victory, and he believed them; they'd been telling the truth about the progress of the battle in the south-east.

His orders were to continue the advance, but they didn't tell him how, without food, without fuel, without ammunition. The sensible thing would be to withdraw and consolidate on a more defensible line, but that wasn't his decision to make. So, they'd hang on where they were, and wait.

He went back to his quarters for the night, a stinking cow shed with a corrugated iron roof that leaked. His sergeant brought him a lump of bread and a bottle of cider salvaged from a bombed pub.

Weber curled up in his bedroll. He was exhausted. He was cold and hungry. He was a long way from home. And it was raining.

46

Brigadier Menzies was ushered into the Prime Minister's room, visibly tired after his trip to Spain and a much-delayed flight home. Churchill also looked physically exhausted, but his eyes shone with the relief of victory won.

"Welcome back, C. Perhaps I should send you away more often."

"Always ready to oblige, Prime Minister. You seem to have had a remarkably good week while I was off on holiday."

"And thank God for it. Eastleigh was a damn close-run thing, but we're on top of the Nazis now. They've shot their bolt, even if it's going to take time to evict them from Kent. Perhaps a damp English winter will help."

"I hear there was high drama at Stratford-upon-Avon as well."

"Indeed! You'd be amazed at the level of support I found there. Mr. Attlee and Mr. Eden were quite effusive, as, I understand, was Lord Halifax in the Lords – though he's off to Washington next week. But enough of England, what did the brave Admiral have to say for himself?"

"Some rather uncomplimentary things about Hitler; not at all uncomplimentary about you. Said he was sorry to hear about Chartwell; asked whether you'd any time for painting these days. He calls you 'the great W.C.' and himself 'the little W.C.' I said you'd be flattered."

"Ah yes – *Wilhelm*. But never mind his flattery, what news? Anything more about the attack on Russia? Is it still going ahead, despite the disaster in England?"

"Apparently so – though, to be fair, his last meeting with Hitler was before the Battle of Eastleigh. At that point, the talk in the OKW was about putting the launch date back by six weeks or so, maybe to the summer. Give them time to replace some of the losses from Sea Lion. Seems shortage of aircraft is their main problem; the losses of armour aren't nearly as significant. Paradoxically, it's worked to their advantage they didn't manage to get the planned number of tanks across the Channel. Meant their losses weren't as bad as they might have been – and they all expect the eastern front will be a tank war. Apparently, Hitler isn't particularly worried about the number of troops lost. Canaris says he's so obsessed with destroying the Bolsheviks that the loss of a hundred thousand men in England, dead or prisoner, doesn't faze him in the slightest."

"C, if ever I get that obsessive about anything..."

"I'll keep a large club handy, sir."

Churchill smiled, but Menzies didn't reciprocate.

"However, he did have some bad news. There was a leak to the Nazis about Ethelred a couple of weeks back, just before the landings. Somebody told them about the reserves we'd built up and scotched the notion there was a split in the government here."

Churchill stayed silent for a moment.

"A traitor? In London?"

"Worse... in the Government. He was quite clear on that."

"A Judas! And well-informed if he knew about our secret reserves. Even accurate, perhaps, about the political consensus at the time – at least before the recent upset. Does he know where it came from?"

"He's fairly sure it was the Butler faction. No names apparently – people tend not to sign these things – but it was the same channel as the messages back in June. I haven't had the chance to check the details yet, but the timing seems to fit with when Rab was told."

There was a deep silence in the room as Churchill contemplated the news.

"So Mr. Butler finally shows his true colours. I might have guessed as much. There's only one word for that behaviour – treason! There may be a right of principled dissent in our democracy, but it most certainly does not extend to helping an enemy in wartime. It may have cost thousands of British lives. He will be held to account."

"Fortunately, sir, it doesn't seem to have changed anything," Menzies said. "Came too late. The invasion fleet was already on its way, and Goering forbade anybody mentioning it to the Fuehrer. Didn't want to upset the poor man!"

"Huh. It is treason, nonetheless. The fact that he failed doesn't make any difference. It just means he won't have those thousands of lives on his conscience as he faces justice. It's time to deal with Mr. Butler and his antics once and for all. I'll speak to Bracken; he may have some other bright ideas, but my own first inclination is the Tower."

Menzies hesitated and took a deep breath before replying.

"Apparently, Prime Minister, whoever did leak the information claims that inviting Hitler to invade England was the act of treason, not trying to stop him."

Churchill growled at the insinuation.

"The hanging judge will decide that, Menzies."

"I'll put a word in for you, sir."

For a moment, there was a dangerous silence, but the riposte seemed to dampen Churchill's spiralling anger. The decision on Butler could wait. He starting firing questions.

"Come back to Canaris. Any more news from the anti-Hitler group? Is the German army with them? How many of the generals? When are they going to act?"

"He says they're going to dispose of Hitler very soon. The army will take the lead, but they have to be careful on the timing... make sure they don't turn him into a martyr. Says we should be ready to respond as soon as they make their move, but not take military action – would just unite the country behind the Nazis again."

"Has he any other suggestions on what we might do?"

Menzies hesitated for a moment.

"No sir."

"And that's all?"

"More or less, Prime Minister."

THE END

AUTHOR'S NOTE

Many books have been written about Operation Sea Lion, both fact and fiction. Other studies include a formal role-play of the battle by the Royal Military Academy at Sandhurst in 1974, enacted with the participation of British and German generals. I have drawn from many of these in my research. However, the seed for my novels was not military speculation, it was an intriguing statement by Winston Churchill in his magnum opus *The Second World War*. The implication was that, contrary to the received wisdom about 1940, the British government was at all times confident of its ability to see off any attempt at invasion – to the extent that "some" people would have been happy to see Hitler try. The uncritical tone of Churchill's words leads me to suspect he was one of the "some".

The six volumes of his magnum opus were written several years after the war ended, and offer many insights. But there is one sensitive subject his history doesn't address in any detail, the political wobbles in the British government in the middle months of 1940. The evidence shows that, in May and June, these were very real. Who is to say that, in the fractured scenario of these novels, they might not have gone much further?

Every novel needs its villain, or two. The readiness of Lord Halifax and Rab Butler to appease Hitler before the war made them the likely candidates. Certainly, once the invasion threat passed, Churchill didn't keep them around for long. He dispatched Halifax to Washington in January 1941 as the new British Ambassador to the United States. A few months later, he moved Butler out of the Foreign Office to the Department of Education. There, his legacy was a positive one; the 1944 Education Act, which laid the foundation for the post-war education system in Britain. In Butler's post-war career, he held all the high offices of state except one. He served as Home Office Minister, Chancellor of the Exchequer and Foreign Secretary. However, he never became Prime Minister. Some people still speculate why.

ACKNOWLEDGEMENTS

How many authors have the luxury of having their editor accompany them on their research trips? My wife, Dee, has been such a support to me. As long as there was a country house or garden in the vicinity as payback, she has been my willing partner in visits to many of the sites featured in the novel. She even arranged flights for me in old World War 2 planes to keep me in period mood. Flying a Tiger Moth over Duxford airfield brought some moments of empathy with the pilots who fought from the base during the Battle of Britain. Perhaps the highlight was a memorable flight in an old Dragon Rapide biplane, in close formation with a Spitfire.

As the novel came together, my children, Alexis and Frances, and my friends, Martin McKenna and Conor McWade assisted me with valuable critiques of the story and with the editing.

My thanks are also due to Andrew Brown of designforwriters.com for the evocative cover design, and to Steve Passiouras of Bookow.com for his expert typesetting services.

For all that assistance, the final product, with any flaws, inconsistencies or errors remains my sole responsibility.

ALSO BY BERNARD NEESON

An Invitation to Hitler

June 1940: Britain stands alone. The army has been routed in France, the survivors barely rescued from the sands of Dunkirk ahead of the approaching panzers. In London, Churchill struggles to impose his authority in cabinet. Some of his colleagues believe there is no alternative but to seek a deal with Hitler.

The RAF is weakening. Mutinies and peace marches are reported across the country. There are hints of disloyalty close to the throne. Britain is on the point of collapse.

Then a shadowy group contacts the Nazis, seeking talks. Who are they? Are there traitors even inside the cabinet?

Who has sent *An Invitation to Hitler?*

Reviews

Amazon Rating 4.6/5.0 stars

'A thrilling read' Historical Novel Society

'Well researched alternative history' Manchester Military History Society

Quarter-finalist in the 2014 Amazon Breakthrough Novel Award

Website

www.bernardneeson.com

About the Author

Bernard Neeson lives in Dublin, Ireland. He took up fiction writing as an interest after a long career in the technology industry, mostly with IBM.

His fascination in the subject matter of An Invitation to Hitler and The Battle for England developed from his lifelong interests in military and political history.

Bernard's first novel, An Invitation to Hitler, reached the quarterfinals of the 2014 Amazon Breakthrough Novel Award, and reached the Top Seller position on Amazon.co.uk in the Alternative History and Political Fiction categories.

When not writing or researching his subject areas, Bernard enjoys sailing in Dublin Bay and further afield with family and friends.

Printed in Poland
by Amazon Fulfillment
Poland Sp. z o.o., Wrocław